HISTORICAL NOTE

When the Roman armies finally captured the holy island of Ynys Mon (Anglesey) in AD 61, they destroyed the power of the Druids who, for centuries, had provided leadership for the Welsh, both religiously and militarily.

After the Roman legions withdrew from Britain in AD 410, they left behind a fractured country divided into fiercely defended kingdoms and princedoms. Eventually, the Saxons became the rulers of England, and nearly six hundred years after the Roman withdrawal, a divided collection of Celts attempted to defend their borders against an enemy that was considerably more united. In Wales, the Celts of the north and those of the south maintained an on-going suspicion and dislike of each other.

Gwynedd was always the most important kingdom of Wales. When the young King Gruffydd ap Llewelyn of Powys claimed Gwynedd, he became the most powerful leader of his time. He reinforced his reputation with his famous victory over the Saxons at the battle of Rhyd-y-Groes, and over the following years he fought and negotiated his way to becoming the first, and only, King of All Wales.

Sadly for Wales, his reign only lasted a bare seven years. With his death in 1063, much of the unity he had created fell apart, and Wales was never completely united under one king ever again.

It is interesting to note that King Gruffydd ap Llewelyn was defeated by Harold Godwinson, the Saxon Earl of Wessex, who was to become King of England three years later. Harold's reign was short. Within a few months, in 1066, Duke William of Normandy, known as the Bastard, who became William the First of England, killed him at the Battle of Hastings.

June 2016.

BARRY MATHIAS

Agio
PUBLISHING HOUSE

PUBLISHING HOUSE

151 Howe Street, Victoria BC Canada V8V 4K5

For information and bulk orders, please contact
info@agiopublishing.com or go to
www.agiopublishing.com
Visit this book's website at www.barrymathias.net and
ancientbloodlinestrilogy.com

ISBN 978-1-897435-96-0 (trade paperback)
ISBN 978-1-897435-97-7 (ebook)

10 9 8 7 6 5 4 3 2 1b

DEDICATION

To Clare

ACKNOWLEDGEMENTS

I am indebted to Clare Mathias for her excellent proofreading, and preparation of the final manuscript; to Pam Hockin for reading the completed second draft, and for her valuable comments. I am grateful to Marsha Batchelor for her imaginative and skilful design of the book covers, and to Bruce Batchelor for publishing my fourth novel and for circulating it in e-book format, which has enabled me to reach a wider audience.

CELTIC DREAMS OF GLORY

There is no present in Wales,
And no future:
There is only the past
~ R.S. Thomas

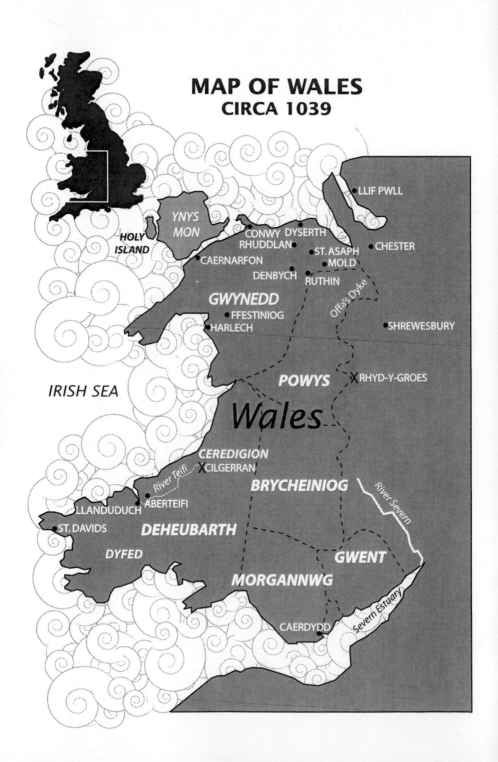

MAP OF WALES
CIRCA 1039

LLIF PWLL

YNYS MON

HOLY ISLAND

CONWY DYSERTH
RHUDDLAN
CAERNARFON
ST. ASAPH
MOLD
CHESTER
DENBYCH
RUTHIN

GWYNEDD

Offa's Dyke

FFESTINIOG
HARLECH
SHREWESBURY

IRISH SEA

POWYS
X RHYD-Y-GROES

Wales

CEREDIGION
X CILGERRAN

River Teifi

BRYCHEINIOG

River Severn

ABERTEIFI
LLANDUDUCH

ST. DAVIDS

DEHEUBARTH

DYFED

GWENT

MORGANNWG

CAERDYDD

Severn Estuary

PROLOGUE

FEBRUARY 1039 – THE ROYAL PALACE AT POWYS

"My Lord King, a messenger from Gwynedd has arrived!" Gruffydd ap Llewelyn, King of Powys, sat up in his chair, and lowered his cup of mulled wine. He was a compact man, yet taller than many Welshmen. He possessed huge strength and energy and, after spending his youth in debauchery, was intent on making up for lost time. He looked enquiringly at his younger brother, Prince Arthwyr. "At this time of night?"

"It must be important." Arthwyr stretched his long legs towards the glowing fire. "Nobody would travel in this weather unless they had to."

"Show him in."

Almost immediately, the messenger entered and bowed to the King. He was a young man, well dressed for the winter conditions, but he staggered slightly and was obviously near exhaustion. Gruffydd pointed to a stool; the man sank down gratefully, and took a deep breath. "My Lord King, Iago of Gwynedd was murdered two days ago."

Gruffydd sprang to his feet. "How did it happen?"

"My Lord, he was killed by a family member over a land dispute."

"Duw. What a waste, he was a good man," Arthwyr said. "Those mountain tribes are forever at each other's throats."

"And his wife and son?" The King stroked his thick beard in an agitated manner.

1

"They have fled to Ireland, my Lord."

"And the murderer?"

"The King's personal guard chased him down and killed him."

After a moment's pause, Gruffydd beckoned to his Seneschal. "Make sure he is well looked after."

There was a silence, as they waited for the room to empty. Athwyr turned to his older brother. "You know what this means?"

"I'm related to the former King Anarwd ap Rhodri of Gwynedd, which means I have as good a claim as anyone else to the Kingdom." He paused, and seemed to grow in size. "I will be King of Gwynedd and Powys. I will be the most powerful king in Wales. We leave tomorrow. I'll rely on you to make the arrangements. Make sure the nobles are ready to ride at first light. I'll take my personal guard, and anyone else with a horse." He laughed. "We must look as though we have the support, even if we don't."

"So, you will want me to come?"

"Of course."

"You remember? I was going to visit your good friend Cydweli, at Rhyd-y-Groes, and see how his fort was progressing."

"That can wait. If I can become King of Gwynedd, I will eventually become King of All Wales."

"Not if the Saxons destroy Cydweli's fort." Arthwyr looked hard at his brother. "Cydweli could well be the difference between your vision of a Welsh nation, and an invasion of our country by the Saxons."

"You're right, my bother, but Gwynedd is the one Kingdom that will always dominate Wales. I cannot achieve my goal without becoming its King. The Saxons will not attack until the snow is gone and the land has dried." He grasped his brother's hand. "Trust me. One thing at a time."

CHAPTER ONE

DEHEUBARTH APRIL 1052

Two men stared anxiously into the fading light, indifferent to the wild splendor of the western sky. The ragged clouds, illuminated by the sinking rim of the sun, glowed in violent reds and yellows while the blackness of the approaching storm slowly dimmed the spectacle. Below them, a rising sea battered the rocks of the low cliff on which they stood, the waves surging and sucking with increasing violence. In front was a small, uninhabited island separated from the mainland by a wave-swept channel less than an hundred paces wide.

"Why haven't they come back? They must have seen how the weather's changing?" The speaker was a short, stocky, bearded man with a large nose and thick, black, flowing hair, graying at the edges. He carried a sword; a heavy silver pin held his close-woven cape together. He punched the air with a clenched fist and looked angrily at his silent companion. "Have you nothing to say, Evan?"

"What's there to say?" Evan shrugged. He was older than Gomer ap Griffith and, although he was taller and stood with quiet authority, a stranger would have noted immediately the coarseness of his clothing and the metal slave band around his left wrist. "Young men live dangerously. You did when you were their age."

Gomer spat contemptuously. "I didn't risk my life for stupid things."

"Yes, you did. All the time. You did so today. You wouldn't be standing here now if I'd not been covering your back."

"All right." He sniffed contemptuously. "That's what I pay you for."

Both men laughed.

Although Evan had been Gomer's slave for most of his adult life, their relationship was one of easy friendship rather than master and servant. Evan had been born a slave, yet throughout his life he had been treated well and lived more comfortably than many peasants. He worked hard for Gomer, acting as a house servant, guard and even adviser. In return, he had been allowed to marry and was even paid a yearly stipend. He could, with his savings, have bought his freedom some years ago, as was his right. But Evan liked his situation, and the owning of money gave him a secret satisfaction. Why use his life's earnings merely to have the band removed?

"If they were my own sons I wouldn't be worrying about them."

Evan smiled. "If they were your sons, they'd be serving with King Gruffydd ap Llywelyn and killing Saxons."

There was a silence as Gomer ap Griffith chewed his lower lip. It would be dark soon and his anger was giving way to guilt. He should never have agreed to the two young men, his dead brother's sons, undertaking such a dangerous mission. If they were drowned, there would be no heirs to the family property; his brother, Cydweli, would turn in his grave. "You're right. If I had sons they would be with the King."

"How long are you going to keep these boys around your apron strings?"

"I've told you before, and I've told them: I will release them as soon as they stop acting as though they were immortal."

"Yet, if they were your sons, you would be proud of their courage and they would be achieving great things in Gruffydd's army." Evan fingered the metal band. "You still blame yourself for Cydweli's death. Yet, you know it wasn't your fault. In the same way, you'd blame yourself if anything happened to his sons. You can't protect young men, unless you want them to behave like your daughters."

"It's getting dark," Gomer said, suddenly changing the subject. "Run back to the horses and get help. Return to the village and gather up some fishermen. We need a boat, if any have survived today's attack. Get ropes too. Hurry now!"

Evan stared intently out at the island and, without a word, turned back towards the path and disappeared into the gloom.

Gomer ap Griffith glared at everything around him. It had been a long and exhausting day but, apart from the stupidity of his two nephews, the result had been very satisfactory. After a decisive victory he had supposed he would be having a well-earned celebration around a roaring fire with beer and venison, not standing impotently on this wind-blasted cliff. He should never have agreed to such a foolhardy scheme. If they hadn't all been so emotionally charged after the fighting, they would have realized; more to the point, he should have realized the stupidity of it.

"Gwriad! Dafydd! Anybody!" His words were snatched away by the wind. He stamped his feet in frustration. If they were to return the way they had gone, they would have to wait until after first light tomorrow for the next low tide. They had not only missed this tide, but also there had been no sign of life since his nephews and his small band of soldiers had disappeared from view, hours ago. His frustration gave way to misery and he sank down on the damp ground.

He sat on his thick cloak and, after cursing the Picts, the weather, and the frustration of his situation, he began to reflect on his life and especially on his much loved and respected younger brother, Cydweli ap Griffith, who had died defending Wales against the Saxons at the great battle of Rhyd-y-Groes in 1039. It had been the most important victory the Welsh had ever achieved over the plundering Saxons. It had all been due to the leadership of the great Gruffydd ap Llewelyn, King of North Wales. "He's a great King," he murmured, "and he won this area from Hywel ap Edwin, even though Hywel was supported by the Danes." He frowned; he had got into the habit of talking to himself. "Then the bastard Gruffydd ap Rhydderch of Gwent suddenly attacked and King Gruffydd ap Llywelyn lost the district of Ystrad Tywi and one hundred and forty of his household guard were killed." That had been in 1047 and since then, and for the last five years, there had been a state of on-going war between Gruffydd ap Llewelyn, who ruled Gwynedd and most of North Wales, and Rhydderch, who now controlled Gwent and some of Deheubarth. "But Rhydderch doesn't control me, or this area," he grumbled. His mind refocused on the earlier part of the day. "Today started badly, then got better," he mused. "If only it had remained so."

• • •

It had been a sun-blessed April day in the year 1052, when Gomer ap Griffith, one of the minor Lords of Ceredigion and Dyfed, arrived at the village of Llanduduch, on one of his periodic visits to the villages and hamlets in his domain. He arrived with a small bodyguard of well-armed soldiers and was accompanied by his two nephews, Gwriad and Dafydd and, as always, Evan, his personal slave.

Gomer liked to visit Llanduduch; over the years had established a friendly relationship with the village elders. It was a well-established community on a steep hillside overlooking the south bank of the River Teifi. It boasted a safe, shallow harbour, and a small, stone-built church, which perched on a rocky knoll above the cluster of slate and wood hovels that composed the village. The inhabitants were poor and, according to their elderly priest, Brother Williams, mainly God-fearing. Fishing was their primary occupation, which required the building of coracles: small round boats with wickerwork frames, covered with woven cloth soaked in tar. These small boats, sometimes big enough to carry two people, were well suited to the river, but dangerous in tidal waters. The village owned only two row boats, each capable of holding four people, but these were considered unsafe on the sea in stormy weather and, because of their value, only experienced men were allowed to use them.

The women wove the local wool, baked lava bread, grew leeks and cabbages, and looked after the children and the cooking. The men fished and occasionally hunted, although all hunting was, in theory, the right of Gomer ap Griffith. On rare occasions, they might be enlisted to help their Lord defend his realm, but for the most part their lives were uneventful and centered on feeding their families and coping with the vicissitudes of the seasons. The Teifi was a good salmon river and the village, being only two miles from the estuary, benefitted from easy access to seafood. There was only a limited amount of corn and barley grown in the area, and the women harvested seaweed that they dried and ground to make lava bread. Up in the bleak hills a few sheep farmers eked out a modest living, while in the damp valleys, which flooded each spring and autumn, small herds of local cattle added some limited amounts of beef and milk to the diet. The cattle were short, black, sturdy creatures that seemed to mirror their owners, and shared their stubborn, truculent natures.

Gomer's party weaved its way past the ancient church with its small bell tower, and began the steep descent down the winding path to the centre of the village. The soldiers hung back, pointing out features of the spectacular view in front of them. Gomer turned and beckoned to his nephews who were riding behind him.

"Blow your horn, Gwriad. Nobody's on watch. You'd think they'd never heard of Pictish raiders," he grumbled.

Gwriad blew two long calls on his ram's horn and stopped his horse to admire the view. He was eighteen years old, and with his jet-black hair and enormous energy, was considered handsome by the local women. He had recently grown a beard, and had persuaded his uncle to buy him a new horse. Being the elder of Gomer ap Griffith's two nephews, he looked forward to the time when he could shake off the control of his gruff uncle. Gwriad was short and thickset with piercing blue eyes and a ribald sense of humour. He was very like his father, Cydweli, who had died in 1039, at the famous battle of Rhyd-y-Groes, near Welshpool. It had been a victory of monumental importance for the Welsh forces when Gruffydd ap Llywelyn, King of Gwynedd and Powys, had defeated the invading army of Leofric, the Saxon Earl of Mercia, killing his brother General Edwin and capturing General Aelfgar, the Earl's son, who had been seriously wounded. This defeat had blunted the ambitions of the Saxon invaders and made their father, Cydweli, a national hero.

Dafydd rode up beside Gwriad. "Does he think the Picts are going to come over the mountains?" He smiled as he surveyed the sparkling river, tracing its path into the wide tidal plain, which led to a narrow estuary with just a glimpse of the blue sea in the distance. Although only a year younger than his brother, he was not so confident. He was taller, leaner and had green eyes and a mass of red hair. The brothers were so different in appearance that some thought it unlikely they had shared the same father. Dafydd was the more bookish one, and unlike his elder brother could read Latin. He always had an opinion and spent his time trying to match his elder brother's achievements. "If a Pictish boat came up river, those fisherman would know. They're not stupid. Which is why they don't post guards around the hillside."

"He likes people to welcome him," Gwriad said, winking at his brother. "Especially the women." They watched as women, children and old men appeared below in the doorways of their houses. "Now he'll be happy. All those people clapping and cheering."

"They'll be happy, too, when they see those," Dafydd said, pointing at a couple of large deer carcasses that were stretched across the front of two of the soldiers' saddles. The riders were close behind Gomer so he could indicate his trophies if he saw someone he recognized. He had been unsuccessful in hunting for wild pig earlier that day, but had been satisfied when he killed the two large deer. It would be enough to feed the village and ensure an enthusiastic welcome.

"They'll be particularly happy to eat the venison," Gwriad said meaningfully, "for as you know they never taste it unless Gomer gives it to them." They nudged each other as they watched their uncle reach the centre of the village; he was smiling broadly and nodding graciously in all directions. Women cheered, children ran excitedly around, dogs barked and geese wobbled away hissing and flapping their wings. The older men greeted him with formal bows and there were appreciative noises when they were shown the deer.

"I'll bet he'll be deep in his cups tonight," Dafydd murmured. "It might give us a chance with the local girls."

"You're too young for that sort of thing. Best leave it to those who know what they're doing."

"I might be younger than you, but I'm taller and better looking."

"I've seen better faces in a pig sty."

They continued in friendly jesting until they dismounted next to their uncle, who completed the formalities of the greetings and introductions. "Their father was my younger brother, the great Cydweli ap Griffith," he said proudly. "He died thirteen years ago, when we beat the Saxons at the battle of Rhyd-y-Groes, under the leadership of King Gruffydd ap Llewelyn." He glared at the elders. "Cydweli was a brave man. None like him." He sniffed, and wiped his eyes. "He would be forty-four years old next month. The finest man who ever lived."

The old men nodded agreement, and muttered, "He was, Lord. He was." They had heard the speech many times over the recent years, but none dare say so. Two young men of the village had died in that epic battle and it was still a fresh wound, even though more than a decade had passed. More important still, was the fact that the present Lord Gruffydd ap Rhydderch of Gwent had, five years ago, expelled the same King Gruffydd ap Llewelyn from the area, which was part of the large principality of Deheubarth. The two Gruffydds had been at war ever since. Gomer had been one of the few local nobles to continue to support Llewelyn: the King for whom his much-loved brother had died.

"When I die, Gwriad here will be your Lord." Gomer sniffed loudly and beckoned to his nephews. "Most of the men are fishing and will be back before nightfall." He had a habit of stating the obvious and making it sound important. He smiled broadly at the assembled women, and while the older ones bowed their heads, the younger grinned impishly at the two young lords.

"How's your wife, my Lord?" a village elder enquired.

The smile on Gomer's face vanished. "She's well. Thank you for asking." It was common knowledge that his wife never left her room, and was cared for by servants. Rumour had it that she was not in her right mind and that Gomer rarely visited her. He glared round at his two nephews.

"Gwriad, take charge of the soldiers and bring in plenty of fuel. Dafydd, you arrange their billets for tonight and fodder for the horses." He nodded to them to come closer. "And keep your hands off these girls. I don't want any trouble with their fathers. Is that clear?" Gwriad nodded diplomatically and made a small bow.

Dafydd looked indignant, but thought better of protesting when his brother nudged him.

"Good, then." Gomer took a deep breath, enjoying his power, and walked off in close conversation with the elders. Behind him walked Evan, slave and best friend, who knew how to protect his master without giving offence. Before entering one of the larger buildings, Gomer turned and glared at the two youths who were enjoying being the centre of attention. "Now!" he bellowed.

They both jumped to attention and strode off towards the soldiers, smiling weakly, trying to retain some modicum of self-esteem.

• • •

THE OUTDOOR FEAST TOOK PLACE in the centre of the village. The weather remained fine and, although the night air was cold, the heat of the fires kept everyone warm. Women roasted the venison on smaller fires and carved the meat onto wide wooden platters. The men helped themselves first and the women served the elderly and the children before finally helping themselves. There were boiled onions, leek soup with lava bread, and salmon for the appreciative soldiers, for whom fish was not a daily diet. Both men and women drank beer, and even the children were allowed a small amount.

Later, amid the shadows and the flickering flames, there was singing and some dancing. One of the soldiers played the pipes, and others played flutes, which they had carved in their spare time. A number of the fishermen owned their own drums, and there was a primitive excitement in the air. Young girls, egged on by their mothers, were the first to dance and eventually some of the fishermen and a few of the soldiers joined in. The young people danced with a reckless abandon, making the most of a rare event. Gomer applauded vigorously and nudged Gwriad who was sitting next to him on a makeshift bench. He had noticed an attractive young woman beckoning to Dafydd. "Tell that brother of yours that he's not to dance, or you either, mind. I do not want to be shown any of your bastards in this village the next time I come here."

Standing behind Gomer, Evan winked at Gwriad, who rolled his eyes.

"Doesn't he know it takes more than dancing to make a child?" he murmured to the family slave.

"Dancing is where you start, isn't it?" said Evan, with a broad smile. He nodded at Gomer. "He's enjoying himself, anyway."

This was the way Gomer always behaved, especially when he had been drinking. Over the years, Evan had acted like an uncle to the two brothers, and there was a strong bond between them. Evan particularly liked Gwriad, with his easy humour, his courage and the fact he never worried about anything. Dafydd was different: he respected his uncle, was easily embarrassed, and seemed to worry about everything. But, even Evan had to admit that Dafydd had the greater intelligence; while Gwriad was the doer, Dafydd was the thinker.

Dafydd watched the girl intently. He did not remember seeing her before, which was strange as she was unusually good looking. Her thick black hair hung loose about her shoulders and was not plaited in the usual fashion. Although not tall, she had large, rounded breasts and broad hips. This was his second visit to this village, and she had not been around two years ago, when he had last accompanied his uncle. He affected disinterest for a while, raising his mug for more beer. But when he next glanced at her she was still staring at him, her face immobile, but her eyes willing him to react. Slowly, her mouth parted and her pink tongue flickered between her full lips. He felt his cheeks flush and an uncomfortable stirring in his britches. He was about to stand up to ease himself, when Gwriad passed on his uncle's prohibition. "He says no screwing the women. He didn't say you couldn't try the men though."

Dafydd fumed silently.

"Give him a bit more time," Gwriad whispered, out of the side of his mouth, "he'll soon be past caring."

Dafydd gave her an apologetic smile, shrugged his shoulders and waited obediently. He watched anxiously as Gomer held out his mug to be refilled. Some of the village elders, sitting on his right, were already nodding and laughing loudly at nothing in particular. They kept waking up, repeating what an honour it was to have their great lord to stay, and drifting off to sleep.

Brother Williams, who considered himself the most important man in the village, always sat on Gomer's right whenever there was feasting. The priest was the only man in the village with any education and he managed the finances of the area, answering directly to his present Lord and, when necessary, to his Bishop, the latest of whom he had never met. He had known Gomer for many years and had been responsible for teaching Dafydd how to read and write in Latin. He had quickly given up with Gwriad, who had always been more interested in physical things.

Gomer belched loudly, rubbed his belly and, with a beatific smile, turned to Brother Williams. "Anything going on I should know about?"

The priest enjoyed his moments of importance and looked gravely at the prancing dancers. "My Lord, I suspect there have been a few deer taken, but nothing serious." He always gave this report, as Gomer would have thought it strange if the village youths had suddenly ceased to carry on an ancient tradition. Brother Williams was also mindful of the fact that he was always given a generous allowance of the meat from any illegal hunting.

"That all?"

"Most of them come to church regularly. If they don't, I remind them, of course."

Gomer nodded grimly, aware that many of the villagers were watching their conversation and wondering if the priest would betray their minor misdemeanors. "Any reports of Picts? I hear their boats have been raiding the coast up north."

"No, my Lord." The priest cut himself yet another slice of venison, and chewed on it reflectively. "I can't imagine they'll venture this far down yet. Not until the summer comes, at least. Then, who knows?" He paused, and took a swig of beer. "It might be a good idea to give the young men some training, once the weather improves. Now, if we had trained soldiers in every village, the Picts would think twice before they risked attacking us."

"I'll consider it." This was not the first time the priest had mentioned training the local youths. Although Gomer liked the idea in principle, he knew he would have to provide the swords and armor, and it cost money. The farmers of the inland villages were able to pay taxes and provide cattle, sheep and pigs in exchange for protection, but the coastal villages were poor; they paid their dues in smoked and salted fish, woven goods and wicker baskets. Only occasionally did traders arrive and pay them money for their fish, and the priest was always around to demand a contribution for the Church.

Gomer knew very well that there was also the necessary payment to be made to soldiers to ensure their loyalty. Every lord understood that when war was imminent, trained soldiers would hire themselves to whomever would pay the most. In contrast, untrained men would always fight to defend their villages and were unlikely to seek employment elsewhere, preferring family and friends to the unknown possibilities of foreign parts. If he provided the training and the weapons the villagers would be able to defend themselves. However, trained young men might be tempted to seek glory and money elsewhere, and at his expense. He drank deeply. No need to think about it now. An alcoholic contentment slowly overtook him, and he did not notice that his mug had been refilled.

Dafydd waited until Gomer's eyes closed. Gwriad turned and leered, did a vulgar gesture with his fingers, and nodded for his brother to leave. They glanced at Evan, who nodded encouragement. Dafydd rose casually to his feet, slipped away into the dark, and made his way to the other side of the fire where the eager young woman awaited him.

"I thought you weren't coming." She tossed her long black hair provocatively. Around them, people were drinking, embracing each other or just staring into the fire. The music was quieter and many of the men were singing drunkenly. Mothers had begun to collect their protesting children and were ushering them off home, while some of the older women continued to serve beer. He stared guiltily about. Nobody seemed to be watching.

"Sorry, I couldn't get away. The old man's forgotten what it's like to be young."

She smiled up at him. "Better late than never, isn't it?" She rested her hand on his arm.

"I'm Dafydd." He felt strangely excited.

"I know who you are. You're a rich boy, who wants a good time." Her hand ran down his chest and stopped, for a moment, on his purse. "I'm Megan, and I like rich, good looking boys."

He reached out to put his arm around her, but she took his hand.

"Come with me," she whispered. "I know a place we can go."

He glanced back. His uncle was dozing; the priest was still eating, and even Gwriad was occupied in a lively discussion with an older woman. "All right," he said, his tongue moving nervously over his lips.

She led him away from the firelight, past the small, ragged houses close to the river, and up across a sloping, rough field. Dafydd looked back to check if anyone had noticed them leave. His eyes had become accustomed to the dark, and he was certain there was no movement behind him. In front, the dim outline of a building loomed up,

"Over here. It's my Taid's barn."

He hesitated when he reached the wide doorway. Around him the field was faintly illuminated by the glow of a partial moon, but the inside of the barn was as black as pitch. He was wondering what would happen if her grandfather caught them. "This will do," he said, suddenly uneasy.

He leaned against the wooden doorway and pulled her towards him. His nervousness made him clumsy, and she fell heavily against his chest. She was shorter than he was, and he felt her large breasts pushing against him. "Don't be in such a hurry," she murmured, clasping her hands behind his neck. "I have arranged a comfortable place, just inside the door here." She rotated her hips sensuously. "What a big boy you are then." She laughed tauntingly, and he felt certain she was much more experienced than he was. He had only dreamed about kissing her behind one of the hovels, but she was indicating something beyond his dreams, or his experience.

So this is it, he thought. He had fantasized about this moment, and especially since Gwriad had described his own adventures with the maids in Gomer's fortress. If his older brother was to be believed, Gwriad had raised the skirts of just about every young woman in the area.

"What if anyone should come?"

"They won't."

"But they might. Perhaps we should stay out here."

"And do what?" She chuckled wantonly. "Are you afraid of me?"

"No, of course not. I just don't want to upset my uncle."

"Upset your uncle? Not frightened of him, are you?" She placed one of her hands between his legs and moved him gently.

He gasped with pleasure. Things were moving too fast. He placed a hand tentatively on one of her breasts. He had never touched a woman in this way, and he was unsure how to proceed.

"Is this your first time?" she said, as though reading his mind.

He grunted, unsure whether to admit to it or not. In recent months he had tried to measure up to his brother's boasting, claiming a number of fictitious conquests of his own, but was unsure whether Gwriad believed him. Somehow, he had never progressed past kissing, and had always held back when the local girls had seemed willing. Even tonight, when there had never been a better opportunity, he was worrying about his uncle.

He was not afraid of him. In spite of his gruff manner Gomer had always treated him fairly. It was simply that Dafydd did not want to disappoint the man who had taken over the responsibility for his welfare since his father's sudden death. He was aware that he respected and idolized his uncle in a way that Gwriad found amusing and incomprehensible. "He's just our uncle, doing what our father would have done for Gomer's daughters in similar circumstances. He treats us well, but he doesn't own our lives."

"Come on," Megan said peevishly. "Or don't you want to?"

"Of course I do." He swallowed loudly. "You're very pretty." The blood was thumping in his neck, and he felt intensely aroused. "You're the most beautiful woman in the village."

"And you're an attractive man." She kissed him, forcing her tongue into his mouth, and biting his lower lip. She pulled him determinedly towards the blackness of the barn.

"No. There's someone coming." It was a desperate attempt to take control of a situation that suddenly did not seem right.

She glanced back. "There's nobody," she said angrily. "What's the matter with you? Your brother never acted like a milk sop." She broke free of his embrace. "He's twice the man you are. You wait until…" She stopped, and gave a small gasp as a light flared up at the other end of the field. "Duw! It's my Taid." Without, a word of parting, she disappeared behind the barn, and he could faintly hear her departing footsteps.

Dafydd stood up straight, one hand on his hip, and tried to look relaxed. He watched anxiously as a dark figure advanced across the field holding a small torch that glimmered in the light breeze.

"Did I catch you in the act, or have you already stolen the virginity of that poor, unsuspecting girl?"

"Gwriad! What the hell are you doing here?"

"Trying to stop you from getting the pox," he laughed. "Megan's the local whore."

"I've never seen her before!"

"That's because she's always been too busy with older men."

"How would you know?" Dafydd clenched his fists.

"Because I had it off with her the last time we came here."

"You encouraged me. You bastard." He lunged at his brother, only to back off as Gwriad pointed the burning embers towards him.

"Calm down, little brother. Gomer is asking for you. I said you'd gone off to relieve yourself." He guffawed. "I didn't tell him how."

They made their way back to the fire. Gwriad whistled tunelessly and Dafydd stomped behind, unable to decide if his brother had rescued him or prevented him from untold pleasures. "How do you know she's got the pox?"

"'Stands to reason. Nobody else will sleep with her."

As they passed the first cottage, a dog growled and Dafydd kicked out at the animal, venting his pent-up frustration. "What does Gomer want?"

"Apart from wanting to make sure you don't provide him with dependent bastards, he wants to talk to us both about some idea of training the local boys to be soldiers."

"He wants us to do it?" Dafydd was incredulous.

"Blame Brother Williams. It was his idea."

"He wants to discuss it now? At this time of night?"

Gwriad shrugged his powerful shoulders. "We leave tomorrow. I suppose he wants to agree something with the elders. That's if they're still awake."

By the time they reached the fire, Gomer had left and most of the villagers had retired to their homes. A soldier was on guard outside the house that Gomer always slept in. He accepted Gwriad's glowing torch and informed them the Lord had gone to bed. They nodded and entered quietly. The building contained only a single room that was lit by a smoking candle and by the glowing embers of a dying fire in the centre of the floor. At one side, Gomer was snoring on a raised palliasse, and beside him, closer to the corner of the wall, was the shape of a woman, her long hair covering her face. His sword, spear and armor were stacked against the other wall, together with the weapons belonging to Gwriad and Dafydd. His two huge hunting dogs wagged their tails in greeting, but did not move from their positions by the side of their master's bed.

"That's lucky," Gwriad whispered. "He might forget about his idea by tomorrow." He tiptoed across the room and collected his weapons and armor. "Just in case we have to fight off the sex-mad women of this place."

Dafydd scowled, but did the same. On his way out, he cast an envious glance at his uncle, and understood why they had separate billets. At the foot of the bed Evan slept soundly, wrapped in a blanket on a pile of rushes.

They carried their weapons and armor to an elders' house close by, where they had arranged to spend the night. Gwriad opened the door carefully and peered in. There was no candle burning and the fire was out; it was impossible to see anything although they could hear the sound of snoring, and the low growl of a dog. They withdrew cautiously.

"You get the torch from that soldier," Gwriad said. "I'd better stay to keep our weapons safe." As usual he spoke with heavy sexual innuendo.

Dafydd returned to Gomer's house, and retrieved the torch from the soldier. He held it aloft as Gwriad peered into their proposed lodging. A number of bodies were lying together on a broad bed. Near them, some small children were curled up on a mound of dried rushes that was shared by a very large dog. It watched them suspiciously and began a menacing growl, the sound blended in with the snores and heavy breathing of the sleepers. Dafydd was aware of a strong smell of beer, fish and stale bodies.

"Arth. Good dog," Gwriad murmured. "Remember me?" The dog relaxed and wagged its tail.

Dafydd shook his head in disbelief: his brother had a way with animals, even wild ones. He wondered if the huge creature was really called Bear? It did not appear to matter. He closed the door and they moved to the space on their left and stacked the armor, swords and hunting spears against the front wall. In the corner was a pile of rushes that had been arranged for their sleeping quarters. He watched as Gwriad pushed the torch into the fireplace and crawled on to the rushes beside him. They wrapped their cloaks around themselves, and within moments were asleep.

CHAPTER TWO

D uring the night, a large galley entered the bay. It came from the north. The Pictish warriors on board had followed the coastline until they reached a small, bleak island, which they had passed to the seaward side to avoid the possibility of rocks. On their left they could see high, dark cliffs that led them to the mouth of the river. On their right, a long, sandy beach stretched away into the gloom and there was no sign of human habitation. They rowed carefully, alert to any danger, and could feel the change in the water as they crossed the bay. After a while they passed into the river's estuary, and were confronted with what appeared to be a wide lake. It was the first time they had explored this area, but the fine weather had enabled them to travel further than they had planned, and they were keen to exploit their good fortune. The eight oarsmen on each side and the large single sail enabled the vessel to move swiftly, aided by the rising tide. The galley held a total of twenty-six men, all of them armed and desperate for plunder.

By the light of the half moon, they stared around trying to locate the main course of the river through the tidal plain. "Keep your eyes open for any gleams of light," said the Leader. He was an experienced seaman, who had ventured into these waters the previous summer. "The tide is already near the flood; we should have been here earlier." He glowered at the straining rowers and nodded to his sergeant. "Keep watch from the bows."

Before long the tide would lessen and the journey upstream would become more difficult. It was essential they find the nearest village before the waters began to ebb. The outgoing current would guarantee a rapid escape, but only as long as the river did not drop too quickly. At first light they would storm ashore, kill the men, rape the women and take whatever they could make use of. Most of them were hardened fighters; it was the way they earned a living.

From past experience they knew that the people of the fishing villages owned nothing of great worth, but there was often a church where a priest, under torture, would reluctantly show them where he hid his money. There were always women to satisfy their cravings, and caches of food and alcohol to renew their dwindling supplies. But most of all, fishing villages contained few fighters and were easy prey. The Picts enjoyed killing, but would gladly avoid the chance of being injured, and certainly did not wish to die. They were tall, muscular men with wild beards and grim faces, and their long, dirty hair pushed out from under their iron helmets. In battle they wore light body armor and carried heavy axes and short swords. Their leather shields were decorated with metal studs, and a few carried javelins.

They travelled cautiously, avoiding the sand banks that lurked beneath the still waters. By making use of the flood they were soon past the wide plain of the estuary. Dark hills crowded down on them from both banks of the river as they peered into the darkness, searching for any sign of life. The Leader steered the galley into the main current, totally focused on the tell-tale signs of the river's movements. As they turned a bend in the river, his sergeant saw a red glow in the distance, high on the right bank. He raced silently back along the boat to the Leader.

The order was passed down the boat to stop rowing and they allowed the tide to take them slowly towards the welcoming light of the smoldering fires. The Leader stared fixedly ahead as the boat moved like a shadow towards the sharpening outline of buildings.

"They've been feasting," the Leader whispered to his sergeant. "I see no guards. Perhaps they're all drunk." He gave a humorless chuckle. "This should be easy."

There was no need to wait for first light to attack; they could see enough by the glow of the fires and were aided by the clear night sky. He calculated that dawn would break soon. If he attacked now he might catch them all sleeping. He edged the vessel into the shallows, hearing the dull sucking sound as the bow bit into the muddy bank. On the right, he could see the outline of two large boats resting upside down on a grassy ledge; on the left, a narrow path weaved its way up to the village.

His men waited and listened. There was no sound. The Leader moved down the boat, quietly issuing orders. Two were to stay behind to guard the galley; two were to destroy the fishing boats. He would lead, and they would follow. The men stood up slowly, unknotting their muscles and reaching for their weapons. They were like hunting dogs about to be released, their breathing loud in the silent darkness. In the moonlight their eyes glowed with excitement. The Leader clambered over the side into the cold water and staggered to the bank, his feet sinking deep in the mud. He dragged himself up onto hard ground and silently waved his sword at his men. Now, they would launch themselves on their unsuspecting foe, and their blood lust would be sated.

The raiders came ashore in two slow lines, struggling against the embrace of the mud, gasping with the effort and the cold. As soon as the first men reached the shore, the Leader, unable to curb his impatience, led them quickly up the steep path to the village. Behind them, the rest of the small army followed in a scattered line, their leg muscles crying out after the long inactivity.

When they reached the first building, a large flock of geese began to hiss and honk. Immediately, the dogs began to bark. The Leader charged through the narrow lane and on into the small square that was lit by a warm glow. Ahead was a path that led to the church, its distinctive shape silhouetted on the lightening hillside. "This way!" he yelled. The time for caution was past.

In front of them an old man lay asleep by the fire. He was awakened by the dogs, and staggered awkwardly to his feet. His eyes widened in fear when he saw the raiders. He turned, but was unable to flee before the Leader's sword cut him down. The Picts raced by and the old man screamed as he fell dying, his voice blending with the increasing sounds of anger and terror that embraced the village.

This was what the Leader craved: the excitement of battle and violent fighting, the bloody killing and after, the sweet taste of success. There would be money in the church somewhere; there always was. He enjoyed killing priests; it was so easy.

The honking of geese awakened Gwriad. For a sleepy moment, he wondered if a wolf was close by. When the dogs began to bark in earnest, he sat up and shook Dafydd. "Something's wrong. Get up. Quick!" He reached for his sword as the door was violently thrown open. The family's big dog barked a warning.

A huge armored figure burst through the doorway. He held an axe in both hands and hesitated for a moment while his eyes accommodated to the dim light. In that instant, the dog hurled itself at the intruder, its deep barking awakening the family. The soldier swung his axe and impaled the animal in mid air, but its weight and acceleration unbalanced him. He bellowed with rage as he staggered back, crashing heavily against the doorjamb, with the dog's dead body falling at his feet. Quickly regaining his footing, he advanced on the horrified family in front of him, unaware of the armed youths behind the door. His swearing gave way to a maniacal laugh when the children began screaming; now, the killing would begin. The adults were yelling a jumble of terrified warnings to each other and trying to edge their backs around the walls, as the horrid apparition advanced on them, lurching across the floor through the dead cinders of the fire ring.

Gwriad sprang forward, unable to contain the yell of loathing that burst out of him. He swung his sword with both hands in a wild undisciplined action, aiming for the head and shoulders of the powerful warrior, whose axe was already raised for a killing stroke. The yell gave the Pict a split-second warning. His survival instincts had been honed by numerous deadly battles, and he reacted instantly. He was turning to his left, the axe already curving round, when Gwriad's sword cut deeply into his left shoulder, missing his neck, but immobilizing his arm. The axe continued its momentum, passing in front of Gwriad's head, but smashing his sword from his grip. Gwriad stumbled and sprawled in the doorway, his arms deadened by the blow.

The soldier, overwhelmed by the pain, roared like a wounded bear. He swayed drunkenly, blood pouring out of his wound, and shuffled forward, mustering his great strength. His vision was blurred, but he could vaguely identify his enemy outlined in the doorway. With a supreme effort, propelled by intense hatred, he raised the heavy axe with his right arm.

The weapon was at its highest point when Dafydd thrust his spear up into the warrior's armpit and through into the neck, severing major blood vessels. The man convulsed and dropped the axe. His blood spurted out over Dafydd, who stood unable to move as he watched the ironclad corpse collapse in front of him.

His brother was instantly on his feet, adrenaline pumping through his body. "Well done, Dafydd! You saved my life, boy." Gwriad rested his hand on his brother's shoulder. It was hard for him to admit that his unworldly brother had bettered him.

Dafydd did not react, but continued to stare at the lifeless invader who, only a moment before had seemed indestructible. He could not believe he had killed this monster. Never in his whole life had he been involved in a fight where people got hurt, or seen a person killed. Now, he was covered in the blood of a man he had speared to death.

"Dafydd! Come on!" Gwriad's urgent voice cut through his trance. "There are more of them. We have a job to do."

As though in a dream he quickly donned his armor, buckled on his sword and, carrying his shield, followed his brother out into the square. Behind them the adults of the meager lodging were stripping the body: the men were arming themselves; the women were wreaking their revenge.

They ran out into the cool air. Dawn had broken and a grey light pervaded the scene, adding a strange quality of unreality to a confused picture. Two houses were burning and a fresh breeze was blowing the smoke across the small square. There was vicious hand-to-hand fighting near the house where Lord Gomer had been sleeping. Four of his soldiers were engaging a large group of Picts in a defiant resistance. There were bodies lying on the ground, and the air was rent with hysterical screams and yells of victory and despair.

"Over here!" Gwriad sprinted across the square towards his uncle's lodging. He noted as he ran that two of Gomer's bodyguard were writhing on the ground, and the remaining two were fighting for their lives against a determined attack by men who were taller and heavier. Still smarting from his first encounter with the invaders, he was desperate to prove himself. He killed the nearest Pict with a spear thrust into his undefended back, but was unable to extract the weapon, and was forced to back away as he struggled to draw his sword, which had somehow become entangled with his belt.

Dafydd raced up, waving his sword and pushing his shield out in front of him. He also had been unwilling to pull his spear out of the giant he had killed, and was still in a numbed state, unable to function, merely following his brother in what seemed an prolonged nightmare.

Three of the invaders turned to face their new enemy, but each relaxed when they recognized they were being challenged by two inexperienced youths. Behind them, the two remaining bodyguards were beaten to the ground, and instantly dispatched. The main body of the Picts charged into the building, convinced there was something of value inside.

The three remaining warriors attacked, two with swords and one with an axe, keen to revenge their fallen comrade. Dafydd shielded his unarmed brother, lashing out with his sword, his speed of action compensating for his lack of experience. A powerful blow from the axe pounded into Dafydd's shield, splitting the leather and forcing the shattered armor hard against him. His arm went limp, and it was only the reflex action of his right hand, delivering a robust strike to the warrior's helmet, that saved his life.

Dafydd backed away as Gwriad rushed forward, attacking the Picts with a terrible anger. He was aware his brother had saved him for the second time. Gratitude and guilt overwhelmed him, for unlike Dafydd, he had received many months of hard training; he had always assumed he would be more than able to defend himself in battle. Yet, when tested he had failed, needing his younger brother to defend him. Such was his passion, that the Picts were forced to give ground and review their earlier assessment. As he drove them back, Dafydd reappeared at his side, hardly able to raise his shield, yet still hacking with his sword, swept up in the adrenaline of the moment. From behind the invaders, Evan appeared, swinging a long oak staff and roaring horribly.

The three Picts were suddenly reinforced by those of their crew who had found nothing of value in the building behind them. In the blink of an eye, the momentum of the battle altered. The two brothers were forced to retreat; panic replaced their former exhilaration as their emboldened enemies raced round to take them from both sides. With a furious cry of rage Evan belayed the Picts from behind, and at that moment, a strident trumpet sounded and Gomer and four of his soldiers galloped up from the back of the building on their tough mountain horses, overwhelming the Picts in a display of power that the savage invaders had never imagined possible.

Amid the smoke and chaos the church bell began to toll, and Pictish horns sounded a retreat.

• • •

As HE RACED UP THE steep path towards the church, the Leader glimpsed a dark robed figure staggering into the building and slamming the door behind him.

"Quickly!" he yelled to the other two who were labouring up the rocky slope, "Quickly!" He was three strides away when he heard a heavy beam slide into place on the other side of the door. Swearing loudly, he threw himself against the oak door, but it was firmly closed. His heart sank as he realized the priest had beaten him to it. The Leader rammed the door with his powerful shoulders, but to no avail. The door did not move. The other raiders arrived and added their considerable strength in a brief onslaught, hoping to push the door off its hinges, but it was beyond them. They looked quickly around for any timber or suitable large stone to use as a battering ram, but they could see nothing in the grey dawn light.

"Use your axes!" The Leader ran to the back of the stone building, hoping to find another entrance. There was none. The small windows, mere apertures, were high in the walls, and offered no possibility of entry.

He raced round to the front, where the two soldiers were smashing into the thick oak with thunderous blows. But the door was well hung, and the oak panels were proving to be stronger than expected. Finally, one axe broke through, splintering the sturdy wood. The Leader gripped his sword in anticipation of the breakthrough. From above the church a bell began to toll, ringing out its message of warning and defiance.

Below, the sounds in the village changed from the expected screams of terror and despair, which accompanied every raid, to the unmistakable sounds of fighting. He stepped back and stared down in amazement at the small square, where armed horseman and foot soldiers were forcing his men to retreat. To make matters worse, he could see a number of his warriors lying motionless on the ground. It was like a bad dream; he had not expected to lose any of his men. Where had these Welsh troops come from?

Behind him the church door collapsed. His two soldiers gave a bellow of triumph, their huge bodies heaving from the exertion. Now they would revenge themselves on the priest who had dared to delay them.

"Back to the boat! Leave it! Back to the boat!" the Leader bellowed, and disappeared down the hill. The soldiers stood immobile, unable to grasp the reason for his behaviour. At that moment, they heard the noise of a pitched battle and realized something was seriously wrong. When they looked down, they too were horrified at the change in events. Their comrades were retreating back to the river, desperately defending themselves against trained soldiers, some on horseback. Fearing for their lives, the Picts began a frantic race down the slope into the small square and were soon embroiled in a deadly melee, each man fighting for his life.

The Leader carved his way through the square, yelling commands, determined to recreate some sense of order among his retreating men. His presence gave courage to the disparate warriors; they began to fight like a team, easily overpowering their inexperienced assailants, but unable to gain the upper hand because of the weight of numbers opposing them. They had lost a quarter of their force. Many of those remaining had sustained injuries, and were unable to fight effectively. Soon they were retreating again, not only because of the attacks by the trained soldiers, but also because of missiles thrown by the newly empowered fishermen. Stones and the occasional arrow rained down on them. Once more, panic set in.

"Back to the boat!" the Leader yelled. His voice resonated over the screams and shouts of the Welsh defenders. In the confusion, the tolling of the church bell and the excited barking of the dogs seemed unnaturally loud. "Get the boat afloat! Hurry!"

The disheartened Picts gathered together and fought a hasty withdrawal, while Gomer led a vigorous attack with his small cavalry. Eventually, the raiders reached the narrow path leading back to the small harbour. The Leader, his sergeant and two others formed a solid wedge, while the rest of his men, many injured, retreated to their boat.

The tide had turned. The water was racing out, leaving the heavy galley beached in the river mud. Its aft section remained in the water, but its bows were firmly embedded. The two men who had been left to guard the boat and the two ordered to destroy the row boats were pushing feverishly against the vessel's bows, unable to loosen it from the grip of the mud. They were almost thigh deep in the sucking ooze and were gripped with an unfamiliar panic. Everything was working against them.

The retreating soldiers threw their weapons into the galley, and joined their comrades in a superhuman effort to release the boat. It was their only hope of survival, and they pushed as a team. There was a sudden choking sound, and the galley broke free from the clutches of the deep mud. The boat lurched back into the main outrush of the river. A cry went up as the empty craft moved suddenly into the current and began to swing backwards towards the distant sea. A small group of Picts managed to climb aboard, but not before the vessel had begun to move down towards the tidal plain.

It took only moments for them to grab the long oars, but it seemed an eternity as they strained to slow the movement of the heavy galley, gradually returning up river to where their comrades were fighting a rear guard action against the furious Welsh. The men at the oars yelled encouragement to their injured companions, who waded, with difficulty, into the foul mud, seeing the boat as their only redemption. Meanwhile, the Leader launched a violent counter-attack up the narrow path back to the village, supported by a handful of his men who were still able to fight.

Gomer's horses were of little use in the confined space, and he was forced to abandon his mount and try to organize his few remaining soldiers for a final assault. Before he could get his men into some sense of order, the fishermen, lusting for revenge, rushed the Pictish leader and his small guard. The Picts were fighters and knew how to use any advantage they were given; whereas the Welsh fishermen had bravery but little else: they lacked armor, heavy weapons or experience. Before Gomer could prevent them, the fishermen rushed onto the narrow pathway, just as the Picts launched their counter attack in a desperate attempt to enable their injured comrades to reach the galley. The Welsh attacked with knives, staves and an odd spear, and in moments their front line was cut down. Injured fishermen staggered back, blocking Gomer's soldiers from advancing. The Pictish leader, seizing the opportunity, led his men in a speedy retreat back to the boat.

"Duw! They're getting away," Gomer yelled. He was so exhausted he could hardly hold his sword. 'Stop them!" He took a deep breath and fell against his horse. 'I'm too old for this,' he thought. He closed his eyes and sank to the ground, with blood oozing out from under his helmet.

"Silly old fool," Evan whispered in his ear. He dragged Gomer out of the melee. "When will you realize you're getting old?" He removed Gomer's helmet, and poured water over the gash on his head. "At this rate, you'll die before me. Then what would I do?"

Gwriad struggled to force his way through the incensed fishermen; many were injured, but unwilling to move aside. Dafydd followed closely behind and, between them, they finally reached the front of the line. Ahead, they could see the remainder of the Picts struggling through the mud to the waiting galley. The brothers led a half-hearted charge to the riverbank, just as the final Picts were pulled aboard. The oars began to strike the water, and the enemy vessel moved slowly, almost majestically, into the centre of the river.

In front of Gwriad was a wide expanse of mud and no way to

stop the retreating Picts. He cursed the river and anything else he could blame for enabling the enemy to escape. The galley was so near and yet beyond his reach.

"If they get away, they'll know where to come back to next time," Dafydd said solemnly.

Gwriad glared at him. "I know that. What do you want me to do? Fly?"

"No! Use the horses. We might beat them to the mouth of the estuary."

"Too late. They're putting their sail up. We'll never get there in time. We'll…" He stopped in amazement as a flaming arrow flew over his head and landed on the galley, causing chaos among a crew that had just begun to look organized.

"Well done!" Dafydd yelled.

Behind him, a small group of fishermen were using their short hunting bows. They fired at their enemies with arrows wrapped in cloth and flaming tar. The tough Welsh fisherwomen were quickly wrapping the sharp ends of the arrows in small pieces of torn material, dipping the arrowheads in tar and lighting them. It was a risky undertaking, and some women did not know how to prepare the tar, passing to their menfolk fiery missiles that were too hot to handle. In spite of this, a cluster of fire arrows was discharged. Most missed the boat, but two scored direct hits on the wide sail, piercing the fabric, and causing small fires.

There was a flurry of activity on board as the heavy sail was quickly dragged down and the flames extinguished, but not before a further volley of arrows hit the boat, some finding human targets. The boat continued its ponderous journey towards the estuary, but had lost its former momentum.

"Back to the horses!" Gwriad yelled, forcing his way through the fishermen, who were cheering their success.

"Quickly!" Dafydd pointed at his uncle's men. Most were exhausted, some had minor wounds, and a number were missing. "Get to the horses. We can beat them yet!"

At the top of the causeway, Gomer had regained consciousness. His huge body was gasping for breath like a mighty bellows; sweat and blood poured down his craggy face. He was standing with his back against a wall, supported by Evan. "You lead, Gwriad. I'll follow. Nothing stupid, mind! Don't risk the men, or yourselves!"

• • •

IT WAS A NEAR THING. The two brothers and the few remaining soldiers of Gomer's bodyguard galloped their horses along the south bank to the sandy mouth of the estuary in a furious attempt to reach the narrow mouth of the estuary before the Pictish galley arrived. But the strength of the outgoing tide and the frantic energy of the rowers enabled the enemy boat to pass through the narrow mouth while the horsemen were still galloping around the edge of the estuary, a full half-mile away.

The Picts reached the presumed safety of the sea as Gwriad and Dafydd and the few soldiers of Gomer's personal guard finally arrived at the mouth of the river. The soldiers were exhausted and clambered down wearily from their sweating mounts, yelling abuse at the departing galley. But the two brothers, gripped by the excitement of the moment, rode their tired horses over the sand dunes and on to the wide beach beyond, where they had a clear view of the bay.

Their side of the mouth of the river was flat and sandy, with only the low dunes to hold back the incursions of the sea. Behind them, deep marshes gradually gave way to scrubby trees as the land rose slowly up to the distant hills on either side of the river. The opposite side of the bay was a stark contrast: high, threatening cliffs and dark rocky inlets lined the barren shore, leading eventually to a windblown headland with a bleak rocky island beyond. There were strong currents racing along that shore that were a constant danger even to the local fishermen who were familiar with the conditions.

"They're going to end up on the island!" Gwriad yelled, waving his bloodstained sword. His blue eyes were wide with excitement as he stared out across the wave-battered bay. He was still pumped with the excitement of the battle, and unable to grasp the magnitude of their lucky escape. The battle could so easily have gone the other way.

Dafydd rode up beside him. He was gasping for breath and,

like Gwriad, still clutched his short sword as if expecting the Picts to return. The energy that had driven him for the past hour was quickly dissipating, but he felt complete in a way he had never felt before. "They may get through the cut, even now," he argued, jabbing the air with his sword.

"They won't dare. They'll try to escape by going round the island and, with luck, they'll hit the rocks. It's low tide. The boat could end up on the hidden beach on the other side."

It was clear that the Picts were in trouble. They had barely enough men to row their heavy vessel; many of the surviving rowers had received wounds from their unexpected defeat. The damaged main sail had been raised, but was causing trouble as the dispirited Picts fought to cope with the rising wind and the unexpected strength of tide and current. They had to use all their surviving rowers to avoid being swept against the cliffs, and their only hope was to get out of the bay and take their chances on the open sea.

The brothers climbed down from their panting horses and spent a few moments stretching their aching limbs and blowing out their cheeks. They untied their thick leather breastplates and removed their domed iron helmets; the shape of them had distant echoes of a Roman influence. They paced about restlessly, like caged animals, staring angrily across the threatening sea at the distant galley. It was close to the rocks, but still moving inexorably towards the headland. Since first light, the weather had begun to close in; black clouds raced across the sky and the waves in the bay increased in strength.

"Look! They're going to pass the cut. I tell you, they could end up on the island." Gwriad stamped his foot excitedly on the hard sand.

"You may be right after all, but there's not much we can do about it." Dafydd replaced his sword in its scabbard, and lay down on the ground. He felt exhausted and every part of his body ached, his arms in particular. He had fought and killed people and, although he experienced the sweet taste of victory, there was also the shock of the event, which was gnawing away at his tired mind. He spread his arms and legs on the sand and closed his eyes.

Gwriad slumped down beside him, sitting with his arms resting on his knees, watching the disappearing galley. He also felt suddenly tired, as though his energy was departing with the tide. They had been so close to destroying the Pictish invaders, and now the victory was incomplete. They had beaten off the unexpected attack, but the main body of the invaders was escaping. He closed his eyes and let his limbs relax. It was all over.

"What are you bloody well doing?" Gomer's deep voice shocked them awake. "Do you think it's all over?" He dragged them to their feet, his huge hands treating them as though they were small children. "Half-wits! Have you no sense? There's a chance they may founder on the rocks around the island. They could all drown, but there may be survivors. If so, we must hunt them down!" Gomer seemed unnaturally energized, as if gripped by a violent ecstasy. "We have no time to lose!"

Beside him the loyal Evan shrugged his shoulders, rolled his eyes and, with a subtle movement of his hand, indicated that they should follow.

The brothers came quickly to their senses. They watched amazed as their unpredictable uncle vaulted back onto his horse and urged his snorting mount across the hard sand and over the soft dunes, back towards the narrow mouth of the estuary. Evan followed doggedly behind.

Moving as fast as they were able, and exchanging glum looks with each other, the two chastised youths collected their equipment, mounted their horses and followed the disappearing riders. By the time they reached the remainder of their uncle's followers, they had regained their youthful energy and were keen to compete with each other in their anticipated crossing to the other side.

At lowest tide, the distance between the two banks of the mouth of the estuary was only a stone's throw, and since the Pictish galley had passed through, the tide had slackened, allowing the horsemen the chance of a cautious crossing. The depth was unknown and it seemed likely the reluctant animals would have to swim. To add to the danger there were steep sandy banks on each side, which made for a difficult ascent from the river.

Gomer ordered two of his men to cross the channel to test the current and the depth. The horses had trouble coping with the difficult gradient, their legs sinking into the soft sand of the steep banks, but the soldiers held on grimly, forcing their unwilling animals to swim across the narrow channel, and after some balking by the desperate beasts, the two soldiers finally reached firmer ground. A big cheer went up from the other soldiers.

Gwriad and Dafydd were the next to enter the water. They wanted to impress their highly-charged uncle, and crossed the deep river yelling and roaring defiance to the Picts, and making the crossing seem of little danger. Gomer was pleased. With Evan by his side, he led the rest of his depleted bodyguard in a safe crossing. Unlike his soldiers, Gomer knew this coast and led them up a narrow path to the beginning of the high ground. From there, they continued uphill until they were at the top of the cliffs, where they galloped across a springy, windblown heath. It was dotted with stunted bushes, patches of briars and wide rabbit holes, which continued to endanger their horses until they were close to the bare headland.

They were all gasping for breath when they stopped. The horses were steaming and the men could feel the heat in their damp clothes. They stared at the gloomy and seemingly deserted island in front of them. There was no trace of the galley and no sign of human activity. Out at sea, the waves had white tops and the wind was increasing.

"Perhaps they missed the island after all," Dafydd said.

"Can you see any sign of them out at sea?" Gwriad sneered.

"They could be making out to sea, hidden behind the island."

"No. We'd see them by now. They'd be going north. In their condition, they wouldn't want to be too far out to sea. I bet you they've ended up on the rocks."

"I agree with Gwriad." Gomer barged his horse between them. "They may have wrecked on the far side. The locals say it's a dangerous place, lots of rocks, but with this low tide some of the Picts may have survived." His hand went to his sword in an involuntary gesture. "It's my worst fear. If some are still alive they may make their way back to the mainland. They're trained killers. Think of the harm they could do."

"Well, there's nothing to be done unless we want to leave soldiers on guard here for a week or more until we're certain they're dead." Dafydd shrugged his shoulders.

"There's a way to the island at low tide," Gwriad said unexpectedly. He jumped off his horse and ran to the edge of the cliff. He paused, and then walked slowly along until he came to a dip in the rock surface. "Here's the way!"

Gomer and Dafydd dismounted and walked up to where Gwriad was staring down. Evan collected the horses, and stood back while his Lord stalked up to the edge of the cliff.

"Do you intend for us to swim, boy?" Gomer asked incredulously.

"There's a ledge that stretches from the base of this cliff to the island. It's easy to cross when the tide's out."

Gomer frowned. "How do you know?"

Gwriad looked uncomfortable. "When I came with you last year, some of the fishermen showed me."

"Another of your foolhardy antics," Gomer grumbled, but he did not sound angry. His attention was riveted on the possible way down the cliff to a small sandy cove at the bottom. Now he knew what he was looking for, he could see there were low rocky shelves appearing out of the water each time the waves withdrew. Further down the channel on both sides, between the headland and the island, the waves were larger, but in this one spot they were less obvious. "I can see the causeway," he said excitedly.

He turned to Gwriad. "You've been over to the island?"

"Yes."

"What happens on the other side?"

"There's an easy climb to the top. The island's fairly flat. Some areas of marsh, a few pools and scrub." His eyes were bright with enthusiasm. "We were collecting birds' eggs. I've seen the hidden beach."

"What's it like?"

"It's very steep. We didn't try to get down. Some of the fishermen go there by boat and pull up on the beach. They catch conger eels in the deep pools." His face became serious. "There's no beach there at high tide. If any of the Picts are alive, they'll have to climb up the cliff once the tide comes in."

Gomer stared at Gwriad, but did not see him. His mind was wrestling with the decision that only he could make. They could set guards for a week, or he could allow Gwriad and a few of the soldiers to check if there were any Picts on the hidden beach. The one thing that was certain, he could not leave the area without taking some action. He could not allow these monsters the chance of survival, and the risk of them killing the local inhabitants. He felt responsible.

"All right, Gwriad, I want you to show my men how to cross to the island. I want you to lead them to that hidden beach and see if any of that scum has survived. If they're alive, kill them somehow. If there's no trace of them, come straight back. Understood?"

"What about me?" Dafydd exclaimed. "I want to go."

"You'll stay with me and Evan."

"I fought as well as anybody today!" He pointed at Gwriad. "I saved his life, twice. I'm as good a soldier as any man here. Uncle, you can't deny me!"

Gomer was startled. Dafydd had never questioned his orders before, unlike Gwriad, who constantly challenged his authority. He looked carefully at his young nephew, and realized he had changed. Gomer chewed his lower lip, a deep scowl on his face. There was a long silence. When he felt he had reestablished himself, he let out a long sigh. "All right, Dafydd, you'll go with your brother. But he alone will make the decisions. Understand?"

Dafydd bowed his head. "Thank you, uncle. I agree." He tried not to smile. He had won his first argument. It was all that mattered.

"Are there any of you men who don't wish to cross to the island?" Gomer glared round at his depleted bodyguard. They all stared back at him. "All right then, you will all follow Gwriad. Leave your horses tied to the bushes back there." He turned his gaze on his elder nephew: he was so like his dead father: strong, dark and with a lust for adventure. A strange lump formed in his throat. Cydweli had been more than a younger brother; he had been his best friend. He cast a ferocious glare at the assembled men. "And don't be long, the tide waits for no man. Understand?" Gwriad and Dafydd bowed quickly and prepared for their expedition.

• • •

THE CROSSING WAS NOT DIFFICULT, the seawater barely reached their knees, but the rocky shelf was slippery underfoot and rogue waves soaked those who were the last to cross. Once they reached the other side, Gwriad led them up a series of rocky ledges until they reached the exposed flat top of the island. They gathered together, while Gwriad checked the numbers. There were eight soldiers, and he noticed that some of them had minor wounds and the last up were drenched and shivering with cold. "You're brave men. Thank you for coming. I'm sure some of you would have preferred to be drinking beer with a wench in your arms."

The soldiers laughed and raised a cheer. They liked Gwriad.

Dafydd stood at the back of the gathering and blew out his cheeks. His earlier satisfaction had faded and he realized he was, once again, merely the younger brother. When he looked back, Gomer and Evan were standing like statues on the headland. He gave a half-hearted wave and moved off behind the small army. He was certain it was a waste of time, but he could not have allowed himself to be left behind.

For what seemed a very long time, they staggered over the rough terrain, their boots sinking deep into mud and shallow pools. Gulls and cormorants swooped above them, their sad calls strangely suitable in this wild landscape. It was an exhausting march, and many of them were slowing up with fatigue. Gwriad finally called a halt when they had covered about three-quarters of the journey. "We'll rest a while," he said, his broad frame heaving with the exertion.

The men collapsed on the ground, ignoring the wet undergrowth. It had been a day of unending physical and mental effort. Some of their friends had died today and others had been left in the village nursing grievous wounds. The surviving soldiers wanted revenge; it was what had driven them to volunteer.

After a short break, Gwriad stood up. "We're all tired. But I know you feel as I do that these devils must be destroyed. It's possible they've all drowned, but if any of them are alive, I know you'll want to help me end their foul lives."

The men gave a roar of approval, and Dafydd wondered how he would have behaved if he had been in charge. No matter how hard he tried to think himself the better man, he could not help admiring his brother.

They forced themselves to their feet, adjusted their weapons, and advanced in a ragged formation across the boggy ground. The storm was increasing and rain began to beat into their faces. The wind came in bursts, forcing them to stagger. There were no trees or rocks to shelter them as they plodded determinedly across the flat landscape, forcing their way through the knee high heather. Eventually, they could see the angry waves in the distance, and knew they had reached the other side of the island. Gwriad turned to his left, and beckoned them to follow; the soldiers were immediately aware of the loud pounding of the powerful sea on their right. After a few paces, Gwriad stopped, dropped to his knees and, lying on his stomach, approached the edge of the cliff. They all copied him, crawling along to a rocky ledge where they could look down. On the hidden beach beneath, they saw a sight none of them had expected.

• • •

BELOW THEM WAS A ROCKY cove with a narrow, steeply sloping shingle beach on which a large broken galley laid side-on against the powerful waves that rolled in from the open sea. Many of its long oars were broken; those that remained intact were facing the increasingly large breakers that thundered into the cove. The power of the waves was intense and each huge surge swamped the vessel, threatening to drag it away from its tenuous hold on the vulnerable beach. Around the galley, a small group of exhausted Pictish warriors tried to pull the heavy boat beyond the grasp of the threatening waves, little knowing that the whole cove would soon be under water. They were a sad group of men; a mere fragment of their earlier selves: no longer the powerful, murdering invaders, but reduced to a bunch of sodden, half-drowned creatures who struggled to preserve their only hope for survival.

The Welsh soldiers stared down silently from edge of the high cliff, noting the steep, slippery walls of the cove below them, and understanding how the Picts were unable to escape. The light was fading and the tide was rising quickly. Mountainous waves roared in, crashing over and around the damaged vessel, then retreating with a dangerous sucking action. Some of warriors fell into the surge and thrashed around, trying desperately to avoid the drag of the outrushing sea.

"What shall we do?" Dafydd asked, his eyes wide with fear.

"Do?" his brother replied, unable to believe the question. "We stay here to make sure none of these murdering bastards survives, that's what we do."

"But, they don't have a chance," Dafydd continued. "I was prepared to fight them, but I never thought it would be like this."

"There's nothing we can do! Even if there was, I wouldn't risk your life or mine trying to save them."

"But, we can't just watch them drown."

"Then, don't watch!" Gwriad was almost speechless with rage.

As he spoke, a huge wave roared into the cove and burst over the boat, engulfing the struggling Picts, and retreating with a ferocious undertow that dragged more than half of them into the merciless sea, plucking the damaged galley from its tenuous hold on survival, and reducing it to a mere piece of floating jetsam. Many of the soldiers still wore their body armor and quickly vanished below the raging waters; a few others struggled about in the maelstrom for some brief moments, before succumbing to the relentless pounding of the waves.

Only a handful of Picts remained. They staggered up the short, steep wave-scoured beach, their boots sinking deep in the shingle. They were barely able to drag themselves above the tenacious clutch of the water. One of them glanced up and, seeing the line of men looking down from the high cliff above, began calling out and waving his arms frantically. His exhausted companions stared up in amazement, their faces betraying both hope and doubt, as a wave surged up to the rock wall of the cove, covering the whole of the remaining beach.

"There's a way down. You said as much. You could save them."

Gwriad glared at his brother. "For what purpose? If we saved any of them, it would only be to hand them over to Gomer to be hanged." He stood up and watched as the broken hulk of the galley disappeared into the tumultuous sea. "These men deserve to die. How can you feel sorry for them?"

Gomer's bodyguard nodded in agreement.

"There's no honour in this!" Dafydd wailed. "I won't be part of it!" He jumped to his feet and stalked off into the gloom, towards the other side of the island. He knew it was illogical, but he could not feel any satisfaction in the death of these men, even though they were his enemy. Killing them in battle was one thing, but watching them drown was inhuman.

Gwriad and the soldiers watched dispassionately, as one by one the screaming Picts slowly succumbed to the rising sea. Eventually, there was just a dark seething cauldron of frothing water, and no sign of the warriors or their vessel. The light disappeared and darkness descended.

"If we hadn't arrived 'til now, we wouldn't have known they'd drowned," one of the soldiers remarked.

"Gomer will be pleased anyway," another jested as they prepared to march back.

"'Saved us risking getting killed as well."

"So, don't get yourself killed on the way back either!" Gwriad shouted, trying to be heard above the roar of the sea. The wind was still rising, and driving rain added to their problems. It would be an unpleasant return journey, especially as they had no light to see by. "Stay together and watch where you tread," he ordered.

He led the way back across the dark landscape, and cursed his brother for storming off. It would serve him right if he got lost. Mostly, he blamed Dafydd for spoiling what should have been a celebration. Their enemy had been totally vanquished. "Drinks are on me when we get back, boys!" he yelled, trying to raise their morale. "We can claim a complete victory! Plenty to tell your girlfriends about."

After a long, tedious and tiring march, they reached the place where they could cross back to the mainland, and found Dafydd waiting for them. He sat brooding in the darkness on a ledge above the swirling waters. On the other side of the channel, they could see torches flaming in the gusting wind, and knew Lord Gomer and Evan were there.

It was full tide. They made themselves as comfortable as possible, knowing it would be a long wait before they could cross back to safety and a warm bed.

"The Picts are all dead!" Gwriad yelled across the noise of the sea. "We're all safe!" He tried to make it sound as if they had played some part in the defeat of their enemy. Gomer would be pleased.

Over the tumult of wind and rain, he heard his uncle's powerful voice: "And about time too!"

Gomer sniffed loudly, and sought shelter under a makeshift awning that Evan had constructed with the help of a group of fishermen. The men had returned with him, carrying flaring torches and food and drink, eager to prove to their Lord their gratitude to him for defending their village. Gomer chewed slowly on cold venison, as he stared out at the dim shape of the island.

"Thank God they're safe," he murmured. "Cydweli would be proud of them." For the last thirteen years, since the great battle of Rhyd-y-Groes in 1039, there had not been a day pass by when he did not grieve for his dead brother. However, his custody of his brother's boys was a welcome consolation for the sons he never had. It would be a long wait until first light. He allowed his mind to review the way the great battle had developed, and his brother's contribution to their remarkable victory. "It was never easy, but it was such a victory," he muttered. "It would have been perfect if only Cydweli had survived."

CHAPTER THREE

1039

They had known for more than a week that Earl Leofric and his Saxon hordes were on the move. King Gruffydd ap Llwelyn had swept down from his northern stronghold among the Snowdonia mountains, in the kingdom of Gwynedd, to oppose the invaders. His supporters had sent out a call for fighting men as his army moved swiftly across the country towards the Welsh borders. With the promise of battle and plunder, many farmers forsook their lands, and the villages near the borders were emptied of able-bodied men. Many were skilled archers, others possessed spears, swords and knives, but most had only a smattering of body armor. The Saxons were heavier and better armed, but they lacked the speed and agility of the Welsh, possessed few archers and horses, and did not appreciate the problems the terrain presented to a large invading army.

Gruffydd decided to oppose the Saxons near the mountain of Corndon, an isolated peak in Montgomery on their mid-eastern border. Historically, it had been an ideal pathway for invaders: once through the passes of the mountain range, the armies could flood into the lowlands of central Wales. In the distance, towards the east, Gruffydd's army could see the gleam of the upper waters of the mighty River Severn. Below them was a steeply undulating tract of heavily wooded ground through which the Camlad River roared on its way towards the marshes of the Severn valley. Behind them were the rugged, wild lands and the deep forests of Corndon, with glimpses of the holy mountain of Plinlimmon, the cloud-covered summit of Cader Idris, and the dark summits of the Berwyn Range.

On a low hill beside the Camlad, the Welsh had established a large fort, with great ditches surrounding it. The soil from the ditches had been used to create a rampart on which a palisade of heavy logs had been erected, forming an imposing stockade over ten feet in height. It was well positioned, for with the hill to climb as well as the deep trenches to cross, the fort presented a problem for any attackers. There were two heavy gates situated on the west side, and a raised platform circled the inside, enabling the defenders to fire down on their enemies. The builders had established a deep, freshwater well, numerous fire pits for warmth and cooking, and many covered areas for sleeping. There was enough space to house a hundred horses, together with feed bins and small fenced areas for sheep and fowl. It had been built the previous summer by his long-time friend Cydweli ap Griffith, and was Gruffydd's largest military encampment. Indeed, it was his only fortification of its type.

During the winter, it had been manned by a formidable group of scouts, who returned to their farms and villages after serving for a month at a time. It was the nearest the Welsh had to a standing army. Those who served in this lonely place had spent their time making small raids into the Saxon areas, stealing animals and possessions, and burning the enemy farms. In bad weather they worked on the defenses, increasing the covered areas and making large woodpiles for fuel. The area was rich in oak, beech, elm and fir, and willows grew in abundance along the banks of the Cordon. The scouts made small wooden shields, great bunches of sharpened staves, and fine bows and arrows. They practised with slings, had archery competitions and were constantly on guard, sending small reconnaissance parties to watch for the inevitable Saxon attack. Now, with the approach of spring, the Saxons were seeking revenge, and Gruffydd ap Llywelyn was keen to prove the burgeoning power of the Welsh.

• • •

FROM A HIGH POINT ON the mountain of Corndon, two men stared out over the Camlad River, and looked down at the newly cleared hill with its powerful fort dominating the wide valley. Rhys had never seen anything like it: below was a fort of such strength and organization that he could hardly believe it belonged to them. He was the Sergeant-at-Arms to Gruffydd ap Llywelyn, the King of Gwynedd and Powys, and had not seen the defenses since their completion. When Gruffydd had ordered its building the previous summer, the King had stayed only long enough to establish the outline of his plans, before moving up to Powys to quell a small insurrection; where the King went, his Sergeant-at-Arms was always close at his side.

Over the winter, Gruffydd had been concerned with establishing a web of local commanders throughout his kingdom who would be responsible for recruiting men when invasion threatened. Rhys had been involved with all the cumbersome details of the organization. The planning had been all consuming, and he had spared few thoughts on this fort on their border. Now, the Saxons were coming; the new Welsh army was assembling, and the King was keen to see how his first line of defense had developed.

"The man's a genius!" Gruffydd exclaimed as he gazed down at the distant fort. "I tell you, Rhys, he's worth an army!"

The King was in his early thirties, taller than most Welshmen, and with strength and energy that exceeded all his followers. He was a natural warrior: brave, skilled with weapons, and with a quick and decisive mind. He had been fighting almost continuously since seizing the throne of Gwynedd a few months ago. Gwynedd was the most important of the Kingdoms of Wales, embracing the wild Snowdonia Mountains, and the holy island, known as the Druid island of Ynys Mon. A flourishing trade with Ireland enriched Gwynedd, and the other princedoms were, for the most part, content to have friendly ties. Gruffydd had inherited Powys on the mid- and north-east border of Wales; after much fighting, he had extended his Kingdom to include parts of the fertile lands of Ceredigion. His aim was to conquer all of the large Kingdom of Deheubarth and thereby control the whole of the north and west coasts of Wales. Now he was preparing to defend both his Kingdom, and the principalities in the south of the country, whose kings were in a temporary alliance with Gruffydd.

Behind him, a host of assembled horsemen fanned out across

the mountain, eager for a first look. For most of them the fort was like a magical creation: beyond their wildest dreams.

"Cydweli did this?" Rhys said, a mixture of amazement and envy in his voice. He looked up at the King who was mounted on a fierce warhorse, which he had captured from a Saxon lord; it was five hands larger than the typical Welsh pony that Rhys was riding, and reinforced Gruffydd's air of leadership. "Cydweli did this?" Rhys repeated.

"Do you doubt it? Did you ever see such a wonderful sight?" Gruffydd stared down, his quick mind noting the defenses, and approving of everything he saw. It had been his plan to establish a fort to control the area of the Cordon Marches, and Cydweli, his friend from Ceredigion, had agreed to take charge of it.

"Sound the trumpets! We will take possession of our fort, and with it, we will break the back of the Saxon army!"

His men cheered, the trumpets sounded, and he led his mounted soldiers down through the dense forests, into the wet valley, and up to the cleared hill on which sat a stronghold that was a key element in his plan to defeat the invaders.

When he reached the fort, the heavy gates were wide open. Cydweli, in full armor, was standing in the entrance with several hundreds of his soldiers formed up on both sides. This was not an army that had a common uniform: only the King's household guard boasted a recognizable unity, with their green and brown uniforms and their bright body armor. Around Cydweli were men who had laboured for months on the building of this impressive fort. Many of them wore animal skins, a mishmash of armor and carried a variety of weapons. But they were keen, loyal and above all, ready to fight for their King and country. Cydweli swelled with pride as his King approached.

"Cydweli, my friend, you have exceeded my expectations. This is a magnificent construction and a true testament to what we Welsh can achieve." He leapt off his horse and strode towards Cydweli who bowed, and with his right arm, indicated the men who were lined up to meet their King.

"It was your idea, Sire. These men and I merely followed your orders."

Gruffydd embraced him in a bear hug and gripped his friend's broad shoulders, smiling ferociously. "Enough, Cydweli. You have created a most formidable fort that will cause our enemy to hesitate in his advance on our land. In that hesitation, we will defeat him. Our victory will have much to do with this fort, the like of which I have never seen." Gruffydd stepped back and unsheathed his sword. "Step forward, Cydweli, and bend your knee."

After a pause, during which Cydweli looked for support from his delighted men, he staggered forward, uncertain if his legs would carry him. He took a deep breath and kneeled before his King, tears of emotion streaming down his flushed face.

"Cydweli, my most loyal and true friend, creator of this fort and most famed among our Welsh warriors, I wish to honour you for your achievements." He rested his sword on Cydweli's head. "Henceforth, you will be known as General of the Welsh Army. The first Welshman ever to achieve this rank. You will be in charge of the defense of our homeland and subject only to me. In all else, your word will be law and your decisions will guide our army."

The assembled men broke into riotous cheering, banging their shields and waving their swords in the air. Behind them, a deafening roar of approval resonated around the valley, as the soldiers united with each other in their enthusiasm for their new General. It was a generous gesture to a proven friend, and a clever political move by Gruffydd, which his Sergeant-at-Arms was quick to appreciate.

"Tonight we feast! The enemy is still days away and we will celebrate the creation of our new fort and the imminent defeat of our enemy!" Gruffydd remounted his horse and, raising his sword above his head, lead his army into the fort.

• • •

THE NEXT MORNING, THE FORTIFICATION was a hive of activity, with men gathering up their gear, grabbing any food available, and streaming out of the gates to form up in columns under the bellowing commands of their sergeants. The horsemen collected their animals, which had been kept in large enclosures outside the fort, and prepared them for a journey. The feasting of the previous night had been a lively, but congested affair, with many hundreds of men eating, drinking and singing within the tight confines of the fort. Many had eventually moved outside to find a space to sleep, and it was obvious to everyone that there were too many defenders to be housed on a permanent basis. They wondered how their King would use them. The latest reports indicated that the Saxons might be expected within the next two days and Gruffydd decided to act quickly.

"I will divide the army into two sections: those who will defend the fort from the inside, and the majority who will fight in the open." He grinned at Cydweli, who was nursing a bad hangover and a hoarse voice from a night of singing and shouting. "You will be in charge of the fort, Cydweli. Keep a number of your trusted men to act as your officers, and I will take the majority of the army and the rest of the scouts."

"How many men will you leave me?" Cydweli sounded concerned.

Gruffydd smiled. "You'll have plenty of warriors, my friend. By the end of today, and early tomorrow, the rest of the army should arrive. Many of the men are past their youth. They are keen to fight, but will be exhausted after their long march. I want them to recover within the safety of the fort; if the Saxons don't arrive for another two or three days, they will have time to build up their fighting spirit."

"You want me to stay inside the fort?"

"Certainly." Gruffydd nodded. "Do not fear, old friend. You will not be denied your share of the fighting. This fort will attract the enemy like bees to honey. They will be amazed when they see it, and will want to destroy it. You will have to defend your fort." He rubbed his hands through his long hair. "It is important that the Saxons are made to believe that all our fighters are inside. You will be in charge of more men than you have ever led in battle."

Cydweli had a reputation as a fighter, and his promotion to General had been well received by the warriors. In the past, however, his battles had been fierce but limited in scale, often involving fewer than a hundred men. Wales was sparsely populated and had no towns like Hereford or Worcester. Large villages, rarely above four to five hundred people, were the norm, and the constant warring between the different principalities was often fought with a limited loss of life. Most Welsh soldiers were primarily farmers; war was seen as a chance for them to have some excitement, grab some loot and return quickly to their hard-pressed families. It was more important to capture your enemy than kill him; slaves were highly valued, and were an essential element of farming.

"I will establish a camp up in the mountains. It is already being prepared. Most of the horses will be taken there." Gruffydd could see the plan unfolding in his mind and his blue eyes were bright with excitement. "Every man in the fort must be able to use a bow or a sling, and there could be some murderous hand-to-hand fighting. You will have to keep our soldiers in the fort, even if the enemy appears to withdraw. With these untrained men, you will have your work cut out: the moment they think the enemy is retreating, they will want to rush out and kill as many Saxons as they can. They must not be allowed to open the gates, for in doing so they will give up their advantage. Remember, the enemy will use every trick to break in here, or encourage your men to chase them."

"You will come to relieve us when the fighting starts?"

"That will depend on the way the Saxon leaders react to this fort. They will certainly attack you. But, if you prove unbeatable, and cause unacceptable losses to their army, they may by-pass you and head for easier pickings." His face was lit up with excitement. "This is my hope. It will depend on you, Cydweli. If you give them a beating, they may not try for a long siege. Their men will be lusting for plunder and for our women, and they will think to destroy you on their return. They will certainly leave enough men to keep you inside while they advance into our country, believing they will be unopposed. With the ones you kill, and those they are forced to leave behind to contain you, we will have reduced their army significantly." Gruffydd rubbed his nose with the palm of his hand, an action he did when he was excited. "If this happens, they will be defeated. I will ambush them and send them reeling back the way they came. That will be the time for you to attack the rearguard. Between us, we will have them surrounded on all sides."

Cydweli licked his dry lips. He had never thought on this scale. His experiences were limited to bloody hand-to-hand fights on horses, or brutish skirmishes among deep forests. "When will you leave?"

"After you and I have agreed our plans, General Cydweli." Gruffydd slapped his friend heartily on his shoulders. "Find Rhodri ap Tewdwr and Emrys ap Mawr and meet me on the eastern side of the fort." He strode off beaming from ear to ear, acknowledging greetings as he went.

Cydweli coughed and rubbed his bloodshot eyes. He wished he had not celebrated his promotion quite so enthusiastically the night before. He was forced to admit he was getting older. Although still a relatively young man, he no longer had the strength and vigor of his younger King. He shrugged his shoulders and screwed up his eyes. When he opened them, he noticed a young scout had stopped, while walking his horse, and was watching him with a smile.

"What are you grinning at? Make yourself useful, boy! Fetch me Rhodri ap Tewdwr and Emrys ap Mawr, and tell them to meet the King on the east side of the fort. If they're not there by the time I get there, I'll have you thrashed!" The youth jumped to attention, gave a lopsided salute and sprang onto his horse. As he trotted off towards the main gate, the youth cursed his stupidity: never get noticed by the nobility.

It was one of the better days in recent weeks, for although the sun had not broken through the dense clouds, there was no rain, and was a welcome change in the weather. Cydweli rubbed his tired eyes and began to focus on a large group of men who were struggling up the hill as though they were climbing the steep side of Cader Idris. Gradually, a face came into view, and Cydweli snapped awake.

"Gomer! Gomer!" Cydweli waved to his older brother, who was riding a tired black horse slowly up the hill towards the fort. Behind him, a sorry-looking band of men trudged painfully up the steep slope; they seemed exhausted. Cydweli rushed forward and waited impatiently for his older brother to ease himself down from his mud-splattered horse. As Gomer's feet hit the ground his brother gave him an enthusiastic hug.

"Give me a moment, Cydweli boy." Gomer cautiously tested his feet, as though uncertain if they would support him. "I'm as tired as a man who's had sex with every woman in the whole village in one night." He puffed out his cheeks. "We've travelled through vile weather for four days without a break. The men were close to giving up, but they've made it, and before the bloody Saxons have arrived, too!" He turned to face his gasping, red-eyed soldiers, who had stopped and of one accord had collapsed on the top of the damp, grassy hillside.

"Well done, boys! Never, in the history of Wales, has any group of farmers and fishermen ever marched so far, in such weather, in order to get killed! I'm proud of you all!"

The men cheered in a half-hearted way and some, finding they had reached their destination, dragged up reserves of energy they did not believe they had. While many just lay on their backs and smiled, others clambered to their feet and stared in joyful amazement at the huge fort in front of them. For most, it was the biggest structure they had ever seen and many of the men whistled and slapped each other's shoulders, delighted their forced march was worth it.

"Gomer, you're my favourite brother!"

"Don't be stupid, I'm your *only* brother." He wrapped his powerful arms around Cydweli, and gave him a familiar squeeze. "Duw! You've developed some muscles since I last saw you. That comes of clean living, boy."

"I never thought to see you before the Saxon scum arrives. Well done!"

"Can you find us some food, and a place to sleep for a while?"

Cydweli beckoned to some of his junior officers who were watching the reunion with interest. "Get these men into the fort. Get them fed and find them a quiet corner to sleep. You, Hywel, you're in charge."

The brothers watched as the men from Ceredigion were led

away into the fort. They could hear the sound of laughter rippling along the tired column.

"Good men, all of them. But I fear some are past their prime." Gomer took a deep breath. "Get me a drink, and some meat," he said to a youth who was hovering near Gomer's horse. "Iorwerth's son, Cadell," he said absent-mindedly. "A good boy, but not much spunk in him." He laid a thick arm on his brother's shoulders. "Eat first, and save the women for later, don't you think?"

Cydweli nodded soberly. "If you can find any, of course. It seems to me that I have forgotten to include such an important element in your welcome." He gazed lovingly at the tired, mud-splattered, evil-smelling man in front of him. It was so good to see his brother again, after almost a year. "How are the boys?"

"Oh, your sons are as fit as fleas and almost as irritating. Gwriad is as strong as a young bull, and has a temper like a cornered boar. Your younger son, Dafydd, who looks nothing like the rest of us, with his red hair and green eyes, is an obstinate little bugger. I spend most of my time lending them the use of my belt on their backsides. But I love them, because that's how you used to be!"

"I don't believe a word of it." Cydweli hugged his older brother so tightly that Gomer had to fight for breath.

"You're right," he panted. "They're good boys and I have been pleased to have them in my house. They miss you mind. Your wife, Elen, misses you also and, as far as I know, has not bedded another man in a whole long year. Although, if I was her, I would shag every male in the castle just to get you to come home."

"I know," Cydweli murmured. He kicked his foot in the mud. "Once this is over, I will return, and be a family man again."

"Again? Apart from staying long enough to make her pregnant, you have never been a family man. Always been off fighting you have. It's lucky for you I like your sons, and my poor wife likes them, too. But, when this fight is over, I want you to come back to Ceridigion with me. There is more to life than fighting, especially at your age."

"You're older than me!" Cydweli retorted. "But you're right." His face creased in a broad smile. "It's very good to see you again and we've so much to talk about." His face suddenly changed as he remembered what he was about to do before Gomer arrived. "Hi, soldier!" he called to one of his scouts. "Round up as many sergeants as you can and have them parade the men outside. Get all the scouts and cavalry formed up as well." He rubbed his forehead and turned to Gomer. "I've a meeting with the King. I'll see you in about an hour." He beckoned to a guard and arranged for Gomer to be taken care of. He slowly moved his head in a circle, his hands on each side of his jaw. "Make sure your young Cadell gets you some decent food." He rubbed his forehead. "Oh, I've got the damnedest hangover."

His brother leaned against his horse and offered Cydweli his leather water bottle. "Still not old enough to hold your drink, or young enough to enjoy it. What a good job I'm here to look after you." Gomer paused, and gazed appreciatively at the fort. "Well done, boy, you've made a fine job of this little castle of yours. I'm glad you learned something from me." He turned to see his slave, Evan, hovering in the background. He carried Gomer's shield and spear.

"Wonderful it is to see you again, General Cydweli." Evan was smiling broadly.

"He just wants to prove that he knows things I don't," Gomer said, pretending to look annoyed. "General, is it? Well, much deserved." He turned back to Evan, "Well, don't just stand there admiring us, man. Get over here and help me get into the fort."

· · ·

FOR AN HOUR GRUFFYDD EXPLAINED his plans to his three officers. He appointed Rhodri to be in charge of the right wing of the army, and Emrys the left, as they faced downhill. "You will each be in charge of hundreds of archers; let them use their slings for closer fighting or when their arrows run out. I will lead the cavalry. Cydweli will defend the fort and, if all goes well, he will lead the attack on their rearguard." His eyes were wide with enthusiasm, as he pointed out the area of the battle on a flat piece of cleared earth. He used a stick to indicate where they would be waiting before they engaged the enemy, and how they would use their forces when the Saxons advanced.

"I want the Saxons to think that all of our fighting men are inside the fort. It will give them a false sense of security. Meanwhile, I will wait hidden with the bulk of the cavalry up in the mountains at the top end of the valley. The foot soldiers will stay back in the forest on both sides of the Cordon valley. Rhodri, you will be on the far side of the river, and when I sound the trumpets you will use your archers. Make sure they begin to appear from the trees. At this time I want you to sound your trumpets; make a lot of noise. Your job will be to stop them crossing the river, especially when our cavalry appears."

He pointed with his stick. "You, Emrys, will be closest to their forces, as they advance. Keep your men in the tree line, do your worst with your bowmen, but don't engage in hand-to-hand fighting. When they charge you, as they will, retreat into the forest until they get lost and lose heart. Then follow them back and repeat the slaughter. Do not engage them in hand-to-hand fighting until you hear my cavalry and my trumpets sounding attack. Before I arrive, I want the air black with arrows. Remember, wait until the trumpets sound, and keep everyone out of sight. I want to create the maximum confusion.

He turned to Cydweli. "I need to believe that you and your men will be able to stop the enemy from taking the fort. If you give them a bloody nose, it is my conviction they will bypass you." He grinned, "I might even give them some encouragement." His face changed and his dark brows lowered. "However, if you begin to lose control; if the enemy breaks down the gates or finds a way over the walls, then, and only then, will you blow your trumpets. If I hear those trumpets I will lead the horsemen down immediately and Rhodri and Emrys will march down on both sides of the river."

Gruffydd looked sternly at Cydweli. "Remember, I want you to sound those trumpets at the first sign of the fort's capture. You will be of no use to me if you and your men are dead. Our only hope is to catch them between us."

Rhodri nodded as he stared up at the mountains. He wondered how long it would take to bring the main army back down the valley. Would they remain under control, or break ranks, eager to get into the fight? It was their nature, and the officers would have a hard time controlling them. He realized how important it was to force the Saxons to bypass the fort and be caught in an ambush. It was the only way to a certain victory.

The King stood up and walked around deep in thought. The others remained sitting. Rhodri and Emrys, who were both in their mid-twenties, squatted on their heels, showing no sign of discomfort. Cydweli, who was not so flexible, sat with one knee on the ground and one raised up, his hands clasped around it. All three remained silent, staring at the rough map, trying to envisage the battle.

After some minutes, without any preamble, Gruffydd began to speak. "The Saxons are under the control of the great Earl Leofric of Mercia; his forces are led by his brother Earl Edwin. For a long time we have taunted him, and it is not surprising he has decided to get his revenge. He comes with huge numbers and expects a total victory. His generals are the Lords Thurkill and Aelfgar, both proven soldiers. We don't know for certain how many Saxons are coming, but some scouts have estimated there could be at least six thousand, probably more. Also we don't know what our final figure will be; men are arriving all the time, but I think we can be certain the Saxons will greatly outnumber us. Their foot soldiers have better armor and their weapons are superior to ours. But we have more horses and many more archers. These, and the element of surprise, will give us victory."

"One last thing," he said after a short pause, "their soldiers probably have more experience of fighting than our men. The majority of our army is not made up of soldiers, just farmers with a need to prove themselves." He gave a humorless chuckle. "They have courage; they love a good fight, but they lack discipline." He looked around at his three commanders. "When we have split up into our four groups, get your nobles to assemble the men and ensure that each man is under the control of a sergeant. Make the sergeants understand the importance of discipline. Tell them to get rid of any who are witless or unwilling to accept orders. Send them home, but make it a public event. Hopefully, a few examples of this humiliation will ensure the rest do as they are told."

"We may lose a few," Rhodri cautioned. "The men don't like authority."

"All the more reason to make them do as they're told. You understand me?" Gruffydd glared at his senior officers. He began to pace around the site. "Like you, I have been in small battles, when the outcome could have gone either way, and when one man has thrown down his weapons and run off. In moments, before those of us who were fighting for our lives were aware, the rest of his friends and relatives had turned tail, like a flock of starlings, causing a total retreat. All was lost, and we were forced to forsake a fight we might have won." He stopped pacing and looked up at the increasingly grey sky. "Better to have half of our army who are prepared to fight until the bitter end, than for us to have twice the number on the field, knowing that half may suddenly desert and cause the rest to fail."

"We could let it be known that anyone who deserts his post will be killed," said Cydweli. They all looked at him in alarm. He noted their surprise. "We will give them the chance to leave before the battle starts, but if they stay, they stay until the end, no matter how the battle goes." He stood up, and gripped his sword. "I only want true Welshmen around me when I fight. The rest can just bugger off home!"

CHAPTER FOUR

Two days later, the scouts reported that a vast army of Saxons would arrive within the next few hours. Gruffydd ordered the scouts to operate in platoon strength in order to annihilate any of the enemy scouts they might encounter. "They must not be allowed to gauge our numbers, nor do I want them having too many reports of the fort. Let it be a surprise for them."

Gruffydd had a final meeting with Cydweli and led his cavalry, numbering more than six hundred, up into the hills. After some delay, Rhodri and Emrys marched their men up both sides of the valley. It took Rhodri some hours to get his men across to the far bank, as the river had become a raging torrent following weeks of intermittent rain. However, with the help of local hunters, he managed to find useable, but difficult fords, and although the men were soaked in the crossing, they all managed to keep their bows and their strings dry. There was a sense of optimism in the air. In spite of the promise of further rain, the foot soldiers laughed and joked their way up the wide, tree-covered valley, eager to get into position.

Finally, with the enemy drawing near, Cydweli ordered the last of the scouts to report to the King. The heavy gates were closed and barred and he arranged for as many soldiers as possible to stand shoulder to shoulder along the line of the emplacements facing east and north. "Let them think, when they first see us, that we are twice the number we are!" Cydweli yelled. Once again, he inspected the whole fortification, checking the reserves of arrows, the piles of sharpened staves, and the mounds of small boulders. He joked with the men, many of whom he had known for years, and like him, were no longer in the first flush of youth. "Remember, boys, we need to stop them getting too close. No need to smell their bad breath!"

Then, the wait began. After an hour, small groups of horsemen could be seen making their way up the valley. They waved swords and some raced to the foot of the hill staring up at the fort and yelling insults. Unable to get any response from the massed Welshmen on the ramparts, they rode back slowly to their emerging army.

Cydweli had ordered that no man was to respond until he gave the order and the sergeants moved among the excited men, reminding them of their duty. "They're like a pack of greyhounds before the hunt," Cydweli joked with his officers. "Let go the leash for a moment and they'll be gone; each one seeking personal glory." He paused, while he thought of his earlier days when he was virtually ungovernable in a fight. He shook his head. "Make sure they get water and something to eat while they're waiting; I don't want their wives to blame me for starving them."

For the next two hours the Saxon horde moved into positions on the east side of the hill. Their massed ranks beat their shields as they prepared for battle and the sound reinforced the reality of their huge numbers. A large troop of enemy scouts galloped past the fort to the north and disappeared up the broad valley. Meanwhile, their leaders positioned themselves out of the range of arrows, but close enough to appreciate the strength of the fort and gain some idea of the numbers of the defenders.

Cydweli moved quietly along the parapets, patting friends on the back and making jokes with those he did not recognize. He watched as the men stared out at the gathering horde and knew what they were feeling. Many were obviously fearful, with no experience of a real battle: their faces were pale and their tongues flicked out over their dry lips.

"You mustn't worry about that lot of thieving drunkards," he said, his deep voice carrying along the rows of waiting men. "The more there are, the more chance you have of killing them. You don't want to return to your families and have to admit that you never had the chance to fight any of them." He laughed loudly.

"Any man who can kill more than I do will win my horse! And I don't fancy your chances." There was a roar of laughter and shouts of "Good old Cydweli!"

He grinned at his brother. "Go along the ranks and speak to them, Gomer. Many of them are likely to pee their pants unless we encourage them."

Eventually, after a tense stand-off, the Saxon trumpets sounded, drums boomed out, and a large group of well-armed soldiers moved at a trot around the hill from the east side to the north, intending to encircle the fort and reach the gates at the western side. Cydweli was standing in the centre of the east wall, staring down on the huge army that was pouring into the flat area below; they flowed across the land like water at high tide.

Once the effect of the massed defenders on the east wall had been achieved, he repositioned his men: the majority was placed on the west wall defending the gates and only a handful on the south side, which was steep and difficult to climb. With the raging river below, it was virtually impossible for the enemy to launch a massed assault on this side.

"We want them to attack us and we want to punish them for trying!" he yelled. "It is our duty to hold this fort. Remember, if they retreat, we do not follow them. I will kill any man who forsakes his post." There was a tense silence. Cydweli waited for his words to sink in, then at the top of his voice he roared: "I love you, boys, and together we will win a great victory! But only if you follow orders. Now, a big cheer for King Gruffydd ap Llywelyn!"

A mighty roar of approval rose up from the fort, causing the Saxons army to look up in alarm.

Below the hill, Saxon officers raced about ordering their men to yell their battle song, and for a short while, both sides roared their defiance at each other. Once the majority of the Saxons army had arrived, their sergeants began to direct platoons of soldiers up the hill towards the fort. They positioned themselves beyond the range of arrows on three sides and, as expected, avoided the south. They quickly assessed it was boggy and slippery at the base of the hill where the river had overflowed, and the steep climb would make the south wall almost impregnable.

The drums stopped, and there was a moment of quiet, before the Saxon trumpets sounded and the drums thundered their call to action. With a roar of hatred, they advanced in their hundreds, their iron helmets gleaming in rays of bright sunlight that occasionally shafted through the grey clouds. As they approached, marching in ordered ranks, they began to beat their swords on their shields like the sound of rolling thunder. The effect was impressive. Many a Welsh defender was heard to mutter, "Oh Duw," and to have his sergeant curse him for his stupidity: "Just 'cos they make a loud noise doesn't mean they can fight."

The drums stopped and the Saxons paused at the base of the hill. At each of the three sides, a huge warrior with gleaming armor and horns on his helmet stepped forward, turned to his men, waved his sword or axe, and roared out encouragement. The soldiers roared back and raced forward as their leaders led them in a massed charge up the hill.

"Tell the sergeants to draw bows and release on the trumpet," Cydweli ordered. He paused until he was sure they were within arrow range, and then he roared, "Sound trumpets!" A thick swarm of arrows darkened the sky, and the Saxon lines faltered as warriors on all three sides fell victim to the deadly arrows.

It was the moment when order gave way to blood lust. The Saxons screamed defiance and charged up the hill into a constant wave of arrows. Many of the leading warriors were killed or injured, but the vast majority reached the trenches just below the palisade, where their advance was slowed. They had not anticipated the problem: the trenches were deep and lined with sharpened staves, causing a multitude of injuries and deaths and throwing the confident Saxons into disarray. The confusion allowed the defenders to fire a further wave of arrows, causing many more casualties. At this point of the conflict, none of the Welsh had been injured.

The Saxons did not possess many archers, but a number were soon shooting from the cover of the trenches and often next to those who had impaled themselves. Within minutes, the attacking soldiers overcame the obstacles and reached the base of the walls. Heaving grappling irons, they lodged the hooks into the tops of the palisade and pulled themselves up the wooden sides, while other soldiers covered them by throwing spears at the defenders. In places, powerful Saxons hoisted friends on their shoulders, who tried desperately to pull themselves over the walls. All the while the Welsh archers continued with deadly efficiency to rake the enemy with their metal-tipped arrows. The losses on the Saxon side were immense, but slowly the tide turned and Welsh casualties started to rise.

At the gates, groups of powerful Saxon warriors tried to batter down the heavy doors with oak logs. Each time they approached they were beaten back with a withering storm of arrows; if they reached the doors, heavy stones knocked them to the ground.

Eventually, on the east wall, some of the attackers fought their way over the palisade and vicious hand-to-hand fighting ensued. The Saxons were tall, heavy men whose strength was far greater than the shorter, wiry men who opposed them. Their body armor was superior, as were their weapons, and slowly their force of numbers began to overwhelm the Welsh defenders.

"Look about you!" Cydweli roared at a group of archers who were aiming at the Saxons below them, unaware of a furious skirmish to their right. "Quickly, boys! They're breaking through!" The archers drew their swords and fought like men possessed, their speed and bravery compensating for their lack of armor.

Cydweli picked up a sharpened stave and forced a tall bearded soldier backwards off the wall. He continued using it as a club, knocking back the helmeted heads that surged up over the palisade.

"Should I sound the trumpets and call for help?" At the sound of the voice Cydweli swung round, his eyes wide with anger. In front of him was his brother Gomer. Blood was running down his face and he was breathing heavily. "There's too many of them, boy. Best to call for help, while we can."

"No, Gomer!" Cydweli yelled. "If we call for help the King will be defeated. Better we kill as many of the enemy as possible. After us, they will advance up the valley and get caught in the ambush. We must not fail the King!" He read the doubt in his brother's eyes. "It's the only way. Take charge here," he ordered.

Gomer nodded his agreement, suddenly too tired to argue.

"You can do this, old man," a voice murmured. He turned to find Evan holding a spear, and grinning from ear to ear.

"What are you doing here? You have no reason to fight. You're my slave."

"I could have bought my freedom any time in the last few years, and you know it. For today, consider me a free man and I promise not to knock your stupid head into the mud."

"You're a bloody awful slave, but I love you like a brother." Gomer gave him a brief hug, and turned to face the furious Saxon attack. By his side Evan, smiling like a half-wit, lunged his spear at a large bearded face that appeared over the parapet.

Cydweli rushed to his left and tried to run along the rampart towards the gates. Ahead of him, the Saxons were gaining the advantage, as a small gang of the enemy fought their way over the walls, forcing back a defiant group of defenders. Without hesitation, Cydweli drew his sword and rammed it into the back of a large enemy soldier who was lunging about with his axe against two smaller defenders. The soldier collapsed. The two defenders turned to beat back another warrior who was pulling himself over the wall. "Use the stones!" Cydweli yelled. He picked up a heavy boulder and hurled it down onto a red-bearded giant who was attempting to lift a fellow soldier onto his back. Both men fell into the mud.

As he ran past the defenders, he sensed that the gates were the weak spot. Although he had some of his best men positioned there, he felt a strong urge to take charge. Around him, his men were fighting magnificently, and he knew that this was the battle that would establish the Welsh as a nation. It was Gruffydd's dream. He would not disappoint him.

He approached the gate from the right in time to see the massive gates buckle inwards as they received a resounding blow from outside. They did not collapse, but it was clear that the enemy had broken their leather hinges, and it was only the oak beams across the doors that were holding the structure in place.

A young officer came up close to Cydweli; his face was firm and he was not afraid.

"What's your name?"

"Ganny ap Mawr."

"I knew your father. You're from Morgannwg?"

The young man nodded.

"You're just the officer I need. Get more men from the areas where the pressure is least. We need them now. Hurry!" The young officer raced away, and Cydweli ran off, screaming for the men to prepare for the fall of the gates. Sensing the impending disaster, soldiers appeared from both sides. They were not young men, but he knew they would not run away.

"Bring up barrels, carts, logs, anything to slow them down if they break through!" He quickly directed his soldiers into formations and prepared for the worst.

Above the gates the defenders had adopted a swift rotation for the bowmen: archers fired, stood back while they reloaded and allowed fresh archers to cover their positions, thereby keeping up a constant barrage of missiles into the one area in front of the gate. With the help of heavy stones, the defenders decimated the Saxons who, only moments before, had seemed certain to force their way into the fort.

A mighty roar went up from the soldiers defending the gates. The Saxons were withdrawing. They had lost many of their leaders in the last attack on the gates and seemed to be pulling back in order to regroup.

Cydweli climbed up onto the ramparts to access the situation. "Well done, all of you!" A cheer went up from the surrounding archers. "Now, quickly boys, prepare for the next attack. They won't give up that easily."

He jumped down from the ramparts and gathered a small group of officers. "Get men working on those gates; prepare a second defense with anything to slow them down if they break through. You, Lord Ganny!" he pointed at the tall young nobleman who carried an axe he had taken from a Saxon. "I want you to get your men mounted on those few horses we have left. If the Saxons break through, you will charge them and force them to retreat."

"Yes, General." Ganny saluted and ran towards the horse

enclosure where fewer than a dozen horses were stabled. As he ran he yelled the names of men whom he knew could ride well.

Cydweli looked in all directions, trying to decide where he was most needed. The south was quiet, and with the temporary lull at the main gate, the Saxon attack had reached its greatest intensity against the north and east walls. He began to run as best he could towards the east side, being aware that the defenders were fighting with unexpected courage and ferocity. Cydweli felt an intense pride in these men, most of whom had never experienced a battle. He decided his responsibility was to support his brother on the east wall, where the fighting had been ferocious. As he ran, he could see many bodies falling from the narrow palisade, and he was filled with a cold fear that the Saxons had overcome the valiant defenders of the wall. Was Gomer still alive? Cydweli felt his eyes water. This was his fort; he was determined to defend it to the last man, even if it involved the death of his older brother and himself. He could see a melee on the ramparts, but he was unable to discern who was winning.

Suddenly, he realized that there was no longer hand-to-hand fighting on the walls and the blare of Saxon trumpets was sounding from all directions. He reached the bottom of the east wall and was forced to stop before a pile of bodies that barred his way, testifying to the fury of the fighting in this area. Amid the corpses were survivors, groaning and screaming with pain. A few were Welsh, but most were heavily armored Saxons. Above his head, there was no longer any sound of battle, just the cheering and jeering of the defenders.

"Dear God," he murmured as he raced up a ladder to the rampart, "can it be true?"

"They've pulled back, boy. You can rest yourself." Cydweli turned to face the speaker and found he was looking into the face of his brother, Gomer. His face was smirched with blood from a small head wound, and his sword had broken at the tip, but he seemed in great spirits. "We gave them a bloody nose all right, boy." Gomer clasped him in a bear hug. "You were right, cariad. If it had been left to me, I would have sounded the trumpets and most likely we would have faced defeat. Worst of all, we would have failed our King, and I could not have lived with that."

Cydweli noticed tears in his brother's eyes. "There's a gwirion brother you are, Gomer." He smiled, "You're the best brother a man could have!" He began to pound the broad shoulders of his life-long friend. "I think, between us, we've saved the day."

Neither man was aware of the blood-splattered face of Evan, who watched the brothers and was grinning like a half-wit. He examined his spear with its chips and its blood stains. "That was the most fun I've had for a long time," he spoke to himself, while around him cheers, trumpets and screams rent the air.

The brothers looked down from the fort and could see the enemy forces falling back and gathering into marching formations. A strong force of foot soldiers had positioned itself on the west side, in front of the gates, and the besieging soldiers were preparing their own defenses. There were huge numbers of dead and injured soldiers on the hillside and, under a flag of truce, the Welsh defenders allowed the Saxons to collect their bodies.

Cydweli and Gomer moved along the ramparts past their cheerful, but exhausted men and watched with interest as their erstwhile attackers built rough barriers on the hill opposite the west gates, and just out of range of the Welsh archers.

"They've taken the bait," Gomer observed, "just like Gruffydd said they would." He felt full of enthusiasm and his mind was refusing to admit how his tired body was demanding a rest. "We will have to give some thought to our breakout from here when their main army retreats. We need to smack them hard and be able to launch a counter-attack." He yawned. "I might just sleep a bit, if you don't mind?"

"Go and find something to eat and rest yourself. I will have need of you in a few hours." Cydweli nodded to himself. "At least I hope I will." He patted his brother on his back and began to lead him towards the ladder.

"Just a moment, boy," Gomer stopped to look across the valley.

Below them, on the north and east sides, the huge Saxon army was reforming and beginning to march up the valley on the right hand side of the river. It was an impressive spectacle. They advanced with their horns blaring, drums thundering, and with their regimented columns of soldiers marching in their hundreds, their armor glinting in the occasional burst of intense sunlight. Behind the marching formations came the cavalry; although not numerous, they brought up the rear with their colored pennants rippling in the gathering wind.

"With luck, they'll return in a less organized fashion," Cydweli quipped, as he descended the ladder.

The young nobleman, Ganny, rode over and dismounted, handing his horse to a scout. He waited respectfully at the bottom of the stairs. As Cydweli descended, he noticed the officer: "Not much action for you that time, Lord Ganny. But there is more to come, believe me."

"Yes, Sir." He looked about at the bodies of the Saxons. "I think we did well."

Cydweli nodded. "Find out how many of our men died, how many are injured and how many can still fight."

Ganny saluted, and hurried away. Cydweli turned to his brother. "This is what Gruffydd hoped would happen," he said, punching his brother on his arm. "They think to keep us locked up in here while they plunder our homeland. With luck and considering the lusty strength of our defense, they might believe that our whole army is here and that we have nothing left to defend our women and children." He rubbed his hands over his tired face. "We have done our part for the moment. We need to rest."

He called to any sergeants who were close, "Tell the men to stand down. Leave only a few guards. Make sure everyone gets food and drink. We could be fighting again before the day is out."

"If we are," Gomer murmured, "it means we'll be winning the day." He yawned, staggered slightly, and was surprised to find strong arms supported him. "Thank you, Evan," he said, without looking round. "Remind me to pay you sometime."

• • •

GRUFFYDD WAITED AT THE HIGH end of the valley and tried to quell the nervous excitement he felt. Scouts had reported a huge Saxon army was attacking the fort. There had been mixed messages:

some suggesting unimaginable enemy losses, while others were describing a wave of Saxons pouring over the breached walls. On a number of occasions he had prepared his cavalry for a rapid deployment, only to rescind his orders on receipt of more positive news.

"Cydweli should have called for help by now," he muttered to himself. At the same time, Gruffydd was grateful that he had not. If the Saxons were forced to leave the fort intact, it meant they would have suffered considerable and, perhaps, unacceptable losses. Then, they would have to leave a sizable force of men to guard the gate and they would be advancing with fewer soldiers, many of who would be tired and dispirited.

He prowled backwards and forwards in front of his temporary headquarters, unable to settle. A meal was left uneaten. His guards prevented anyone from approaching, and he found himself waiting impatiently, as scouts galloped up and were taken away to Rhys, his Sergeant-at-Arms, for interrogation. He knew Rhys to be a good man: dependable, loyal and, above all, a great friend, who was proud to hold the post of Sergeant-at-Arms. But, like many of his experienced officers, Rhys was no longer in his youthful prime. It was as though Gruffydd had inherited an experienced team of advisers and soldiers, all of whom were old enough to be his father.

"Good news, my Lord," Rhys panted as he rushed towards Gruffydd. "Cydweli has beaten them off. We don't know any details of the Welsh losses, but the Saxons have taken a drumming. As you predicted, they have left a small force to guard the gate and keep our surviving defenders inside. The rest of the Saxon horde is advancing up the valley." He took a deep breath. "The scouts report the enemy has a strong group of mounted scouts and many of the officers ride horses, but they have few heavy cavalry. Those they have are guarding the rear. The bad news is, that in spite of considerable losses at the fort, they are approaching in huge numbers. Many of their companies were not involved in the attack on the fort, and are fresh for battle. They are advancing with trumpets and drums and waving their flags as though they had already won a great victory."

"That is what I would have expected, Rhys," Gruffydd said impatiently. "They hope to scare off any small bands of soldiers who stand in their way, by giving the impression they are invincible." A small grin appeared on his face. "I think we will encourage them in that thought." He beckoned to a party of scouts who were waiting close by. "Tell Lord Meilyr ap Ithael to collect fifty horsemen, and wait for my signal. Also, get messages to Lords Rhodri and Emrys. Tell them the Saxon army is coming, and remind them of the importance of maintaining discipline. No one is to attack until I sound the trumpets. No matter what they might see. Tell them that." The scouts bowed and ran for their horses. 'So far, so good,' he thought. 'If we can hold them here, and force a retreat, then we have a chance of destroying their whole army.'

In the distance he could see Lord Meilyr, on a white horse, marshaling his group of cavalry. Within moments, the riders were sitting quietly on their mounts, in ten lines of five. Meilyr positioned himself at the front of the detachment and sat perfectly still. When all was quiet, he looked towards the King. Many of the riders were carrying lances with pennants fluttering in the rising breeze. They looked impressive as the first few drops of rain began to fall.

Gruffydd raised his right arm, held it for a few moments and then brought it down in a sudden, dramatic gesture. Lord Meilyr raised his arm in acknowledgement and led his men down the valley at a gentle trot. "A good man, one I can trust," he murmured. The Saxon army was still more than two miles away and well out of sight, and he knew he must have patience.

Beckoning to Rhys and his personal guard, Gruffydd led the way to a small escarpment about half a mile from the camp. He looked down at the broad valley stretching away beneath him. Behind, low cloud had begun to fade out the summits of the high mountains. On the tree-clad slopes of Cordon, mist was forming in the lower gullies. He could still see where the river ran fast through the thickly forested valley and through occasional narrow ravines, where the water thundered through its craggy enclosures. In other places, the rocky banks were barely above the thundering water and the sides were wet and slippery. After the recent rains, the river was difficult to cross and Lord Rhodri had needed to use local guides to get his men safely to the other side: an advantage the enemy would not enjoy. Once over, the Welsh archers had melted into the trees, and Gruffydd found it hard to believe there was an army hidden along the rocky banks.

He knew that Lord Emrys was well positioned among the dense forest on the slopes facing down along the wide path that led up from the fort. Emrys had his orders, and Gruffydd was confident the young lord would follow them to the letter.

"It is most unlikely that the Saxons will be able to cross the river in any numbers and Rhodri's men will be able to put their bows to good use." Gruffydd pointed to a large smooth rock in the centre of the river, about a mile from their eerie. "When the Saxons reach that point, tell the trumpeters to sound. I will lead the cavalry, but only after the archers have done their worst." He looked thoughtfully at his Sergeant-at-Arms. "You will take charge of the reserves. Do not use them unless you see us in retreat."

Rhys nodded. He was both relieved and disappointed. As an older man, he was thankful that he did not have to fight next to his youthful King, who seemed to have an infinite store of energy and strength. Rhys remembered that, as a younger man, he also could fight all day and still be willing to travel miles and fight some more. But now, he knew Gruffydd valued him for his experience and not his ability in the front line. Although part of him wanted to be fighting besides his King, he knew he would be more use defending him if there was the possibility of defeat.

"You can depend on me, my Lord."

"I know I can." He clasped Rhys' arm in a tight grip. "Together we will win a great victory. We must. For if we do not, the whole of our beloved Wales will be open to these murdering fiends." He stared down the valley, conscious of the increasing rain. "I think the weather will be on our side as long as the archers keep their bowstrings dry." He could feel the pulse beating in his neck, and realized he was anxious to get started.

They watched as Lord Meilyr and his fifty horsemen took up their position on the trail near the rock in the river. They waited patiently, as the noise of the advancing army began to reverberate in the valley.

"Fetch the trumpeters, it is almost time," Gruffydd said to Rhys. He indicated to two soldiers, who ran back towards the camp.

"From now on, you will be in charge." He smiled encouragingly at Rhys. "I will lead the cavalry. Remember, don't sound the trumpets until the marching soldiers have reached that flat stone in the river. You will see Meilyr conduct a disorganized retreat. Ignore it. If the enemy's cavalry attempts to follow Meilyr's men, take no action. Wait until the marching columns have reached that rock, then sound the trumpets, and continue until our archers, on both sides of the river, are fully involved."

"I will, my King."

Gruffydd smiled. "Once my cavalry are engaged, be prepared to use the reserves, but only if you see us retreat."

"I understand." Rhys bowed as Gruffydd swept past, his mind already focused on the battle.

. . .

LORD MEILYR AP ITHAEL CONSIDERED himself a fine horseman. He loved hunting, and was popular with his friends. In his early adolescence, he had been part of a spirited group of youths who, sheltered by their noble connections, had gained a reputation for drunkenness and for taking advantage of young women. Most notable in this group was Gruffydd ap Llywelyn, whose parents and relatives were frequently outraged by his dissolute behaviour and yet, after the unexpected death of his father, were equally amazed at the change that occurred in him. Virtually overnight, once he had a role to play, Gruffydd became an astute ruler of North Powys. As he established himself, his friends quickly became his loyal supporters. Meilyr was one of a number of young nobles who saw in Gruffydd a king who could lead them to greatness, and whom they followed without question.

Meilyr turned to face his men, and raised his voice to carry over the roar of the river. "We'll wait until the enemy scouts comes into sight and then charge towards them. I imagine they will be surprised and will retreat to fetch reinforcements. As soon as their cavalry appears, I want you to act as though you can't control your horses and don't know whether to charge those bastards or retreat." He raised his eyebrows. "That shouldn't be difficult!" A roar of nervous laughter rang out. "Once their scouts and cavalry appear, yell insults, wave your weapons and, at my command, we will retreat in confusion."

"And then?" A voice called out.

"We will lead them to the top of the valley, where the King's cavalry will destroy them. It is our job to prevent any of them escaping over the mountains." He gave a roar of laughter. "Don't you worry, boys, you'll get your chance for glory!"

They stared down the valley and waited for what seemed to be a long time, but was less than it would have taken them to drink two flagons of beer. There was a light rain obscuring the track ahead and when a small detachment of enemy scouts appeared from around the bend, about four hundred paces away, there was surprise on both sides.

"Charge!" Lord Meilyr roared. The startled scouts quickly turned their horses and retreated before the rush of the Welsh cavalry. Once they had disappeared around the bend in the track, Meilyr slowed down and eventually brought the cavalry to a halt.

"Trot back up the hill, boys, until we get past the steep bit, just past the bend here." He glared at them. "And do as you're bloody well told!"

There was much smirking among the horsemen. Most were young nobles, unused to taking orders and for some it was their first real fight. As Meilyr trotted back to their earlier position, he reflected on the chances of these untrained youths following his commands. They formed up in some semblance of order and he took his place at the front of the lines.

"Be ready!" he yelled.

Almost immediately, a large formation of scouts and cavalry came galloping round the bend. There were at least three times the number of Meilyr's riders, and they were less than four hundred paces away. After a brief display of chaos, some obscene gestures and loud name-calling, the majority of the Welsh horsemen raced away up the hillside, provoking a huge roar of derision from the Saxons.

Meilyr stayed back to ensure the hot heads in his group would not hang back too long. But true to form, a group of five lingered, waving their swords at the advancing scouts in a show of bravado. "Move! Damn you, boys! Go now!"

But it was clear that they had left it too late. A cluster of Saxon riders was ahead of the main body, urging the horses to their maximum. As they advanced they lowered their lances, forming a deadly phalanx. The young Welsh riders, seeing their mistake and realizing their imminent danger, tried to turn their horses. But there was no chance of escape.

"Too late! Turn and face them!" Meilyr shouted, and charged at the leading Saxons. A vivid shaft of sunlight burst through the grey sky, reflecting on his armor and his polished lance. His white horse seemed ghostly in the strange light and the leading Saxons slowed in spite of themselves. Behind him, there was a moment of confusion, as the five riders tried to make sense of the quickly changing scene. Four of them, after a guilty look at each other, raced up beside their leader while the fifth, panic-stricken, turned his horse and fled the scene.

Only two of the four had lances, the others had long swords. All carried round shields and wore light body armor. There was a furious engagement as the two groups met and for a moment Lord Meilyr's men were successful, killing and injuring many of the leading scouts. But, once the initial clash was over, the lances were useless in the resulting melee, where only their swords could be used. There was a brief, desperate fight, but the outcome was clear once the main body of Saxons arrived. When Meilyr was killed, only one of the Welsh riders managed to escape the massacre, and he galloped away, bleeding from numerous wounds. As he escaped up the valley, he could see his erstwhile friend disappearing into the gloom.

The Saxons were convinced the Welsh were finished and the ease with which their cavalry had been overwhelmed encouraged a headlong charge up the valley. In the distance the main group of the Welsh were still visible and the two separated riders were like bait to the hunters. They passed a rock in the river, unaware of the hundreds of archers hidden in the trees and, as they approached the summit of the mountain, they saw the retreating Welsh horsemen pause, yell obscenities, and begin, once more, to retreat in disarray and gallop out of sight.

"We have them! Spread out!" the Saxon leader waved his sword to encourage his men, whose horses were beginning to blow. He was convinced that the Welsh were only good for hit-and-run attacks, but in a real battle he was sure he would win the day. If he could destroy the remains of their paltry cavalry, he would be well rewarded, and he looked forward to the bloodshed that would follow the rout. He galloped over the summit of the high ground and onto a large flat plateau, which was surrounded by dense forest. Two hundred paces away, the Welsh horsemen had formed up as though to charge.

"They don't learn," he said to one of his officers, "but we will teach them." He stopped his horse, and stood up in his saddle, as the rest of his horsemen arrived. "Kill them all!" he yelled excitedly and urged his tired horse into a final gallop.

"My Lord!" An officer was pointing frantically behind him, and soldiers on both sides were suddenly reining in their mounts. He stopped his horse, and glancing back saw hundreds of Welsh cavalry closing in fast from both sides. He could not believe they had so many horsemen. A cold feeling passed over him as he realized that he and his men were surrounded.

"Turn back!" he yelled. "We'll fight our way back!" But, in the increasing noise of thundering hooves, the roar of battle and the screaming of the wounded, his orders were heard by only a few. His men had lost their momentum and the Welsh took advantage of their confusion.

Led by Gruffydd, the Welsh drove a wedge into the Saxon ranks, using their lances to great effect, while denying the surrounded Saxons the use of theirs. The ambush had been a complete shock, enabling the Welsh, with their fresh horses and overwhelming numbers, to gain a decisive victory. His soldiers wanted to fight and Gruffydd's cavalry was soon able to overwhelm the tired and confused Saxons. Nevertheless, some of the enemy, despite the futility of their resistance, continued to battle on until they were killed or wounded.

In the final stages of the battle, the Saxon leader sought out Gruffydd, who was easily recognizable as he insisted on wearing a thin crown over his helmet. The warrior carved a passage towards the Welsh King , and was only a few paces away when a spear was thrust into his lower back. He collapsed over his saddle, toppled to the ground, where he was trampled to death by the hooves of the terrified horses. His surviving followers saw him fall, lost hope, and the battle was quickly over.

"Take prisoners!" Gruffydd bellowed. He was unaware of the death of the Saxon warrior who had intended to kill him.

Rhys had kept the reserve force back from the fighting and now galloped up. "What are your orders, my Lord?"

"Disarm them. Make use of their weapons. Tie up those who can still fight. Mount guard on all of them, including the injured." He gave Rhys a wolfish grin. "That was good. It shows what we can do with a bit of planning! I'll move into position now with the cavalry, you take charge behind us."

Rhys frowned. "I'm sorry to report Lord Meilyr's dead!"

Gruffydd bit his lip, and said nothing until he had composed himself.

Rhys waited until Gruffydd looked directly at him. "Two of his horsemen arrived just before the Saxons. I arrested the first youth for cowardice, the second, badly injured, told us of Lord Meilyr's death."

"I will deal with these things later." He trotted away towards his cavalry and signaled to an officer. "What are our losses?"

"Only ten killed, my Lord, and about forty wounded. Some of those can still fight," the officer reported. He indicated a large subdued crowd of prisoners. "We have captured about sixty of them, some badly injured. The rest are dead!" He was breathing quickly, still recovering from the intensity of the fighting. "We can certainly make use of their horses!"

Gruffydd nodded. The excitement was fading. He wondered grimly if he knew any of the dead men; he would certainly miss Lord Meilyr, who had been his friend for many years, and questioned how many others he would lose. He received a brief report of the reasons for Lord Meilyr's death and was saddened by the futility of it. He was unsure how he would deal with the coward; for the moment, the youth would remain in fetters under Rhys' control.

"We are ready, my Lord," a young officer bowed his head. Gruffydd moved forward to the front of his assembled cavalry. Many of the horses were still trembling and, although some of his men were displaying temporary bandages, all seemed in good spirits. A few were remounted on the larger Saxon horses, and feeling proud of themselves.

Gruffydd took a deep breath; it was not the time for mourning or revenge. He flashed a broad smile at the assembled cavalry. "That was just a taster of what is to come!" Gruffydd shouted, his deep voice cutting through the rising wind. "You've done well. With God's help, we will gain a great victory." There was a roar of agreement. "In a short while their marching columns will reach a point in the river where our archers will make them sorry they ever stepped on our land!" A loud cheer went up from the assembled horsemen. "You will hear our trumpets and will know the battle has started. When the archers have done their worst, we will finish off the invaders and any who escape us will find Lord Cydweli waiting for them!" There was another loud cheer. "Good luck. Fight well. Make Wales proud of you. And remember, we do not retreat!"

Gruffydd turned his horse and moved slowly into position on the brow of the hill. It was one of the longest public speeches he remembered giving. He preferred action to words.

• • •

THE SAXON GENERALS WERE UNHAPPY with Leofric, the Earl of Mercia. He had given the overall command to his brother Edwin, who had appointed his friend Thurkill and his nephew, Aelfgar, son of Leofric, as his seconds in command. The generals all agreed that they would not have allowed the fort to remain as a constant reminder of the Welsh presence. They argued that their weight of numbers would have won the day and the defenders, believed to be the only organized military force in Wales, had to be defeated to allow the invasion to continue without further resistance.

Lord Edwin had stated that the capture of the fort was not worth the wasting of more warriors. He insisted that a small contingent of their troops could starve the defenders into submission, while the main army devastated central Wales.

"We will teach them a lesson," Edwin said, as he lectured his officers prior to the invasion of the Welsh borders. "For many years the Welsh have made innumerable small attacks on our towns and our farms. They are not worthy of being considered a nation. They are only a band of cattle thieves who like a quick fight and then they disappear back into their cold mountains." He paused to create a dramatic effect. "They can keep their bare, inhospitable mountains. We will take their rich valleys and show their women what real men are like!"

There had been a resounding thunder of approval.

But the fort had been an unexpected problem. When the initial attacks had failed to take it, the Generals Thurkill and Aelfgar had urged Edwin to bypass what they considered an irritant.

"It's of no importance," Thurkill said. "The Welsh have poured all their meager resources into this one defense. All their real soldiers are imprisoned in that fort. If we keep them locked up, they will run out of food and water, while we destroy their country."

"I agree," the younger Aelfgar nodded. "We have enough men to conquer their undefended lands, and we will leave garrisons to ensure that they never cause us further problems. We will destroy the fort on our return."

Edwin had ordered the army to advance. In spite of his generals' protests, he had left only a relatively small contingent of soldiers to ensure that the remaining Welsh were confined within their fort.

"They're beaten," Thurkill said. "We have shown them the power of our army. I imagine they're grateful they don't have to meet us in another battle."

"My brother Leofric would have liked to have been here," Edwin said. "I am grateful that he has allowed me, with your help, to finally eradicate this Welsh irritation."

The other generals laughed, in spite of themselves.

"We will ignore their little fort. We will advance into their country, while their warriors," he rolled his eyes, "are imprisoned in their own jail."

At the time, the speech had gone down well. But, once they had left the meeting, many of the senior officers had expressed concerns over the strategy. Edwin was known as a general who avoided fighting and preferred to give orders from his command post. Although none of the other officers would call him a coward, he was thought to be fastidious and obsessed with small details. The general agreement was that if he had not been the brother of Earl Leofric, he would never have reached the rank of general. In contrast, Thurkill had a reputation for bravery that bordered on stupidity, and only his friendship with Edwin had enabled him to remain in the role of second-in-command.

General Aelfgar was aware that these officers considered him to be too young and inexperienced to be in such a senior position. He returned to speak privately to his uncle. "Our officers seem to think the Welsh might have other soldiers, who could ambush us in this valley," Aelfgar said cautiously. He was keen to give the impression that he was not a young hothead.

"They're a nation of farmers," Edwin replied. He gulped down a cup of wine. "They have no standing army. Whatever real soldiers they could put together, they've imprisoned in that fort of theirs. The forces they have left will be of no consequence."

It was at that moment that a report was received that a small Welsh squadron of horseman had been defeated and the Saxon cavalry was in hot pursuit of the main body. "There are less than fifty of them, my Lord, and they are running for their lives," a junior officer announced.

"That proves my point," Edwin said. He smiled confidently. "We will advance up the valley and begin a systematic destruction of this odious country."

He stood at the entrance to his tent and chewed reflectively on some roasted fowl, while the generals made their arrangements. He wondered how his brother, Leofric, would reward him. Perhaps, he would ask to be Earl of Wales. Edwin scowled at the leaden sky: it always rained in this God-forsaken country.

CHAPTER FIVE

W hen the Saxon regiments, marching six abreast, reached the point where the track passed the rock in the raging river on their left, they heard a sudden roar of trumpets echoing out from the top of the valley. They smirked. The Welsh were beaten and would need more than trumpets to save their undefended country.

At that moment, the sky went dark with arrows. Soldiers screamed as death rained down from above. Immediately, the ordered ranks raised their shields; under the urging of their officers they faced towards the left where Welsh archers had appeared on the other side of the river.

The Saxons advanced to the edge of the swollen torrent, where they waited as arrows swept down from a rain-laden sky. The occasional shafts of sunlight had vanished as dark clouds began to obscure the mountainsides, adding a sense of gloom and dread to what had been an otherwise triumphant advance.

The officers urged the reluctant soldiers across the cold, limb-grasping river. Some were swept away. Others, more by luck than judgement, found ways across the raging waters and staggered breathless onto solid ground. Immediately, they began to form up for an attack on the vulnerable bowmen only fifty paces away, who continued a rapid hail of arrows. It was at that point that Lord Emrys' bowmen unleashed their arrows from the deep forest slopes against the undefended backs of those Saxons who had reached the opposite bank, or were still crossing. The Saxons were caught between a seen and an unseen enemy and panic set in. Those who were trying to ford the raging river were uncertain whether to continue or turn back, and their officers gave conflicting orders.

The senior Saxon officers quickly understood the situation. Those on the main track launched a counter offensive against Lord Emry's men, who continued to use the forest to their advantage. The Welsh archers were able to fire and quickly retreat up the treed slopes behind them, while the heavily armored Saxons plunged like leviathans through the dense undergrowth, determined to destroy this unexpected opposition, yet unable to make contact with it.

At the bank of the river, the Saxons had been halted. Those warriors who had crossed suffered under a hail of arrows as they tried to advance on the massed archers. Finding themselves vulnerable to arrows from both sides, they retreated back across the dangerous river. Once again, a few were dragged under the raging torrent, their heavy armor making it impossible for them to combat the overwhelming surge, but the majority were able to reform back on the bank and shelter under their long shields, while their officers waited for reinforcements.

The constant advance of fresh troops, and the quelling of panic by the officers, gradually turned the tide against Lord Emrys' archers, who were forced to retreat away from the main battle, drawing hundreds of Saxons deep into the dark forest that clothed the steep sides of the valley. Lord Rhodri's archers advanced again to the edge of the river's bank. Shielded by the raging waters, they began a deadly assault on the ranks of advancing troops.

Once the Saxons had dislodged Lord Emrys' archers and their rear was secure, fresh troops began a second attack across the river with some limited cover from their own archers, who were few in number and lacked bows as strong as the Welsh. Lord Rhodri's archers again retreated to the safety of the trees to fight a rearguard action against the well-armored Saxons. But the battle began to shift in the Saxons' favour. New companies of soldiers were still arriving. Behind them came their well-equipped, but limited, cavalry. There was some confusion where they could be best used and eventually General Thurkill decided to lead the horsemen up the valley to destroy any remaining resistance that might have gathered there. He was a brave man, but had a dread of arrows, and was looking for any chance to extricate himself from this tawdry battle that lacked nobility.

As he prepared to depart, he handed over the responsibility for the mopping-up operation in the valley to the young, inexperienced General Aelfgar. Although of equal rank, he had understood from Lord Edwin that he, Thurkil, was to make the major decisions, while giving the impression to the other officers, and particularly the men, that Aelfgar was, in all ways, his equal.

"You are prepared to take full responsibility here?"

"Of course." Aelfgar was keen to prove himself.

"Good. Follow me, as quickly as you can. We need to get the troops out of this hellhole of a valley."

He climbed onto his horse and was about to give the order to advance, when a sudden hail of arrows descended. For a short while there had been no arrows, and with the imminent advance, the Saxons had relaxed their guard. There were screams and loud swearing as the missiles struck home. Suddenly, Aelfgar was no longer by his side.

"General Aelfgar!" he bellowed. He turned in his saddle to see the young general struggling to control his horse, which had taken an arrow to its neck. Aelfgar was a large youth. When his horse reared up in its death throes, he crashed down onto the stony track like a sack of wheat, his right leg trapped under the weight of the falling animal. His men shielded him from the deadly arrows as they struggled to free him. After his release, he was in great pain and his crushed leg prevented him from standing. His face was ashen and he did not speak, seemingly unaware of anything around him.

"Find the General a horse, and escort him back to the safety of the forces with Lord Edwin," Thurkill ordered. "When we have finally destroyed these savages, we will have time to assess his injury." He looked around and noted with satisfaction that his soldiers were quickly establishing themselves on the far bank of the river and that the danger from arrows had lessened. The officers had, at last, regained a semblance of order. He felt confident he could still lead the cavalry in a successful mopping-up operation.

"Give a full report to Lord Edwin and tell him we have regained control. Tell him I am leading the cavalry to destroy the remnants of the Welsh fighters." He glanced at the young commander, now no more than another injured soldier. "Promoted before his time," he murmured. He watched as Aelfgar was firmly secured on a fresh horse; he seemed unconscious. Thurkill avoided the eyes of his officers. There was no time for emotion. He pointed at the assembled officer core. "Clear the valley on both sides, and take care of the General." An arrow narrowly missed him and he felt a strong urge to leave the deadly confines of this gloomy valley.

The rain had become a deluge, pounding on the armor and transforming the track into a rushing stream. In all directions, water raced in rivulets down the uneven surfaces. It was hard to believe there was so much water. The sky darkened and low clouds obscured the sides of the mountain. A sharp breeze had arisen and it was becoming more difficult by the moment for the Saxons officers to clearly assess the situation: the landscape would fade and, almost immediately, come back into view.

"You're in charge until I return!" he yelled at a senior officer. "Send up a strong column behind me. They must guard the way ahead and not allow any of the Welsh archers to reform." He looked back down the track, and was suddenly aware of the huge losses his army had sustained. Bodies were piled up along the river's banks and behind him soldiers were dragging their comrades to the side of the track to allow others to march past. "Kill all the Welsh!" he bellowed. "Spare nobody!"

He gave his horse a savage kick, and cantered up to the front of the Saxon cavalry, which waited in sodden lines. The riders were facing into the rain. Many were slouched forward in their saddles, trying, in vain, to shield their eyes. The majority were the sons of nobles, and had looked forward to the battle as a chance for excitement and an opportunity to gain a reputation for bravery and courage. The past hour had been an uncomfortable, dreary time when they had risked death from the sky but had been given no chance to fight their enemy. As General Thurkill took his position at the head of the column, they braced up in their saddles and hoped for action.

He wiped the rain from his eyes and cursed the weather that seemed to be in alliance with the enemy. "Forward!"

After a short canter the Saxon cavalry had to settle for a brisk trot, unable to push their horses any faster up the steep waterlogged track that wound its way up the valley. On their right the dark forest seemed impenetrable, and on their left the river roared past with increasing ferocity and all the time the rain pelted down on them like a curse from the Gods.

"When we reach the top of this track, we will assess the situation!" Thurkill shouted. His voice was snatched away in the roar of the wind. The nearest officer nodded, hoping he had understood the message.

As they turned a bend in the track, everything changed. Without any warning, they were overwhelmed by hundreds of Welsh cavalry. In moments, the track was a mass of swords, horses, blood, and death. While the Saxons fought desperately, the sheer numbers of the Welsh decimated their column, and not one of the Saxon cavalry survived.

In his last moments, Thurkill tried to rally his beleaguered troops, but to no avail. Some tried to retreat, but the track had been blocked; some tried to force their way through the massed enemy, but were soon cut down. Thurkill fought bravely, yelling his encouragement into the raging wind, but succumbed to warriors attacking from all sides.

When the brief, violent battle was over, Gruffydd walked his horse through his emboldened army. "We have won a small engagement!" he bellowed, his voice cutting through the wind and pummeling rain. "Now, the main battle is about to begin and I want you to listen!"

The soaked riders drew near, their hearts thundering in their chests. They had experienced a complete victory and most would have been happy with that. If it were not for Gruffydd, their King, they would have turned for home, happy in their part of a victorious skirmish; wanting to return, without injury, to their homes and wives.

"You have done well, my friends! But, the main battle is ahead. We will charge down this track and defeat the Saxon hordes. We must have victory! Total victory! And God help the coward who tries to desert us at this time!"

Many of the noble horsemen swallowed hard. This was not what they were used to. War was a game. War was when soldiers, farmers and slaves were slaughtered, it was a time to show brief bravery and return to one's adoring family, unscathed.

"If any one of you deserts us at this time, I have ordered the reserve cavalry to cut you down!" Gruffydd glared at his rain-battered army. "This is a new age! We are going for total victory! You are the heroes of Wales! We will win!"

A huge roar went up from the assembled horsemen. Even those who had heard nothing of the king's speech, knew instinctively that they were committed.

"For victory, and for Wales!" Gruffydd roared and led his cavalry at a trot down the flooded track.

• • •

THE FINAL BATTALIONS OF THE Saxon army reached the rock in the river. On both sides of the track, the earlier companies of the Saxons were engaged in a bloody and uncomfortable series of skirmishes with the retreating Welsh archers. The officers of the fresh troops halted them and waited for orders.

Edwin, their commander-in-chief, answerable only to his brother Leofric, was unhappy. He had assumed that by the time he arrived, the battle, such as it was, would be over. He was appalled to see his nephew, the young General Aelfgar, draped unconscious on a horse, and furious when he realized that if General Thurkill failed to return from his misguided advance up the valley, then he, Edwin, brother of the great Earl Leofric, would be responsible for this rapidly developing disaster.

"What are the latest reports?" he demanded, glaring at his divisional staff. He had established his headquarters well below the area of fighting, and insisted on platoons of crack troops being redeployed to guard all sides of his camp. "I need to know why we are still fighting these savages? Why are they still opposing us?"

"General, we are almost in total command of the field of battle," an officer stepped forward. "General Thurkill is ahead destroying any remaining opposition, while our forces on both sides of the river have turned a weak ambush into a rout." He smiled, wanting Edwin to remember him when the honors would be allotted after the war.

"So, why has General Thurkill not yet returned?"

The officer gave an ingratiating smile. "It's almost certainly because of the weather, my Lord." He looked to the other officers for encouragement, and finding none, continued his impromptu assessment of the situation. "We have superior numbers, better weapons and experienced troops." He smiled confidently. "They are only a rag-tag band of farmers. They are bound to be defeated, and then we can march out of this accursed valley, and into the Welsh hinterland." He bowed his head. "We await your orders, my Lord."

Edwin scowled; he was aware that the other officers were not as happy with the situation as this coxcomb in front of him. "What's your name?" he demanded.

"Ethelbert, my Lord."

"Well, Ethelbert, as you are so sure General Thurkill is on his way back from a victorious encounter with these Welsh farmers," he winked at some of his officer friends, "I want you to lead those men," he pointed to the front battalion of fresh troops, "to meet the General and relieve him of his prisoners." He glared at the unhappy officer. "Go, now!"

The officer quickly saluted, gathered a party of junior officers, and hurried towards the waiting troops. Edwin watched him depart, suddenly aware that he could no longer see the opposite side of the valley. He stepped out of the cover of his tent, followed by his senior officers, and stared up at the thick mist that had cloaked the track. The top of the valley was completely obscured. The forest on his right was wreathed in grey plumes of mist that slowly enveloped the trees from the bottom upwards. It was a depressing scene: there was no hint of sunlight in the dark, leaden sky. Torrential rain battered on his armor like an insane drum beat. His wet cloak stuck to him and he felt the deluge was diminishing his authority. He would have preferred to stay under the cover of his tent, but he sensed the need to be seen to share the army's misery. This was not how he had imagined it would be.

"What is your assessment of the situation?" Edwin demanded of the waiting officers.

One of the older, more experienced men stepped forward. "General, it is impossible to make a true assessment in these conditions. We have no clear idea of the success of our forces on either side of this valley, not since the rain and mist swallowed them up. Our soldiers are fighting in thick forest where they are at a disadvantage, and where their officers are unable to direct them. They have, however, forced the bowmen to retreat from their earlier positions. In this weather there is no longer any real threat from them, so I suggest we sound the recall and march out of this accursed valley."

"Yes," Edwin nodded. He chewed on his thumb. "But what happened to the scouts? Where are Thurkill and his cavalry? Why have there been no reports?" He stared around angrily at the officers, who shifted uncomfortably. Getting no response, he returned to the older officer. "Well?"

"We can only assume, my Lord, that they are pursuing the remnants of the Welsh horsemen." He paused and looked around for encouragement. "The performance of the Welsh, earlier in the battle, indicated they have no real cavalry."

"Do you all agree?" Edwin glared at his rain-soaked officers. There was a rapid nodding of heads. "Well, if you think there is no real opposition, then we will continue forward." He felt more optimistic. "Sound the advance!"

As the officers marched off to arrange their formations, he placed an affectionate hand on the shoulder of the older officer. "You will take charge of the recall of the soldiers on both wings. Do not sound the trumpets until the main army, under my control, is well up the valley. Make sure they reform in their companies, and send me a report of their losses."

"My Lord, the men will have been fighting for some hours. Some will be injured; all will be exhausted. Do I have your permission to rest them before we follow your advance?"

Edwin chewed on his thumb. Why did they always ask questions?

If things went badly, he did not want his orders remembered. "Yes, of course. But remember, you will be responsible for the rearguard, and for protecting the supply wagons." He could hear the trumpets sounding the advance. "I leave you to determine what to do with the injured." As he stalked away towards his horse, he tried, unsuccessfully, to remember the name of the officer.

Ethelbert wished he had kept silent before General Edwin. He came from a noble family and had only wanted some mention in dispatches; something to prove that he had been noted by the generals as an officer who had fought well in the defeat of the troublesome Welsh. His father had been a great warrior, and in his middle age was forced to stay at home as a result of his old and numerous injuries. In his enforced retirement, he relived his life through the achievements of his many sons. Ethelbert knew he did not measure up to his father's expectations. In spite of his inexperience and inner terror, he understood that this was a chance to prove himself.

He urged his junior officers to maintain the marching pace regardless of the steep slope and the torrential rain. "General Edwin expects us to capture the heights, and ensure the safety of the rest of the army. Keep them moving!" he shouted. But, in the back of his mind, he wondered if he should have relied on the name of General Edwin to make his point. He knew his father would have given the order in his own name. "Move on! Damn you!"

The junior officers rode up and down the marching columns, hitting out at any soldier who seemed to be holding back. Ethelbert felt better. He pulled his horse to the side and watched the lines of soldiers marching past; rank upon rank of hardened fighters, their armor and weapons glistening in the wet light. There was no doubt that he could achieve a reputation in this campaign. What had been a sudden nightmare back at headquarters could become an overwhelming victory. All he had to do was maintain an air of authority; his junior officers would do the rest.

He stood up on his saddle. "Forward to victory! Today you will achieve greatness!" he yelled. The massed ranks of bearded, almost identical soldiers trudged past, seemingly unaware of his presence. Somehow, his words had not sounded the way he had intended. He was grateful that the wind had drowned most of his speech.

He turned to his aide. "Ride ahead and report back to me of the situation at the front."

The rider trotted away and Ethelbert drew his waterlogged cloak around him. Ahead, the steep track bent to the right, and beyond, the mist obscured the mountains. He wiped his wet face. When this was over he would deserve promotion, if only for his suffering in such foul weather. His father would be pleased.

Suddenly, he was aware of a cataclysmic change, as though an earthquake was tearing the world apart. Ahead of him a wall of riders was breaking through the marching columns like scythes cutting corn. There was immediate chaos and the marching ranks disintegrated. Soldiers fell before the sharp hooves of the Welsh cavalry, their riders cutting a bloody swathe before them. The Saxons tried to fight, but their tight formations prevented them from using their weapons effectively. Many sought safety behind their shields, taking up a series of disjointed defensive positions. In moments, panic set in. The previously ordered ranks of foot soldiers became a desperate mob, shoving each other aside as they sought safety or a space to fight. Behind the front ranks, fear spread like a wild fire. Many at the rear of the bunched army turned back, some intending to reassemble once they could make a space, others, lacking officers, succumbed to flight, unable to control their need to seek the safety of the main army.

Ethelbert drew his sword and urged his horse towards the left side of the track, close to the bank of the swollen river, where he tried to lead his small group of junior officers in a counter-attack. The heavy horses had difficulty maintaining balance on the slippery rocks. His attempt to charge the enemy failed to achieve any real momentum uphill before the Welsh cavalry were upon them. He felt his mouth go dry as a wave of screaming Celts, many with lances, galloped down the edge of the steep track, forcing their way towards his small group of horsemen. The light Welsh horses were surefooted, enabling their riders to use their weapons to deadly effect, and the Saxon horsemen were hopelessly outnumbered. Ethelbert was appalled to see the ease with which his small company was overwhelmed. He did not want to die. He turned his horse sharply to escape the ferocious onslaught. But it was impossible. He found himself surrounded by a tight knot of Saxon foot soldiers, all seeking to make a stand around him. With his back to the enemy, he tried to push his way through the wall of shields, yelling at the soldiers to give way. In the chaos of the fast changing situation, his men refused, looking to him for the leadership he was so willfully lacking.

The wild forward motion of the Welsh charge swept aside any opposition. A savage blow to his armor knocked Ethelbert from his horse before he could turn to face his opponent. As he collapsed from the saddle, his left foot caught in his stirrup and he ended hanging upside down, while around him men fought and died. He attempted to use his sword to cut the leather, but only managed to cut the belly of his horse. The terrified animal reacted instantly and, regardless of the close, heaving mass of Saxon soldiers, leapt forward, its huge hooves raining death on the men directly in front. Ethelbert was dragged into the seething mass of humanity and trampled to death under the iron boots and dying bodies of his men. As he died, the battalion he had commanded fractured, broke, and disintegrated into a leaderless rabble.

• • •

INSIDE THE FORT THERE WAS an air of expectancy. Most of the men had fed and gained some rest, and were prepared for the next stage of the battle. The driving rain had begun to lessen in its intensity, as the sombre clouds lifted. Up the valley, the tendrils of mist were retreating and those on watch at the fort were aware of the gradual reemergence of the track along which the mighty Saxon army had marched some hours before. All felt it was possible that the weather could improve: the rain might stop, even the sun could appear before the end of the day.

"We have only a brief hour or two before darkness," Gomer murmured. "With luck the sun will come out, and give us a few more minutes of daylight."

He watched the Saxon guards, as they stared back from behind their makeshift defenses in front of the west gate. They were just beyond effective arrow range, but to keep them alert, Cydweli allowed some of his strongest archers to loose the occasional arrow from different places on the ramparts.

Cydweli smiled. "The men would like the sun to break through. They would see it as a good omen."

"What about those devils?" Gomer nodded towards the Saxon force that was intent on keeping them within the confines of the fort. "Will they attack the gates, do you think, or wait until their army comes back down the valley?"

"I think they're happy to wait it out," Cydweli said. "I know I would be."

There had been no letting-up in the Saxon activity behind the barrier of fallen trees and rocks they had assembled in front of the gates. The Saxon generals were convinced that the main element of the Welsh army was confined within the fort. They assumed there had been a great loss of life within this unexpectedly strong fortification, and that Welsh losses were equal to, or more, than their own. The remaining officers had been ordered to keep the remnant of the Welsh army within their own fort, where they would either run out of food and water, or would be easily destroyed when the might of the victorious Saxon army returned.

"Come with me," Cydweli said. He climbed quickly down from the rampart, checked the defenses around the west gate, and climbed the ladder up the south wall. Gomer found himself puffing like an exhausted horse as he staggered up the steps. He was followed by the ever-faithful Evan, who carried a Saxon axe.

Gomer turned to glare at him. "What the hell are you doing with that?" he growled. "You're a slave, man. You're not expected to fight."

"I can fight if I want to, my Lord," Evan responded with a hint of sarcasm.

"Well, don't swing it near me. You've no more idea of fighting than my daughters."

"I promise not to cut your head off, my Lord. You owe me too much money."

Gomer frowned, smiled and gave Evan a powerful thump in his chest. "You'll do, old friend. Just don't bloody well get killed."

Only a handful of soldiers guarded this section and they saluted Cydweli with obvious enthusiasm. Unlike the other walls, this had seen little action. The soldiers, while grateful to be alive, were keen to be involved.

Cydweli returned their salutes and beckoned to his brother to join him. They stood together on the narrow palisade, staring down at the steep rocky slope that fell away to the raging river below. "Can you see any Saxons on this side?"

"No, of course not. They couldn't mount an attack up this slippery slope. They'd all drown."

"Indeed. And that is why the main body of our men will leave this fort from this side."

Gomer looked amazed. "How?"

"I built this fort," Cydweli said. There was no longer a smile on his lined face. "I knew, eventually, that we would have to defend it. I also knew that any fort could be subject to siege. I realized the west gates would be the most vulnerable, and that the east and north side would be subjected to heavy attack. However, with the south side close to the river, and with this steep slope, I was certain it was unlikely to be seriously attacked. I have built it such that we can remove a section of the wall and launch a sudden assault on the enemy."

Gomer shook his head. "You never cease to surprise me, little brother."

Cydweli pointed to a narrow, rock-strewn ledge that ran along the side of the fort, above the river. "That would be a suicide path for the Saxons, but for us it is a way to launch an unexpected attack on their flank." He moved around the rampart until they were facing the Saxon emplacements opposite the west wall. Beneath them the gates were being reinforced. In the courtyard a strong barricade had been erected to oppose the enemy if they broke through.

"I do not intend to wait until our forces come to rescue us, or for the Saxons to return in force to crush us." Cydweli stared bleakly at the mist-shrouded valley, where the light was slowly increasing.

"Llywelyn said to wait until the Saxons were in retreat, or to prepare for a siege if he was beaten." Gomer spoke with a quiet intensity.

"There's no point in our remaining like captives. We must do our fair share." He stared at his brother, his mouth a tight line. "Now listen carefully. You will lead the attack from the west gates and the archers will provide cover. Once you are engaged, I will launch the main attack on their flank." He smiled as he visualized the scene. "With luck, they will not be expecting you to open the gates. You should catch them off-guard. I am hoping my attack will cause such chaos they'll run away."

Gomer remained silent for a moment, unable to present a realistic argument. He nodded his agreement and pretended to check his equipment. Behind him, Evan smiled. He relished a good fight.

They returned to the officers who were assembled near the gate, where Cydweli explained his plan. Finally, he turned to Lord Ganny, the young mounted officer. "As soon as you see them fleeing the battle, that is when you and your few cavalry attack them from behind. Understood?"

"We will look forward to that, General."

"Good man. Get into position now and wait until Lord Gomer leads the attack from the gate. We'll not sound trumpets to begin with. We'll try to catch them unprepared. I keep hearing trumpets up the valley, which I'm sure is a good sign." He looked around at the tense faces around him. "Today is the chance for each of you to be a hero. Don't let me down. Remember, your wives and families are relying on you to defend them from the Saxons."

There was a growl of agreement, and, after some embracing, each officer returned to his men with a spring in his movements.

"I reckon you could persuade a cockerel to lay eggs," Gomer muttered as he moved towards the west wall.

• • •

WHILE GOMER INSTRUCTED THE SERGEANTS around the gate,

Cydweli prepared his officers for the surprise attack around the side of the fort. He revealed a secret only a few were aware of: a number of seemingly stout poles in the middle of the south wall were not fixed deeply in the earth, as they appeared to be, but were merely resting on the surface and would be easy to remove.

At the west gate the guards, who could be seen by the enemy, were slowly reduced in number. Gomer encouraged the remainder to appear sleepy and bored. The Saxons duly noted the reduction in activity above the gate, and on the north and east walls.

Cydweli spoke to his closely packed troops. "Once our west gate is opened, the Saxons guards will sound the alarm, but with luck most of their men will be resting. Lord Gomer will charge out of the gates, form up his men as if to attack the Saxon barricades, then he will falter and will tempt them to leave their defenses. At that point, we must move quickly into position. It's vital that we're not seen, so that once the Saxons have committed themselves, we hit them hard on their right and from behind. With luck and your bravery, we should be able to overwhelm them. Then, with our bowmen on the palisade adding to the chaos, and with our small cavalry, I'm certain we will force them to flee."

There was a muted cheer, as men moved into position. Those who were alert would have noted that the rain had stopped and the sky was revealing streaks of blue.

• • •

THE SAXON OFFICERS OUTSIDE THE fort were tired from their long march and their fierce and unsuccessful attack on the Welsh stronghold, but they were confident that their enemy was in a similar state and had suffered huge losses. "They will not be a problem until night falls," a senior officer remarked, as he watched the apparently exhausted guards on the fort's ramparts. "Stand down half of the men and give them time to rest and prepare for a night assault."

The other officers were in full agreement, and were happy to pass on orders that pleased their disgruntled soldiers.

The dark clouds lightened, giving way to pockets of blue sky, allowing the sun, unseen for days, to shine briefly with an intensity that was magnified by the rain-drenched landscape. Staring into the low sun was difficult. The Saxon guards positioned themselves with the light to the side and behind them as they looked east at the fort. The brightness made the shadows darker and these factors helped Cydweli and his small army to advance unseen along the sides of the steep ravine, until he judged he was behind the Saxon emplacements. The thunderous roar of the raging waters covered the sounds of their advance. After much slipping and silent cursing they were eventually in position.

They waited with pent-up energy for Gomer to lead his attack through the main gates, while experienced officers silenced the huffing and puffing of those young men who had never been in a real battle. The tumult of the river continued to cover their advance. Eventually, Cydweli and his officers reached a vantage point where they could observe the Saxon camp. The Saxons had been lax in their defense: all of their guards faced the fort and many of their soldiers were asleep; the rest, sitting in small groups, were eating and drinking as though there was no possibility of fighting.

From a raised rock some fifty paces behind the camp, it was possible for Cydweli to assess the number and the preparedness of his enemy. He smiled encouragingly to his officers; they passed this down to the impatient men waiting in the cool space of the ravine. He wondered what was delaying his brother, and realized Gomer would need to be certain that Cydweli's forces were in position before he began his assault through the gates.

"Do any of you have a flag?" he whispered to his nearest officer. "Anything we can wave?"

The officer shrugged his shoulders and, once more, passed a message down the line of men. Eventually, a bright colored cloak was handed to him. Cydweli tied it to a spear and, with three of his officers, advanced to a point behind the Saxons where he could be seen from the fort. He cautiously raised the improvised flag and began to wave it slowly from side to side. There was an immediate reaction on the ramparts of the fort. In moments, before the Saxons had any warning, Gomer launched his assault.

The huge gates were forced open before the inattentive guards had realized what was happening. The Welsh stormed out of the fort. They formed up in a line, beating their shields, while on the walls of the fort the trumpets sent out their challenge. Behind them the heavy gates were shut tight.

"They're trying to escape!" The Saxon officers yelled abuse as they ran through the sleeping ranks of soldiers. "Quickly! You're dead men if they get away!

"No!" Another Saxon officer shouted back as he watched the Welsh begin a slow advance forward. "They intend to attack! Form up! Form up!"

There was chaos in the Saxons' camp. Many soldiers, half asleep or midway through a meal, were forced to run to their positions. Officers were screaming orders and contradicting each other. The soldiers hastily buckled on their armor and grabbed their weapons, as they raced from their encampment. They formed up in hastily arranged groups, quickly massing along their makeshift barricades, trying to understand what was happening.

"Are they mad?" the senior officer exclaimed as he stared out at the Welsh soldiers. "There are so few of them. We outnumber them by at least four to one!"

The Welsh advance slowed to an uneven stop midway between the fort and the Saxon emplacements. It was as though their officers had only now realized that they were so heavily outnumbered. The soldiers, however, continued to beat their shields with their swords and spears, and to yell at their bemused enemy, as though they were confident of their ability to win. Some of the younger Welsh turned and bent over to display their bare buttocks, causing a roar of outrage from the Saxon defenders at the insult.

"They've stopped advancing! Their commander appears to have changed his mind," an officer said as he pointed at the confused melee a hundred paces away. "Can they really be this stupid?"

Behind the Welsh lines, the gate of the fort began to slowly open and junior officers could be seen ordering their men to retreat. Some soldiers began to shuffle back a few paces, while behind them, a small group of archers fired a volley of arrows over their heads, inflicting the first casualties. This convinced the Saxon chief of the need for action. He gave the order to advance and leave their fortified positions.

With a huge roar, a wave of well-armed giants clambered over the logs and branches that had formed their defenses. They charged towards the Welsh forces, which immediately began a rapid retreat towards the open gates of the fort. The Saxons were encouraged by the pitiful behaviour of their enemy. There was fierce competition to get past the barricades and take part in the intended massacre. The bloodlust was so strong that none looked behind, nor did they have any thought of doing so.

Cydweli swept silently across the deserted camp, leading his untrained soldiers who had been ordered to keep silent until they reached the Saxons, or risk unspeakable punishment. He caught the enemy on their right as they were bunching up waiting their turns to break through their own defenses. Many died without knowing where the danger came from. Those who recognized the threat were so crowded they were unable to immediately defend themselves.

At that moment, a second force of Welsh troops attacked from behind, wreaking panic along the whole of the Saxon line. Fierce hand-to-hand fighting began, and the wave of Saxons advancing on Gomer's forces was reduced to a mere ripple, although those in front were confidently unaware.

In front of the walls of the fort, Gomer turned his men from retreat to attack, as he had always planned to do. They had just enough time to form up before the charging Saxons were on them. Huge in size, and protected with heavy armor, the Saxon vanguard attacked the smaller Welsh, who tried to maintain a shield wall to stop them. The weight and strength of the invaders was such that the Welsh lines were forced back. The centre appeared to collapse completely, with their soldiers retreating to the sides, and allowing the Saxons a clear advance on the open gates. Dozens of their soldiers raced into this apparent breach, determined to reach the gates before they could be closed.

One moment the Saxons were charging an open gateway, the next it was filled with cavalry galloping towards them. The armored horses scattered the attackers, who found themselves surrounded on three sides. In spite of the unexpected reversal in their fortunes, the Saxons fought with a reckless bravery. They faced the riders with a confidence in their strength and armor, and would have destroyed the small cavalry contingent if it had not been for the vigorous attacks on their flanks. In moments, the Saxon advance halted. It was soon merely a desperate rump, unable to cope with the fierce assaults on all sides. But, in the fierce fighting, Ganny was seriously injured by an axe blow to his thigh. Despite the wound he continued to fight.

Behind them, the second wave of Saxons had realized the real danger, had regrouped and launched a violent counter-attack on Cydweli's forces. What had been a massacre by the Welsh, in moments became a bloody battle with much of the advantage returning to the Saxons. The officer in charge was a big man with a dense, red beard and arms the size of most people's thighs. He carried a huge axe that he used with the strength of two men, and a long, metal-studded shield. The giant seemed almost indestructible, like a mythical demon, hacking his way through the poorly armored Welsh forces, causing fear and panic in their lines.

"With me!" Cydweli yelled, as he tried to encourage his inexperienced troops. He screamed orders to his junior officers in a vain attempt to reverse this Saxon advance, which threatened to turn his attack into a rout. It was clear the huge officer was leading the Saxon's counter-attack. He was creating order where before there had been chaos. Cydweli watched with anger and a sense of impotence as his men scattered before the onslaught.

A few of his friends and officers answered his frantic calls. With their support, he led a furious charge at the wedge of Saxon fighters that was decimating his troops. Within a heartbeat, he was facing the Saxon leader who towered above him. There was no time to reflect on his actions. He was committed. Cydweli attacked with a speed and resolve that caused the giant to hesitate. He lunged with all his strength at the Saxon, but his sword stroke was deflected by the man's thick armor and the force of the blow shattered the blade.

"A sword!" he yelled, dropping the useless weapon. "Quickly!" He raised his shield to protect himself and attempted to regain his balance, as the Saxon's heavy axe bit through the thick leather of the shield, smashing him to the ground, leaving his left arm numbed and useless. He quickly rolled to his right, narrowly avoiding the next blow and became entangled in a melee of charging feet and injured and dying men. Above him the giant swung his axe, clearing a space through the Welsh soldiers as though he was scything wheat. Cydweli glanced around desperately seeking a weapon, but in the turmoil he had become separated from his officers. He sprang to his feet in time to dodge the next blow, but as he drew his dagger, he was barged from the side and was unable to position himself to avoid the sharp axe, which almost cleaved his head and right shoulder from his body.

The Saxon raised his powerful arms above his head. He waved his huge axe, roaring his victory for all to hear. He knew he had killed a Welsh leader, and sensed the battle had been settled in that action. As he raised his arms for yet another deafening roar of triumph, Gomer, advancing from behind, thrust his sword into the giant's armpit. The blade passed through his lungs, cutting a major artery. The warrior staggered, his cry of victory becoming a death rattle. He dropped to the ground, next to the lifeless body of Cydweli.

With the fall of their champion, the Saxon forces disintegrated and, as they retreated in disarray, the injured Ganny and his cavalry struck them from behind. Few of the Saxon besiegers survived. Those that did fled for their lives, uncaring for the fate of their fellow Saxons.

Around the fort, the Welsh soldiers wreaked their revenge on any injured Saxons unable to retreat. "We take no prisoners!" Gomer had yelled in his despair. In his arms his beloved brother laid dead, his head cleaved nearly beyond recognition. For Gomer, no victory would be enough. With Evan's help he insisted on carrying his brother's body back to the fort, where he laid him down on the floor of a cart. "Stay with him," he ordered Evan. With tears running down his face, he gathered his remaining officers together and urged them to reassemble his small army.

The sun faded as low cloud returned, and soon the mist was rolling back down the valley; a useful cover for the Welsh, but a grim warning for their enemy.

For General Edwin, the day's reversals had come as an unbelievable shock. When his foot soldiers had retreated down the valley, he ordered his personal guard to execute them. "We will not tolerate cowards!" he had screamed.

When the injured Aelfgar, his nephew, was returned to the base camp, Edwin blamed his friend Thurkill for not taking more care of the young officer. But when confirmed reports came of the annihilation of his army's cavalry and the death of Thurkill, Edwin knew he had to take responsibility, however unwillingly.

"We will advance on their fort," he announced to the assembly of his shaken and confused officers. "Once we have taken it, we will destroy the remains of the Welsh army." It seemed quite simple.

"My Lord," an officer protested, "our soldiers are in full scale retreat!"

"We do not retreat!" Edwin roared. "I will kill the first officer who deserts me. You will stop them and you will reform the army. This is only a temporary setback. My personal guard will protect you!" He stared them down, and the officers rushed out of his tent knowing they faced their worst nightmare.

As the grey light began to dim, the desperate officers, with the help of General Edwin's personal guard, managed to regain some semblance of order among the retreating Saxon troops, who were fleeing down the valley as though they had an army of devils behind them. Momentarily emboldened, the dispirited troops were able to form a shield wall and withstand a massed charge by the Welsh cavalry, who appeared out of the gloom in a solid wall of horseflesh and spears. After a short, savage encounter, in which the Saxons found themselves fighting for their lives in a desperate defensive role, the Welsh cavalry quickly withdrew. They stopped about two hundred paces away, milling about like a disorganized rabble.

"We've beaten them back!" Lord Edwin shouted. "Prepare to charge!"

"No, my Lord," an officer protested. "We must maintain our positions. They want us to break ranks."

"Do as I order!" Edwin screamed. He knocked the officer to the ground, and glared round at his other officers. "I am your general. You will do as I command." He kicked out at the fallen officer. Nobody was going to tell his brother Leofric, the Earl of Mercia, that he, Edwin, had failed in his courage.

"Charge them down!" he yelled, and urged the officers to move the dense ranks of their foot soldiers into a gradually accelerating wave of iron and muscle. The Welsh retreated a short way and again faced their enemy, as though unsure how to react. At this point, Welsh foot soldiers appeared on both sides of their cavalry, encouraging the Saxons to completely break formation in their eagerness to vent their frustration on the elusive Celts. When they were less than fifty paces away, Welsh archers emerged from the woods on the right of the Saxon advance and began a systematic assault on the dense, but mainly undefended ranks. Many in the front rows, and those on the right, fell to the hail of arrows, stalling the furious advance, causing those behind to become entangled.

Edwin led a small group of mounted officers, and forced his way to the left of his forces, intending to lead his personal guard around the side, away from the deadly archers and towards an advancing wave of Welsh foot soldiers. His attention was diverted by a powerful Welsh cavalry charge down the centre that threatened to divide his army. But, it was not until an officer grabbed his arm that he became aware of hundreds of Welsh fighters advancing up the valley, led by a handful of cavalry.

"We're surrounded, my Lord!"

"Gather our horsemen, we will meet them head on."

The officer tried in vain to alert the other horsemen. However, they were already engaged in a frantic rear guard action against wave after wave of Welsh foot soldiers, which were linking up with their cavalry and seemed to be attacking from all sides.

Edwin knew that if the Welsh forces, advancing rapidly up the valley, reached the main battle, then all would be lost. "Follow me!" he screamed to his personal guard. He assembled more than two score of horsemen, and he charged down the track in a desperate last attempt to reverse the defeat threatening his army.

As he closed the distance between himself and the advancing Welsh, he saw the small group of their cavalry form up and take a position between him and the mass of their foot soldiers. "Straight through them!" he yelled.

Ganny was only seventeen years old. He had never fought a battle in his life and was so tired, he could hardly stay upright on his saddle. The day had been a series of violent engagements; he had been continuously involved since first light. He had survived the attack on the fort without a scratch, but had sustained a deep wound to his thigh when he had led the cavalry through the gates of the fort. Ganny had continued to fight until the Saxons had retreated, driven by excitement and nervous energy, unaware of how much blood he had lost. Now, he was being called upon to lead a final charge to destroy the remnants of the Saxon's cavalry, or die in the attempt.

His eyes refused to focus and he could not feel any sensation in his left leg. The wound in his thigh was throbbing so badly that he groaned in agony every time his body was shaken with the movement of his horse. He raised his sword in his right hand, the signal to advance. Then, with an effort, he urged his blown mount into a canter. He was driven by a grim determination, and led his few cavalry towards the enemy.

Behind him, Lord Gomer was ordering them on. He had acquired a spare mount from an injured noble, and was using action as a way of blotting out his intense sadness over the death of his brother. "One last charge, my boys, and we will drive them out of Wales! No cowards, now!"

He kicked his tired horse into action and rode closely behind Ganny, trusting in the young man's ability to lead. The small force broke into a gallop, charging towards a Saxon cavalry troop led by an imposing officer on a white horse. Suddenly, Ganny tipped sideways, dropped his sword, and fell out of his saddle into the direct path of the Welsh cavalry. In a brief moment he was under the charging hooves, and was unrecognizable when the dead were later counted.

Gomer had never led a cavalry charge in battle. In truth, he had never fought on a horse before. But, there was no turning back. He knew that King Gruffydd ap Llywelyn needed him if victory was to be secured. It was enough to quell his fears and convince him of the necessity of leading the diminutive Welsh cavalry. But, more than this, was the need to be avenged on the invaders who had killed his beloved brother. "Onward!" he cried.

Leading the advancing Saxon horsemen was a tall, well-armored knight who rode a fine horse, but for all his obvious signs of leadership, seemed awkward and almost amusing. He held his lance as though unsure of its weight, and he bounced in his saddle like a rider unused to a cavalry charge.

The two leaders clashed some distance in advance of their advancing forces. Gomer easily deflected Edwin's spear with his small shield, and was satisfied to see his own lance take the Saxon Lord in the throat. In moments it was over. The Welsh cavalry charged past and engaged the Saxon horsemen in a furious skirmish, which was quickly settled as the advancing Welsh foot soldiers surrounded and overwhelmed the remains of the confused enemy.

Gomer was driven by anger and a wild excitement. He led his men in a dramatic charge into the virtually undefended Saxon headquarters. General Edwin's remaining guard was slow to comprehend the immensity of their defeat. They stood staring helplessly at the advancing Welsh soldiers as they swarmed into the dead general's camp. The servants ran away and the soldiers, unable to find an officer to lead them, deserted. Before the long day was over, the remnants of the great Saxon army, whose soldiers had considered themselves invincible, were fleeing back over the border. More than half of their forces lay dead or dying in the Welsh hills. The rest, leaderless and defeated, returned back to their families, unable to explain their historic reversal.

It was a brave officer who reported the defeat to Earl Leofric. "Your son, Aelfgar, was injured, my Lord. I am told that the Welsh King intends to ransom him, when Lord Aelfgar has recovered from his wounds."

The Earl had received other reports of the defeat, but nothing about his son. "You're sure he lives?"

"Yes, my Lord." The officer chewed his lower lip. "He fought well, my Lord."

"I'm sure he did." The Earl sat staring, unseeing, into the roaring fire. His palace had become a cold and barren place. Outside, the rain pelted down and a strong wind moaned in the shutters. He knew he should not have entrusted the army to his brother. Edwin had always been an administrator, not a general. But with such an army, how could he have failed? He turned to face the officer. "General Edwin is confirmed dead?"

"Yes, my Lord. He died leading a cavalry charge in the final moments of the battle." The officer clasped his bandaged left arm that was oozing blood.

Leofric nodded grimly. "You've done well. Get your wounds seen to. I will promote you when you have recovered." He turned back to the fire. "Come to me tomorrow, I want to know more details about my son."

• • •

THAT NIGHT, KING GRUFFYDD AP Llywelyn celebrated with his troops in the damaged fort. Fires burnt high, the fighters relaxed with roasted meat and beer, and up the valley the peasants took their revenge on those Saxons who were unlucky enough to have remained alive.

"We have won our greatest victory ever!" Gruffydd's voice boomed out across the packed fort. "You all played your part in this historic battle, and you're all heroes!" Hundreds of Welsh voices joined together in a prolonged cheer. "But many of our friends and relatives did not survive!" There was a sudden silence. "But we will remember them in the days to come, when we tell our families of this momentous day. One name in particular will always be mentioned. The man who built our fort and trained many of you to become soldiers! The man who led the defense of this fort and defeated the Saxon attempts to destroy it. It was he who ensured our great victory. He was the first General of the Welsh Army, and he died defending his soldiers. My great friend

Cydweli ap Griffith!" A roar of approval rose up like a roll of thunder, continuing until the King raised his arms for silence. "I will commission a great stone to be erected here in his memory. When men pass it in years to come they will remember General Cydweli!" There was another burst of enthusiastic cheering, which gave way to the one word: "Cydweli!"

"But there is good news also. We killed General Edwin, the brother of Leofric, Earl of Mercia, and General Thurkill, his great friend." A loud hoot of derision went up from the soldiers. "But most importantly, we have the Earl of Mercia's son! Lord Aelfgar. He's badly injured, but if he recovers, I will ransom him for his weight in gold!" The yelling and banging of shields continued for many minutes.

Gruffydd waited patiently for the men to settle down, knowing it was their way to show respect for the passing of a great hero, and to feel a sense of revenge for his death. Finally, he raised his arm for silence.

"And worthy also of our praise is Cydweli's brother, the indomitable Gomer ap Griffith!" The King took hold of Gomer's left arm, raising it high above the heads of the applauding men. "From henceforth, Gomer ap Griffith will be known as the Lord of Deheubarth, which includes both Ceredigion and Dyfed!"

Gomer had little memory of the following hours, as he struggled with the loss of his brother and the furious celebrating of his friends and survivors. But he did remember that shortly before exhaustion overwhelmed him, Gruffydd had gripped his hand and spoken with warmth and intensity. "I'm in your debt, Gomer ap Griffith. By making you the new Lord of Deheubarth, I am giving you both an honour and a problem, my friend." He placed a powerful arm around Gomer's shoulders and gave a self-conscious chuckle.

"You know, of course, that Hywel ap Edwin has set himself up as the self-styled King of Deheubarth?"

"It did occur to me, my Lord." Gomer eased his tired body from the heavy embrace of the King and turned to face him.

"He did not fight with us today, and he will pay for it." The King grinned like a large boy caught stealing apples. "Your problem is that Hywel will not wish to give up his title. You will have to fight him for it, if needs be."

"There's no love lost between Hywel and my family. We've crossed swords before."

"There will be even more reason for him to hate you once he hears I have appointed you in his place."

Gomer rubbed his tired eyes. "No matter. With this army, we'll dispose of him very quickly."

Gruffydd slowly shook his head. "No, my friend. The army will disband tomorrow; the men need to get back to their families," he paused, "and I leave tomorrow with my personal guard." His blue eyes flashed. "News has just arrived that some in Gwynedd wish to take advantage of my absence. I must return immediately."

"In this time of your great victory?" Gomer spat on the ground. "Don't they realize that you have destroyed an enemy that would have taken everything from them? This is the greatest victory Wales has ever had. Those vipers, who refused to fight beside us, now stab you in the back!"

"Gomer, you know this is how it has always been. The nobility have always warred with each other, like dogs fighting for a small bone. But eventually, I will defeat them all, one by one. I will become the High King of All Wales!"

"Amen to that."

"Tomorrow, I will be returning to defend what I have created." He patted Gomer on the shoulder. "But you, my friend, will have to seize your new honour with your own men," he smiled broadly, "and with my blessing. If Hywel proves a hard nut to crack, I will come to your aid in due course." His eyes wandered over the firelight. "But first, I must teach the rebel lords of Gwynedd that it is dangerous to cross me."

• • •

1052

GOMER STARED, BLEARY-EYED AT THE dim outline of the island in front of him. It would soon be day, and his nephews would return.

'And I'm still not Lord of Deheubarth, no matter what Gruffydd promised,' he muttered. He took a swig of wine. However, he had to admit to himself that Gruffydd had, two years after the battle, finally helped him become the Lord of Deheubarth. In the year 1041, true to his promise, King Gruffydd had enabled Gomer to defeat Hywel at the battle of Pencader, and Gomer had become the Lord of Deheubrath, and Hywell had been forced to flee Wales.

Three years later, in 1044 the self-styled King Hywel had returned to Deheubrath with a strong Danish fleet, to regain his kingdom. There had been a bloody battle along the banks of the River Teifi, and the villagers of Llanduduch had fled to the hills. Upriver, the town of Aberteifi had been put to siege. Then, King Gruffydd had suddenly appeared with a large army and had soundly defeated the Danes. In the bloody battle, Gomer had killed his rival Hywel, and retained his title of Lord of Deheubarth. It was that year that Cydweli's long-suffering wife, Len, had died, and Gomer had taken over the fathering of his brother's sons.

But, in 1047, after only three years, Gomer had been forced to give up his title when Gruffydd ap Rhydderch of Gwent, in association with certain disgruntled nobles of Ystrad Tywi, attacked Deheubarth unexpectedly, and killed 140 of King Gruffydd's personal guard. The King had been staying with Gomer at Aberteifi, and had been forced to flee the area and regroup in the northern mountains of Gwyneth. Gomer had retreated south to his family home near St. David's. During the next five years, there had been numerous small fights between the soldiers of the self-styled King Gruffydd ap Rhydderch and Lord Gomer's men aided by King Gruffydd ap Llywelyn. Eventually, Gomer had regained control of much of the southern area of Deheubarth, including Llanduduch. However, now in the year 1052, Gomer was still trying to regain his lost title, while his enemy Gruffydd ap Rhydderch continued to hold Aberteifi, and the northern parts of Deheubarth.

'But that bastard Gruffydd ap Rydderch can't last for ever. Soon King Gruffydd will help me unseat him. When he finds the time.'

He scratched meditatively under each arm, forcing his aching limbs to work. "Evan!" he roared. "Where are you?"

"Where I always am," Evan replied from outside the tent; there was a hint of amusement in his voice, "ready to serve you, my Lord."

"Well, do something useful then and tell those bloody heroes on the island to get back over as soon as possible. I want a warm bed and some hot food."

"And perhaps some strong drink?" Evan suggested.

"Well, of course!" Gomer bellowed. "Use your sense, man. I don't have to tell you everything."

Evan nodded and walked over to the cliff edge with a grin on his face. 'He's in good voice,' he murmured to himself. 'Nothing much the matter with him. Tough as old leather.' He glanced back down the headland and was surprised to see a small group of horsemen emerge from the gloom; they were advancing rapidly over the difficult terrain.

He ran back to Gomer's makeshift tent. "My Lord!" he yelled. "Horsemen approaching!"

Gomer emerged quickly, his sword drawn, and beckoned to the fishermen who were sheltering beneath their cloaks. "Form up behind me!"

The strangers approached at a steady trot. None of them was holding a weapon. It was clear they did not intend to launch an attack. The leader was a large bearded man, who wore a heavy mail hauberk and rode a huge destrier that towered over the other horses. Behind him a soldier in expensive armor carried a lance with a pennant displaying a red dragon.

"My Lord Prince Arthwyr?" Gomer was amazed.

"Gomer, you old devil. I hear you've been murdering Picts?"

"What brings you here, my Lord?"

"You're a hard man to find. But my elder brother, the King, wanted you to know the good news as soon as was possible."

Gomer's eyes widened. "Good news is always welcome," he said cautiously.

"Gruffydd led an invasion of the Saxon county of Herefordshire over a week ago and we defeated a mixed force of Norman mercenaries and Saxons." He climbed down from his horse and embraced Gomer in an enthusiastic bear hug. "We pillaged the towns and the countryside and Gruffydd has enough gold to pay for a permanent army." He stretched his arms. "Do you have anything to drink?"

"Not much." He handed his jug to the Prince. "We came here as soon as we could after the battle in the village. I wanted to make sure those Pictish murderers didn't end up on the island. What remains of my personal guard are over there now." He pointed across at the shadowy huddle of men on the other side of the gap. "We'll be able to celebrate our two victories, indeed."

"Gruffydd wanted you to know that he has not forgotten you. He's grateful for your continued support. As soon as he is able, he'll help you defeat Gruffydd ap Rydderch and return your property to you. In the meantime, I and my men will return to Llanduduch, where we can rest up." Lord Arthwyr ap Llywelyn drank deeply. "The King's men will soon return to their families to show off their loot. It might be a while before he can reestablish his permanent army." He placed a large hand on Gomer's shoulder. "But he's not forgotten you."

"That's good. As long as I'm still alive to enjoy it." Gomer gave a roar of laughter and took back the jug. He turned to Evan. "Go on ahead and make sure there's a hot fire, cooked food and plenty to drink." He placed a fatherly arm around the Prince. "Now, you must tell me all about your battle and then I'll tell you about mine."

CHAPTER SIX

1055

It was a foul night. The cold rain lashed the riders mercilessly, and the wind howled so loudly that they were unable to communicate with each other. They were approaching their destination, making their way along known paths in thick darkness, determined to be in position before dawn. There were more than two hundred horsemen, each heavily armed and riding strong, mountain ponies. In spite of the grim weather and the hard journey along rough mountain paths, there was a sense of determination and confidence in the small army. They bunched up in a large ordered group, as the leading horseman stopped in a natural opening in the dense forest.

"Where are the scouts? Damn them! They should be here by now?" The speaker, Gruffydd ap Llywelyn, King of Gwynedd and Powys, a tall, thickset man was now in his late forties. He was unmistakable with his wild black beard and big features. His dark eyes flashed in the light of a flickering torch that he held above his head, and his deep bass voice cut through the wind. He sat astride a tempestuous black destrier, much larger than the native horses and there was no doubting who was in charge of the small army.

"We've made good time, my Lord. They're reliable scouts. They should arrive at any moment." Rhys, his elderly Sergeant-at-Arms, smiled in the darkness. Unlike his volatile Lord, Rhys was an easy-going, friendly man who possessed a quiet confidence in his own abilities and was a good judge of men. He was, like many of his race, short and muscular, and a deep believer in the importance of family, friends and freedom. Like Gruffydd, he hated the Saxons, but was content to follow rather than lead. He worshipped

Gruffydd, whom he considered to be Wales' greatest leader ever, since he defeated the Saxon invaders at the great battle at Rhyd-y-Groes sixteen years ago.

He still vividly remembered the turning point in the battle when Edwin, the brother of Leofric, the powerful Earl of Mercia, was killed. With his death, the death of General Thurkill, and the capture of the wounded General Aelfgeat, the Earl's son, the remains of the once great Saxon army had fled back across the border. It had been a remarkable victory; the greatest defeat of the Saxons in the long history of the Welsh defense of their homeland. As Rhys waited patiently on his horse, he reflected how, since then, the battles had been mainly between rival Welsh nobles, who often named themselves as kings and wasted the nation's blood in their envious and jealous squabbles. Wales needed a single strong king who could unite the whole country, and he hoped to see that happen during his lifetime.

At that moment, two riders approached and identified themselves. They quickly dismounted and approached the King.

"Well?" Gruffydd demanded. It had been a long ride and he was keen to engage the enemy.

"My Lord, the traitor, Gruffydd ap Rhydderch, is camped along a hillside above a stream. He has a large force of mercenaries, and many impressed local men who have no wish to fight. He expects to engage Lord Gomer at first light, and is confident of victory."

"He has more men than Gomer?"

"Yes, my Lord. Lord Gomer is following your orders. He has given a challenge to the traitor, and is advancing with only a small force. Gruffydd ap Rhydderch believes Lord Gomer is an old man who has lost his judgement."

"What about Lord Gomer's young friend, the Saxon Lord Aelfgar?"

"He's in position, my Lord, with a strong force consisting of his personal guard and the rest of Lord Gomer's men. He is placed to prevent the enemy from retreating back to Aberteifi."

"Good. You've done well. Take ten men and cover our advance. When this is over I will see you are both well rewarded." The two scouts returned to their horses, their faces flushed with pride.

The Sergeant-at-Arms nodded to himself. What a change around. Sixteen years ago the Saxon Lord Aelfgar, son of Earl Leofric, the powerful Earl of Mercia, had been seriously injured in the great battle of Rhyd-y-Groes. Now he was fighting alongside the very King who had been his enemy. After the battle, Lord Gomer had taken the wounded Aelfgar back to his home, where the young man had slowly recovered, and during which time he had been well treated. He became friends with Gomer's two nephews, Gwriad and Dafydd, who had been mourning the loss of their father, Cydweli. They came to admire the handsome Saxon Lord. Aelfgar had spent much of his time acting as a surrogate brother to the two boys. Rhys looked around and by the light of a flaring torch identified Gomer's two nephews among the riders, both now grown into manhood: the short, stocky Gwriad and the tall, lanky, red-haired Dafydd.

"Give the order to advance," Gruffydd ordered his Sergeant-at-Arms. "Douse the torches, and remind them to travel in complete silence." He motioned to a broad rider with a large beard: "Arthwyr, you old goat, I want you by my side."

"Of course, King Gruffydd," he spoke with heavy irony. "Where else would a younger brother be?"

• • •

ON A HILLSIDE NEAR THE ancient village of Cilgerran, close to the upper reaches of the River Teifi, the massed forces of Gruffydd ap Rhydderch, the self-proclaimed King of Deheubarth, had been in position since first light. A mixture of Saxon, Norman and some Pictish mercenaries reinforced the centre and both wings. They were well armed, experienced warriors, who would fight for whichever Lord would pay the most. King Gruffydd ap Rhydderch was confident that he had their loyalty. If they helped him defeat the upstart Gomer ap Griffith, they would be worth the cost. He had also placed a strong contingent of the 'foreigners' to cover the rear of his battle line to act as a reserve and, more importantly, to ensure that the local men did not desert. He was aware that his new taxes were unpopular, but being disliked had never concerned him. Knowing that the locals called him *Gelen*, which translated meant *leech*, was a source of pride. "I will suck them dry," he joked to his nobles.

He sat comfortably on a large horse that he had chosen more for its placid nature than its experience in battle. It was not his intention to fight; he paid soldiers for that. From the top of a broad, rolling hill he could look down on his forces and control the conduct of the battle; although once the two sides were engaged, he knew he would have only limited control. There would be a short, bloody encounter: one side would lose heart and turn and run, and the other side would give chase and capture as many of their enemy as possible. Slaves were worth more than the weapons and armor of the dead. In Wales there was always a shortage of men to work the land.

"Lord Gomer's forces are approaching, Lord!" One of his younger officers pointed excitedly to the skyline of the low hill opposite. Soldiers were beginning to emerge from the gloom. He could make out the red and green of his opponent's flags. It was still raining and he could hear the muted roar of the swollen stream that divided the wide valley. Overhead, low dark clouds obscured the higher ground and the October sun was unlikely to appear.

He watched with interest as Gomer's forces began to form up. There were only a few on horse and they remained at the top of their hill, as he and his more numerous cavalry waited on theirs. He had received reports that Gomer's army was comprised entirely of local men, as Gomer was unable to afford mercenaries. He guessed only a few of these would be trained soldiers. Gelen sneered as he assessed the opposing army: it numbered less than a third of his; only the soldiers in the centre wore full body armor and, apart from the front row, the wings of Gomer's ragtag army seemed to be composed of lightly clad archers.

What was the old man up to? Gelen knew that his main enemy, King Gruffydd ap Llywelyn, was fighting an insurrection in the mountains of Snowdonia. So, there would be no help for Gomer from that quarter. He smiled when he recalled how he had defeated the Northern King eight years before, and had become King of Deheubarth. The great Gruffydd ap Llywelyn had come to pay a courtesy visit to his vassal Lord Gomer and had brought fewer than 200 soldiers with him. He had believed the area to be friendly and was quite unprepared when Gelen had marched from Gwent and ambushed him with superior forces. In the short, bloody battle, Gelen killed 140 of Gruffydd's personal guard, and forced Gruffydd to flee back to Gwynedd. Today, he mused, I will finally rid myself of this meddling old fool, and then the great hero of the battle of Rhyd-y-Groes will have no support in this area, and will be forced to remain in his mountain wilderness.

"Why don't they attack?" he asked his senior officer.

"I don't think they intend to, my Lord. They can see how much we outnumber them."

Gelen rubbed a leather glove over his wet face in a gesture of irritation. His men were well positioned on this hill, and he had hoped Gomer would have attacked and been slaughtered: he was known to be an impulsive old man, whose bravery was often depicted as rashness and stupidity. "He'd certainly have attacked if he'd been able to gather more men," Gelen muttered.

Both sides had begun to yell insults at one another. Some of Gomer's archers had unleashed a few arrows to test the distance. Most had landed short, and this had produced a roar of derision from the mercenaries.

"Do we attack them, my Lord?" The officer, a young noble, was excited, as were all of his officers. They were raring for a fight, like young hounds that have the scent of prey and are tugging at their leashes.

"I am Gruffydd ap Rhydderch, King of Deheubarth," he snarled. "I will give the orders when I see fit."

The officer nodded his head and looked straight ahead.

Around him, Gelen could hear the restless stamping of the horses and the mutter of the other officers, all local nobles, and most lacking real experience. War was just a game to them. He spat into the mud that surrounded their horses. He knew he could not keep the hired soldiers standing on this hillside for much longer. They had been keen to form up before daylight, but now they were becoming unsettled. If he gave the order they would swarm down the hill. With their superior numbers, they would almost certainly overwhelm Gomer's men.

So, why did he feel so unsure? He noticed how both of the wings of the opposing army had fixed sharpened poles in the rocky earth to slow down the cavalry and allow the archers some defense. Did it matter? The mercenaries would destroy the centre in their first charge. Then, the archers would be massacred. His cavalry would soon route Gomer's horsemen, who did not appear to number more than two score. Perhaps it was merely disappointment: he hated giving up his strong defensive position. He imagined the problems the enemy's archers would cause as his men were slowed down crossing the stream. They would have to storm up hill to engage the enemy. So what? They were professionals; they knew how to fight.

For the first time in his memory, he felt strangely uncertain. There was something wrong. It was almost too good to be true. He called his senior officers around him. "Do the scouts have any new reports?"

They all shook their heads, unwilling to tell him that no scouts had reported in the last hour. It was not important. The battle was about to start; they wanted to fight.

At that moment, a wave of Gomer's bowmen rushed down to the stream and unleashed a flurry of arrows at the massed ranks of Gelen's army, causing random deaths and injuries. An angry ululation arose from the frustrated mercenaries, who possessed few bowmen. The arrows continued to wreak havoc and it was clear that the situation could not continue.

"All right. Attack!" Gelen shouted petulantly. He felt he had lost control of the situation. But his good humour returned as he watched the enemy bowmen race back to their positions, away from the dark wave of his army as it raced down to the stream. A few of his soldiers fell as they crossed the water, but the majority roared up the hill towards the fixed ranks of Gomer's men-at-arms. They looked unstoppable.

"Their cavalry is moving to our left!" an officer yelled, pointing to the two score of horsemen who appeared to be intent on crossing the stream above the fighting. He shook his head. Surely, they were not intending to engage his powerful cavalry? "They must be suicidal!" He bellowed. He had not intended to involve his nobility until after the main battle was over, when they would be useful in the mopping-up of any isolated patches of resistance and in capturing those who tried to escape.

Gelen pointed to his senior officers. "Destroy them!" The cavalry quickly formed up in rows, gathered speed and charged down the side of the hill, angling themselves towards the oncoming riders, who had crossed the stream and formed up some five hundred paces away. Gomer's horsemen appeared to waver: they moved around each other, waved their weapons at the oncoming cavalry, then turned and galloped back the way they had come, like a disorganized rabble.

It was an unbelievable scene. Gelen's remaining officers almost choked with incredulous laughter. "The cowards! They've no more sense than chickens!" they yelled, as the pitiful group of horsemen raced back up their hill. Unlike his officers, Gelen did not share in their hilarity. This was not the way battles were fought. It was as though his cavalry was being tempted to follow. He looked back at the main battle, where Gomer's centre was slowly giving ground, and their archers on both wings were retreating to positions behind the men-at-arms. There at least, there was no doubt of the outcome.

"The day is ours!" an officer chortled. He waved his sword above his head.

"It's too easy," Gelen muttered. "They're up to something."

The officers exchanged glances. What more could Gelen wish for?

His gaze returned to his cavalry, which was moving fast up the far side of the opposite hill and parallel with a low plateau down which the stream flowed. They rode in a large tight formation and were quickly closing on their retreating enemy. On the brow of the hill, Gomer's horsemen suddenly stopped and turned to face the advancing throng. At that same moment, hundreds of horsemen appeared along the plateau and charged down on the left flank of Gelen's cavalry, catching them completely off-guard. Their tight formation prevented them from avoiding the deadly line of lances that sliced through them, creating panic among men who only moments before had felt supremely confident.

"It's King Gruffydd ap Llewelyn!" an officer shouted pointing at a cluster of flags with the unmistakable red lions on a gold background.

Gomer felt his mouth go dry. He watched as his long-time enemy burst through the melee and galloped across the stream, accompanied by a strong force of cavalry. The King was in full armor on a mighty destrier, and was carrying his family's famous long shield of red and gold with its four horizontal lions. He was using his long sword to devastate the fast fading opposition. There was no doubt where he was heading.

Everything had changed almost in the blink of an eye. Gelen gritted his teeth in frustration as he saw a further army of foot soldiers advancing rapidly up the valley. The men were well armed and occupying both sides of the stream, confronting the mercenaries on their right flank and preventing an escape route. Elements of King Gruffydd's cavalry, having overwhelmed Gelen's horsemen, had turned their attack on the mercenaries' left flank. The foreigners knew how to fight, but their resistance was brief and bloody. An organized retreat soon became a chaotic, hopeless rout, as each man tried to save himself. The mercenaries knew that there would be little sympathy for them if they dropped their weapons and tried to surrender. Some fought to the death, while others dropped their heavy shields and ran off in all directions.

"What are your orders, my Lord?" There was panic in the voice.

Around Gelen, his knights were barely controlling their desire to flee and he knew he had one last chance. "We will meet them head on!" he bellowed. "If you leave the field, they will hunt you down. If we kill Gruffydd, they will lose heart, and we can still win the day!" He waved his sword and pointed it at the on-coming cavalry, led by the Northern King, who was galloping up the slope like a man possessed.

"Kill him!" Gelen screamed. He urged his horse down the slope in a final gesture of defiance. He was unaware that only a few of his personal guard had followed his example. Many of those who had joined him lost heart and turned back before the two enemies met.

Although unwilling to risk his life needlessly, Gelen was a dangerous adversary when forced to fight. He was strong, skillful with a sword, and fearless when cornered. He slewed his mount across the path of Gruffydd's destrier, rose up in his saddle, and delivered a savage backhanded blow at Gruffydd's head. If it had connected, it would have changed the outcome of the battle, but the Northern King had fought in many such fights. He parried the blade, his strong arm reverberating with the impact of the weapons. His huge warhorse, trained for battle, reared up and struck Gelen's untrained horse with its powerful ironclad hooves.

Gelen barely managed to jump free as his animal fell to the ground, its powerful legs flaying out in a paroxysm of pain. He aimed a wild, revengeful blow at the towering destrier, but was kicked by his own horse, lost his balance and did not see Gruffydd's sword before it slammed into the thick armor on his left shoulder. He was knocked down, but regained his feet before Gruffydd had dismounted. The two men faced each other, surrounded by a dense wall of Gruffydd's officers. Both men were breathing heavily. Gelen clasped his sword in his right hand; his left arm hung uselessly at his side and he was vaguely discomforted to note that Gruffydd was left handed.

"Surrender, Gruffydd ap Rhydderch!"

"Never!" Gelen gasped, and rushed forward, swinging his sword wildly in a frantic last effort. Instead of retreating and parrying the strokes, the Northern King sidestepped his adversary and dealt him a ferocious blow to the back of the neck. Gelen staggered. His body collapsed forward. Gruffydd reversed the sword's direction to a deadly upward movement. His blade cut up below the helmet and Gelen died before his body hit the ground, his head almost severed from his body.

Lord Gomer, who had entrusted the mopping-up to his two nephews, arrived in time to see Gelen die. He paused for a moment and gazed down thoughtfully at his dead enemy. His gaze shifted to the victor. "Well fought, my Lord King! Now, at last, I can be Lord of Deheubarth!" Gomer gave a roar of delight. He dismounted and clasped King Gruffydd in a ferocious hug.

"Enough, you great bear! Give me time to breathe." He bent

double for a while, then placed a mailed glove on Gomer's shoulder. "Now, there's only Morgannwg to persuade, and I will be King of All Wales."

"You will, my King. Wales needs a strong leader, although I am now a spent force." He gave a dismissive shrug. "However, my nephews are strong and young enough to be of use to you." He waved toward Gwriad and Dafydd, who could be seen across the stream, organizing the disarming of the captives. "Those two, the sons of the great Cydweli, will serve you well, King Gruffydd."

The King nodded. His eyes roamed over the field of battle. Many had died, but his army had won a decisive victory. There were still some isolated fights continuing between mercenaries, who had nothing to lose, and Welsh soldiers who wanted them dead and were determined to take their weapons and armor. But the battle was over, and the rebel Gruffydd ap Rhydderch lay dead at their feet.

One of his officers rode up on a spent horse, dismounted and knelt quickly in front of him. "My Lord King, I have sad news."

Gruffydd stared down at the rider, recognizing him as a friend: "Give me the news, Vernon, who's dead?"My Lord, your brother, Prince Arthwyr ap Llewelyn, is dead. He died bravely, leading a charge against the foreign mercenaries." The officer began to weep. "He was my friend, my Lord. Wales has lost a great man."

"He died saving Wales!" Gruffydd yelled. He shook his head and fought back the tears. "He died fighting for me and for all of you!" He sniffed loudly. "We will not forget my bother, Prince Arthwyr ap Llewelyn. As fine a brother as any man could be." He stared angrily around, as if challenging anyone to contradict him. After a short pause, he raised his sword above his head. "May this be the last time that I am forced to kill Welsh men. May this be the last time Welsh Lords employ mercenaries to kill my countrymen. Let there be peace!"

There was a huge roar of assent and Gwriad and Dafydd kneeled in the mud, alongside a host of other officers. As one voice, they yelled, "King Gruffydd ap Llywelyn! King of All Wales."

CHAPTER SEVEN

1056

The south-west peninsula of Deheubarth was reminiscent of a foot sticking out into the Atlantic Ocean. It was a favourite destination for the two brothers, who, although different in temperament and ambition, shared an admiration and love for this wild landscape.

In the brief time since their Uncle Gomer had finally become the Lord of Deheubarth, their lives had changed considerably. Gwriad, now a thickset man of twenty-four years of age, had become a firm friend of King Gruffydd ap Llywelyn. After winning a number of minor military engagements, he had been promoted to General, in charge of the defense of the whole of the south-west of Wales. Dafydd, a tall, thin aesthete, had been recognized for his academic abilities and had recently become the King's Secretary.

It was mid-afternoon on a warm spring day as the two sons of Cydweli rode down into the Glyn Rhosyn valley and could see, in the distance, the famous St. David's Cathedral. It had once been a monastery founded by David, Abbot of Meneria, in the middle of the sixth century. He had been being credited with a number of miracles, and was eventually made a saint. Over the next 400 years, he had come to be considered the most significant of the Welsh saints. As they gazed down on the ancient building, it was possible to see the recent changes and additions that had been made. It was no longer a stark, lonely building with a few meager huts surrounding it. Instead, it had become the central point of a collection of stone buildings housing an increasing number of monks. A large walled garden could be seen on the south side.

They had been riding hard since first light, and apart from some brief stops to eat and relieve themselves they had had enjoyed little opportunity to talk. This was the first time they had met in more than a month, and they allowed their weary horses to champ the moist grass, while they took a moment to admire the picturesque scene before them. There were few buildings of any architectural note in Wales and it was always a surprise to reach one. They had travelled for hours across a lightly populated landscape with only occasional small villages and bleak, lonely farms. It was good to have arrived.

"What a beautiful sight," Dafydd said. "You can see why this is the most important religious place in Wales."

"The Druids wouldn't agree with you," Gwriad replied with his usual sardonic humour. "If you travelled to their holy island of Ynys Mon and mentioned St. David's, the Druids would think you had a leek in your head." His reference to the symbol of St. David was not lost on his brother.

"You never take anything seriously, do you?"

"I don't take religion seriously, that's for certain. I leave that to you. But I do take women seriously."

"No, you don't. You have a new woman every week."

"Usually two, at least." Gwriad always enjoyed baiting Dafydd, whom, he suspected, was still a virgin. "And, unlike you, I take great care not to get killed in battle. It was a good job you gave up trying to be a soldier, or I'd be travelling by myself today."

"Who's Angharad?" Dafydd asked, keen to change the subject.

There was a slight hesitation. "Just a woman. Why?"

"You were discussing her with Gomer when I arrived at Ceredigion."

"Correction. He was discussing her with me." He raised an enquiring eyebrow.

"I came in at the end of your conversation and Gomer seemed upset?" Dafydd was beginning to suspect he had touched on a raw nerve.

There was a long pause. Gwriad's horse shook its sweat-covered head to remove the irritating flies. "It seems I have ruffled a few feathers. Or to put it another way, her father is insisting I marry his daughter and has sent a message to Gomer." There was suddenly no trace of humour in his voice.

Dafydd turned in his saddle and examined his brother's bearded face. He was staring ahead and his blue eyes gleamed in the bright sunlight. His full mouth was set in grim, resentful line, quite unlike his usual light-hearted attitude.

"Do you love her?"

"She's very attractive."

"That's not what I asked."

"I love women. I always have. Angharad is no different to any of the others. It's just that I have known her for a while now." He glared at the distant buildings. "But I had no intentions of marrying her."

"Is her father important?"

"Aye, now you have it." He blew out his cheeks. "Her father is Cadell ap Bleddyn."

"Duw!" Dafydd's eyes opened wide. "King Gruffydd's revered Seneschal?"

"Not only that, but he is also the father of the beautiful Ealdgyth."

"Another of your conquests?"

"Don't be stupid. You must know who she is?" Gwriad stared in amazement at his brother's blank look. "You're the King's Secretary! Do you spend all your time with your head in a book? She's tall, slim, has long black hair, amazing eyes, and loves to dress in blue. She's been in Court a lot recently."

"Ah, yes. Now I know whom you mean. Yes, she's very beautiful. I didn't know she had a sister."

"Ealdgyth's likely to become the next Queen. Gruffydd is besotted with her. He will soon announce their engagement."

As the implications of this sunk in, the expression on Dafydd's face changed from a casual smile to a deep frown. "You have been bedding the future Queen's sister? The daughter of the Seneschal?"

"Yes." He breathed out loudly. "When I first met Angharad, she was travelling with her father and we became lovers. She was as keen as I was. Of course, I knew who her father was, but there didn't seem to be any harm in it. I'd never met Ealdgyth and, until recently, neither had Gruffydd."

" But you knew Angharad was the daughter of Cadell ap Bleddyn?"

"Of course I did. I just said so." Gwriad sounded irritated. "Many of the noble women have lovers. I imagine I wasn't Angharad's first." He glanced at the censorious expression on his younger brother's face. "I forget how innocent you are."

Dafydd blushed. "Being such a man of the world would also appear to have its problems."

Gwriad looked uncomfortable. "I wasn't going to tell you until I had sorted out the situation with our uncle. In his mind it's simple: I have a responsibility to marry Angharad, because her father is a friend of his and there would be a big falling out if I refused."

"But if you agree, you will become Gruffydd's brother-in-law by marriage. He will think you are politically ambitious, maybe dangerously so. However, if you refuse, you could be seen to be insulting Cadell ap Bleddyn's family and, by implication, casting doubt on the King's future wife. What an interesting situation."

"Interesting situation! Are you mocking me?"

"No. I leave the mocking to you, brother." He stared down, unseeing, at the stone buildings around the Cathedral. "Would you like some advice?

"Why not? It can't be worse than Gomer's vituperation." Gwriad had always liked words, and although he could not read Latin, he could speak it to some extent, and could read and write in Welsh. He would frequently use his extended vocabulary on Dafydd whenever he felt the need to remind him he was not a complete gwirionyn.

"It's not a question of not marrying her. Cadell will feel highly insulted. He will complain to Gruffydd, and you will lose his favour and will almost certainly be demoted. Also, Gomer will never forgive you for insulting his childhood friend and disobeying him. He still thinks he's responsible for us."

"But if I marry her, as you rightly said, Gruffydd will be suspicious of my motives. He has been a friend to me. But, he is the King and is merciless towards those whom he thinks might threaten his power. As my brother, you could suffer as well."

"Not if you marry Angharad first," Dafydd said. He displayed, at times, an unexpected tact and statesmanship, which is what had first brought him to the King's notice. "If you approach the old Seneschal as though you always intended to ask his permission to marry his elder daughter, he will be delighted. I imagine he is not unaware of the King's interest in his younger daughter, and the last thing he would want is to have anything happen that would cast a shadow on the prospect of him becoming the King's father-in-law. He will be as keen as you to have an early marriage with Angharad and, certainly, before the King asks to marry Ealdgyth. If you act quickly, all can be saved and Gruffydd will accept you as part of a family he wishes to embrace."

Gwriad scratched his beard in a meditative manner. "Well done, little brother, you might have saved my skin." He leaned over and placed his gloved hand on Dafydd's shoulder. "I suppose it's about time I settled down and Angharad is a good catch for any man. Of course, she may say no."

"Is that likely?" Dafydd was conscious again of how little he knew about women.

"Well, as far as I'm aware she's not carrying my child. She could say no; she's a very independent woman."

Dafydd grinned. "Well, the sooner you find out the better then. It's a long journey back to Gwynedd and I imagine you'll want to stop at Gomer's castle on the way and make him think you are carrying out his orders. He will be so pleased, he will almost certainly pay for the wedding!"

In decidedly better humour, the two brothers cantered down towards the cathedral gate.

They had sent a messenger to Bishop Hywel advising him of their visit. Monks quickly appeared and took charge of their horses and their weapons. An elderly monk, Brother John, directed them to the Bishop's walled garden. They entered through an iron gate, and just inside was a stone ledge on which were two bowls of water, soap and towels.

"Please refresh yourselves," Brother John said. "The Bishop will meet you over there." He indicated a secluded corner at the other end of the garden, where carefully pruned bushes surrounded three leather chairs and a round oak table with wine and cakes.

"The Bishop is at prayer and will meet you presently. He asks that you will enjoy the wine and the food while you wait." With a brief bow the monk took his leave.

It was a well-established garden with grape vines growing on the south-facing wall; a number of fruit trees and bushes were dotted around. The brothers removed their heavy hauberks, loosened their tunics, and washed themselves with considerable enjoyment.

"Now I feel able to discuss the King's business on a more equal basis," Dafydd said, as he dried his face. "I hate stinking like a shepherd."

Gwriad nodded, and restrained himself from his usual brotherly insult. "I'm glad we have some time for you to explain to me this business in detail. Bishop Hywel might raise some unexpected problems."

He walked over to the table, poured two cups of wine, devoured three of the flat currant cakes, and had refilled his wine by the time Dafydd joined him.

"You will need a clear head, brother, so don't indulge yourself too much," Dafydd warned. Although he was aware he sometimes sounded like a mother hen, he secretly envied Gwriad's lusty approach to life: he so obviously enjoyed eating, drinking, fighting and womanizing, and never suffered the moral and social pangs that inhibited others.

As usual, Gwriad took no notice and refilled his mug. He knew his brother had always been a worrier and one who found it difficult to relax. Settling comfortably into a chair, he carefully observed Dafydd, who was sipping his wine and admiring the bouquet. "It's for drinking, not sniffing it up your nose. There's no doubt you need a sexy woman, boy. Some regular shagging would do you a lot of good."

Dafydd colored up and quickly glanced around the garden, horrified that the Bishop might have heard. Reassured, he sat on the edge of a chair, eager to change the subject. "As I mentioned to you, the King wants to unite Morgannwg into the rest of his realm. It makes sense. It is the only part of Wales outside his direct control. Since the death of Gruffydd ap Rhydderch, that self-styled King of Deheubarth, the Princes of the south-east of our country have remained quiet. They know they cannot raise an army large enough to resist the King if he decides to invade, they continue to fear the Saxons, yet they want to keep their power. For nearly two years they have failed to agree among themselves and now the King's patience is exhausted. "

"I know all this."

"The King is not prepared to wait any longer," Dafydd continued. "He has ordered them to meet here in four weeks and take their vows of loyalty."

"I know that too."

"What you will not know is that Gruffydd will arrive with all his lords and a large army, and having obtained the submission of the Morgannwg Princes, he intends to have a Coronation. He wants to be crowned King of the Britons, which is why I am here to see the Bishop and arrange the details. He asked for you to come to this meeting to represent his military power in this part of his kingdom."

Gwriad sat up and lowered his cup. "Why didn't he tell me this?"

"Because you were on patrol in Ceredigion, and he knew I would find you."

"Does Gomer know?"

"No. Gruffydd only decided recently. You know what he's like, he decides on something and it has to be done immediately." He chewed thoughtfully on a cake. "Gomer will be very impressed when you tell him, especially as you are going to follow his advice and get married."

A solitary golden eagle circled overhead and Gwriad watched it thoughtfully. "Suppose the Princes of Morgannwg do not submit to Gruffydd?"

"They'll agree. He intends to let them know he's bringing his whole army."

"They haven't agreed in the past, why should they now?"

"Since you took over as General of this area, you've changed Deheubarth. Now there are regular patrols, and your soldiers are a constant reminder of the strength of the King. Before the death of Gruffydd ap Rhydderch, this area was friendly towards the Princes of Morgannwg. Now, they can see the power and reality of the King. With the exception of the Prince Rhys Fachan, the other princes are willing to join a united Wales."

"Rhys Fachan has always been a problem. I can't see him changing. It's very likely he will defy Gruffydd." He watched the eagle glide away towards the coast. "Rhys is an unpleasant man and I will look forward to crossing swords with him. I think his people will not mourn him."

"We shall see. The King wants to avoid a fight."

After a long pause Gwriad relaxed back in his chair. "Why King of the Britons? I thought Gruffydd wanted to be called King of All Wales?"

"We discussed this. He thinks King of the Britons will impress foreign kings. It allows him to contemplate forming an alliance with the kingdom of King Mark of the Cornovi tribe. Although, by crowning himself King of the Britons, he is claiming to be the paramount leader of Mark's kingdom." Dafydd shrugged his shoulders. "We're all Celts."

"Are you referring to what the Saxons call Cornweal?"

"Indeed. It's the kingdom of those Britons at the end of our Island that the Romans never conquered and neither have the Saxons. Gruffydd intends to use the Church to encourage their Saint Geraint to unite them all in a holy war against the Saxons."

"Will King Mark agree to this?"

"Who knows? One thing at a time." He nodded his head; he was enjoying himself. "Your news about Ealdgyth makes me realize that once Gruffydd is crowned he will need a wife to produce an heir. There is no doubt that he will want another big ceremony; a wedding to be remembered and one to impress our neighbours."

"It will cost money." Gwriad rose to his feet and casually checked the garden. "This Bishop will need paying."

"Quite right. More money than Gruffydd has in his treasury.

Which is where you come in, brother." Dafydd finished his wine and poured them each another cup.

"He wants the Saxons to pay?" Gwriad touched cups with his brother in a silent toast.

"He wants you to assure the Bishop that the money will be forthcoming. I am to encourage him with his discussions with Saint Geraint."

The gate opened at the end of the garden and a smiling elderly bishop approached them.

Gwriad bowed and muttered, "The poor man doesn't know what is about to hit him."

"Don't you believe it," Dafydd hissed as he bent from the waist. "The Bishop is not a man to be trifled with."

• • •

JUNE 1056

RHYS FACHAN WAS A COLD, unemotional man, whose grim, lined face was a warning to anyone who thought they might appeal to his humanity or generosity. He rarely discussed his thoughts and had little time for anyone who could not advance his fortune or increase his power. Uninvited guests were casually insulted or publicly humiliated by Rhys, who would refuse to speak to them or acknowledge their presence. He was the most influential of the Morgannwg Princes. Without his unrelenting opposition to King Gruffydd, the others would have agreed to the concept of a paramount ruler immediately following the defeat of Gruffydd ap Rhydderch.

Rhys had summoned the Princes to his castle, which crowned a small hill overlooking a winding river. Although a warm day, his great hall was still cold; it was a drab room with a recently lit fire that smoked and gave out little heat. A line of servants stood near the main door, staring ahead as though they were statues, and by a side door stood his elderly chamberlain. There were no decorations on the walls; the room was empty apart from a large oak table, a throne chair at one end, and a scattering of smaller chairs and benches around the fireplace.

Prince Fachan, as he liked to be called, remained seated behind the long oak table, while three nobles stood like underlings in front of him. He was glaring at them and waving a long, gnarled finger, as though they were naughty boys caught stealing fruit. "The longer we hold out, the greater the chance that Gruffydd will get killed by one of his many enemies," he said, his voice harsh and deliberate. "There's no need for us to hurry to answer him." He gave a contemptuous grunt that was the closest he ever came to a laugh. "He can wait until we are ready to discuss his ideas. The longer he has to wait, the better for us."

"We have to agree to meet him at St. David's at the end of August," Prince Anarwd ap Tewdwr observed. He disliked Rhys intensely, but was cautious of his unpredictable nature.

"I did not agree," he hissed. "We don't have to bow and scrape to this Northern upstart!"

"He intends to have us swear allegiance to him in front of the rest of the Welsh nobility. It will be a great occasion. After the ceremony, he will have a Coronation to crown himself King of the Britons."

"And do you intend to go?" Rhys' tongue moved in and out of his narrow lips like a viper's.

Anarwd nodded, and looked to the other two Princes for support. "We have no choice. He intends to bring his army with him."

"He doesn't want another Welsh war," Rhys snarled. "If he did he would have invaded us before now." There was a long pause as Rhys stared grimly at each of the young men. "We'll go to St. David's, but we will take our own armies. We will negotiate from strength, not weakness. I'm prepared to sign a treaty of alliance with him, but I will not agree to him being ruler of Morgannwg." He wiped the sweat off his face, although the room was cool. "We're Princes, stretching back to King Morgan Mwynfawr, who was not called 'Great in Riches' for nothing!"

He slammed his fist on the table in front of him. "He united the kingdoms of Glwysing and Gwent to form our Morgannwg. For more than two centuries we have withstood invasion and outside threats. We do not bend our knee to this Gruffydd ap Llywelyn!" He stared angrily into the eyes of each of the three Princes; each looked away. Rhys knew they would desert him.

He resorted to his customary war of silence and watched the three younger men shuffle awkwardly, each waiting for the other to reply. Eventually, Prince Anarwd, the most senior of the three, broke the tension. "I will not bring war to my people."

"He'll not risk war with us!" Rhys yelled. "If we stick together he'll back off. Gruffydd hopes to frighten us. He wants our lands. He won't bully me!"

I trust Gruffydd. He can unite all of Wales. He will be the first king ever to have done so." Anarwd was supported by low murmurs of assent from the other two nobles. "A united Wales will save us from the Saxons. They would love to see us continue in our customary manner of bickering and fighting our neighbours. You must join us and present a united Morgannwg."

"I must do nothing of the sort!" Rhys jumped to his feet, the veins stood out on his forehead. He pushed back his heavy chair that crashed to the floor. His face was contorted with rage and his eyes bulged. The three Princes backed away from the table, uncertain as to what violence he might level against them. He had been known to kill servants with his own hands when his temper was unleashed. "No one will tell me what I must do! I am Prince Rhys Fachan. I go my own way!" He was breathing heavily, but with a great effort. He turned away and stared out of the window behind him. After a long pause, he faced the three men and indicated for a servant to pick up his chair.

"You may be right," he nodded at the Princes and sat back on his chair. "I will think on it." He made a dismissive gesture with his hand.

They bowed and walked towards the main door, exchanging surprised looks.

"Prince Anarwd!" Rhys called. "A moment with you, if you please." He nodded to his chamberlain, who disappeared out of a side door.

The two younger men exited quickly, glad to escape. Anarwd

paused by the door, wondering what had caused Rhys' sudden change of attitude. His left hand touched the hilt of his sword in an involuntary gesture. Breathing deeply, he crossed the room.

"I'm sorry," Rhys indicated to a servant to bring up a chair. "I have a short temper. Please sit. I was not thinking clearly." He seemed ill at ease and his eyes kept darting to the side door.

Prince Anarwd sat down cautiously. He knew from past experience how Rhys' moods could change. "Thank you, Prince Fachan. You wish to speak to me, alone?"

"I lose patience with those young Princes. They know nothing. But you," Rhys paused as his chamberlain entered carrying a tray with two goblets of wine and some bread and cheese, "you're different. I respect your views." He nodded to the chamberlain, who laid the tray carefully on the table between them. He glanced at his Lord and bowed his way out, beckoning to the other servants to follow him.

When the last servant had closed the door behind him, Rhys cleared his throat and handed a goblet to Anarwd. He sat back in his chair and stared at his hands, then began to nibble a piece of cheese in a distracted way. "I think, if we work together, we can persuade the King to leave us be and, in return, we can agree to his claim to be King of All Wales." He nodded at Anarwd's goblet. "Drink up. A toast to better times." He raised his drink.

"Indeed," the young Prince raised the goblet, then slowly replaced it on the tray. "Perhaps, this would be a good time to agree our boundary problem?"

Rhys stared at the tray. "Boundary problem?" He became suddenly alert.

"Indeed, Prince Fachan. I refer to the question of who owns the forest on the other side of the river." He smiled. "My father left it to me, but recently, I believe you have made a claim for it?"

Rhys stood up, replacing his goblet on the tray. "It's not a recent claim. Your father and mine never agreed on its title, but it's obviously in my territory."

"Why is it obviously so?"

"The curl of the river makes it so!" Rhys exploded. He pushed back his chair and stalked over towards the window that overlooked the river. "Look!" he said, jabbing his finger towards the distant forest. "You can see the way the river bends." He was so focused on the scene, that he failed to notice Prince Anarwd exchanging goblets. "How can you claim to own that forest, when any fool can see it's mine?

Prince Anarwd pretended to look out, as Rhys continued to point his finger furiously at the scene. "You have been hunting in my forest for years. I want you to stop." His face turned towards the younger man. "There's no boundary problem!"

"Perhaps you're right," the young man sounded suddenly weary as he returned to his chair.

"Well, I am." Rhys said triumphantly. A sudden thought came to him as he returned to the table. "Anyway, we won't argue about it. We have more important things to discuss." He sat down and raised his goblet. "To better times between us!"

"To better times!" Both men drank deeply and Anarwd watched with interest as the exultant expression on Rhys' face became one of fear.

"What have you done?" he gasped. He stared bewildered into the dregs of his goblet and slammed it on the table. "You've tricked me." He pushed himself from his chair, and clutched his throat, staggering backwards. White saliva trickled out of the corner of his mouth and his gnarled hands clawed the air like a baited bear. He began choking and clutching at his chest. His dark eyes rolled upwards and, with a horrible gargling noise, he collapsed backwards onto the stone floor.

• • •

JUNE 1056 WAS A BUSY time. The complex arrangements for the Coronation were planned and set in motion, and with the unexpected news of Prince Rhys Fachan's death, the last obstacle to Gruffydd's ambition to become King of All Wales and King of the Britons, was removed. The King had moved quickly. He invited Prince Anarwd to meet him at his palace in Rhuddlan. From the moment he arrived, the young Prince had been lavishly feted, and it was made clear to him that he had become a very important noble in the hierarchy of Wales.

"Prince Anarwd, I can't tell you how pleased I am," Gruffydd said. He had invited the young Prince to his newly constructed Palace to impress him and to listen, first hand, to the remarkable story of Rhys' death, and of Anarwd's narrow escape. "You are a very resourceful man. I need people like you around me. I will accept your oath of allegiance at the ceremony at St David's Cathedral, and I will in turn proclaim you Prince of Morgannwg and General of the Army of the South-East." He beamed with pleasure and handed a cup of wine to Anarwd. "To your good health and success." He winked and nudged him. "And you don't have to exchange the wine cups!"

The two men felt comfortable with each other: both coming from similar aristocratic families, and both knowing how to command men and give orders. Gruffydd was in peak health in his forty-ninth year: a powerful man with a thick, trimmed beard, penetrating blue eyes, and huge energy. It was said he could start early, train with a sword and shield for hours, then hunt all day, and dance and celebrate at night. He was a man of enthusiasms and became easily bored, and many claimed it was his ambition that had prevented him from marrying.

By contrast, Anarwd, the younger man, was taller and slimmer. He wore his dark hair long, and women thought him handsome. He was, like Gruffydd, an energetic man: well trained in marshal arts and a fine horseman. Unlike Gruffydd, he loved reading and could play the harp. He was reputed to be quick-witted and interested in government; his people considered him a fair and honorable ruler, loyal to his friends, but unforgiving of those who broke his trust.

"My Lord King, I should, in turn, like to toast you: to the future King of the Britons, and King of All Wales. Long may you live!" They emptied their cups.

Gruffydd placed an arm around Anarwd's shoulders. "Bring as many soldiers as you are able. I want to impress not just the local people, but all the great and wise who are coming from other countries." He grinned, "Now that I know Morgannwg is on my side, your army is most welcome. It will be the first time in living memory that the families of the North and the South of this great country will meet in friendship." He moved away and refilled their wine cups. "However, it is important that we show strength with that friendship for ,sadly, not all of our nobles can be trusted."

"I will bring a goodly number, my Lord," Anarwd replied. His face was suddenly solemn. "However, I must leave a strong force to guard our borders. When the Saxons hear of your Coronation, they might be sorely tempted to intervene."

"Indeed." He nodded thoughtfully. "But I want you here. Leave one of the other Princes in charge. You decide which one, and make him your second-in-command."

I would chose Prince Rhys ap Mawr, he's reliable and has a good record of administration. Of course, I will have to find something for the other Prince, Rhodri ap Williams. He's the youngest of us, but very ambitious."

"In which case, bring Prince Rhodri with you. He can also give me the oath of allegiance, and I will think of some responsibility for him." He sipped his wine thoughtfully. "I will also conjure up some title that will impress him. The last thing we want is another dissatisfied young noble. I should know: I was one once."

They both laughed.

"Let me show you the rest of the palace. I want you to meet my secretary, Dafydd ap Griffith. It would please me if you two got to know each other," he said meaningfully.

CHAPTER EIGHT

Angharad, the elder daughter of Rhys ap Bleddyn, the King's Seneschal, was a strong, independent woman, and one year younger than Gwriad. She was not as beautiful as her younger sister Ealdgyth, but she had a vivacious and passionate nature that was not lost on the unmarried nobles who came to her father's house. However, she also possessed a powerful personality; this, combined with a lively intelligence and an overt sexuality, tended to frighten off those young nobles who considered that their wealth, their courtly manners, and their good looks should be enough to attract any woman.

"They're all so boring," she would say to Teifryn, her friend and confidant. "They think their ability to fight each other and butcher innocent creatures is an attraction that no woman can resist."

"Most women don't have your high standards," Teifryn would respond. "But, I wouldn't wait too long before you find your perfect man. You may not have noticed, but the years are passing you by."

"That applies to both of us." But even as she joked with her friend, she was reminded of her father's increasingly strong pressure for her to get married. "Do you want to be an old maid?" he was in the habit of saying whenever another prospective young noble had been sent packing.

Teifryn's father was a local Lord, who had been killed in a land dispute when she was a small child, leaving her god-fearing mother and a bevy of aunts to raise her. As an only child in an all-female household, she had experienced very little male company, and tended to view men in a romantic and unrealistic way, and was easily embarrassed. She had recently become friends with

Angharad, and they both enjoyed riding, hawking, and other outside pleasures. Angharad was lively and entertaining company, but Teifryn could not help but be jealous of her easy familiarity with men. Moreover, she did not appear to be remotely envious of her startlingly attractive younger sister.

In the early summer, while Teifryn remained on Ynys Mon, Angharad had accompanied her father on a visit to the fortress at Harlech. It was there she had met Gwriad. Both had been immediately attracted to each other. He was not her first lover, but unlike the others, he had not disappointed her. She had returned to her home consumed with desire, and unable to think of anyone or anything else. It was not surprising, therefore, that she soon unburdened herself to Ealdgyth.

Her younger sister had been unusually enthusiastic when she discovered Angharad's affair with Gwriad. In the past she had delighted in flirting with any man who showed an interest in her elder sister, and had been shocked when she had come to realize that men whom she had assumed were in her thrall were previous lovers of Angharad. Consequently, when she began to enjoy the attention of the King, she worried over the possibility of her future being ruined by the behaviour of her sister. When she heard of Angharad's passion for Gwriad, she decided to take matters into her own hands and was able, without any difficulty, to let her father know of Angharad's affair with the King's new General. Ealdgyth was aware of her father's ambitions for her and knew she was his favourite. "If General Gwriad were forced to marry Angharad, and quickly, there would be no scandal," she said, innocently. Her father nodded and sent an immediate message to his old friend Gomer, the Lord of Deheubarth.

The next day, unaware of her father's knowledge of her affair with Gwriad, Angharad arranged to go riding with Teifryn. High clouds studded a bright sky and the heather was springy under the hooves of their horses. After a brief canter to some high ground where the view was idyllic, she told of her meeting with Gwriad and pretended it was just an innocent flirtation. "You've met him in Court, I suppose?"

"Oh, yes," Teifryn replied casually. "Another soldier."

"Do you think him handsome?" Angharad asked, piqued by her friend's lack of interest.

"Middling, I suppose."

Angharad glared, although she knew Teifryn was deliberately provoking her. "I think he's good looking. He's strong, witty, and he thinks I'm very attractive."

"So, his eyesight isn't very good then?"

"Stop being silly and tell me what you think of him."

"Well," Teifryn said thoughtfully, "I've only met him the once. He seemed much like all the other young nobles you have dallied with in the past. I gather he likes hunting and killing people, so you'll soon find him boring."

"I will not! And what makes you think he likes killing people?" Angharad slapped one hand into the palm of her other, a habit she had when she was angry, or feeling awkward.

"You don't become a General just because the King likes you. Do you? I have heard that he is quite merciless in battle. He slices people he doesn't like into little pieces." Teifryn had become a great admirer of Angharad, who was quite unlike any unmarried woman she had ever met. She was independent, fiery, and very well read. Teifryn, who did not possess the voluptuous body of her friend, had an equally intelligent mind and was thought by some to be pretty. But, as is often the case with innocent young women, she loved to tease her friends, although secretly she wished she had an admirer as attractive as Gwriad.

Angharad sniffed and decided to alter the direction of the conversation. She turned to her friend with an impish grin. "I can assure you he's very good in bed." She could not stop herself from smiling broadly as she thought about him.

"Shame on you!" Teifryn sounded genuinely appalled. "And you the daughter of the Seneschal."

"I don't believe you're such a prude."

"I'm not a prude," Teifryn said defiantly. She could feel her face reddening. "I just don't think it's right to do that sort of thing before marriage. And you certainly shouldn't boast about it. You'll get yourself a reputation."

"You're beginning to sound like an English nun," Angharad

gave a rich, throaty laugh. "I think you've had lots of boys, really. Haven't you?"

"I have not!"

"What about Iorwerth? I've often seen you two together."

"He's just a friend. We talk about things." She turned her head away. "He's not even kissed me."

Angharad nodded. Her father had mentioned Iorwerth's intention to become a priest, but he had felt unable to do so because of his sick mother. "He feels he must wait until after her death before he takes holy orders." Her father had also hinted that Iorwerth liked men rather than women. She decided not to pursue the matter. "I'm sure there are others?"

"No, there are not. And even if there were, I would not let any man have my body until after we were married." She stalked off the path, and stared moodily at the distant mainland mountains across the straits.

Angharad sat down on the grassy hillside and watched her friend and mused at how little she knew about her. They had been friends for less than a year and had always enjoyed each other's company. Both had complained about the lack of marriageable men. In a light-hearted way, they had discussed their hopes and dreams. However, Angharad had not revealed the details of her occasional sexual encounters, suspecting her friend might not be of like mind. As the daughter of the King's Seneschal, she had a position to maintain. While other women in the court circle, mostly married, had thinly disguised affairs, it would have outraged her father should he ever have discovered her promiscuity.

She blew out her lips. Gwriad had changed everything. He thought like her in so many ways: he enjoyed the sensual pleasures of life and, unlike her previous lovers, he did not make her feel guilty or wanting. She regretted mentioning him to Teifryn. It had been a stupid boast, but she had so wanted to share the excitement she was feeling. She stood up and walked slowly over to her friend and placed an arm round her waist.

"I'm sorry I mentioned it. I didn't think you'd mind."

"It's your affair, not mine. But I would hate you to get yourself a reputation."

"We won't mention it again."

"Will he marry you?"

"Who says I want to get married?"

"You might have a baby."

"I take care not to."

Teifryn felt the heat come back to her face. She had no idea what Angharad meant, but did not want to appear stupid. "Good." She took in a long breath to cover her embarrassment. "Will you marry him if he asks you?"

Angharad slapped her hand in her palm. "I haven't thought about it," she lied.

• • •

IN THE LARGE HOUSE OF Cadell ap Bleddyn, the King's Seneschal, the servants were in a high state of simulated activity, taking a sudden pride in each activity they performed, and taking a long time to do it. Each was trying to listen in to the conversation between their master and the King's General for Ceredigion and Deheubarth.

"What's happening? Why is General Gwriad ap Griffith here?"

"He's come to ask for the hand of one of Cadell's daughters."

"Which one?

"It's obvious, you gwirionyn, he's come for Ealdgyth. She's the most beautiful woman in Wales."

"She's not the eldest though. Angharad is. He's obviously come for her."

In the great hall, Cadell was in good humour. Although the young upstart had dared to take his daughter's virginity without his knowledge, he was here at last to ask for her hand in marriage, and before it was too late. All would be well. After all, Gwriad was not a bad fellow. Young and reckless, but the King thought well of him, and he had a position in society. Best of all, the equally reckless behaviour of his elder daughter would not, after all, bring ruin to his dreams. His favourite daughter, the beautiful Ealdgyth, could still be the wife of the great King Gruffydd and there would be no slur on the family name.

"I'm happy you wish to marry my elder daughter, Angharad."

He raised his cup in yet another toast to Gwriad, who raised his in return.

It had been a difficult interview. For a moment, Gwriad had wondered if the Seneschal had any idea that his daughter was having a lusty affair with the man who now came to ask for her hand. Gwriad had made the formal proposal and Angharad's father had reacted as though quite unprepared for such a request, yet his surprise seemed tinged with relief.

Eventually, he had called in servants, arranged for a sumptuous meal, and together they had drunk a lot of wine, which was not Gwriad's normal tipple. As the evening had progressed, there had been no doubt as to Cadell's wholehearted approval of the union.

"You are a young man, but the King thinks well of you." The Seneschal's words were blurred. He drank deeply, and nodded contentedly towards Gwriad, who was having trouble keeping his eyes open. "I think my daughter," he paused as though trying to remember which daughter he meant, "will be happy to ashept you. I'll tell 'er tomorrow." He dropped his cup, his head slumped forward, and he collapsed back into his chair.

Gwriad carefully returned his unfinished wine to the table and rose to his feet. An attractive woman servant offered to show him to his sleeping quarters.

"Thank you. But, I think I'll take a walk outside before I sleep."

"I've made a bed up for you, my Lord, through there." She pointed to a recess at the end of the hall.

He thanked her and walked towards the main door. He stopped to watch as four strong servants lifted the unconscious Seneschal out of his chair. He did not awaken as they carried him off into an adjoining room and the servants continued with a lively discussion, confident they would not be overheard.

"I'm sorry, my Lord, they get a bit excited by family news." The woman smiled. "It's almost as though they were members of this family and not just servants."

"What family news?" Gwriad gave one of his engaging grins.

"Why your news, my Lord. They couldn't work out which of Lord Cadell's daughters you wished to marry. Typical men."

"Ah." He nodded sagely. "But you had worked it out?"

"I'm Angharad's maid. She tells me everything," she said meaningfully.

"Where are Angharad and her sister? I thought they would appear at the dinner?"

"As soon as he knew you were coming, Lord Cadell sent them on a visit to the nunnery at Penetrate."

"I see. How long will they be there?"

"Until you've gone." She glanced around. "Lord Cadell doesn't trust his daughters to be under the same roof as you, my Lord." She giggled and tossed her hair.

"What's your name?"

"Elen, my Lord."

Gwriad looked into her eyes. He liked women with a sense of humour. At another time and place he would willingly have enticed her into his bed. "I want you to answer a question," he said, giving her a silver coin. "Will Angharad agree to marry me, do you think?"

The woman pocketed the coin, and dropped him a small curtsey. "She will, my Lord, and not just to please her father."

"What does Ealdgyth think?"

"I think she's relieved, my Lord, to have her elder sister married off."

"Oh?" Gwriad raised his eyebrows in feigned innocence.

"With no disrespect, Sir, she's very ambitious, and has her eyes set on the main prize. She would never have forgiven her sister if Angharad had caused a scandal." She gave him a knowing look, curtsied, and walked away.

Outside, Gwriad breathed in deeply, savouring the cool air. He realized with some consternation that he was not completely at ease. Although his passion for Angharad was as strong as ever, he was beginning to understand that he had little choice in the matter of his intended marriage, and everyone was aware of his predicament, except the King.

Gruffydd had other concerns on his mind. He was to be crowned King of the Britons in late August, after months of careful preparation by Dafydd. Following the ceremony at St. David's, the nobility of Wales would pledge their allegiance and, for the first time in living memory, the country would be peaceful and united. Gwriad was arranging the military presence, but his mind was focused on his forthcoming wedding.

• • •

THE WEDDING WAS TO TAKE place in late July in the small church at Aberteifi in the territory of Ceredigion, and with almost undignified haste. The Seneschal had made it clear that the Cathedral of St. David was out of the question, as only kings and important princes were married there. Gomer, in a rare gesture of generosity, suggested that the wedding might be held in his local church. From Gomer's point of view it saved him a long journey up to Gwyneth, and the Seneschal was keen to get the marriage accomplished with as little fanfare as possible. He had chosen a time when the King would be involved with Irish trade negotiations, and unable to attend the wedding. His wife-to-be, although the sister of the bride, had persuaded Gruffydd not to cancel the negotiations, and had assured him that Angharad would understand, as would Gwriad.

Gwriad was unconcerned, especially as his uncle had agreed to pay for the ceremony. Yet, it annoyed him that he had not been asked for his opinion on many of the arrangements. Gomer had hinted that the Seneschal was making it clear that he was displeased with his daughter's behaviour, and was keeping the celebration to a minimum.

"I feel as though I am being herded into this marriage, regardless of my thoughts on the matter," he said to his brother. Dafydd was dressed for the occasion in a new robe, and wearing a silver insignia betokening his membership of the King's inner circle.

It was the first time Dafydd had been asked to take part in a wedding. It was not only his brother's big day, but many of the most important local lords would be watching his performance, knowing he was the King's new Secretary. It was important to him that the ceremony was seen to go well.

"But you told me you love Angharad, and she loves you? The King has sent his regrets. What further compliment can you require?" He pretended to look amazed. "I have it on good authority that Gomer has agreed to help his friend, the Seneschal, by agreeing to pay for the feast at his castle. You can't ask for more than that."Gwriad ground his teeth in frustration. "Don't you understand? I love Angharad, but that doesn't mean I want to marry her! The only reason I have agreed to this religious travesty is that Gomer wants it to happen to save his old friend from ridicule. Angharad's sister wants it to happen so she will not be prevented from marrying the King. For all I know, the King wants me to marry Angharad to save the reputation of his chosen wife, and, if I don't agree, I might lose my command and fall from the King's grace."

"What about Angharad? Does she want to marry you?"

"Of course she does! Why wouldn't she?"

There was a pause, broken by a low chuckle. "Oh, Gwriad. You are unbelievable! Has it never occurred to you that you are so lucky? Most men would lose a hand to have your chances." Dafydd shook his head. "You will marry Angharad, who is a fine woman. You will remain as General for Deheubarth, where your uncle watches out for you. You are among the most trusted of the King's inner circle, and yet you want more?"

"And you don't understand I had no choice!" He exhaled loudly, and reached for the wine jar, to find that it had been replaced with water. "Where's the wine?"

"You don't like wine," Dafydd reminded him. "And above all, you must be totally sober for your wedding." He patted Gwriad on the shoulder. "You'll be fine. Just convince yourself you've been very lucky, and enjoy what God has given you, in spite of your transgressions."

"You sound like a bloody priest!"

Dafydd looked wistful. "With my luck with women, I might just as well be a priest."

Gwriad felt somewhat mollified. "Well, be content that your clean living has not forced you into a unforeseen marriage."

"I've never seen you nervous before," Dafydd joked, as he helped his brother dress for the wedding. He was wearing light body armor under a red cloak. In his left hand he carried a polished helmet as befitted a General, with a leek attached to indicate a man about to be married.

"I'm not nervous," Gwriad said. "I'm just angry that I have been forced into doing something that I wouldn't have done, had it not been for Gomer and the King."

"And the Seneschal."

"Yes, and his younger daughter. I understand she stoked the fire."

"Our father would be proud of you," Dafydd said, changing the subject.

"That is the sort of statement that people make when they don't know what else to say."

"You knew him better than I did. But I know he would have been be pleased to think that his elder son was a General for King Gruffydd, and helping to ensure a lasting peace between the warring factions of Wales."

"All right, he would have been proud. But, I still feel I shouldn't have to get married."

"And Angharad?"

"She feels the way I do. We would have been quite happy continuing as we have been. We do not have to get married to increase our love for each other."

Dafydd attached a golden lion pin to connect his brother's robe. It was a family treasure that had been passed down to the first son for many generations. "You are no longer free to do as you wish. You know this to be true. Ever since you agreed to be the King's General for the South-West, you became a part of the government of this country. People look up to you. You must set an example."

Gwriad did not reply.

"But you know this, you don't need your younger brother to remind you." He handed Gwriad his sword. "I think you also know that Angharad wants to get married. Like you, she is a free spirit, but she is happy to be getting married to you. It's important to women, even those as outrageous as Angharad." He slapped his brother on the back. "Don't spoil her day."

Gwriad cleared his throat. He had never understood his

brother's reserve regarding women, but he respected his intellect and his ability to see the simple truth in things.

"Well said. I will bite my lip, smile with my teeth and try to make Angharad happy."

He walked to the door and ordered some wine. When it arrived he poured two cups. He handed one to Dafydd, who regarded it doubtfully. "One last drink as a free man!" Gwriad raised the cup, and smiled roguishly. Then he frowned at his brother. "Whatever this marriage brings, Dafydd, I hope nothing will come between us."

Dafydd took a sip of his wine, and returned his cup back on the table. " He stared into his brother's bright blue eyes. "Never. You can always count on my support." Outside, there were the sounds of music and the hubbub of many people. "Whatever happens to us in our lives, I will always be your true friend and true ally."

For the first time in his life, Gwriad was overwhelmed by his brother's passion and sincerity. "Thank you," he muttered. He grasped Dafydd's hand. "You never cease to surprise me." He cleared his throat. "And I won't let you down. Ever."

• • •

"You look lovely," Ealdgyth said reassuringly, as she adjusted Angharad's veil. "He's a very lucky man."

"You can relax," Angharad said. "If it wasn't that most of the people gathered here know that the King is keen on you, they might think you were the blushing bride." She waved a hand at her sister. "No, don't argue. We both know you are delighted in my forthcoming marriage to Gwriad, because it ensures you can approach your wedding to the King next year, without any worry that I might cause you an embarrassment."

Ealdgyth gave one of her rare smiles. "All right. You know then that I was the one who told father? And I agree: I knew he would force Gwriad to marry you. But you can't say you're unhappy with the result?"

Angharad regarded her sister thoughtfully. "I will admit I am more than happy, but I'm not sure that Gwriad is. He would have been content to have me as his mistress. He's not a man to be tied down."

"You would not have agreed to be his whore!" Ealdgyth looked genuinely shocked. "You have more self-respect than that."

"I would never have used that word," Angharad said, threateningly. "We would have sorted out our lives. This way, we feel that we have become puppets in a power game outside our control."

There was a long hiatus as Ealdgyth concentrated on putting a final touch to Angharad's veil. "We will be the most powerful family in Wales."

Anghard snorted. "Is that what this is about for you? Power? I'm marrying for love."

"If you were not my elder sister, I would instruct you in some of the basic tenants of life."

"If it was not for my love for Gwriad, my concern for his chosen career, and also my consideration for our father, I would walk out of this wedding and you would have to cope with the problems that would cause." Angharad stood up and glared at her sister. She was conscious that her sister was taller, more self-assured and definitely the only one of them who could be called beautiful. "After today, never try to manipulate me or Gwriad ever again!"

• • •

THE SMALL CHURCH AT ABERTEIFI in Ceredigion was packed for the simple wedding, and officiated by Bishop Hywel of St. David's, who was Gomer's friend. Angharad glowed with pleasure throughout the service and, in spite of himself, Gwriad was delighted to see her so happy. Ealdgyth was the maid of honour; everyone agreed she outshone the bride, but she did nothing to take away from her sister's occasion.

After the exchange of rings, the smiling couple walked slowly down the narrow church, acknowledging their friends and the local nobility. An open wagon took them to Gomer's castle where a lavish feast was arranged. At the high table, Gomer placed Gwriad and his new wife in the seats of honour. He placed himself next to Angharad, with Dafydd next to him. Lord Cadell ap Bleddyn, the King's Seneschal, was on Gwriad's left, and next to him was the radiant Ealdgyth, with the sombre Bishop of St. David's next to her. Lord Cadell's wife had died giving birth to Ealdgyth, and Gomer's wife had, as usual, been unable to attend the celebration. Both men seemed happily liberated.

There was music and lots of singing. Wine and beer were consumed in huge quantities, and the food was plentiful. It was clear that Gomer had added greatly to the frugality of the Seneschal's contribution.

"I hope your husband realizes what a lucky man he is," Gomer remarked gallantly.

"I believe he does, my Lord," Angharad said with a twinkle in her eyes. "I hope he remembers what a generous uncle you have been to him."

"I doubt it," Gomer said as he glanced around the room and assessed the number of people who were feasting at his expense. "I leave that to you to remind him." He raised his goblet. "To you, Angharad. I couldn't have hoped he would marry a better woman."

She leaned over and kissed his cheek. "You're a fine man, Gomer ap Griffith. I'm grateful for your support."

Gomer realized that his eyes were watering and lowered his head. 'I'm drinking too much,' he thought. He turned quickly to Dafydd, who was slowly working his way through a plate of oysters. "Your turn next," he muttered. "It's about time you found yourself a good woman."

"I'm sure there are many good women around, Uncle. But, I never seem to meet them." Dafydd shrugged.

"That's because you spend your time reading books and writing reports." Gomer shook his head, his white hair falling across his face. "You've done well for yourself. I'm proud of you." He sniffed loudly and wiped his nose on his sleeve. He always became emotional when he drank too much. "But, I want to see you and Gwriad with sons before I die." He glared around in case anyone had seen the tear course down his cheek. He placed his large hand on Dafydd's arm. "Remember, you're only young once. When I was your age I had been married for three years and had two children." He drank heavily from his goblet. "All daughters. Mind you, they're good girls." He seemed to lose his concentration and stared down at his plate.

"Your daughters do you proud, uncle." He and Gwriad had grown up with them and had treated them like sisters. He tactfully omitted any reference to Gomer's mad wife. "You'll soon have to find dowries for them." Dafydd had meant the comment to be a compliment, but it was clear that Gomer took it otherwise.

"More money," he said mournfully. He slowly emptied his goblet, sank back in his chair, and closed his eyes.

Dafydd looked anxiously at his uncle, and then saw Angharad smiling at him. "See the effect I have?" he jested. "No wonder I'm not married."

• • •

IT WAS NOT UNTIL LATE August that Gomer was finally able to summon Gwriad and his new wife to his castle at Aberteifi. It was a fine summer's day and the weather had remained hot and dry. Swallows hunted for bugs in the cloudless sky, and there was a sense of peace and wellbeing as farmers prepared for the rare chance of ample crops.

King Gruffydd had been officially crowned as the King of All Wales, or as he preferred: King of the Britons, barely two weeks ago at St. David's. Although Gwriad had been part of the great swearing of allegiance, his mind had been focused on his new wife. He knew that King Gruffydd saw the Coronation as a purely political event: a necessary precursor to the knitting-up of the former princedoms into a legal framework, as arranged by Dafydd. "When I get married," he had announced, with his usual enthusiasm, "then, I will have a proper Coronation at the same time. I will have the whole of Wales involved. This ceremony is for the nobles, so that they can understand that I am their King."

Now, two weeks later, when all excuses had been exhausted, Gwriad and his new wife, accompanied by Dafydd, approached Aberteifi Castle. The atmosphere was tense, in contrast to the natural world around them.

Gwriad had finally agreed to this visit, after sending numerous excuses to Gomer. These ranged from his need to help Angharad set up home in their new house at Llanstephan on the south-west coast, to his seemingly constant need for military maneuvers, and finally the King's Coronation. Gomer was pleased to see him, yet angry at what he perceived to be a lack of gratitude. The wedding had cost him more than he had expected. He felt slighted by Gwriad's coolness. It did not occur to him that his favourite nephew objected to being forced into marriage, no matter how successful that marriage had become. Gomer expected his family members to respect his wishes and he was not used to having his requests brushed aside.

Angharad understood the situation. "You must go and see your uncle," she insisted. "He's an old man, and you are not showing him the respect he feels you owe him."

"He's got to realize I'm no longer his responsibility." Gwriad was drawing up plans to attack the Saxons through the Camlad valley, a reversal of the Saxon invasion that resulted in the Welsh victory of Rhyd-y-Groes. In his mind, it would serve as a firm warning to the Saxons of the growing might of the Welsh under the Kingship of Gruffydd ap Llewelyn.

After a formal welcome, Angharad had departed with her maid, Elen, to unpack. She sensed the men needed to discuss their differences on their own. Things would not improve until Gomer had been able to express his dissatisfaction.

"Well?" Gomer said, glaring at Gwriad. "You're now a wealthy, married man with a good position in society. You are loved and trusted by the newly-crowned King who, for reasons beyond my comprehension, has asked you to be his best man at the wedding next year. I take it you have agreed?"

"Of course. It's a high honour," Gwriad responded. It suddenly occurred to him that Gomer might have expected to be chosen for this role. He noticed that Gomer looked older, even frail, and for a moment regretted his deliberately avoidance of his uncle since the wedding.

Eventually, it had been Dafydd who had insisted that the situation could not continue. "If you agree to visit Gomer, I'll come with you. He isn't as well as he was. He thinks you're insulting him." Dafydd had been to visit Gomer recently, and was troubled in the change in the old man. In just a few weeks, he had lost weight; he was no longer the larger-than-life character that Dafydd remembered throughout his childhood.

"It doesn't seem to bother him that I'm no longer under his control. He still wants to order me about as though I was a small boy."

"Please, see him for my sake."

So, a week later they arrived at Gomer's castle.

"I'm very grateful for your generosity, Uncle. If it were not for you, I could not have afforded to get married." He glanced at Dafydd, who was pretending to be somewhere else.

"Well then, just remember that," Gomer said. It was at this point he began to suspect a double meaning in Gwriad's easy compliment. It was pleasantly cool in the big hall, yet Gomer felt hot and bad-tempered. "How is Angharad then?"

"As you have just seen, she's in excellent health."

"That was not what I meant, and you know it!" Gomer roared. He was increasingly conscious that he had passed the normal lifespan for men, and was slowly becoming more aware of his frailties. He found himself gasping for breath, but was unwilling to acknowledge it. "Is Angharad happy? Does she love you?" He stood up to reinforce his question.

Gwriad expelled his breath loudly. "Yes, Uncle, she is happy. We are both happy. Because you paid for my wedding does not mean that I have to give hourly reports of our behaviour."

"You may be the King's General for this area, but you are still my nephew. I am still your Guardian!" Gomer was aware that he was shouting and he was trying to remember why.

"You ceased to be legally in charge of me, some years ago," Gwriad retorted. "I am grateful for your help and the protection you have given me since our father died. I'm conscious of the respect I owe to you as my Liege Lord, but I didn't need you to interfere with my choice of wife!"

"I saved you from humiliation!" Gomer was red in the face. "If the King had heard from his Seneschal that you had tupped his daughter, and were refusing to marry her, the sister of the woman he, the King, wanted to marry, where do you think you would be now?" Gomer raised his right hand to his chest. He had a numbing pain in his left arm. "Your father left your future in my hands! I don't intend..." He suddenly staggered, and crashed to the floor.

Dafydd, who had been observing the increasingly angry confrontation between the two people he loved most in the world, was first to reach Gomer. He turned the old man onto his back. Gomer was breathing rapidly, his face was wet with sweat, yet his wrist felt cold when Dafydd checked for his pulse.

"Uncle. Are you in pain?"

"Remember your father," Gomer whispered. "He was a good man. The very best." He closed his eyes, his breath coming in irregular gasps.

"What's wrong with him?" Gwriad knelt down beside Dafydd. He had always respected his uncle, but had never loved him in the way his younger brother had.

Tears were coursing down Dafydd's face. "It's his heart. He's had a sick heart for years."

"Oh?" Gwriad felt unable to respond. "I didn't know." Yet, he must have known as Dafydd had, but it had never occurred to him that this powerful, domineering old man would suddenly collapse like a wooden building whose beams had rotted through.

Gomer's eyes flashed open, and he stared angrily at both his nephews. "Promise me," he rasped. His lips continued to move, but he spoke no words. He fought a private battle to complete his sentence. "Always...support King Gruffydd." He grasped Gwriad's hand in a vice-like grip, and tried to sit up. "Make your father..." His eyes bulged, and spittle flecked his convulsing mouth. "Proud!" he roared, and his head collapsed back on the reed-strewn floor.

There was a long silence as they stared down at the still body. The angry features seemed to compose themselves as their uncle took his last breath. Behind them, servants arrived and stood in a shuffling, murmuring group. Evan, who had been out of the room, ran forward, and knelt down behind Gomer's head.

Eventually, Gwriad released his hand and stood up. He had seen many men die, but this had been the first time he had felt emotionally involved. He gently patted Dafydd's shoulder. It was an awkward gesture, but he felt strangely alone.

"Oh, Gwriad!" Dafydd rose quickly to his feet and embraced his shorter brother, which Gwriad reciprocated. Both realized that it was a long time since they had shown such physical affection for each other.

"I'm going to miss him. You knew our father better than I did; you probably miss him more. But, Gomer was like a father to me. Now, we have only each other." Dafydd turned to look down at his dead uncle, as Evan gently closed the staring eyes. Gomer's slave and lifelong friend gave himself up to his own personal misery; tears were running down his beaklike nose.

The two men watched as Evan, sobbing uncontrollably, wiped Gomer's face and straightened his clothing.

"He's also part of our family," Dafydd said. For as long as he could remember Evan had been an important element of his childhood.

"Don't forget Angharad. She's part of the family too," Gwriad said defensively. He beckoned for the servants, and began to make arrangements to have the body moved. "Although I was angry with Gomer for forcing me to marry Angharad, she's a fine woman." He blew out his cheeks. "I feel bad that we argued. He was right, and I was not prepared to admit it."

Angharad entered quietly and knelt down beside the body. She held Gomer's left hand. "God bless you," she murmured.

Evan rose slowly to his feet. "I loved that man like a brother," he said between sniffs. "Especially since the death of Cydweli. He was the only family I remember." He bowed towards the two brothers and supervised the servants as they carried Gomer's body away. Angharad hurried off to break the news to Gomer's daughters. She realized as she went that Gomer's mad wife was now their responsibility.

"Who's going to provide Evan and his wife with a home?" Gwriad raised his eyebrows.

"He can buy his freedom anytime he wants," Dafydd said. "I know he has enough money. He and his wife could buy their own farm. I could arrange that."

Gwriad shook his head. "It's not what he wants. He's older than

Gomer. He's spent his life looking after this family. He's not a farmer."

Dafydd nodded. "You're right. After all he's done for our family, especially for Gomer, we can't just forget him." He wiped his eyes. "Will you give him a home? This castle will become yours. You will be the new Lord of Deheubarth. This is where he belongs." He placed his hand on Gwriad's shoulder. "Besides, if you have a big family of boys, you'll be glad to have him around."

For the first time since their arrival in the castle, both men smiled.

· · ·

DAFYDD WAS DRESSED FOR TRAVEL. His thick cloak hung from his slim, wide shoulders, down past his knees; he wore a short sword at his hip. He was cheerful for the first time since Gomer's death, finally coming to terms with his loss. The funeral, however, had been a small family affair, in spite of his protests.

"Gomer was one of the most important men in Wales. He deserves a great funeral," he had argued.

Gwriad did not agree: "The King is preparing for his Coronation. He and his Northern lords are settling yet another dispute in Gwyneth. They would be unable to attend. This is a family affair; we should treat it as such."

"Our uncle and our father made history at the battle of Rhyd-y-Groes. Cydweli was remembered after the battle, and the King raised a memorial for him. Gomer should be remembered in the same way. We should not ignore his importance because we have the King's Coronation to plan. Our father is remembered. Gomer should be, too."

Gwriad nodded. "I agree. Cydweli is a household name, although the promised stone that Gruffydd was going to erect has still to be erected." He raised his eyebrows in a meaningful way. "Be that as it may, memorials are for the living, not the dead. We will not forget Gomer, but outside this area he was just another Lord. A lavish funeral will do little to change that." He looked to Angharad. "We will arrange this funeral for ourselves, his family, and the local people. It's all we can do. I believe it is all Gomer would have wanted."

After further discussion, and with the gentle urging of Angharad, Dafydd had agreed to the arrangements. Gomer had been buried in the grounds of the castle, which he had fought half his life to acquire.

"Remember, Brother, this is your home as much as mine," Gwriad said. "When Gomer left it to me, he left it to both of us."

"I'm not wanting to own half of it," Dafydd said. "I keep telling you, I am well accommodated by the King. Gomer left you his castle because you're the elder. You are also a married man. Angharad here can keep an eye on Gomer's daughters!" He laughed. "That is not something I wish to take on." He frowned and turned away. "It must have been a relief when his wife died?" He spoke softly.

Gwriad nodded. Gomer's wife, whose name they never used, had died within hours of Gomer. It was both a deep sadness and a great relief. "It is. Yet, I remember her before her illness; she was our new mother when we were still young, and she was very kind to us. Me in particular."

"And now you have a wife to be proud of. I envy you."

"Luckily for me, she likes you too. Otherwise, I would probably have to boot you out." Gwriad hooted with mirth, much of it an emotional release.

"You could try," Dafydd quipped, "but your wife might realize she had married the wrong brother." He was finding it easier to be in Angharad's company, secretly delighting in the cuddles she gave him.

Angharad entered the room and embraced Dafydd. "You need to find a good woman," Angharad said, taking hold of Dafydd's hand. She was genuinely fond of this gauche young man who seemed supremely confident in all respects, except with women. "I'm sure there are many noble girls wasting away, because you never notice their existence."

"I assure you, Angharad, I do look around. Often I admire a pretty face. But, I never know what to say to them."

For a moment he looked quite vulnerable; Angharad changed

her tack. "When the right one comes along, you'll know what to say." She winked at Gwriad. "Now, Dafydd, when can we next expect you?"

"I'm not sure. It depends what the King wants me to do."

"It's my birthday in late October. Now, promise me you'll arrange to be here. It won't be the same without you." She flashed her eyes and gave him a kiss on his cheek."

Dafydd blushed and nodded his head. "All right. I promise. If your sister is coming for your birthday, I expect the King will come too? In which case I will come as part of his entourage."

"Gruffydd will come like a bee to a honey pot," Gwriad said. He gave Angharad's body an appraising look. "He might even notice how lucky I've been?"

Angharad leaned across Dafydd, and pressed her husband's nose. "He will only have eyes for my sister." She took hold of Dafydd's hand. "Tell me if you see any likely women, or even any unlikely ones!" She chuckled. "I'll introduce you." She squeezed his hand.

"Get on with you," Dafydd said. He knew he was being teased; he was beginning to get used to it and liked her witty banter. "Goodbye for now, sister-in-law, or should I say Lady of Deheubarth?" He squeezed her hand and winked. After a few words to his brother, he went down to the courtyard where his horse and a small detachment of soldiers awaited him.

"I think you're having a good effect on him." Gwriad placed his right arm around her waist and waved with his other. They stood in silence as Dafydd rode out of the castle.

"He's a fine man. I don't know how he ended up with such a sex-mad brother like you."

Their laughter echoed as they made their way to their private room. The servants nudged each other and made vulgar comments, as the uninhibited sounds of rampant love making emanated from the room.

Later when their passion was spent, Angharad lay contentedly in Gwriad's embrace. They had restrained themselves during Dafydd's short visit, but with his departure they had made up for lost time. Gwriad was just slipping into a relaxed doze, when Angharad nudged him awake. "I've got an idea," she said triumphantly.

"Give me a chance, woman," Gwriad groaned, his eyes tight shut. "I need a few minutes."

"Not you, silly. I have an idea for Dafydd. I think I know just the woman for him."

"Oh, good," Gwriad replied sleepily, and promptly forgot about it.

• • •

ON A WIND-SCOURED CLIFF, HIGH on the island of Ynys Mon, two women sat easily on their horses, admiring the view. Below them, long slow rollers crashed on the jagged rocks, the surf exploding into the air. Mournful gulls circled above and in the west a threatening cloudbank darkened the horizon. They turned their mounts, and began a slow descent to a farmed valley beneath.

"I would love to come to celebrate your birthday," Teifryn said. Her eyes were bright with excitement. "I enjoyed your wedding, but there were so many people there, and I hardly had a chance to speak to you. But your birthday will be much smaller, I take it?"

"Oh, yes. Only our special friends and family will be there." Angharad looked up as a red kite circled the farm they were riding past. "And, of course, the King."

Teifryn tried not to over-react to the news. She should have realized that Angharad's sister was going to be there. Recently, the King was always in her company. "Of course," she murmured. "Are you sure I'll be welcome?"

"Welcome? I'm inviting you. Don't worry about standing on ceremony for the King. Gruffydd will hardly notice you. He is totally besotted with Ealdgyth. Since his Coronation, and the swearing of allegiance by his nobility, he has thought of nothing else."

"Is their marriage date settled?"

"Oh, yes. The Cathedral is booked for next May. Gwriad's brother Dafydd is in charge of the nobility's side of the arrangements, as he was for the brief Coronation. He was telling me the King wanted to get married before Christmas, but the Bishop refused. He said it would be unwise to risk bad weather."

"How can he do that? I thought he would have to bow to the King's request?" Once again, Teifryn realized how little she knew of what went on outside of her own small, comfortable world.

"Bishop Hywel is a powerful man. He represents the Church in Wales and, in theory, the Cathedral is his." She stopped to watch a red kite streak from the sky and disappear behind the stone wall of a farmyard. There was an instant cacophony as startled hens flew up in all directions. In moments the kite reappeared with a struggling chicken in its powerful claws. "Like the chickens, we live in dangerous times and power is an interesting balancing act: The King needs the support of the Church, and the Church needs the King's protection; both have to dance around the other, keeping their differences concealed. It would not do either of them any good if the people suspected a lack of unity."

"But why would the Bishop worry about the weather?"

"Because he wants to ensure the Cathedral will be packed with the noblest blood in Wales to witness the occasion, and there will be hundreds of common people outside enjoying a day off work. Also, the Bishop rarely has such a chance to demonstrate his power. He needs time to prepare: he wants to give important clerics from France and Ireland an invitation. It takes time to arrange these things. Dafydd tells me that he and the Bishop have convinced Gruffydd that a short wait will be worth the huge political value of such a wedding. There has never been a King of All Wales. Unlike his political coronation, this will be a memorable event. It will also give the ordinary people a chance to see their new Queen and how beautiful she is."

Teifryn nodded thoughtfully. Although well educated, and able to read and write both Welsh and Latin, she was quite unaware of how married people behaved or how power was acquired and exercised. Through her friendship with Angharad, Teifryn was gradually realizing that her life had been unusually comfortable and restricted. She had never been asked to make important decisions, protected from the real world by her wealth and her many female relatives. As Angharad had pointed out, there were dangers in the world. If she was not to be as vulnerable as a chicken cooped up in the farmyard, she had to step out into the real world and make use of the wealth and education her family had provided. "I shall look forward to your birthday."

"So shall I," Angharad said. "I know you've seen my husband at Court. You may even have been introduced to him?" Teifryn nodded. "I have told Gwriad what good friends we are; he is looking forward to getting to know you."

"And I him."

"Have you met his brother Dafydd?" she asked, casually.

"I know who he is. He's often with the King. He's the King's Secretary."

"Have you been introduced?"

"Um, no. He always appears very busy. He doesn't seem to have time to engage in social chit-chat." She patted her horse's neck. "I think the King keeps him hard at work."

Angharad twisted in her saddle to get a good look at her friend and saw no hint of irony. "Does he ever dance?"

"I don't think so, or if he does, I have never seen him. But you must know more about him than me. He's your brother-in-law." She spoke with such innocence, that Angharad coughed to cover her smile.

"The reason I ask is that I too know almost nothing about him. I think he's shy."

"Really?" It had never occurred to her a man could be shy. She had assumed it was a female trait.

"Well, see what you think of him when you come to stay. He's promised to be there. I will be interested in anything you can find out about my mysterious brother-in-law."

"I will. I'll do my best." Teifryn sounded quite enthusiastic, totally unaware that her friend was biting her lip.

• • •

OCTOBER 1056

WITH SOME REGARD FOR THE accommodation and provisioning of his Court at Aberteifi in Ceredigion, the King had restricted his party to Dafydd, Ealdgyth and her father, Lord Cadell, a small assortment of Gruffydd's Northern noble friends, and their wives and servants. Angharad and Teifryn had travelled ahead with Gwriad and his personal guard to prepare his castle for the birthday celebrations. When the King and his consorts arrived three days later, everything was ready to receive them. Gwriad had dismissed most of his uncle's servants, who had become too fixed in their ways to accept new ideas; he had replaced them with a well-drilled selection of his own choosing.

The royal party was greeted by roaring fires throughout the castle and by the aroma of baked bread and roasted meats. They arrived tired and wet after a long ride along the coast road from Llanbadarnia, more than twenty-five miles away. They had started from the King's palace in Rhuddlan nearly a week before, enjoying the warmth of a late summer. But, after two days, autumn arrived with a sudden cool spell, followed by days of continuous rain.

In spite of their ordeal, everyone was recovered and in good spirits by the time the feast of welcome was served. The main hall was bright with torchlight and candles, musicians played, while servants rushed about with laden platters of food and jugs of wine and beer. Fresh rushes covered the stone floors and a variety of entertainments were promised. At Angharad's request, no dog fighting or bear baiting had been arranged.

At the top table, Gruffydd, in rich robes, sat in the centre with the beautiful, but unemotional Ealdgyth on his right, and the lively Angharad on his left. Gwriad, looking impressive in his new uniform, sat next to her with an excited, but uncertain, Teifryn on his left. She was grateful to find that Dafydd was on her other side. Although she did not know him, he was a welcome alternative to the dominant Gwriad, who after a brief welcome was totally taken up with his new wife, and was conversing humorously with the King. There were some customary toasts to start the feast, and after the King had toasted Angharad, the eating commenced.

Gwriad had ensured that there was a bountiful array of meats, fish dishes, soups, breads, cheeses and sweetmeats, with enough beer and wine to satisfy twice the number of guests. As he had said jokingly to Angharad, "I will put on a feast fit for a king. The cost will make Gomer turn in his grave."

"Are you enjoying yourself?" Teifryn asked. For, after formal introductions, Dafydd had not spoken. She remembered that Angharad had said he was shy and decided she would lead the conversation, as the silence was becoming embarrassing.

"Enjoying myself? Oh, yes. Indeed." Dafydd felt his face glow in the flickering light. He raised his cup to his mouth and drank deeply. He was beginning to favour wine over beer, but was always careful not to drink too much. He cut himself a morsel of meat. "Angharad looks very happy," he added, trying to think of something to say.

"She looks lovely," Teifryn said, with a hint of envy in her voice. She chewed reflectively on a chicken leg, as she waited for Dafydd to continue.

"Yes, indeed," he replied with unnecessary emphasis. He glanced around the great hall, desperately looking for something to comment on. "The musicians play well."

"I like music. Do you play an instrument?"

Dafydd took a long drink. "I play the flute. Not very well," he added modestly. "And you? Do you play?"

Teifryn's face lit up in a broad smile. "I love playing the harp. My mother and my aunts all play the harp." For the next few minutes, she described her life on Mon, and how her father had been killed. It was the longest speech she remembered having with a man only slightly older than her; furthermore, he seemed to be hanging on her every word, listening attentively as he ate.

She asked him about his work as the King's Secretary. He explained it was not as exciting as it might appear. He wanted her to continue talking and asked her how she had come to know Angharad.

As she talked, Dafydd relaxed. He began to enjoy her conversation, realizing she was talking about something real, not the inconsequential chatter of the women who decorated the

Court with their silly fashions and their vicious gossip. He watched her animated face, noting her attractive features: the pale blue of her eyes, that contrasted with the glossy black hair she wore in a long braid, her small white teeth, and the determined chin. She did not have the ample, wanton beauty of Angharad. For that, Dafydd felt grateful. He found his brother's wife almost scary with her voluptuous sexuality.

"My father died when I was a small boy," he said. "You will have heard of Cydweli? She nodded. "He died in battle." He never knew how much detail to give when he mentioned his father. Dafydd was very proud of being his son, but did not want to give the impression of boasting. "My older brother and I were brought up by our Uncle Gomer, who used to own this castle. He died recently." He felt uncomfortably emotional and emptied his cup. It was immediately refilled. "His wife died soon after. Those are his unmarried daughters over there." He pointed to two attractive women who were clearly enjoying the company of a group of young men at a lower table.

"Why aren't they married?" Teifryn asked. They were about her age, and she had begun to think herself an oddity.

"They never had a chance to meet young men when Gomer was alive. He kept them on a very tight rein." He drank in a meditative way. "He was like that with us too. But, unlike me, Gwrlad always did what he wanted to do. He never minded how much he annoyed Gomer." Dafydd noticed his cup was empty again and prevented an over-eager servant from refilling it. He took a deep breath. "Normally, I avoid celebrations like this."

She felt pleased he was confiding in her. He was so unlike his brother. Dafydd was taller than most men, with unusual green eyes and a mass of unruly red hair. She noticed his long, sensitive fingers and his somewhat pointed nose. She found herself gazing at his wide mouth. "Why did you come to this celebration, then?"

"I had no choice!" he laughed. "My brother insisted I come, and Angharad can be very persuasive." His eyes moved to where Angharad was rocking with laughter at something the King had said. Even Ealdgyth was smiling.

Teifryn followed his gaze. "Yes," she said thoughtfully. "She is a most unusual woman. I am fortunate to be her friend."

The King's story had finished and Gwriad half-turned to pick up his wine. He smiled wickedly at her. "And she thinks highly of you too!" he boomed. Before Teifryn knew what he was about, he leaned over and kissed her on her cheek. He peered round at Dafydd. "Another lucky man, ay?" Then, with an obvious wink, he returned to listen to what his wife was saying.

Teifryn was both surprised and flattered, but noticed that Dafydd had a stern look on his face. "Your brother knows how to charm a lady," she joked.

"As you get to know my brother, you will discover that he can't resist a pretty face," he said grimly.

"Well, thank you, Sir." She adopted a pose, and fluttered her eyes.

"Oh, I didn't mean…I mean I did mean. I mean you are…" Dafydd was overcome with embarrassment and desperately signaled for a servant to refill his cup. He drank deeply, wondering how to proceed, unsure whether he had shocked her or pleased her.

Teifryn was delighted to receive the compliment, even if it was unintended. She sipped her wine to give her courage and placed her hand over his. "I think you're a handsome man. I'm delighted to be in your company."

Dafydd was lost for words. He blinked, and his mouth opened and closed, like a fish. He swallowed quickly, determined to take control of the situation before she changed her mind. Gently, but firmly, he placed his other hand on top of hers. "I'm not very experienced with women," he murmured.

"Nor I with men." She smiled. He noticed how beautiful her teeth were. Dafydd felt enormously happy. He was aware that the wine had taken effect and he was giggling like a young boy. For once in his life, he was in the company of a woman who did not make him feel uncomfortable. Instead of wanting to escape, he felt a great desire to stay and she seemed to be equally eager to remain.

It was at this point that the King stood up. Everyone rose

quickly. "We will have dancing!" Gruffydd roared. He had drunk more cups than he could remember. But, unlike most men, he did not stagger or feel sick, nor did he become maudlin.

"My brother and the King share the same ability to drink copious amounts of wine," Dafydd confided to Teifryn, enjoying the fact that she was nestled against him. "Other men collapse or feel ill, but both of them become wildly energetic, until eventually they get sleepy, and are carried to their beds with smiles on their faces."

The King took Ealdgyth's hand. Amid much clapping and cheering, he led her down to the centre of the hall. The trestle tables and benches were quickly moved and the musicians took up their places below the high table. Pipes, drums, flutes and string instruments began a lively jig. Gruffydd and Ealdgyth led the dancing with a wild display of bravado on the one side and determination on the other. Eventually, the King indicated that others should join them; the room erupted in a colorful melee of happy and semi-intoxicated people.

Apart from the Seneschal, they were the only ones left standing at the high table. Dafydd was breathing quickly and watching the dancers with a mixture of envy and fear.

"And you?" Teifryn nudged him.

"Me?" he rubbed a hand over his fevered brow.

"Yes, you." She gave him an appraising look. "What happens when you drink?"

"I don't normally drink very much. It doesn't agree with me."

She nodded encouragingly and gave his arm a squeeze. "I never drank wine until I attended Court." She noticed he was looking uneasy. "Do you dance?"

Dafydd slipped his arm round her. "Yes," he said defiantly. "I haven't danced much, but I know how to." He gazed anxiously at the frenzied actions of the dancers. "Would you like to dance?"

Teifryn looked up at him. "I would like to dance, with you," she said daringly.

CHAPTER NINE

LATE NOVEMBER 1056

It was unusual for invasions or even small battles to take place in winter. Those leaders contemplating going to war were forced by the unpredictable weather to wait until the snow had melted in the passes, and the ensuing floods had abated in the low valleys. Picts did not venture onto the dangerous seas, and the Saxon lords spent their time feasting in their warm halls. However, for the majority of the people in both the Welsh and Saxon lands, winter was a time of hunger and cold, when people sat around their smoky fires, venturing out only to protect their animals from the wolves or defend their food stocks from robbers.

On a whim, following Angharad's birthday celebrations, King Gruffydd had travelled from Rhuddlan, where his new palace had been built, to Morgannwg. He took with him his household guard and took possession of the castle now belonging to Prince Anarwd ap Tewdwr, the new General of the South-East and Lord of Morgannwg. Anarwd had been given the castle following the death of the hated Prince Rhys Fachan, and was honored to receive the King, grateful to have his obvious support.

Gruffydd wanted to familiarize himself with this most recent of his Welsh possessions. He intended to stamp his authority on those local lords who were slow to accept him. He was also keen to meet Prince Rhodri ap Williams, the other power in the region, who, with Anarwd, had suffered under the tyrannical reign of Prince Fachan. He had hoped to meet Prince Rhys ap Mawr, Prince Anarwd's second-in-command, but the noble was ill. Gruffydd understood this was a frequent event.

"Rhys is a good man. I would trust him with my life, but," he paused, "he's not very strong." Prince Anarwd clapped his hands to indicate the commencement of the feast. The gloomy, damp hall of Fachan's era had been transformed into a warm, welcoming room. A high table had been constructed and trestles and benches had been crammed in to accommodate as many local nobles and landowners as possible. A huge fire heated the room to the discomfort of those closest, while musicians played in a far corner.

Ealdgyth and Angharad had remained at Gwriad's castle at Aberteifi. So, without an obvious partner, the King sat with Prince Anarwd on his right and Prince Rhodri on his left. Their wives sat next to them with Gwriad and Dafydd on either side, with the Bishop of Llandaff at one end, and a local priest at the other.

After the usual small talk, the King concentrated on Prince Rhodri. He liked the look of the younger man: he was alert, confident, and seemed to have a lot of physical energy. But, he was just the sort of man who could be a danger if unemployed. "I understand your family has always owned land by the sea?"

"Yes, my Lord." Rhodri wondered where this was leading.

"Do you own a boat? Are you experienced on the sea?"

"Many of my villagers own boats. I have sailed and rowed since I was a child. My father encouraged trading with Brittany, but it was never very successful."

"Why was that?" The King seemed genuinely interested.

"We don't build very big boats in this area. There has not been the demand and we lack the skills and the money to finance such building. Most boats are built for local fishing and, what with pirates and bad weather, it's a risky business." He drank slowly, knowing all eyes were on him. "I have thought, perhaps, that we should build some galleys, war ships, as the Picts do."

"For what purpose?"

"To defend our ports and to escort our small trading vessels. Perhaps, when we have captured enough money, we could build a fleet that would prevent the Saxons from using the great River Severn to supply their towns that threaten our borders."

"Indeed." The King rested his hand on Rhodri's arm. "You have my attention." Someone raised a cup in a toast and Gruffydd raised his. "We will talk more of this."

Rhodri took another long drink and, keeping his face impassive, turned to his wife. "Catrin, I think our King likes me. If all goes well, we might eventually regain our rightful position in Morgannwg. If that bloody Fachan had succeeded in killing our friend, then the King would soon have replaced our Prince Fachan, and I would have become the new Lord of Morgannwg." He patted her hand, and winked. "Find out as much as you can from Gruffydd's so-called Secretary. I am particularly interested in what he expects from his new Lord of Morgannwg." He glanced at Dafydd. "I think a woman could easily get him to talk."

Along the table Gruffydd was talking to Prince Anarwd. "Tell me about Morgannwg. Are the people content? What problems have you encountered since you became Lord of this region? I need to know these things." He paused and glanced back to where Prince Rhodri was talking to his wife. "I also want your frank assessment of Prince Rhodri. You have known him for a while. Can he be trusted? Will he cause us a problem?"

"My Lord, I have known Rhodri since we were boys. He's very ambitious." He ran his hand down his smooth face. "He wants to be the Lord of Morgannwg. If I am to rule this area without constantly watching my back, I need to use him in a position he will find acceptable."

"What would that be?"

"You gave him responsibility for the coast, and to prevent invasion. That excited Rhodri at first, but he now sees the threat of invasion from the sea as negligible: the Saxons have few boats of any size. He soon discovered that without a deep chest of gold, he could achieve little to improve our coastal defenses. I believe he is in need of a real challenge, or I will become the focus of his energy. He is a good man in many ways, but I fear his ambitious nature."

Gruffydd picked up his wine cup and studied Prince Anarwd over the rim. "I hear you. If I had wanted him as Lord of this area, I would have appointed him. You have my full support to take what action you deem necessary." He smiled around the room, and raised his goblet. "To Welsh unity! May the North and the South be forever forged into one united Wales. Let us work together to increase the safety and the wealth of our people," he glanced casually in the direction of Prince Rhodri, "and let us not be divided by ambition or petty feuding." He locked eyes, and raised his eyebrows a fraction.

The Prince gave a weak smile and finished his wine in a single gulp. "Perhaps I'll wait to see what he offers me," he muttered to Catrin. "Perhaps we won't worry for the moment."

. . .

THE SNOW ARRIVED UNEXPECTEDLY EARLY. By the beginning of December the roads had become impassable. Gruffydd had been convinced that the early snow would soon melt, but the weather had worsened and he had finally accepted the fact that he must wait until the weather improved before it was feasible to travel. He was confident he would soon be able return to the castle in Aberteifi and rejoin his future wife, but his planned Christmas at his palace in Rhuddlan seemed doomed.

One morning in early December, with the roads blocked with snow and long journeys impossible, Gruffydd entertained the local bishop on a short journey to the coast.

"I've noticed that the sea is very calm at this time of the year," Gruffydd said. He was standing on a snow-covered cliff looking out over the wide channel leading to the mouth of the great river, known locally as the Severn.

"It is always the way following snow, your Majesty," the Bishop of Llandaff said. "In this area, unlike the high ground, we have two or three cold weeks without wind or high seas. I have lived here for most of my life. It has rarely been different."

Gruffydd nodded thoughtfully. "Do the fishermen go out?"

"Indeed, my Lord. It is a necessary to prevent starvation. Although in this windless weather they are unable to travel far."

"Do trading boats from Brittany travel up the Severn to the Saxon lands at this time?"

"Yes, indeed. There are some in the port of Caerdydd at this moment. I believe they have been there for a while, waiting for a favourable wind." He licked his finger and raised it in the air. "I believe there is a slight breeze. This could be the start of a change in the weather.

"How far is Caerdydd from here?

The Bishop scratched his nose and wondered why the King should be so interested. Perhaps it was just idle curiosity? He pointed towards the east. "You could travel there in about half a morning, especially now that the paths near the sea are fairly clear, unlike further inland."

"Thank you for your information, Bishop. I will be making a contribution to your church." The Bishop bowed slightly and withdrew with his usual confidence. It had been a worthwhile outing.

The King watched him go and beckoned to a soldier who was holding the bridle of his horse. "Fetch General Gwriad and also the Prince Rhodri."

The soldier bowed, handed over the reins, and marched a short distance to where Gwriad and Prince Anarwd were waiting, their breaths steaming in the cold air. While Anarwd checked his animal's health, Gwriad had remained in the saddle, spending his time instructing a contingent of the household guard on the finer points of guard duty. "And remember you're not here to admire the view. At all times you must be prepared for the unexpected. I know the Saxons don't fly, but be ready in case they learn how to." The men laughed. Gwriad was popular as a General; a man who was as tough as metal, but who had a sense of humour, and never put on airs. "Stay here and remain alert and don't freeze your balls off."

Anarwd walked over to Gruffydd. "Prince Rhodri has taken off with a group of friends to inspect a small village of his to the west. Shall I send for him?"

Gruffydd stood looking out at the quiet waters. "No. I may talk to him later."

"My Lord?" Gwriad dismounted. He stood by Anarwd, who gave a slight shrug of his shoulders. "The weather might be changing, my Lord. The road will soon be open to Gwynedd, and if not, we could always stay in my castle at Aberteifi." There was an optimistic note in Gwriad's voice; he was missing Angharad.

He knew Ealdgyth would still be there and hoped it would be provide a suitable incentive.

"The men need some action, and I need to fill my coffers." Gruffydd looked suddenly animated. "We will take a ride to Caerdydd," he said. "I understand it's a short journey from here and may prevent me from going mad with boredom. Also, I have an idea." He swung easily into his saddle.

"My Lord?" Gwriad was puzzled. Everyone knew the roads were still almost impassable. No General would ever consider trying to move an army in these conditions.

"We will travel to Caerdydd. Once I have seen what's there, I will explain."

"My Lord, I can tell you anything you want to know about Caerdydd." Anarwd seemed at a loss to understand why the King would travel any further in the biting cold, when roaring fires and hot food awaited them back at his castle.

"I'm sure you can. But I need to see it for myself. I have an idea that might advance our country's power and catch the Saxons off-guard." He turned to Gwriad. "I might also have a plan to keep the young Prince Rhodri busy." He rubbed his hands and stamped his feet. "Let's away before our soldiers freeze their bums to their saddles."

Gwriad was about to make a lewd joke, but decided against it. He helped the King on to his destrier, and remounted without comment. He had come to know that Gruffydd's taciturn behaviour always preceded a plan of action, and it was best to keep silent. He signaled to his sergeant to bring up the soldiers, quickly catching up with the King and Prince Anarwd.

They journeyed on a wintery path, deep in snow, that wound its way along the twists and turns of the coastline. It was a bleak area; there was little evidence of habitation. Eventually, they reached a wide shallow river, and followed the path north along the western bank until they came to a ford, where they crossed without incident. The path turned F, rising up along the side of a bare white hill, with the river below. Soon they were on high ground looking down on a small fishing port. It was surrounded by low hills, and to the east, was dominated by the ruins of an old Roman fort. On its western side the river, known locally as the Taff, flowed into the sea. A sturdy stone breakwater protected the harbour, and small fishing boats were pulled up on a sandy beach. Inside the breakwater, a stone quay led onto a sturdy wooden wharf, along which were moored three trading vessels. Two were typical small Breton boats, called Crayers. They possessed only a single mast, and although very slow in the water, had the advantage of a big hold and were capable of transporting a sizable cargo. The third boat was larger, with two masts, a foresail, and with a small raised deck at each end to repel pirates. It was known as a Nef. It had a rounded stern and bow and was often referred to as a Roundship. Although faster than a Crayer, it was not as stable.

"What do you know about boats?" Gruffydd asked as he studied the ships. He had the eyes of a hawk, and could see, very clearly, for a long distance.

"Very little, my Lord," Anarwd replied, "Some of our soldiers come from fishing families; they might be able to answer your questions? It's a pity Prince Rhodri isn't here. He knows about boats."

Gruffydd did not reply, but continued to observe the harbour. He noticed that there was some activity around the Nef. "Quickly!" he yelled at Gwriad. "Send the Sergeant down to the wharf with half of the men. Tell him to occupy each of the boats. He's not to allow any of them to leave. He's to arrest anyone who objects. I want you to take the remainder of the troops, circle round the village, and come in from over there." He pointed to a track at the other side of the port. "I don't want any of the sailors to escape. Use whatever force you have to, but avoid bloodshed if possible."

"My Lord?" Anarwd looked shocked. "This is a peaceful village."

"I need those boats, and I don't want anyone to let the Saxons know. Stay with me, Prince Anarwd. I will need your thoughts in due course."

Gruffydd continued to survey the harbour as Gwriad instructed the Sergeant and, having divided the column, led half of them at a gallop along the brow of the hill. The Sergeant led fifteen of the well-armed royal horse guards down to the port at a fast trot. Their approach was noted. In moments, the quiet village was transformed to a scene of panic: women screamed and grabbed their children; men yelled at each other and ushered their families into their houses. A crowd of men poured out from the single alehouse and raced for their boats. The Sergeant reached the village and galloped along the quay, quickly overtaking many of the fleeing sailors. Some were pushed off the edge of the quay into the water, others stopped, holding up their hands in surrender. A few reached their ships and tried to cast off. There was a brief, but furious, struggle, and the two Crayers were soon occupied. The Welsh soldiers vaulted off their horses, knocking the frightened Bretons into submission, while the villagers sought the safety of their houses.

However, the crew of the Nef was in a different position. The Bretons had been preparing to leave when Gruffydd's forces arrived and were able to cast off before the Welsh troops reached them. The sailors, using oars, pushed the vessel away from the wharf, where it rocked aimlessly in the enclosed harbour. Abandoning their long oars, they concentrated on raising the sails, which partially filled in the light breeze. The vessel began to move very slowly along the side of the breakwater. As it approached the harbour opening, it gradually gathered speed. The Bretons roared insults at the soldiers on the smaller Crayers.

Gwriad galloped down the hill at the other end of the village, and intercepted a gang of local men who were trying to escape. He was arranging their capture, when he saw the problem in the harbour. "Gwilym! Aeron! Sion! Bryn! To me, boys!

He urged his horse into a gallop. With a handful of his men close behind, he raced down the hill, entering the village at the far end of the quay that connected with the wharf. He veered to the left. Soon he was on the uneven surface of the breakwater where he was forced to slow his horse to a trot for fear of injuring the animal. The Sergeant had been fully involved with securing the Crayers. He seemed unaware that the main ship was escaping. As Gwriad and his men passed above, the Sergeant looked up, realized his mistake, and vented his frustration on the disarmed sailors.

"Quickly!" Gwriad yelled at his men, as he urged his reluctant horse along the breakwater. On the wharf beneath him, panic had set in among the horses abandoned by the soldiers in their rush to capture the boats. Some of the beasts bolted to the end of the lower wooden wharf in a vain effort to join their companions, who were moving above them. Others reared up, knocking sailors and soldiers into the dark, cold water.

The Nef, meanwhile, had reached the mouth of the harbour, and the crew was forced to alter the sails to accommodate the direction of the slight breeze. For a moment, the ship slowed, almost stopped, wallowing only a couple of arms' lengths from the end of the breakwater. Some members of the crew were trying to reset the large oars in their rowlocks and Gwriad knew that once they could engage the oars, the boat would soon escape. He urged his horse over the last few uneven paces, dismounted and without a pause for thought, launched himself into the air. He dropped like a sack of onions down into the well of the sluggish ship.

Gwriad landed awkwardly, stumbled, but instinctively drew his sword as three of the sailors rushed him. They were poorly armed with small knives, and one had a long oar. Behind him, he could hear other troops crashing on to the deck. He lashed out with his sword and the sailors quickly gave way, realizing that they had no chance against well-trained soldiers. Immediately, Gwriad limped to the stern, where the captain was cursing as the breeze failed and the ship slowed to a stop: it was unable to pass out of the harbour and rocked gently in the quiet sea. There were two other sailors next to the Captain. One was armed with a sword, the other with a knife. In moments, the man with the sword was bleeding on the deck and the other retreated as Gwriad, in a mad rage, lurched forward and placed his sword on the Captain's neck.

"Stop!" he yelled. "Turn back!" The Captain understood Welsh, for it was little different from the language the Breton's spoke. He raised his hands before him. With a series of foul oaths, he ordered his crew to return to the harbour. Under the prompting of drawn swords, the sailors were forced to use their long oars to return to their mooring.

Eventually, all three boats were secured to the wharf and their crews were marched along to the quayside. Each of the

Crayers had a crew of six; the Nef held eleven, and they stood in a sullen bunch, uncertain what was to become of them. The three Captains were outraged over their treatment. Although prisoners, they continued to protest loudly.

Gruffydd had watched the capture of the ships, noting the leadership exhibited by his General. Gwriad had been a good choice. Interestingly, if it had not been for Gomer's insistence, he doubted if he would have chosen Cydweli's son, no matter how famous his father had been. He walked his horse down to the village with a satisfied air and congratulated the Sergeant on the success of the attack. Apart from the sailor on the Nef, there had been no serious injuries. The wounded man was taken into the alehouse, where a buxom young woman agreed to treat him. His wound was reported to be minor, but the voluble cries from inside the building suggested otherwise.

The King dismounted and addressed the Sergeant. "I want you to assure these men they will get their ships back after I have borrowed them." He paused over the word 'borrowed', as though enjoying a private joke. "Tell them, I will want them to unload their cargos, and store the goods in the village. I want the Captains to give me some idea of how many horses and soldiers each boat can accommodate. They will take my soldiers, and me up river to the Saxon towns, where they were intending to go. We will leave tomorrow if the wind improves. If they agree to my terms they will be well paid, and their cargos returned. But, if they prove difficult or unwilling, I will reduce them to slaves, seize their ships, and confiscate their cargos. Make that clear to them."

While this was being explained to the Bretons, Gwriad had been supervising the rounding up of the horses, many of which were still highly nervous. Luckily, none were injured.

Gruffydd patted Gwriad on his back. "I thought I would have to find another General when you tried to fly!"

"It was a good thing I didn't think too much about it, my Lord," Gwriad said. "I have never been much good in boats."

The King grunted. "I think we can all learn to manage when we need to," he said ambiguously. "Let us inspect these ships. We might learn something."

They were sturdy craft, well built, and in good condition. Each carried mixed cargoes, mainly barrels of wine, sacks of onions, rolls of fabric and heavy metal goods.

"They're unexpectedly roomy," Gruffydd remarked, "especially for a short journey." He turned to Gwriad. "Unloading all this should keep the crew busy." He moved slowly around each ship, feeling the ropes and sails and testing the movement of their tillers. "I've always wanted to own a boat. In fact," he squinted his eyes, "I think we should have a royal fleet that could defend our shores and protect our traders." He stared, unseeing, at the quay, where local inhabitants were cautiously opening their doors and discovering that the soldiers were not brigands but part of the King's retinue. Most of them had never seen their previous lord, Prince Rhys Fachan; to be told that the King of All Wales had come to their small village was almost beyond their belief.

"If I can build a fleet of warships, our enemies will think twice before they attack us from the sea."

"Does that happen often?" Anarwd looked glumly around. He was not comfortable near the sea.

"Not often from the Saxons, but the Picts are a nuisance, especially around Mons. In this area, we could establish a fleet that would control all the trading up the Severn. It would prevent the Saxons from reinforcing a land invasion. Then, with our new-found wealth we may be able to establish a second fleet off Gwynedd and deal with the Picts and the pirates from Ireland." He scratched his large nose absentmindedly. "This could be the start of a new era. We have been poor for too long."

Gwriad nodded in vague agreement, knowing he would never wish to be involved. For him, fighting took place on a horse and on firm ground. Prince Anarwd looked equally unimpressed.

"Meanwhile," Gruffydd turned to Gwriad, "I will return to the castle with the Prince. Get back as soon as you can and bring the Captains of these ships with you: it will ensure the crews behave themselves. Pick four of our men to guard them on the journey and leave the rest here. Tell the Sergeant there will be no stealing, drunkenness, nor the molesting of any woman. I will personally punish any man who disobeys me. Tell the local people we will return tomorrow and I will pay for the cost of the soldiers' rations."

He climbed back onto the wharf, and mounted his destrier. The villagers had never seen such a huge animal. They could easily believe that this impressive man, who sat comfortably upon it, was a King. However, they had no idea why he had attacked the traders. Looking down at the villagers, he saw their confusion.

"I am King Gruffydd ap Llywelyn. I am King of All Wales!" he bellowed. He paused to let his words sink in. "These men," he pointed to the forlorn bunch of Bretons, "have been trading with our enemies. I know they trade with you, which is why I am not taking their cargos, but I am using their boats. You will give hospitality to my soldiers and I will repay you. Tomorrow, I will be looking for volunteers to man these vessels." He stared angrily at each adult male, then turned his horse and departed with Prince Anarwd and a small retinue.

The Sergeant listened carefully to Gwriad's orders and looked thoughtfully at the small ships. "I've never been on anything bigger than a rowboat," he mused. "I hope we don't have to fight on the water, my Lord."

"I agree," Gwriad said emphatically. "It's against my religion, as well."

• • •

GWRIAD'S FIRST THOUGHT HAD BEEN to lock up the sea captains, and let them suffer for a night, as punishment for trading with the enemy. But, during his return journey to the Morgannwg castle, he listened to their explanations, and changed his mind. They maintained they were just traders, who had always dealt with both Welsh and Saxon merchants. They worried that if their boats were used to attack the Saxons, then they would never be able to trade with them again.

"Perhaps, you should limit your trading to Welsh ports only?"

"That would be a big loss to us, for Welsh villages and ports are poor in comparison to the Saxon towns," the Captain of the Nef explained. "We do not just sell our goods, we also trade. The Welsh have little to trade."

"What do the Saxons have to trade with?" Gwriad asked. He was vaguely insulted by the assertions that Wales had little to offer.

"They have many animals: cows, sheep, goats and hunting dogs. Their women produce fine weavings and they have many metal workers and skilled artisans who create pottery and wood items."

"We will talk further about this," Gwriad said.

He moved up to the front of the column and considered the situation. He knew that Gruffydd would not have thought of attacking the Saxons by boat if he had been in his snow-bound palace in North Wales, as previously planned. This raid was to raise the morale of his personal guard, to fill his coffers with plunder, and most of all to enable him to strike at his enemy and shake off the boredom of inactivity. Gruffydd had avoided unnecessary bloodshed at Caerdydd, because he did not consider the Bretons to be his enemy, and he had indicated that their ships and their cargos would be returned to them. However, it did occur to Gwriad that there was a strong chance one or more of the ships might be destroyed in the raid. If Gruffydd returned empty-handed, the Bretons' cargos might not be returned to them, no matter what assurances they might have received.

His thoughts moved on to the raid itself. If the captains could be persuaded to share their knowledge of the Saxon ports, they needed to know it would be worth their while. These men should be our friends, he mused, not treated as enemies. He would ask Dafydd for his thoughts. His brother was back at the castle, catching up on the legal aspects of the King's recent incorporation of Morgannwg into a unified Wales. He spent much of his time with the Bishop of St. David's clerics, and with certain monks whose duties concerned the history and ancestral rights of the nobility of Wales. Dafydd was so interested in his work that he seemed unaware of the enforced boredom that plagued others, especially the King.

Finally, his mind turned to the almost certain attack on the Saxons and the use of the small ships in Caerdydd harbour. He was never afraid in battle, but how would he cope on that huge expanse of water? What would happen if a storm blew up? How would the horses be kept calm, and how would they be unloaded?

He had no experience of this type of warfare. His stomach twisted in a tight knot. But, at the back of his mind, he knew, as one of the King's Generals, he would have no choice.

Back at Anarwd's castle he arranged for the ships' Captains to be fed and kept under light guard, while he sought out his brother before reporting to Gruffydd. He discovered Dafydd in a small council chamber, where he spent much of his day, and explained the King's plans and his own concerns.

"It's a fine idea," Dafydd said, ignoring his brother's surprised look. "By attacking them at this time of the year, it demonstrates that the King has the capability. If we are to defend our borders, we must initiate the action, not wait for them to attack us."

"I agree," Gwriad said slowly, realizing he should never underestimate his brother. He poured himself some wine and stood staring out of the narrow window. "But what about the Bretons? Do we want another enemy?"

"Certainly not. Nor do they want to increase the dangers to their trading. I believe they would be happy to trade only with us if we could guarantee them a safe and bountiful partnership." Dafydd had, over recent months, begun to sound more and more like an experienced councilor. Gwriad had ceased to mock him, even in jest.

"How could we do that?"

"It's now a possibility since the King acquired Morgannwg. Up until recently we have traded only through the northern ports of Gwyneth and Ynys Mon. However, with the unifying of the country, the King could encourage the southern princedoms of Gwent and Deheubarth and even Brycheinog to sell their goods in all the ports from here along the South Coast." He tapped his nose dramatically. "The Council has been working on such an idea. The minutiae of such a plan does not interest the King, but he is keen to increase our wealth, if only to be able to pay for more mercenaries."

"What about the present situation? If we are to make use of these ships in Caerdydd, we need their Captains to agree to sail them, which is doubtful. After all, they risk losing both their boats and their reputations with the Saxons."

"I think we must convince the King of their undoubted use and get him to see the long-term benefits of a signed agreement regarding their employment. He should offer guarantees of reimbursement for loss of their boats or their trade."

"Will he agree?"

"He will, if you can plan a successful raid with them, and I can show him how this is just the start of a huge trading partnership." Dafydd's eyes took on a faraway look. "Increased trade will mean wealthy merchants, and merchants can be taxed. The King will agree to the plan." He took a long and thoughtful drink, rolling the wine gradually around his mouth. "However, I will persuade him that he cannot risk his life on an unimportant raid. He will object, of course; he's bored and desperate to kill Saxons. But, I will inform him that Ealdgyth needs his presence, and will be travelling down from Aberteifi. As King, he should not be risking his life on the uncertain waters of the Severn. The arrival of Ealdgyth will save him losing face."

"Is Ealdgyth really coming? In this weather and on these tracks?"

"I doubt it." Dafydd gave a dry laugh. "She'll almost certainly have changed her mind. But the raid will be over by then."

• • •

"OVER HERE," THE CAPTAIN OF the Nef whispered. He pointed to a small bay on the starboard side, just visible in the fading light. It had taken them longer than they had imagined. Gruffydd's plan to arrive in the late afternoon, raid the Saxon settlements, and return to the ships before dark, had proved impossible. At the start of their expedition a rising tide had balanced the outward flow of the great river, but the wind had been inconsistent and the small ships had made little progress. However, with the imminent change of tide, a strong breeze had pushed them up stream until they had reached the point that the Captains had agreed would be a good place to beach the ships and disembark the unsettled horses. It was shortly before the outgoing tide would cause them a problem.

Gwriad looked back, uncertainly, down the vast expanse of the shadowy estuary. The water was calm, but it was the unknown that worried him. He was still recovering from the shock of the extraordinary event they had experienced a mile down the river's estuary.

Conditions throughout the voyage had been calm and it was just as he was beginning to feel more confident that the Captain of the Nef had pointed out a strange wide wave roaring up behind them. If there had been other waves, Gwriad would not have been so concerned, but this wall of water had appeared out of nowhere and was advancing quickly above a flat sea. He had time only to warn his men to control the horses when it reached them, raising the ships up more than the height of a man. The small armada rose up, surged forward for a short distance and dived down, before settling back into a disturbed sea with the sails flapping, and the vessels rolling from side to side. Gripping the transom, Gwriad watched amazed as the wave continued on into the distance. It stretched from one side of the estuary to the other. The Captains had seemed to enjoy the experience, cheering and gesticulating at each other. The sailors in the ships had laughed at the terrified soldiers, many of whom had lost their balance and fallen, screaming, in a struggling pile on the crowded deck. The horses had panicked, and it was a while before they could be settled. The event had increased the tension between the soldiers and the crew.

"What was that?" Gwriad demanded.

The Captain shrugged his shoulders. "It's nothing. It happens at high tide."

"You could have warned me!"

"It would only have made you more nervous." He turned his attention to studying the approaching bay.

Gwriad remained angry. "Will it happen again?"

"No. Not until the next high tide." The Captain spat into the water. "You're lucky. These are good conditions."

"Get yourselves ready!" Gwriad yelled at the soldiers. It was unnecessary, but it made him feel better.

"You realize that the ships will be stuck here for half a day, before the next full tide?" the Captain said, shrugging his shoulders and looking unapologetic; he was not responsible for the tides.

"I understand," Gwriad said. "However, we'll need all of that time to complete our raid." He breathed out deeply, allowing the tension of the past few hours to subside.

The journey had been stressful; the wave had added to his fear. Neither he, nor the majority of his small army, had ever travelled any distance by boat. He had spent much of his time concentrating on the heaving of his stomach, avoiding the undignified vomiting by many of his men. But it had been a near thing.

He assigned a handful of archers and men-at-arms to prepare to secure the bay as soon as the ship grounded. "Remember, keep quiet. Only yell out if there are Saxons waiting for us."

The men nodded. Like him, they were eager to get back on land. The ship grounded surprisingly quietly on the muddy beach, and the soldiers jumped down into the quagmire, waded ashore, and rushed off into the gathering darkness. There was complete silence in the bay, as if everyone was holding his breath. The breeze dropped. Soon there was just the splash and occasional whinny, as a horse was brought ashore.

"Light up," Gwriad whispered, and soon there were fiery torches along the small beach, encouraging the two Crayers to land safely.

After the ships were quickly unloaded, the soldiers and twenty horses assembled on the beach. The ships' Captains were in agreement that the nearest Saxon settlement was less than a mile up the river. "It's a large village with a useful harbour. I've tied up there many times," one of the Captains of the Crayers said. The others agreed.

"Y'ave until first light to get back t'our ships," another said. "By then tide'll be in full flood. The sooner we gets afloat the better."

Gwriad understood they were still hoping their ships would not be identified.

"The reason we've brought the horses is to make the Saxons think we've travelled over land to attack them." He spoke loudly to the assembled soldiers and seamen. "We will attack on horse. The foot soldiers will follow, set light to the buildings, and take anything of value. We need to create panic. The cavalry will move on up the river to attack any Saxon habitation we come to. By first light we must all be back here. The Saxons must be made aware of our power to attack at will. Until now, they have been the ones who invaded us. Now we invade them!"

His speech produced a muted cheer from the shadowy shapes in front of him. Having left a few soldiers to guard the beached ships and their crews, he galloped off with his small detachment of cavalry. The foot soldiers followed at a run. They were keen to find Saxon homes, for this was their chance for plunder, their chance to raise themselves from poverty in a single night.

• • •

THE SAXON VILLAGE WAS CELEBRATING a feast day when Gwriad and his cavalry arrived. The light from the fires and the sound of music and singing could be heard from a distance. Gwriad did not consider the women or their families; this was an attack on his enemy. These were the Saxons who plundered his people and destroyed whole villages. They were his enemy, and they would all die.

The cavalry galloped through the village, killing the unarmed men and creating panic among the women, the children, and the old folk. Gwriad stopped at the edge of the village, regrouped, and returned for a second charge. This time, the surviving Saxon men were armed and prepared to die for their families. A short, bloody battle ensued, until the Welsh foot soldiers appeared attacking the Saxons from the rear. In moments, it was all over. Gwriad led his horsemen on to the next village, while the foot soldiers destroyed any last opposition, and began a systematic plundering and burning of the village.

"Burn their boats!" he yelled. The Sergeant raised a hand to show he had heard. They galloped off along a well-used track towards the next habitation. Only the Captain of the Nef had accompanied Gwriad; the other two Captains had remained to guard their boats, along with members of their crews.

"What does this prove?" he asked, when they stopped in sight of the lights of the next Saxon village. "You kill them. You take their few possessions. You return to Wales. What have you achieved?

"It will have made them fear us, like our people fear them." Gwriad spat angrily into the dark. "For years we have waited like pigs in a sty, knowing they will eventually come to kill us. Each year, when the weather improves, they have attacked our homes. Now, with Gruffydd ap Llywelyn, the first King of a united Wales, we have the power to hit back." He glared at the flickering lights ahead. "And we will hit back!"

The Captain shrugged his shoulders. As long as he was on the winning side he did not care; morality was for the rich.

The assault was sudden and unexpected and the Saxons were quickly overwhelmed. The Welsh cavalry, led by Gwriad, rampaged through the village, killing those who opposed them and setting light to all of the buildings.

"The fires will alert their local army," the Captain commented. He had watched the attack from a small hill; once the fighting was over, he had found Gwriad. "We should return to our ships before daybreak."

Gwriad knew he was right. He was experiencing an aching sense of disappointment. There had been no glory, only a bloody massacre. Gruffydd's dream of revenge had been brutally accomplished; but, now that the excitement of the attack was over, he was left with a hollow sense of achievement. The people he and his men had killed were poor farmers and artisans. It was unlikely any of them had ever set foot on Welsh territory, or killed Welsh women and children. They were just the victims of war.

He rode slowly out of the devastated village. Bodies lay in small piles and every house was alight. Stray dogs barked, and he tried to shut out the sound of a child screaming in one of the burning houses. The foot soldiers had not arrived. Gwriad knew they would be returning to the ships with their plunder from the first attack. He looked around. They had killed every man they could find and many other members of this meager habitation had been slaughtered. There had been some spirited resistance and his twenty horsemen had been reduced to twelve, and some of them were nursing injuries. But, all of the surviving horsemen carried plunder, and considered the raid a fine success. Gwriad carried only his bloody sword. "Enough!" he shouted. "We return to the ships!" He urged his tired horse into a canter beside the Captain; behind him, the remains of his cavalry followed.

"So, it was a victory!" Gruffydd roared, clapping his powerful hand on Gwriad's shoulder. "Why are you so depressed? You lost a few soldiers, but that was to be expected. All three ships returned, which I did not expect." He stared into Gwriad's eyes. "You've done everything I wanted you to achieve." He handed him a cup of wine. "You have no idea how I wanted to be with you. If it had not been for the affairs of state which your brother keeps reminding me of, I would have shared your victory."

"Almost certainly, my Lord, the Saxons will seek revenge and attack the south of our land, once the weather improves."

"Perhaps. But I have plans to attack them on a number of fronts. It is my intention to play them at their own game." He began to pace the room like a caged wild cat. "I am going to establish a Southern army, with a strong cavalry wing under the control of Prince Anarwd. I have given him military control of the lands that belonged to Rhys Fachan, and I have made him a General. If Deheubarth is attacked, his cavalry will support your forces; if Morgannwg is attacked, he will be able to hold the area until you arrive. The other Princes have been told, and given other responsibilities." Gruffydd rubbed his large nose thoughtfully. "It is my hope that if I keep these young Princes busy, they might leave each other in peace. We shall see."

It was a sound plan and Gwriad was grateful to have another army between his Deheubarth forces and the Welsh border. During the rule of Prince Rhys Fachan, the princedom of Morgannnwg had been a law unto itself. "When will this happen?"

"I have given the order. Thanks to Prince Anarwd, everything should be in place before the good weather returns and the Saxons try to cross our borders." His face split into a wide smile. "But, I have an even better idea! Can you guess?"

Gwriad shook his head. "You're going to attack Hereford again?"

"Perhaps, but that's not it. I'm going to build a Welsh fleet that will be based at Caer Myrddin, or Caernarfon as some of our Lords call it, and maybe at Conwy as well. I will attack the Picts and the Irish before they reach our shores; I will protect our trading partners, and I will make them pay for this protection. When I have more money, I will establish a second fleet at Caerdydd and use the ships to bring war to the Saxons who live near our borders along the Severn River." Gruffydd was obviously enthralled with his plans, and Gwriad nodded agreement, although he had heard from his brother that the first fleet was to have been built in the Caerdydd area. Once again, the King's first concern was for Gwynedd.

"Would you not get richer pickings from the Bretons and the Saxons?"

"Maybe." Gruffydd looked shifty. "I think it best that Gwynedd gets the initial ships and the trade that will come from this." He looked defiantly at Gwriad. "As King, I must defend my base and keep my local Lords indebted to me. Southern Wales will get their ships as soon as I can afford them."

Gwriad smiled. As far as he was concerned he had no desire to fight on the water. "In the meantime, I will prepare my army for our next attack on the Saxons?"

"Indeed. From now on, it is our turn to steal their cattle and plunder their homes. The days are past when we wait for them to attack us. From now on, we will attack them on land, where they are strong, and on the water, where they are weak. We will divert their trade. Instead of being the poor, underfed Welsh, we will meet them with full bellies, and with weapons and armor that are as good, or better, than theirs."

"This will cost money, my Lord." Gwriad felt obliged to point out. "Where do you get the money for the first ships?"

Gruffydd moved towards a small table where a detailed model of the country had been created. "Which is why we will soon start to attack their towns from Oswestry to Hereford. When spring is here and the ground has dried, I want you to bring your Deheubarth army to meet me at Offa's Dyke, opposite the Saxon town of Shrewsbury. There is a cleared break in the wall there. We will pour through into their rich lands and strip them of their wealth." He pointed out the places as he spoke. "This model is the combined memory of many people. This shows the mountains and the rivers of our land and all our important places." He pointed to the northern border, and a raised line that curved its way down to the south. "This is Offa's Dyke."

"I have not encountered it," Gwriad said. "My campaigns have all been in the South, or within Wales itself."

"It's a remarkable creation, named after a Saxon King of Mercia, who had it built about 250 years ago. It consists of a ditch and a high earthen rampart. The ditch is deep and quite wide and faces us, with the rampart behind. It allows the Saxons to see into Wales. The ditch slows down any attack, especially by our cavalry." He pointed to a cut in the line. "Here is where we have slowly filled the ditch by removing a part of the rampart. Over the past two and a half centuries, much of the dyke has been worn down, or removed by farmers, but it still remains a formidable obstacle if the Saxons decided to defend it. Which is why we will attack them before they're prepared. After my wedding, we will launch our attack as soon as the weather permits."

Gwriad stared at the model. He felt excited; it was what he wanted to do. "I will immediately begin assembling horses and supplies and preparing the Army of the South-West." He frowned. "However, it may be difficult to assemble a large body of soldiers: the local landowners will worry about their tithes, as the majority of their income is from farmers. The farmers will want to begin plowing and dealing with their newborn lambs. It's a difficult time of the year for them to be leaving to fight. It's different when they are fighting to defend their homes."

"Tell them we're going to attack a rich Saxon town and they will take home more wealth than they can make in a lifetime of farming. Besides, slaves do most of the fieldwork in the farms in your area." He rubbed his nose thoughtfully. "Perhaps we could get the Bishops to help? As you know, the Church gives terms of slavery as a form of religious penance for those whose sins are considered serious. I will ask the priests to be particularly zealous in the next few months." He roared with laughter. "It's about time we had some more religious observance in this country, especially among the farmers in your area, and especially among strong, witless young men and Irish itinerants. Land is useless without the people to work it. We have never produced enough food to allow us to have a standing army. That must change."

Gwriad nodded. His family had always had slaves; most were local people who had committed crimes, itinerant beggars, or men and women who had fallen foul of the ecclesiastical laws. The Church, for all its faults, was seen by most of the peasants to be a powerful and important element in Welsh life. Bishops encouraged their priests to consider imposing penalties of slavery for crimes against God. It was understood by the Church and the landowners that providing a slave to a deserving farming family, was a sure way of increasing the revenue to the local Church, while reducing the problems caused by disaffected youth. There were also slaves that were the result of wars: both local battles between tribes and larger conflicts with invaders and pirates. Evan, Lord Gomer's lifelong friend and slave, had been a young boy when his whole family had been condemned to slavery after a local insurrection. While Gwriad would admit that most slaves were not treated as well as Evan had been, he had no reservations in agreeing with the King's plan.

"We'll take wagons to carry our supplies. On our way back, we'll ensure that the majority of the gold and silver is carried in these wagons and ends up in my coffers. I will allow young boys to accompany their fathers to our border, where they'll wait for our return to help with driving the cattle and sheep to all parts of Wales." Gruffydd's deep voice reverberated around the hall. Gwriad could tell he was thinking aloud, his huge enthusiasm drowning any objections. "I'm also going to promise the men that their families will be looked after if they are killed or injured. What do you say?"

"It's a good idea. Men won't desert if they know they are going to be rewarded; and their families will breathe easier with your promise of protection."

"Yes," he nodded, pleased with Gwriad's reply. "I'm going to encourage the Bishops to come to the border with us to bless the campaign."

"They'll probably send their priests instead," Gwriad jested.

"Of course they will," Gruffydd laughed. "But they won't be

able to complain of being ignored." He poured more wine. "To victory in war and in marriage!"

"To victory in war and marriage, my Lord." The wine was good and Gwriad sipped it with approval.

"From the Captain of the Nef," Gruffydd murmured. "He felt obliged to leave me a barrel or two."

"Dafydd tells me that planning for your wedding is well advanced and the plans also include a second Coronation?"

"Indeed. I want to reinforce the fact that Wales is now one country." He emptied his cup and placed it down on a table, "Oh, Gwriad, I have such plans! I want you to line the road to Saint David's Cathedral with as many foot soldiers as you can equip. I will journey down through Wales with hundreds of horsemen. Soldiers will ride ahead to prepare the people in every nearby village, so they can see me, and know that I am their King and can protect them. Every Prince and Lord will be invited. They will come with their own households. Dafydd has appointed a team of men and women to arrange the feeding and accommodation of them all."

"What does the Bishop think of all this?"

"He's delighted. He has invited priests from France and Ireland, and all of Wales. It's his great opportunity to show how powerful he is. No doubt he will expect gifts from all the Princes and Lords. He's as keen as I am to create a spectacular occasion, but Dafydd is insisting on a balance between my nobles and the clergy. Given the chance, Bishop Hywel would fill his church with foreign priests." Gruffydd laughed. "Dafydd is insisting the Bishop arrange the accommodation for his own priests. Unlike me, he can afford it!

CHAPTER TEN

MAY 1057

The wedding was an historic event. Dafydd's organization succeeded even beyond his own expectations, melding the sacred and the political in a unified service, in which the King was married and his kingship of all Wales publicly acclaimed. The cream of the Welsh nobility packed the Cathedral, almost shoulder to shoulder with more priests than Wales had ever seen in one place. Hundreds of soldiers lined the route of the procession. Gwriad had ensured that many more took on the task of corralling and controlling the huge crowd of excited peasants and lesser lords who flocked to the peninsula from all parts of Wales. Even the weather cooperated. A week of dry weather preceded the event, with brilliant sunshine on the day. The Bishop stated that his prayers had been answered, while the Druids on Ynys Mon claimed otherwise. But the day had not been without certain dramatic incidents.

"There must be thousands of people here," Ealdgyth gasped as she approached the Cathedral. She was traveling in a specially built wagon with Angharad beside her, her lady-in-waiting sitting opposite, and with Teifryn beside her. The wagon was sumptuously adorned with expensive fabrics. Behind on a fine destriers, rode King Gruffydd and Cadell ap Bleddyn, his Seneschal and the proud father of Ealdgyth. Both men were richly dressed: the King in gold and purple, and the Seneschal in red with a blue cape. Behind them rode Gwriad in his bright armor, with two other Generals: Prince Anarwd of Morgannwg, and Owain ap Cynan from Gwynedd. Behind them, in order of seniority, rode the most important Princes with their wives and daughters following in wagons.

Flags and pennants flew, soldiers paraded, and the huge crowd roared its approval. For a moment in time, the color and splendor of the occasion convinced the Welsh they were no longer a poor nation, but one that had finally achieved greatness.

"It's a pity you have to share your wedding with the King's Coronation," Angharad said innocently.

Ealdgyth's eyes flashed, but her face retained its fixed smile as she waved at the cheering crowds. "At least I didn't have to rush mine to preserve my good name."

Angharad swallowed loudly and turned to wave at the sea of happy faces that stretched up towards the Cathedral. 'We may be sisters,' she thought, 'but once this afternoon's ceremony is over, Ealdgyth will be Queen and I, the elder sister, although married to the top general, will have to watch my tongue.'

"My dear sister, never forget that I am doing you a big favour. Left to ourselves, it is likely that Gwriad and I would not have married, or at least, not for a long time."

"You will think differently when he gives you a child," Ealdgyth retorted.

"From what I hear, your future husband has plans for himself and Gwriad that do not involve either of us. With both men constantly at war, it is unlikely that we will start families in the near future."

"Really?" Ealdgyth's face broke into a genuine smile. "I have plans of my own, sister. I will have an heir sooner than you can imagine." Before she could elaborate, a huge roar broke out from the crowds.

"We're almost there, my Lady," Teifryn said, the flush on her face not only from excitement.

In spite of the uplifting atmosphere of the occasion, a small frown crossed Angharad's face and she looked quizzically at her sister. The wagon stopped and Ealdgyth licked her provocative lips and smiled back. With a slight tilt of her head, she stood up confidently to acknowledge the crowd, as her lady-in-waiting began to arrange her elaborate dress in preparation for her descent from the wagon.

Ahead, the King and his senior Lords dismounted and paraded into the Cathedral. Gruffydd strode down the aisle, staring straight ahead. He was an impressive figure with his thick black beard, his shoulder length hair, and his powerful physique. He wore a richly embroidered gold tunic with a thick purple cape, a color so rare in Wales, and so expensive, that it confirmed the King's power. He did not appear to be in any way overawed by the event, nor did he acknowledge any individuals in the thick throng of his most important Lords. The Bishop was standing at the top of the steps in front of the altar, flanked by an army of his most senior clerics, who stood on either side, each trying to give the impression that they were of some importance. Gruffydd advanced down the aisle with a grim countenance, and at a speed that caused his followers to quicken their pace. Gwriad, marching two paces behind him on his right, could hardly suppress a grin as he imagined the less physically active members of the possession struggling to keep up.

Near the front, on the right hand side, Dafydd was checking off the stages of the ceremony in his mind. He felt uncomfortably conspicuous in the bright robes that Ealdgyth had presented to him and which Gruffydd had insisted he wear. "You are my Secretary; only you and the Bishop have any idea of the arrangements. I want people to understand who you are, and how important you are to me." With such high praise, Dafydd had no other option but to forsake his drab clothes and present himself like a foppish courtier.

"You'd think he wanted to get it over with, the speed he's moving," a nobleman remarked in Dafydd's ear. "He can't wait to get to his Coronation."

"Ealdgyth won't allow him to hurry," Dafydd replied, confidently looking around. "This is her part of the day. She'll keep him waiting, you'll see.'

Dafydd was proved right. Ealdgyth refused to enter the Cathedral until her robes were exactly as she wanted them; her long train was laid out without a crease. When she finally entered with her coterie of women-in-waiting; she processed slowly down the aisle on the arm of her father. A hush descended on the packed Cathedral. Gruffydd was standing in front of the steps leading up to the altar, which was ablaze with candles and gold. At his right, one pace back, stood Gwriad, suddenly conscious of the huge honour the King had bestowed on him. The Bishop, in all his finery, waited patiently, like a statue, while the King shuffled restlessly in front of him.

Finally, Gruffydd was unable to restrain a quick look over his shoulder. His grim face slowly creased into a wide smile, as he saw how beautiful Ealdgyth looked. She paraded slowly towards him, beaming with happiness, and took her place by Gruffydd's side.

The wedding ceremony took longer than expected as the Bishop, reveling in his position of power, delivered a long and turgid oration about God, belief, and the need to support the Church. Eventually, he remembered the reason for the occasion, finally speaking about marriage, kingship, and the Welsh nation.

"That must rate as the longest speech ever delivered at a wedding," the nobleman muttered, and Dafydd nodded his agreement.

After the exchanging of rings and the fervid acknowledgement by the congregation, Gruffydd and Ealdgyth paraded slowly, at her speed, from the ornate altar with its tall, golden candlesticks to the great, carved door. Outside, they climbed onto a raised dais where they could be glimpsed by the hundreds of enthusiastic soldiers and commoners. After a short bout of waving, they returned to the main door, where they began a gradual procession back to the altar. Two ornate thrones had been placed in front of the steps. It was in these thrones that Gruffydd and his new wife were proclaimed King and Queen of All Wales. It was the most magnificent occasion in Welsh history, and as Gruffydd remarked: "We are a strong nation and getting stronger. If we can stop the deadly disagreements between our imbecile princes, who are only concerned with their petty power, we could become a nation able to retake the lands that should belong to Wales and defeat the bloody Saxons once and for all."

• • •

IT WAS THE MOST COLORFUL and well-attended event in living memory. The celebrations went on for two days before the families began to return to their farms, while many of their men folk started a brief military training before the proposed march to the border. The weather was unseasonably warm and dry. Even the strong winds that frequently buffeted the peninsula were pleasantly absent. It had been a mammoth achievement. It had succeeded on many levels; most of all was Gruffydd's desire to be accepted as King of All Wales and King of the Britons, and to be seen as their King by as many of his nation as possible.

"Well, brother, you can take a well-earned rest," Gwriad said, as he touched cups with Dafydd. "It went well. Although there were times when many hoped the Bishop would lose his voice." He emptied his cup of wine. "You managed to achieve what Gruffydd wanted, which was a spectacle that nobody will forget for a long time."

Dafydd nodded contentedly. "I'm pleased it's over. Now I can get back to doing the things I really like working on."

"The laws and history of Wales? Rather you than me."

"However, it's your turn now, General," Dafydd gave a mock salute. "Will you be returning with the King and his Court to Gwyneth, or are you leaving your lovely wife to the attentions of your younger brother?"

"Angharad would eat you alive," Gwriad smirked. "Believe me, I speak from experience."

Dafydd felt a heat rise in his cheeks and cursed his inability to discuss sexual matters on an even plain when talking to his experienced brother. "You're right, of course, and I wouldn't have time anyway, not now that Teifryn is after me." He knew it sounded a feeble boast and was grateful that Gwriad did not pursue the matter.

"I'm here for a few days to organize the local men into some sense of how soldiers fight wars." He rubbed a calloused hand over his weather-beaten face. "You have no idea how stupid the average peasant can be when it comes to holding a weapon. They seem to think that by having a piece of leather armor, they are somehow protected from any injury. If you order them to pick up a sword, they are more likely to cut off their own limb than frighten an enemy." He paused, shaking his head. "I'm convinced that for most peasants, war is a game. They think if they agree, or are forced to attack the Saxons, they will all return with immense wealth. No matter how often I tell them they may die or lose an arm or a leg, they still hold fast to the belief that, in spite of their stupidity, they will live to return laden with gold."

Gwriad began to pace the room like a hunting dog on a leash. "We were lucky. The Saxons did not try to take advantage of the celebrations, which puzzles me. If I had been in their position, I would have launched an attack, if only to make a dent in Gruffydd's political achievements. Even the weather was ideal for an invasion."

"For an invasion to happen, there must be a leader," Dafydd said, thoughtfully. "From what I hear, there is a power struggle going on between those Saxon Lords who support their King Edward, and those who think he is weak, mad with religion, and too close to the Normans."

"You might be right. I've heard such rumours, which is why Gruffydd believes this is a good time to attack the enemy while they're divided. There is also the fact that our exuberant King needs money to finance his other plans. When do you leave?"

"Tomorrow. The King is enjoying a last day with his new wife. Then the Court returns to Rhuddlan. He's sent his Northern officers ahead to complete the mobilization; he hopes to begin an advance towards Offa's Dyke shortly after his return."

Gwriad nodded. "I have a few days to complete some minimum training of the local men, and pry some more peasants from the grasp of their land owners. Not all of them support Gruffydd, just like not all of them favoured Gomer." He clasped his sword's hilt. "But they'll bloody well do as I tell them, or they won't have any land to own!" He took a deep breath. "Then, I march them to the border and hopefully meet up with the King, who will have joined the army of General Owain ap Cynan and the men from Powys. You will have heard that Prince Anarwd, General of the Southern Army, will be marching up from Morgannwg after he has arranged for some reserves to guard the area? If our sergeants do their job, we should be able to mount the largest invading force in our history."

"I wish you well. It will mean a lot to this country if you're successful." Dafydd sipped his wine, while Gwriad refilled his cup. "In a way, I wish I were with you." There was a wistful quality in his voice. "You do exciting, physical things, while I fight my battles in words and written agreements."

"I'm pleased to know you'll be holding the fort for us," Gwriad said soberly. "You're about the only one who will remain at Court who can be trusted."

There was a short silence as each man reflected on the days ahead. "Many of the people believe that we're about to achieve the greatness predicted by Merlin," Gwriad said. "What do you think?"

Dafydd nodded. "I agree. I think Gruffydd could turn out to be our greatest King since the famous days of Arthwyr." He rubbed his hands up his clean-shaven cheeks. "But there's so much left to chance. We're committing the majority of our forces in one place and there is a great danger in that."

Gwriad nodded. "We have discussed it. If the Saxons did launch an attack in the South, we have some forces remaining. Also, we could redirect the cavalry, if necessary."

"What happens if the Saxons are expecting you and have their forces defending Offa's Dyke?"

"There is a large part of the Dyke that has been destroyed. We will direct our archers to rain death on those who defend the nearby ramparts, while our cavalry breaks through the gap and attacks them from behind." He shrugged his shoulders. "We will deal with problems as they arise. What we have this time, as never before, is a large army of men, many of whom are well-armed and trained both to fight and to follow orders." He had a faraway look on his face. "I think we will surprise them. They will have heard of Gruffydd's wedding and will be convinced that he's enjoying his new wife. We will hit them hard and destroy Shrewsbury and the surrounding countryside before they know we have invaded them. When they counter-attack, we will have retreated to the Dyke, where we will use their defenses against them."

He stood up and grasped his brother's shoulders. "Look after my wife and the Queen." He winked lasciviously. "Don't take too long before you get Teifryn into bed. Women get impatient, you know." He strode out of the room, his laughter echoing on the stone steps.

Dafydd looked furious, then thoughtful and finally, with a grin on his face, he went in search of Teifryn.

● ● ●

IT WAS MORE THAN TWO weeks before the King and the three armies came together a mile away from Offa's Dyke. The weather had changed; torrential rain and wind made life miserable for the massed warriors. At last, before Gruffydd was entirely convinced that his army was marshaled, he instructed General Gwriad to lead the combined armies up to the imposing barricade that separated Wales from Saxon lands. The ground was waterlogged, and those who were unlucky enough to be at the back of the army, found themselves trudging through mud a foot deep. For this reason, the army spread out as it advanced, and there was a resulting lack of cohesion.

The ancient Dyke was unfortified, as Gruffydd had hoped. From the top of the embankment he could see into Saxon land and it was not encouraging. There was no sign of human habitation: waterlogged fields, dark forests and swollen streams barred their way.

"Forward!" he yelled, his voice barely reaching the nearest battalions. The officers were ready, and anticipated his hand signals. They knew, as he did, there was no turning back.

The first large village they encountered was Alberbury, an ancient settlement that had existed long before the coming of the Saxons. Many of the inhabitants had fled, and the Welsh met with little resistance. The rain continued to pelt down and a thick mist made it difficult for the officers to keep a tight reign on the disparate elements. If it were not for the presence of the King and his strong personal guard, some of the soldiers would have settled personal and historic grudges. As the light faded, the army set up its camp in and around the village. The King had ordered his officers to warn the men that they were to spare the women and children, on pain of death. The animals were rounded up and the young sons of the soldiers proudly led them back over the border, eager to get the praise from their families; many were hurrying, hoping to return to gather up more of their enemy's goods.

Beneath a leather tent, Gwriad and some officers stared out at the gathering gloom. Around them a sea of mud and the constant rain had made the lighting of fires difficult; groups of soldiers huddled together finding whatever comfort they could. A cool wind had added to the problems and it was only the prospect of loot that unified the men.

"The King says we can allow pillaging, but they can only take what they can carry. No deserting and no setting fire to buildings." An officer gave a humorless laugh. "Since when has warfare been a party game?" He pointed to billowing smoke at the far side of the village. "An army this size is impossible to control."

"The warning will be out and Shrewsbury will be expecting us tomorrow," another officer complained.

'They'll not have any idea of the size of our army," Gwriad countered. "They'll take back reports of just a small Welsh raiding party, whose aim was to attack the village. The Saxons have no means of knowing that we intend to attack their town. They'll think we'll be drunk on our small success and preparing to flee back over the border. " He swirled the wine in his cup. "In fact, I would not be surprised if the Saxons of Shrewsbury do not launch a small counter-attack to drive us away." He gave a wolfish grunt. "Tomorrow, we rise early," he looked out of his tent at the pouring rain, "not that many of our soldiers will have slept much in these conditions. We'll be prepared to confront their soldiers before they understand what they are up against."

Towards dawn the rain stopped and first light revealed a clearing sky and the chance of a warm, bright sun. The Welsh soldiers took what sustenance they could, doused their fires and prepared for the fighting ahead. There had been a few who had decided that this was not the way they wished to fight. But, their retreat had been prevented by a determined squad of cavalry under the direct control of Gwriad.

"You men have a choice," he said, looking down from his saddle at the miserable bunch of deserters. "You can either die here, cut down by your friends, whom you wished to desert. Or you can return to your sections and fight like the Welshmen we know you are. If you try to desert again, and are lucky to escape justice from my patrols, you will return to your villages as craven cowards. When this war is over we will visit every village and make your cowardice public knowledge, and we will punish you."

There was a groan of despair from the twenty or so captives. This was not how they had imagined it would be. In their minds it would have been a pleasant march to the Saxon lands where they could have stolen a cow or a pig and guided it back home. Only a few of the deserters had thought of actually fighting, and few of these farmers were equipped with anything more than a pitch folk or a long knife.

"Now listen to me!" Gwriad bellowed. "I know you're not soldiers, but I need every one of you to convince the Saxons that we have a mighty army. The trained soldiers will do most of the fighting, but you will support them. You will help me, and King Gruffydd, show the Saxons that we can form a large army that will match anything they can assemble. That is your role! If we take Shrewsbury, as I am certain we will, you will have the chance to take from our enemies and return to your homes like rich men."

A small cheer went up from the cowed prisoners.

"So what is your decision? Those who will fight for Wales, move over there." He pointed to the right of the group. "Those who remain cowards, stay where you are and my cavalry will slaughter you!"

He was not surprised when the whole group rushed to the safety of the area he had indicated.

"You are good Welsh men!" he roared. "Like me, you will support King Gruffydd. Together we will return to Wales as heroes."

There was a roar of approval. Those who had assumed they were doomed realized that they had a chance to redeem themselves and bring back riches to their families.

"Take them to the front of the line," Gwriad hissed to his officers. "I am not risking them deserting again."

The large and extended army moved like a dark cloud towards Shrewsbury. As Gwriad had expected, a small army of Saxons left Shewsbury to defeat what they had imagined would be a minor border incursion. Gwriad's scouts were able to prepare the Welsh army long before they met.

"What is the latest news?" King Gruffydd asked, as he trotted up to General Gwriad and his officers.

"They have sent out about two hundred Saxon foot soldiers and a handful of horsemen. They think we are just a few marauding Welsh bandits. We are about to destroy them, my Lord." Gwriad revealed his teeth in a snarl. "Then we will advance quickly on Shrewsbury and we should be upon them before they know their fighting men have been defeated."

Gruffydd's face was as expressionless as a piece of slate. "Well done." He turned his horse to watch the massed sections of Welsh foot soldiers march past. "Who gave the order to burn the houses in Alberbury?"

Gwriad's confident smile disappeared. "There was no fire when I left the village. The soldiers had been warned as you ordered." His brow furled as he thought about the situation. "Prince Anarwd's men from Morgannwg followed us and your men from Gwynedd followed them."

Gruffydd lowered his head. "I suppose I have to expect this. The people of Morgannwg have suffered over the years from Saxon attacks. Their families were always butchered. Their women and their children were murdered in cold blood. Their men seek vengeance." He placed his hand on Gwriad's leather glove. "Am I expecting too much of my people? I had hoped we could fight their men, steal their riches and their animals, and somehow leave their women and children alone." He took a deep breath. "We are like all soldiers: we rape, plunder and murder, and eventually we die."

Gwriad watched in silence as the King turned his huge horse. Followed by his personal guard, he cantered away towards Shrewsbury. 'It could well have been the men from Gwynedd, not those from Morgannwg,' he mused. 'But, best to believe it was those from Morgannwg.'

Shrewsbury was overwhelmed before the guards realized that they were under attack. The town's best fighters had left to destroy, as they thought, a small invading force of impoverished Welsh farmers. The main gates were opened when carts of seemingly dead and injured men sought refuge. The gates remained open as the laden carts rumbled through. It was at this point that guards on the walls identified a large army approaching, and the Saxon volunteers rushed up to man the walls.

Suddenly, the seemingly dead Saxons in the carts became alive. Before those on the walls could react, the gates were forced open, allowing the huge army of the Welsh to enter. It was a day of horror for the inhabitants of Shrewsbury. Hundreds of battle-crazed Welsh soldiers rushed through the town, killing all the men and subjecting their women to rape and vicious death. Children were mindlessly murdered, the houses were pillaged, and many were set alight. For most of the soldiers the town was the biggest they had ever seen and held the promise of unimagined wealth and long awaited revenge.

"Why is the city burning?" Gruffydd bellowed. "I gave orders that there would be no burning."

"You also gave orders, my Lord, that the women and children were to be left alone." Gwriad replied. "But there is no way to stop a victorious army from committing atrocities. It's never been possible in history, and it hasn't been possible now."

"These are Welshmen, my people!" Gruffydd yelled. "I did not expect my people to behave in this way."

"My Lord," Gwriad wailed, "did you really expect that these men would forgive the hundreds of raids that the Saxons have made on their families?" Gwriad was exhausted with the non-stop decisions he had had to make in the past few hours. "For decades the Saxons have slaughtered their families. They have burnt their homes, humiliated their women, and murdered their children. This is their chance to show that they are not without spirit. We must not judge them. You, my Lord, must not condemn them for their inability to reach your high standards. They have beaten the Saxons. They want, for once, to get their revenge."

Gruffydd bowed his head, and said nothing.

"We've taken Shrewsbury, as you hoped we would. By tomorrow, we will have confiscated everything of worth, and the town will burn." Gwriad held out his hand to his King. "Forget the murders and rapes. Our men will not be controlled: they are soldiers, or farmers or even slaves; they have never had the chance to hit back at the people who have oppressed them for years. This is their moment and it is yours. You will be remembered as the King who defeated the Saxons and brought riches to Wales. Nothing else is important."

Gruffydd did not reply. He sat on his horse, staring at the huge fires that burned out of control. "I had thought to spare the women and children," he muttered and turned his horse back towards Wales. "We are better than this!" he roared. "We will be strong, but we will also be humane. In future we will teach our soldiers how to behave." He walked his huge horse slowly along the road down which they had previously advanced. His personal guard formed up behind him. "This will not happen again!"

"And rain will not fall from the sky," Gwriad muttered. He turned to his officers, "Start the immediate evacuation of the town. By tomorrow, the Saxons will have gathered their forces. I don't want this raid to end with a massacre of drunken Welsh peasants!"

• • •

In late November, Ealdgyth gave birth to a son. Some people counted on their fingers, but none wondered aloud if the child was born prematurely. Most just smiled.

"Congratulations, my Lord," Gwriad bowed before a radiantly happy Gruffydd.

"A boy! A healthy boy!" The King handed a cup of wine to his friend and most dependable General. "I have an heir, Gwriad, and such an heir. I have named him after your father, Cydweli. Cydweli ap Gruffydd. Are you pleased?"

Gwriad beamed. He had not known the King's intent. The honour was such that he was unable to reply.

"I can see you're pleased. Your father was a great man. He inspired me. Without him, and his amazing fort, we would not be here today." Gruffydd drank deeply. "My son is a real boy. You should see the size of his... arhum." His words faded away as Ealdgyth entered carrying the baby. Already the child was feeding well and seemed large for his five days.

"Husband, I hope you're not still celebrating the birth of your son?" She gave one of her rare smiles. "The nation needs your attention, Gruffydd. Leave the child to me."

Gruffydd put an arm around his wife and tickled the red-faced infant, who slept contentedly in his mother's arms. "He's a handsome fellow and I can't wait to get him on a horse."

Ealdgyth pouted. "Surely, my Lord, I can have the child to myself for a few years before you make him into a soldier?"

"Perhaps, just a few years then." His face creased in pleasure. "But he's already large for his age. I think he'll become a brave warrior, and a powerful king." He kissed Ealdgyth on her cheek. "You are a fine woman and a worthy Queen for Wales. You will produce a line of strong males, who will keep this country safe."

"Perhaps I should produce only girls from now on, so there is no competition for your attention, my Lord."

The King frowned. "You are right, of course. Strong males are always fighting to achieve the top position. But, I need more boys, in case anything should happen to Cydweli. It is always best to have a number of heirs. I will keep them in order, never fear."

Gwriad watched this exchange with amusement. He was in no hurry to start a family. He suspected Angharad was of the same mind. "My congratulations to you both." He stared into his wine. "My father would be greatly honored. I'm sure Cydweli will grow up to be a fine son of a remarkable marriage."

Ealdgyth glowed; it was rare that a man included a woman in such a compliment.

"Your wife is lucky to have a man who thinks of women when he thinks of power."

Gruffydd gave his wife a thoughtful glance. The barb had not missed him. "I have decided," he said with some emphasis, "that you will be present at the next meeting of the Grand Council. We will be deciding on our next moves against the Saxons." He tugged on his full beard. "It will be interesting to have a woman's point of view."

"Eventually, I would like you to include other women in your Council." Ealdgyth did not appear to have received the news of her inclusion as of particular importance, and Gwriad noted the way she manipulated Gruffydd, who seemed, now that he had a male heir, to be willing to grant her every whim.

"Perhaps, my Queen, you should give some thought as to the women you would like to propose." Gruffydd turned to Gwriad. "In the meanwhile, you and I will have another look at that map. Let's see if we can predict the next incursion by the Saxons."

CHAPTER ELEVEN

MAY 1061

After a series of resounding defeats, the Saxons remained behind their borders. Instead of attacking the Welsh, they began to prepare for their incursions. The border lords quickly established a local militia in each village, and provided trained soldiers from the nearby towns. The plan was to gather the local men together and form a strong opposition to any invading forces. But, no matter how they tried to resist the Welsh, there was no let-up in the Celtic attacks. Some were small-scale, resulting in the loss of animals and the occasional death. Others were devastating blows to the Saxon economy with a grievous loss of life.

"We're losing the battles on the border, my Lord," the elderly Saxon officer reported. Bron had been recently promoted to the new position of Intelligence Officer. He was keen to show his mastery of his subject. "They manage to assemble large numbers. They know where and when to attack us. It was not like this before their King Gruffydd ap Llywelyn became King."

"So, you think this is entirely due to their King Llywelyn?" Harold, the Saxon Earl of Wessex, leaned forward in his carved chair. He was eager to know the details, and to evaluate the officer's information. Harold was a giant of a man. He was strong, ruthless and ambitious: all qualities that marked him out as the most powerful of the Saxon Earls. He was the eldest of four brothers, and his family, the Godwinsons, was second only to the King in influence.

"The younger officers would say so," the older man replied, "but I would think it has much to do with one of their new generals. There is one named Gwriad ap Griffith. He's the son of their long dead General Cydweli. You will remember, my Lord, he was the one who built that remarkable fort and was responsible for our defeat at Rhyd-y-Groes in 1039? This is his son. I believe he's responsible for most of our problems.

"Is he responsible for the attacks on our villages near the Severn River?"

"I believe so, my Lord, but I have also heard of a General called Rhodri ap Williams. The Welsh now have a fleet of ships along their south coast; they have been involved in the recent attacks along the Severn, and his name has been mentioned. The Welsh also have a larger fleet operating from somewhere in the north of Wales. Recently, they have defeated the Pictish raiders, attacked ports in Ireland, and have started to create a large trading empire which should have been coming to us."

"So, if we wanted to hurt the Welsh, an attack along their north coast might be the best way to go?"

"It would go against the normal thinking," the officer conceded. "We have always attacked the south of their lands, or through their middle. Shrewsbury has been the furthest north, because beyond there, the land is difficult, and we have Offa's Dyke to protect us. There are few settlements of any note between a village called Llangollen and a northern coastal village named Dyserth. It is believed that the Welsh keep their fleet somewhere between Dyserth and their holy island of Ynys Mon. The most likely ports are Conwy or at an old Roman fort called Segontium."

"I've not heard of it."

"Its other name is Caernarfon."

Harold gave a dismissive grunt. "So why haven't we attacked them before along this northern coast?"

The officer looked uneasy. "Because it is a difficult landscape, my Lord. There is little of value along the border." He took a deep breath, "It's difficult to invade this part of Wales. We would be exposed to ambush in many places along the way and we would have to advance a long distance into Wales before we would come to any place of importance. Perhaps the first place would be the village of Mold, which is called Yr Wyddgrug or High Hill, but it is merely a poorly fortified cluster of hovels." He noticed Harold drumming his fingers and moved on quickly. "It's ideal country for their type of fighting and would almost certainly be a disaster for any Saxon invasion." He avoided the Earl's penetrating stare. "We do not have the ships to attack their fleet at sea, or carry out an attack on their ports."

"So you wouldn't advise an attack on the North?" Earl Harold Godwinson curled his lip. He was the great Earl of Wessex, the most powerful man in Saxon England, other than King Edward, who was known as The Confessor. He resented the recent Welsh attacks; they were an affront to his authority. "What would you advise?"

"I would advise an attack on the ports of South Wales. They think they have control of the waters of the Severn. If we built enough local ships we could defeat their boats, ravage their villages, and take the war back to their heartland."

"We have ships already, don't we?"

"Yes, my Lord, but they are based in London and York. They are needed there to resist pirates. Also, those in London are old vessels. We have nothing of note that we could use on the Severn. We need to build new ships."

"Do we have the men who can build these ships?" He glared at the officer. "Do we have the ports where they can be built?"

The officer knew his future depended on his answer. "We do, my Lord. I would be honored to take on this task."

The Earl was fast losing patience. He had other concerns besides the wretched Welsh, who continued to irritate him like the flies in summer. "All right. Arrange for the building of these ships. I will provide the money. You will be responsible for their building and the manning of these vessels. Send me word when you are ready." He stood up, "Bron, I have promoted you to be my Intelligence Officer, but I will carve you into little pieces if you fail me."

The officer quickly bowed his way out of the room, leaving Earl Harold to stare angrily at the closed door. He turned to a heavy oak table, which was littered with scrolls, and leather bound books. With a deep sigh, he selected a parchment with the King's seal. Another complaint about the Welsh, no doubt, or perhaps a request for more money to help build England's biggest building: the Abbey at Westminster in London. He broke the seal and read, with annoyance, a long report of how helpful the Normans were being in the construction of the Abbey, which, at that time, was the only building in England based on the Norman architectural style, much favoured by William the Bastard of Normandy. At the end of the letter was a familiar criticism of his brother, Tostig, the Earl of Northumberland.

Edward the Confessor was old for his years and was intensely pious, hence his name. But, he was devious. He left much of the maintenance of order in the country to Harold, who was beginning to think of himself as the next king in waiting, in spite of a rumour that Edward had promised it to William of Normandy. The King had sworn to the Church to be celibate and, although married, had not, therefore, produced an heir.

The Lords of England were preparing to claim their rights when he died. Already there were murmurs of discontent, not least from Harold's brother Tostig, whose abilities did not match his ambitions. Harold had persuaded the King to give Tostig the important title of the Earl of Northumberland, in the hope that his brother would be satisfied and put his enormous energies into supporting Harold, instead of constantly opposing him. However, Tostig had failed miserably in his attempts to stop the incessant invasions by the Scots. He had become hugely unpopular with the local people on whom he relied, and who had expected him to defend them. He was known to be a cruel and oppressive ruler. The area was frequently in revolt.

"Brandon!" Harold yelled.

Immediately, his personal servant entered.

"Send a messenger to my brother Tostig. Tell him to report to me within the week! Find my brothers Gyrth and Leofwine and ask them to attend me immediately."

His servant bowed and departed without a word. He knew it would be unwise to remind the Earl that his brother Tostig had refused an earlier summons. It was rumoured among the household that the younger brother feared assassination.

Leofwine, Harold's youngest brother, was the first to arrive. He was a handsome man, shorter and lighter than Harold, but with a shrewd mind and a reputation as a fearless warrior, deadly with a sword. He was happily married, popular among the local lords, and content to rule an area to the south of London, with no ambitions other than to maintain the power of the Godwinson family.

"Don't tell me, it's Tostig again?" he joked as he embraced his brother. Noting the fixed frown, he tossed off his thick cape and perched on a stool.

Harold passed to him the King's letter. "Read it for yourself," he growled. "The fool called a meeting of some northern lords and tried to get their support to oppose me when the King dies. Reports reached the King, who blames me for giving Tostig the Earldom. He demands that I punish him."

"Let the King punish him." Leofwine had little time for weak rulers.

"The King has no interest in fighting, or in doing anything that takes him away from his prayers, his new Cathedral, or his Norman guests." Harold began to pace the room. "As you know, I am the King's right hand. I carry out his orders and in return he grants me most of my requests. He also blames me when things go wrong."

"If he's wanting you to arrest Tostig, would he take away his Earldom?"

"Not in so many words, but it could happen. Our brother is his own worst enemy. He promised, if I gave him Northumberland, to defeat the Scots and make the North the envy of England. He has failed. The Scots have run rings around him, raiding far into the South, and avoiding him where he is strong. They are attacking him from behind his own lines, and laying waste to rich farmland and burning villages in previously safe areas. His generalship is being openly questioned. Some Lords refuse to be led by him."

Leofwine removed a whetstone from a shelf and returned to his stool, where he began to slowly sharpen his sword. "If he loses his Earldom, our family will lose influence."

"If he continues to be defeated by the Scots and plots treachery, he will deserve to be removed. There will be nothing we can do about it."

The door opened and Gyrth, the third of the four brothers, entered with his usual diffidence. He was the tallest of the family, but did not possess any of his brothers' physical aggression or, at first glance, any of their innate confidence. He had soft dark eyes, was awkward with women, and was the first of the family to take Holy Orders. Gyrth was much liked by the King. He had been rapidly advanced in the Church, despite the opposition of the local bishops, and shared the King's enthusiasm for the new Cathedral. He had frequently acted as the peacemaker between Harold and King Edward.

"Come in, Gyrth. We are in need of your good council." Harold rubbed his hand down his thick beard, concealing his smile; he was aware that he always spoke to Gyrth in a way he never did with his other brothers. He never swore in front of him, or made lewd jokes. There was something about this awkward, gentle giant that he found worthy of respect. "Wine?"

Gyrth shook his head.

"I will, now that you're offering it!" Leofwine said, good-humouredly. He stood up, embraced Gyrth, and helped himself.

"I understand you wanted to see me?" Gyrth gathered up his robe and eased himself into a chair.

"We do," Harold said, including Leofwine, who made a face. He explained the latest situation regarding Tostig. "So, what would you do in my place?"

"He's plotting against the King?"

"He's plotting against me. It seems that no matter how often he fails when he is given a position of power, he still wants more. No matter how unsuited he is for it, he dreams of kingship. He's a danger to our family and to our country."

"Which means he's plotting against the King." Gyrth's face seemed to harden. For a moment, he lost his amiable countenance and revealed an unsuspected strength. "He must, therefore, be banished."

Leofwine stopped rubbing the whetstone against the blade and stared at Gyrth. Harold, who was pouring himself some wine, paused in the act. There was silence, as if each man had been struck dumb.

"I had thought to advise the King to deprive him of his Earldom and bring him back to London." Harold filled his goblet.

"To do what? Foment more trouble?" Gyrth examined his large hands. "The King could have him locked away in some deep dungeon and forgotten. He has committed treason; he could be put to death. Advise the King to banish him. At least our brother will live, and live free. With God's blessing he might become a better man."

"But what if he doesn't reform himself?" Leofwine replaced his sword in its scabbard. "Abroad, he could stir up all sorts of trouble. If he remained with us, at least we would know what he was plotting."

Harold nodded in agreement. "I know our brother is in league with the Norman bastard, William. He visited him a few months ago. He would find a sympathetic friend if he fled to Normandy. Also, reports have come to me that there is some agreement between Tostig and the King of Norway. In spite of my desire to rid us of our problem brother, it is a dangerous move to banish him. One, that could result in even greater difficulties. Unlike us, he does not consider our family. He is driven only by ambition. We all know how unsuited he is to coping with responsibility."

"The best thing would be for the King to invite him down to London to discuss the Scottish problem. Once he is here we could insist that he spends more time under our control." Leofwine raised his eyebrows in a knowing way.

"But, would he come?" Gyrth opened his huge hands in a shrug.

"He might," Harold said thoughtfully, "if the King invited him." Harold agreed with Leofwine. They must preserve the influence of the family, in order to further his own ambitions. Harold knew the time had come to take a stand, even if that meant casting his brother Tostig into a prison.

After his brothers had departed, Harold reviewed his situation. He knew he would, eventually, have to challenge the Welsh upstart King Gruffydd ap Llywelyn. But first, he must settle his on-going feud with his brother Tostig and ensure that the King continued to see him, the Earl of Wessex, as the most devoted of his supporters. Harold hated the Normans. They were beginning to exert too much influence on Edward. The Cathedral at Westminster was only one example of how Norman ideas were becoming increasingly more acceptable among the English nobility. But, in spite of his objections, he knew he must appear to support Edward. The King's approval was vital to keep the other ambitious Lords under control.

His scribe entered and bowed. "You sent for me, my Lord?"

"Yes. Write to the King as follows..." he took a deep breath. "My Lord King, I write this as a token of my affection and support for you." He took a long breath. He hated having to abase himself before a man he despised. Edward the Confessor was a weak King, who had spent twenty-five years of his earlier life seeking refuge in Normandy. It was no wonder he admired everything Norman. "While I know your Highness is much involved with the creation of what will be the most important building in England, I respectfully ask for you to send me the money to enable me to deal decisively with the Welsh problem. My King, you will remember that Gruffydd ap Llywelyn, who calls himself King of the Britons, is engaged in on-going attacks on our borders. Without your help I am unable to pay the soldiers who can repel these onslaughts.

"With your blessing, my King, I promise to defeat the Welsh and bring glory to your reign.

"I remain, your most devoted and loyal supporter,

"Harold Godwinson, Earl of Wessex."

. . .

1061

"WE HAVE HAD NEARLY FIVE years of the reign of our great King Gruffydd, and we have never had such crops, such peace and such happiness."

Dafydd looked up from his writing. "Teifryn, my love, you are beginning to sound like a priest." He smiled at her. They had been married less than a year, but it had been the happiest time of his life.

"I'm just happy." She ran her right hand over her rounded

abdomen. "You promised, as one of your husbandly duties, to take me for a walk."

"And I will, just as soon as I finish this report for the King."

"I think this baby will make a big difference in our lives. I hope you're prepared for that?"

There was a pause as Dafydd gave the report a final check. "Your life will certainly change. However, babies do not seem to have made a great difference to the Queen's life. She travels constantly with Gruffydd, and her nurse looks after the two boys."

"A nurse and a host of servants," Teifryn agreed. "And a company of hand-picked guards. The young Princes get a lot of attention from everyone except their mother."

"She's the Queen; she has a lot of responsibilities," Dafydd replied, defensively.

"I understand she might be expecting another?"

"So Gruffydd told me, but that might be mere optimism. He is keen to secure his bloodline." He smiled at Teifryn. With a few weeks to go, she had achieved a rounded appearance that he liked. "You were quite skinny when I first met you," he joked. "Just look what love can achieve."

"You're a lovely man, but it seems unfair that I have to do all the work," Teifryn replied. "If I have to carry our child for all these months, then you will be expected to be an enthusiastic father."

"And I will be!" Dafydd was secretly amazed how marriage and fatherhood had happened so easily. For years he had worried about women, sex and becoming a father; it had all suddenly fitted into place. His courtship of Teifryn had been wonderful. He had fretted about what to say, how to accomplish his first sexual encounter, and had been convinced that he would not measure up to any woman's expectations. He had come to understand that, unlike the voluptuous Angharad, Teifryn was as innocent and unworldly as he was. Together, they had explored, enjoyed, and overcome the problems of partnership. As he grew into his role as husband and lover, he realized that it was his brother, Gwriad, who had given him such an inferiority complex: Gwriad was the sexual athlete, the brave fighter and the fearless leader. He had been Gomer's favourite and, although Dafydd had always loved his brother, he had at last reached the stage in his life when he no longer felt inferior to him.

He stood up and embraced Teifryn. "I'll be a remarkable father, whether you have a boy or a girl."

"Good. I think I am going to produce a girl."

"We need lovely girls in this world; the more the better. The fewer boys, the fewer wars."

"Do you really believe that?" Teifryn looked him straight in the eye.

"I do. Can you imagine what the world would be like if we had an excess of Gwriads. I love him dearly, but he is never happier than when he is killing some benighted Saxon, or having unbelievably outrageous sex with Angharad. When he's not fighting, he drinks himself stupid and eats prodigious amounts of food. For men like Gwriad, the world is never enough. He must keep challenging himself." He mused a moment. "I try to imagine him as an old man. What will he do with himself?"

"Your brother is a fine man, but I would hate to have him as a husband."

Dafydd slipped his arm around her shoulders. "I would hate you to be his wife; I would always be thinking how he didn't deserve you."

They kissed gently. He realized he was truly happy.

"Why do you think they've not had any children?" Teifryn asked, enjoying his full attention.

"I don't know. Perhaps they don't want any."

"The way they carry on, I would have thought it was impossible to avoid."

Dafydd rubbed his chin, thoughtfully. "Are you suggesting that they can't have any children?"

"Angharad is my friend, but I know she had a number of lovers before she married Gwriad."

Dafydd remained silent. He felt he was treading on thin ice: if Angharad could not have children, would that affect their marriage? He hoped not. He was very fond of Angharad, although he could never imagine having her as a wife. She had always been kind and warm towards him and, in his inexperienced days before he met Teifryn, Angharad had never made him feel awkward. Since meeting Teifryn, he had come to realize that their meeting was entirely due to Angharad, and he would always be grateful to her. "Not everyone has children. They seem happy enough," he murmured.

"I agree. I just hope that Gwriad is not disappointed."

"I hope Angharad isn't disappointed as well," Dafydd said. "She's a fine woman and I love her spirit and her..." He stopped with a stupid smile on his face.

"You love her outrageous behaviour?"

"I suppose I do. But I am so grateful that you love me. I could never have coped with her as a wife." He ran his hand down her arm. "She is ideal for Gwriad, and he for her. Perhaps they don't need children." He began to laugh. "It would slow them down, and the world would be the loser. There are very few people who create such a stir, but they make the rest of us grateful for our more balanced lives."

"When I have our child, our lives will be far from balanced," Teifryn said contentedly.

• • •

AUGUST 1062

THE MOUNTAINS OF NORTH WALES were bleak and forbidding, even in the warmth of summer, and people who inhabited the narrow valleys and the bare hills were unlike those who lived in the wet, fertile lands of Deheubarth and Morgannwg. They were harder, leaner and more warlike; a proud, aggressive people who frequently went hungry and relied heavily on their sheep flocks and root crops. In some areas, they mined for small amounts of gold and copper and for slate for their houses. Around their dangerous coastline, fishing was important, but there was seldom enough. The winters were severe, life expectancy was low, and men were easily drawn to quarrelling. War, with its excitement and the chance of loot, was a constant attraction to a people who had so little.

In the home of the dead Iago ap Idwal, there was great lamenting by his family and, in contrast, a riotous drunken celebration of his life by his friends and soldiers. The Snowdonian tribal chief had been killed in a foolhardy uprising against King Gruffydd ap Llywelyn. Apart from his family, there were few who would genuinely grieve his passing.

His body was laid out on a bare table in the main room. His family wept as they worried about their future. His friends and followers enjoyed the free beer, said the required words, and most felt a sense of relief that Iago ap Idwal would no longer endanger their lives.

"My father was a great man!" his eldest son Cynan wailed. He had been drinking heavily for most of the day. "He was not afraid to stand up to the tyrant Gruffydd. My father was brave. He did not bow his head as many of you have done." He pointed his hand at many in the room.

"Hush, now," his mother hissed. "Your father is lying there in state. These people have come to remember him and pay him respect. I will not have you cause trouble."

"Enough!" Cynan yelled. He was finding it difficult to focus and could not remember how much he had drunk. "I am the eldest son of the great Iago ap Idwal. I am Cynan ap Iago, and proud of it. My father did not accept the tyranny and oppression of Gruffydd ap Llywelyn, our so-called King of All Wales. And I," he staggered as he waved his hand at the packed room, "will get my revenge on this murderer."

"You're a good boy," his uncle said, as he maneuvered him out of the door. He liked Cynan, but the boy had always been a problem. "Your father, my brother, was a good man. But you must know that he was not the best of leaders. He would not want you to follow in his footsteps." He pushed Cynan out of the door.

When the cold night air hit him, Cynan took in a deep breath. He was promptly sick. He staggered to the edge of the yard and heaved up in a seemingly unending series of vomiting. After a while he staggered to the animal trough and washed his face. He was barely aware of the full moon or the silent figure of his uncle standing close by.

"I will get my revenge." He rubbed his face and tried to stand up straight. "My father was murdered!"

"Your father was a fool!" His uncle roared. "King Gruffydd liked him, trusted him and promoted him. How did your father, my brother, respond? He decided he wanted to become King of Gwynedd. He was a fool! Few believed he was worthy. He ignored my advice, ignored the advice of his friends, and challenged Gruffydd to mortal combat. But only when he realized that the King had twenty times the men he had."

"Gruffydd refused to fight my father in single combat! He's a coward and a murderer!"

"Why would our King fight single-handed with a rebel? Your father and his motley crowd, who don't merit the name of an army, brought this upon themselves. You couldn't even call it a battle! He sold his life, and those of his friends, for nothing. It was always his stupid pride that drove him." He gripped Cynan by his shoulders, and forced him to stand up straight. "Now you listen. I loved your father. But, he was an egotistical fool and nobody except your mother and your brothers thought he was a great man." He shook Cynan furiously in an attempt to make him sober up. "You are like him. If you continue to rant your foolishness, you will die young." He frog-marched Cynan back to the trough, where he ducked his head into the green water. After a number of immersions he dragged the youth out and sat him down on a hay bale. "I'm leaving tomorrow to pledge my allegiance to our King. If you have any sense you'll do the same." He walked back towards the house. "As you're too drunk to bury your father with due ceremony, I will attend to it."

Cynan sat with his head in his hands and heard the door close. "I will never forgive Gruffydd for killing my father," he muttered. "I will get my revenge. I will." He collapsed forward and lay in a pool of his own vomit, while on a bleak hillside his father was buried with the traditional ceremony due to a tribal chief.

• • •

SEPTEMBER 1062

THERE WAS A ROARING FIRE in the royal bedroom; expensive candles illuminated the rich tapestries on the walls, and the fine drapes on the bed. Around the floor, woven carpets added to the warmth of the room, regardless of the unseasonably cool wind that beat against the closed shutters at the window.

"You've done well, Ealdgyth." The King ran his hand over his wife's flat stomach. "Two healthy boys and still the most beautiful woman in the realm." He frowned, "I was sorry you lost the third child."

"I was sorry too, my Lord. But, we do have two strong boys to secure the bloodline." She stretched. "I have done well, because I have married the most famous King in Welsh history," she purred contentedly. They were lying naked on the wide bed, listening to the moaning of the wind, enjoying the heat and the comfort.

"Are you happy?"

"Blissfully. Are you?

"Of course. Why shouldn't I be?"

She ran a finger down his rugged face. "You are rarely like this, Gruffydd. I have seen you in recent days when you have been far from happy. You don't laugh as much as you used to. You act as though you have the burdens of the world on your shoulders."

He sighed deeply. "I have such plans for this nation. But I know, even as I strengthen the army and increase the wealth of my people, there are still those who plot against me."

"Perhaps you need to make changes?"

"How so?"

"If people stay in important positions for too long, perhaps they may come to think that they should be even more important?" She spoke with such guileless innocence, that Gruffydd listened. If she had argued forcibly to win a concession, or pleaded her case, he would have been alert and certain to question her motives. But Ealdgyth knew her husband and rarely tried to achieve anything in a hurry. She knew that she must slowly introduce an idea, so that eventually Gruffydd was convinced that it was his. In this way she increased her power.

She continued her plans the next day when she and Gruffydd were walking along the cliffs near their palace. It was rare for her husband to find the time for relaxation during the day, but her hints that she felt ignored had prompted him. But, even the grandeur of the scene and the closeness of his wife did not prevent him from being absorbed with his own thoughts. The defeat of the rebellious Iago ap Idwal had brought him little satisfaction. He had trusted the tribal chief. He was disappointed and baffled by his treachery. It was a waste of Welsh blood and had destroyed the peace that had existed for the past three years.

Ealdgyth was also lost in thought, as she considered her next move.

Her father, Lord Cadell ap Bleddyn, had served for years as Royal Seneschal for the Llywelyn family. First, when Gruffydd's father had been King of Powys, and then with Gruffydd, after he had become King of Gwynedd and Powys, and eventually when he was King of All Wales. It was her ambitious father who had arranged for her to visit Court and had indulged her in everything. But once she was Queen, she did not want the old man forever checking on her. He had served his purpose. Over many weeks, she had maneuvered Gruffydd into thinking that Cadell was too old to carry such a responsibility and, as his daughter, she was certain he would be glad to be released from his burden. Gruffydd had agreed to replace the old man. The next day he had discussed the matter with his Secretary, and Dafydd had spoken against such a move.

"Cadell is entirely reliable and, although he is old, his job is administrative and largely ceremonial," Dafydd had argued. "I believe he has a number of useful years ahead of him."

Ealdgyth was furious when she was told, especially as she had successfully planted the name of Rhys Gwynedd in Gruffydd's mind. "You will be aware of his talents," she had suggested, "he is a rising star, and will bring some new ideas as to the running of your increasingly large household. Also, he is a Powys man." She did not mention that she found Rhys physically attractive. Her maids looked after the children for most of each day, and she was frequently bored when Gruffydd was travelling around the country. It was a situation she intended to alter, which was why she needed to move her father out of the Court. To have Rhys as the Royal Seneschal would enable her to have frequent meetings with him, without raising any suspicions.

Gruffydd's thoughts returned to his Seneschal. "I am not going to retire your father. He can stay on for a few more years."

"Oh, my father will be so disappointed!" she said when she heard the news.

"Why so?" Gruffydd asked. Dafydd had convinced him that the old man was desperate to hang on to his job.

"My Lord, I know you think you are doing the best for him, but he is an old man. He has told me he wants to spend more time with his grandchildren. He will never admit that the job is too much for him. But, as his daughter, I know he yearns for a quieter life. He is afraid he will miss those precious years of our children's childhood."

"Dafydd thinks he will see this as a criticism of his decades of loyal service."

"Cadell is a proud man," she agreed. "But, if you arrange a feast in his honour, he will know you have his best interests in mind."

Gruffydd rubbed his nose with the palm of his hand. "This will make him happy, think you?"

She slipped her arm through his, as they stood looking out at the sea. "I will prepare him for your decision. When he knows you are holding a feast in his honour, and that he will have more time with the children, I know he will be delighted."

"Good. I will tell Dafydd I've changed my mind." He kissed her gently on her forehead and led her back to the castle. His thoughts had moved on to other more pressing matters.

"Did you say you had somebody in mind to be the new Seneschal?" she asked, making it sound as though it was a vague memory.

"Yes. Rhys Gwynedd. Didn't you say he was a rising star?" He gave her a thoughtful glance.

"Did I?" she said, as if it was of no importance. "Perhaps my father might have mentioned that to me?" She gave Gruffydd one of her powerful smiles, displaying her fine white teeth and making her eyes come alive. "Anyway, whoever you chose, my Lord, will be acceptable to me."

"Good. Talk to your father. I will speak to him later, after my meeting with Dafydd." Most days he found time to meet with Dafydd and to be brought up to date with the affairs of state. "You make the arrangements for his feast. I'll summon Rhys Gwynedd; his appointment will go down well with his family. I need a few more local men around me." He hurried away, leaving Ealdgyth to ponder her future.

She stared, unseeing, as huge waves buffeted the craggy cliffs. On reflection, Ealdgyth realized how close she had been to failure. She blamed Dafydd, who seemed to have opinions on everything. If she were to increase her power and obtain the freedom she desired, then Dafydd would have to go. She had never liked him: he was too self-righteous, too priggish, and too intelligent. Just to prove her power, she had focused her attentions on him soon after her marriage, as it would have been useful to have her husband's Secretary in her thrall. But, Dafydd had seemed oblivious to her wiles, and had suddenly taken up with Teifryn, another person who noticed too much and had made little effort to be the Queen's friend.

The Griffith family were a threat to her plans: it was bad enough having her sister marry the King's favourite General, a necessary stepping stone to her becoming Queen, but to have Gwriad's brother become the King's incorruptible Secretary, had not been welcomed. "They have too much power," she complained to Rhys Gwynedd, when they had last met. "If anything happened to Gruffydd, one of those brothers would steal the throne."

"If anything happened to Gruffydd, then you would continue to reign in his stead, until your son, Cydweli, was old enough to assume his rights," Rhys said. "The King is often in danger. You should either get to like the Griffith brothers, who will be obliged to support you, or you must seek to appoint your own people in Court."

She touched his face. "Such good advice, my Lord, and such fine features." She gave him a long knowing look. "I think I must find you a suitable occupation in Court. Then, you can continue to give me," she took a deep breath, "good advice."

• • •

KING EDWARD THE CONFESSOR WAS admired as a holy man, but despised as a King. He was pious and humorless, more often on his knees in church than attending meetings to guide the running of England. But those Lords who were closest to him blamed him most for his vacillation. He would avoid making important decisions, yet could, in an impetuous moment, reverse long-held agreements with those who might have disappointed him over some minor issue. Like many weak rulers, he would lash out at those he distrusted or envied. He was particularly aggressive towards those who threatened his religious tranquility.

"I will not put up with the Welsh any longer!" he ranted. Harold, among other important Lords, bowed his head in agreement. "Their constant attacks in the west are preventing me from raising the money I need to finish my Cathedral at Westminster." He glared at Harold. "You must stop it. Use all the men you can gather, and invade their country. Continue the invasion until you have killed their upstart King. I want the head of Gruffydd ap Llewelyn!"

The assembled Lords bowed to hide their smiles. All knew that if this could have been achieved, it would already have been done. They understood that their King had no concept of how difficult it was to attack the Welsh, who knew how best to defend their rugged country. They muttered their agreement, knowing that it was only a question of providing the King with enough money to complete the huge Cathedral of Westminster. He would soon forget about the Welsh.

"I will defeat the Welsh, my Lord King," Harold responded, shocking the other Lords. "If you will provide me with the money to pay the soldiers that I will need, I will guarantee a final solution to the problem of King Gruffydd ap Llewelyn."

There was a long silence as Edward attempted to stare down the Earl of Wessex. He knew that if any man could defeat the Welsh it was Harold. But, the Godwinson family had always been a thorn in his side. Early in his reign he had banished Harold's father for disloyalty and, although the family had in recent times,been more pliable, he still distrusted them. Then, there was Tostig, whom he should never have made Earl of Northumberland. Eventually, he dropped his eyes, knowing that in spite of his need for money to complete his Cathedral, he must enable this man, whom he did not like, to solve the ongoing and increasing problems on the Welsh border.

"Very well, Earl Godwinson. I will provide the money to pay your soldiers to defeat this Welsh upstart King. But if you fail, you will carry the full expense of the campaign."

"My Lord," Harold kneeled before his King, "I will be successful, and you will soon have the revenue from the West to enable you to complete your Cathedral."

There was applause from the other Lords, who were delighted to see that Harold, who many felt was too ambitious, had committed himself to a mission that all believed he would be unable to complete.

The King placed his hands together, and thanked God. No matter what happened, Edward knew he would be the benefactor. If King Gruffydd were defeated, it would please his Saxon realm. The captured Welsh gold and materials would pay for the expedition, and provide him with much needed money for his church. If Harold were to be defeated, it would remove a growing threat to the King's authority. It would allow him to move against other members of the ambitious Godwinson family, who would have to pay for their brother's failure. By taking on this risky adventure, Harold would be fully occupied. He would have no time for his constant plotting, of which the King was well informed. In the unlikely event of the Earl being successful, it might be necessary to eclipse his popularity with accusations of treason. Edward raised his head and smiled benignly at Harold: "May God bless your enterprise. May all be for the best."

The Lords met secretly after the audience with the King and were keen to express an opinion.

"Harold will either die in the attempt, or be dishonored. Serve him right. Either way, we'll soon be rid of his arrogance, and it will put an end to his hopes of being the next King."

"Our next King will most certainly be that Norman bastard, William of Normandy. I know for a fact that Edward has promised the throne to him."

"Our King is besotted with anything Norman."

"I don't agree. If Harold manages to defeat the Welsh King, then we can all look forward to a Godwinson on the throne." There was a gasp from some, and derisive laughter from others.

"The King doesn't trust Harold Godwinson. He has definitely promised the throne to the Norman."

"Our pious King will promise the throne to anyone who will allow him to complete his Cathedral and leave him to his holy prayers," another added, with heavy sarcasm.

"What should we do?"

There was a hiss of frustration.

"We do nothing!" an older Lord exclaimed. "Either, Harold will be defeated, which is most likely, or if he succeeds in killing the Welsh King, we'll all benefit. Edward, our holy Confessor, will have to pay for Harold's expenses. He will need our support to continue with his absurd Cathedral. I suggest we leave Harold to sort out his problems and wait for our beloved King to approach us. When he does, then we will have some say as to whom our next monarch will be."

The meeting ended; the Lords dispersed to their castles, leaving the lesser folk to try to assess the personal repercussions of their lords' decisions.

"If it's going t'be war," a stable hand said, "then my folks in Bristol will suffer."

"Everyone suffers in a war," an old farrier asserted. "I've bin in a number of battles on the border wiv Wales, an' I never benefitted from any of 'em."

Harold, aware of the Lords' meeting, and had positioned his servants to report the outcome. "Most of 'em think ye will fail in ye war with them Welsh, my Lord," a servant reported. "They thinks no man can beat that Gruffydd, an' they'd all be 'appy if ye was to be beaten." He glanced cautiously at the Earl. "I thinks, m'Lord, they be worried ye might be the next King."

Harold passed a coin to the servant, who bowed his way out. "I think they have every reason to worry," he murmured, as he poured wine into an ornamental challis. He drank slowly, reflecting on the changing situation. The King, although married to Edith, the daughter of the previous Earl of Mercia, had sworn to the Church to remain celibate, and no hoped-for successor to the throne could be forthcoming from those loins. Harold knew that if he could defeat the Welsh King Gruffydd, he would achieve huge popularity among the people, and would become the most likely successor to the English throne. There was a wave of anti-Norman resentment sweeping the country, which he could make use of.

There was much to do. In recent months he had spent his time in London, ensuring his position at Edward's palace, while testing the waters regarding his popularity among the other Lords. His family problems had also engaged him; he cursed his inaction. He was, he realized, unaware of the latest local reports from Wessex. He needed to be brought up to date about the rumours from Wales. If he was to take advantage of Edward's promise to pay for the removal of Gruffydd, then he needed to act quickly, for there would be nothing gained if Edward died before he had defeated the Welsh.

CHAPTER TWELVE

OCTOBER 1062

King Gruffydd sat on his embossed throne. He surveyed his Generals and his most intimate advisers, who were gathered in the great hall of his palace near the coast of North Wales. It was one of the periodic meetings that Dafydd, his secretary, had advised him to have. It was also an unusual gathering, in that Queen Ealdgyth was not present, nor any of the other senior women of the realm. Unlike many nations, the Welsh royalty and Lords included their wives in most of their social and political activities, not confining them merely to the raising of children and the organization of the kitchen.

"It is not possible for you to be aware of all the information that you need to rule this country, my Lord," Dafydd had advised. Gruffydd had listened, as he frequently did, when his Secretary proposed an idea. "If you gathered together those of your subjects who actually know what they are doing, as against the merely decorative members of your Court, you will learn what is really going on around this emerging nation. You will be able to tell them what you want them to do."

Gruffydd surveyed the gathering. Before him was the cream of Welsh society; he knew each man and his individual worth. He stood up and raised his arms above his head. "Welcome to you all, my most valued and loyal friends. Wales is doing well, better than at any time in its recent history. Our borders are secure, our soldiers are well armed, and our people are no longer suffering from starvation and Saxon and Pictish raids." There was a roar of approval; he waited until the hubbub had settled. "Today, we will hear reports from our three Generals, from our two

220

Admirals, and from those of you who can tell us of local successes and tribulations." He glared round at this group of chosen men, daring any of them to make fun of his statement. None wished to trivialize the King's words; it was due to Gruffydd that each man lived in the style to which he had become accustomed and, with God's help, would continue to enjoy.

Gruffydd nodded contentedly at the serious faces in front of him. "We have many heavy burdens. We need to employ your several minds to reach the best conclusion. However, we live in a golden time, my Lords. I intend that we will continue to enjoy this age of Welsh dominance for many years to come."

There was, once again, a huge roar from the assembled Lords.

Gruffydd sat back in his throne. "I call upon Prince Anarwd of Morgannwg, General of the Southern Army, to tell us of the situation in Morgannwg."

The Prince, a tall lean man, now in his late thirties, marched up to a space near the throne, bowed and turned to face the gathering. "Since General Gwriad attacked the Saxon villages along the Severn six years ago, the Saxons have been more interested in protecting what they own, rather than attacking us. This has given me the time to establish a permanent army. Whenever I am running short of funds, I plan a raid with the Admiral of the Southern Fleet, Rhodri ap Williams. We take from the Saxons their gold and animals to finance the very army that opposes them." There was a roar of laughter, which seemed to surprise the Prince. "I will leave the description of the Southern Fleet to the Admiral, but I am happy to report that Morgannwg has never had such an army or such a time of peace."

He turned to Gruffydd. "My Lord, it is your leadership and your imagination that has created this Golden Age for Wales. I am confident in the strength of my men, and in our ability to repel any local invasion that the Saxons might attempt." He faced the assembled nobility. "We are strong because, at last, we have one King, three armies, and two fleets! Never, in the history of Wales, have we ever been so united or so strong!"

He was a humorless man, who took his new responsibilities seriously. He fixed his sober gaze on certain faces in the assembly.

"Let none of you ever think to weaken us by ancient grudges or old, unimportant blood feuds." He bowed to the King and returned to his place.

There was a long period of cheering and clapping. But amid the patriotic fervor, there was a small number of Lords who gave half-hearted agreement, wishing they had more influence and secretly hating Prince Anarwd for his success.

Eventually, Gruffydd stood up and thanked the General. "It is welcome news to know that our constant enemy, the Saxons, have met their match in the South." He turned to his left. "I call Lord Owain ap Pasgen, General for the North, including Gwynedd and our holy island of Ynys Mon, to give his report."

Owain was a typical Celt: a short, stocky man with long raven hair and bright blue eyes. He was a renowned fighter, and had been elevated to General after his years of passionate support for Gruffydd. He was in his early forties and had a reputation for hard drinking and for being a notorious womanizer. He assumed his place amid resounding cheers from the Northern lords. He bowed to Gruffydd and took a deep breath before speaking. "The Northern Army is strong. It is a powerful deterrent to the Saxon raids that used to plague us. Most of the standing army serves for two months at a time during the two months before and after Christmas, when little farming is done, and when they can be used for training and guard duties. From then on, we demand their service for a month at a time to enable them to keep their farms running. We pay them well. I train them hard. With the King's approval, I punish severely those who fail in their duties." There was a pause before the assembled Lords cheered and stamped their feet in agreement. Owain ap Pasgen was known for his brutality and, although Gruffydd gave him public support, he had warned him, in private, of the dangers of being too hard on his men.

At their last meeting, Gruffydd had spoken privately to his long-time friend, while Dafydd listened behind a curtain. "Remember, Owain, we are a free nation. I want my countrymen to fight for me because they respect and love me as their King, not because they fear me, or my Generals." He had stared hard at his friend, forcing him to drop his eyes in submission. "I don't want to hear any further reports of you beating men to death for failing to attend your muster. In some cases their wives had recently died; they were trying to keep their families together. You must give punishment on an individual basis, not as a rule." He took a deep breath, and his face relaxed. "I promoted you to General because I have known you a long time. You are loyal and fight well. But, you must now learn how to administer justice while establishing discipline fairly."

Owain had agreed, although a part of him had rebelled. Severe punishment was the only way he knew how to establish discipline. He did not care if the men hated him, as long as they feared him enough to follow his orders. He bowed his way out of the meeting room, but showed no sign of repentance.

"He could be a danger to you, my Lord," Dafydd had warned, as he emerged from behind the curtain. But Gruffydd had always been greatly influenced by family and by long-time allegiances. He shook his head slightly.

"His family has always been friends with my family. I know he makes mistakes, but as Wales increases in strength, and I continue to expand my powerful grip on this wild country, he will, eventually, learn how to command."

"I pray so," Dafydd responded. "But, I suggest you keep a close eye on him. It might be best to appoint someone you can trust to report back on Owain's behaviour. In the long run, he could prove to be a problem.

"Perhaps." Gruffydd stared unseeing at the setting sun. "But I need men like him. Those who will fight for my cause to the last drop of their blood." He walked back to his chair and sat unmoving for a while. "If I expose his violent excesses, I will alienate him and all of his family and friends. I need a secure defense in North Wales. If he and his followers deserted, I would be hard pressed to defend my Northern realm."

"If he murders your friends, their families will quickly cease to support you. I urge you to appoint someone whom you trust to report back on his excesses."

"You may be right," Gruffydd replied. Yet, even as he spoke, he dismissed the idea.

Back in the Great Hall, General Owain completed his report and, smiling broadly, returned to his place. Gruffydd watched him closely. He wished he had listened to his Secretary and kept Owain in the middle ranks. It was always easy to advance men, but any demotion would be certain to cause offense. He glanced at Dafydd, who was silently recording the meeting, and who looked up at that moment. Gruffydd nodded slightly. Dafydd, conscious of the dozens of eyes in the room, returned his eyes to the vellum on which he was writing, his face expressionless. He would arrange for Owen to be watched.

"I call upon Lord Gwriad ap Griffith, General for the South-West and Mid-Wales, for his report. There was a loud roar of approval. Gwriad was popular with the Lords: he was known as a brave fighter and a successful leader. The younger nobility admired his courage, his humour, and his choice of wife. The older Lords remembered he was the elder son of the great General Cydweli, although Gwriad and Dafydd had kept the family name of Griffith on the insistence of their uncle, and in respect for the unique stature of their father. The surname Cydweli , for their family, would end with his memory.

With his usual light touch, Gwriad gave a lively account of a number of small incursions his men had made into Saxon lands. He made passing reference to a small uprising in Brycheinog, where a newly appointed young Lord had tried to steal his neighbour's lands, and would be spending some time in a castle prison. "He did not seem to understand that we don't behave like that any more. But after a while in chains, I think he'll learn." There was a howl of laughter, and much stamping of feet. He bowed to the King. "With your agreement, my Lord, I will send him to you at the end of his stay in prison, so he can renew his Oath of Loyalty." The King nodded, but the smile on his face was short lived, as Gwriad moved on to describe the recent battle with Iago ap Idwal in the mountains of Snowdonia.

"I was pleased to be able to play my small part in the destruction of Lord Iago ap Idwal, who attempted to seize Gwynedd. He was utterly defeated by King Gruffydd and his personal guard. The battle, I understand, was soon over." He bowed towards Gruffydd. "Iago and a few of his remaining supporters fled south, where I, and part of the Army of the South-West, was waiting for him. He refused to surrender and died after a very brief skirmish. Following his death, his followers laid down their arms and were marched back here to await the King's punishment." Gwriad smiled at the King. "I think I can safely report that we will not have any further problems from Iago ap Idwal. Another man who failed to understand that we don't behave like that anymore."

Gruffydd clapped his hands. Then, his face became suddenly severe. "Iago and the young Lord from Brycheinog have learned that I will not suffer insubordination. General Gwriad speaks true: those days are past." He stared grimly at the assembly. "We made ourselves weak in former years, fighting among ourselves for meager gains. That time is over!" He stood up on his raised plinth and stared down at his nobility. "I know that among us today, there are still those who would, given the chance, try to replace me as King; or, at the lowest end of the scale, try to steal their neighbours' cattle!"

There was a sudden silence. All whispering and joking stopped. Without exception, the Lords stared at Gruffydd, some like rabbits before a weasel, as though their most intimate thoughts had been exposed.

"Those days are passed!" he bellowed. "If any man in this hall ever plots against me, I will destroy him and all of his family. None of you will ever challenge my right to rule this country. I have shown you that we can survive only if we are united. Under me, you are wealthier than you have ever been. Your wives and children are safe from invasion, rape and pillage. We are strong, and I intend to keep it so. I will deal with any opposition, from any of you, with the most severe punishment. Do you understand?"

There was a shocked silence, as the assembled Lords slowly digested the warning. In the past it had been their privilege and expected right that each noble, upon the death of his father, would to try to expand his control and wealth at the expense of his neighbours. Those who were nearest the border were the most circumspect, knowing that they would need help from their nearest Lords if they were to survive the constant Saxon attacks. Yet, each Lord had inherited the belief that he could be a king. Until Gruffydd ap Llewelyn, no local king had ever been King of All Wales. They might protest in private and complain of Gruffydd's dictatorship, but none could deny that their lives were easier and richer under his rule. He was the King of All Wales.

Gruffydd knew he had achieved his aim. Without further comment, he called for Prince Rhodri ap Williams, Admiral of the Southern Fleet. He was the young man, whose father, although noble, had been a small landowner near the coast, and from whom Rhodri had gained his love of the sea and his ability to captain a boat. He had made a meteoric rise in Gruffydd's embryonic fleet, after a series of successful engagements with Saxon galleys and French pirates. However, Gruffydd remembered, there had been a time when Rhodri's own ambitious nature had threatened to disturb the fragile peace in the Southern area following the death of the hated Prince Fachan. Gruffydd had taken the advice of Prince Ganny ap Mawr, the new Prince of Morgannwg, and had given the young Prince a responsibility that he had embraced with huge enthusiasm. As Dafydd had dryly observed: "It is easier to use ambition than confront it."

"My Lord King," Rhodri bowed and turned towards the Lords. "We have an expanding fleet of ships, which for the past four years have been protecting the Southern areas. In that time we have learned the skills of fighting on the sea. Our ships have become larger and more effective, as the boat builders become more proficient at their trade. When we first launched our attacks on the Saxons along the Severn, we relied on foreign boats to convey our fighting men to their destinations. Now, we have our own ships that can challenge any enemy vessels. We continue to improve these ships, we dominate the waters of the Severn, and bring considerable wealth to our country." He raised his hand to accept the thunder of approval from the assembly, much of it the result of the awkwardness caused them by the King's speech.

"I am grateful to Prince Rhodri ap Williams for his continued success on the Severn, and his ongoing protection of our Southern ports." Gruffydd stood up and smiled confidently. "For his continued improvement in our navy's strength, his loyalty to me, and to our country, I give him the lands of Llantwit Major and Margam, forfeited to me by Prince Rhys Fachan, who died before he was able to become a part of our united Wales." None was certain if the King had made a joke, and no one laughed. Gruffydd nodded his satisfaction as the Admiral bowed and returned to his gathering of friends.

"Now, I call upon our Admiral for the Northern Fleet, Elwyn Davies, to give his report for our Northern Coast."

Elwyn was a large man in his mid-life, whose family had close ties with the Llywelyn family. He had been one of Gruffydd's wild friends in their younger days. He was an able commander and seemed born to the sea. Under his leadership the Northern Fleet had expanded; it had won most of its engagements against the Pictish galleys, and the trade with Ireland had increased. It was rumoured that Admiral Davies was a favourite with the King.

"My Lord," he bowed to Gruffydd, "I have to report that we now have twenty large galleys patrolling the seas around the Isle of Yns Mon. They are protecting the trading passages to Ireland. Our ships are well manned and well armored; we can defeat anything that the Saxons or the Picts can send against us. For the first time in our history, we have become a powerful nation on the sea. From our ports in Conwy, Caernarfon, and the holy island of Ynys Mon, we can escort our trading ships, preventing the piracy that used to threaten our survival."

There was a resounding cacophony of applause from the nobility: many of them were heavily involved in the new trade with Ireland. Elwyn bowed and returned to his place.

Gruffydd rose from his throne, fixing his gaze on the faces before him. "You are Welshmen," he said, his voice loud yet controlled. "You have witnessed the reports from our Generals and our Admirals. You know, as I do, that we have reached this point in our elevation to greatness by being united. However, our history is a constant list of internecine struggles, where one lord attacked and stole from another. All of that, I repeat, is past! With the blessings of all true Welshmen, I tell you that I will not allow the past to threaten the present!" As he spoke, Gruffydd was conscious of the fact that Dafydd had written these words. He realized the voice of moderation sounded better than his own belligerent way of speaking, and attacking individuals by name. It meant the same, but to the listeners it was softer and more acceptable.

"In this year of 1062, I, Gruffydd ap Llywelyn, King of All Wales and King of the Britons, am the first king in the history of this country to be King of a united Wales. I promise you, my nobles, with your support this fine nation of ours will continue to be a unified country, where peace and honest trade will enable us to protect our borders from our enemies. United we are unbeatable!" He raised his powerful arms above his head, as the whole assembly erupted in a vocal explosion of support.

Gwriad was standing close to his brother and could not resist muttering: "Well done, my young brother, you seem to be having a positive influence on him. I don't think he threatened any of the assembled families by name? Is that a record?"

"Tread gently, brother," Dafydd murmured out of the side of his mouth. "Gruffydd is no man's puppet. I write the stuff, but he decides which parts he will use."

The King left his throne and began to move among the Lords, pressing the hands of many and sharing a joke with those who deserved to be noted, mainly Northern Lords. The hall was filled with sound, enabling the brothers to talk without the chance of being overheard.

"Tell me about Iago ap Idwal," Dafydd said as he acknowledged a friendly wave from Elwyn Davies, the Admiral of the Northern Fleet.

"He was no more than a drunken boaster," Gwriad replied. "He thought that simply by saying he could defeat Gruffydd, he would achieve the result. Gruffydd led the Northern Army with General Owen ap Cynan from one side. I closed the trap from the other. He wanted to keep an eye on Owen. The last thing Gruffydd wanted was for Owen to kill innocent families and cause more unrest than he was intending to put down. It was not a battle, more a slaughter, but Gruffydd showed what he could do. There is no doubt that he still enjoys a fight. As for Iago, he has always been a pain in the arse. The wonder is he lived so long. His son Cynan is of similar ilk; I dare say I will have to knock some sense into him before long. As the elder of his family, he has less sense than my hunting dog and I hear that he is vowing revenge. He is the sort of Welshman who gives us a bad name."

"Is he likely to be a problem?"

"Not unless the country falls apart." Gwriad nodded to Prince Anarwd of Morgannwg, who was a friend of his, and continued his conversation. "We have some fine men in positions of power. If Gruffydd can keep their friendship, then the likes of Cynan ap Iago can whistle in the wind. He is a drunken idiot, who has no more idea of leadership than a chained bull."

"I have heard that he has a following?"

"Perhaps," Gwriad grudgingly admitted. "But, only among the young and the disinherited. His following is a poor rabble of hill farmers and discontented half-Welsh. Their fathers were Irish traders and pirates. They hate Gruffydd because he has prevented them from raiding their neighbours as they used to do."

"Should we deal with him now, when he is still young in the art of rebellion?"

Gwriad looked at his brother in amazement. "You've changed, Dafydd. There was a time when you protested the fact that we did not risk our lives to save some murderous Picts from drowning. Now you're suggesting that I link up with General Owain ap Pasgen and round up some minor discontents because they could be a problem to us in the future. I could just as well round up half the nobles in this room."

Dafydd stared at Gwriad and did not blink. "My job is to protect Gruffydd. I have become his eyes and ears. I will do anything to ensure that he is safe, and his dream for Wales is achieved. His dream is my dream. I want a safe, strong country for my daughter."

Gwriad smiled in true admiration. "I feel I am still the person I was when you and I were chasing the Picts after their attack on Llanduduch. I was a loud, confident lout, always looking for a fight or a good woman. Well, I found the good woman," he added hastily, "and thanks to Gruffydd, my desire to fight has been rewarded. But you," he thumped Dafydd on his back, "you have transformed yourself from the innocent, puritanical, pain-in the-arse, to a confident, political schemer who is the planner and the manipulator of the King himself."

Dafydd grinned back. "Don't let the King hear you, or I'll lose my job." He clasped his brother's arm.

"How's your daughter doing?"

"Tegwen's doing well. She's a big baby, and very demanding. Teifryn adores her, but she's a bit disappointed because Tegwen's got black hair, and hasn't inherited what she calls my distinguished red." He paused, waiting for the expected reaction. He was not disappointed.

"Distinguished?" Gwriad mimicked. "The poor girl will never know how lucky she is not having a head of hair that looks as though it's on fire."

Dafydd accepted the brotherly taunt and his eyes turned towards Gruffydd, who was holding forth to a tight group of special friends. His face became serious. "There is something that I have heard that I want to discuss with you."

"Yes?" Gwriad noted the tone of Dafydd's voice. "You've heard from one of your spies from across the border?"

"Indeed. But not one given to passing on false news." He glanced around to ensure they could not be overheard. "I hear that the Saxon King, Edward the Confessor, has decided that we have become a threat to his throne."

"Is that all?"

"As you know, the man who is really running England is the Earl of Wessex, Harold Godwinson. I understand he's been entrusted with the removal of our King."

"The removal?" Gwriad bellowed, and quickly smiled back at those Lords who had looked his way. "Do you mean Harold intends to send an assassin to murder our King?"

"I don't know." Dafydd's gaze darted about the assembly. "All I know is that this Harold has been ordered to kill Gruffydd by any means." He looked into his brother's eyes. "I do not think this is a false report. I am convinced that we must prepare for an attempt on Gruffydd's life, from a full-blooded invasion, to a single man who has already inveigled his way into the Royal Court, or will try to do so in the future."

"We can't discuss this here. We'll meet at our family castle. I leave for home tomorrow. Perhaps we can travel together. Angharad will be delighted to have time with Teifryn; both women will love to have the time to coo over Tegwen." He clasped his brother's hand. "Let us assume there is no immediate danger. I will alert the King's personal guard to be on an even higher state of preparedness. We need time to think this through. There is no doubt that this Harold is a dangerous man. I have heard he has ambitions to be King of England."

"I know it on firm account that Edward the Confessor has promised the English crown to William the Bastard of Normandy." He rubbed his red hair absent-mindedly. "I have considerable interest in that Norman Earl. He is a rising star. Already, I hear that there are murmurs of discontent in the Saxon capital of London."

"Why?" Gwriad asked. He was aware that, unlike his brother, he knew little of the outside world. Dafydd was in constant receipt of information from paid spies, merchants, and even priests. He had become far more than a mere Secretary: he kept a careful record of all reports that could affect the safety of the King, and the security of Wales.

"Edward the Confessor, who does little other than kneel and pray in his personal church, is spending enormous amounts of money on the building of a huge Cathedral in an area of London called Westminster. It will be the largest building in the country. It is another reason why he wants Earl Harold to defeat us and steal whatever wealth we have to help him to afford this huge and costly building." Dafydd nodded to a minor noble. "I imagine your recent raids and our warships' control of the seas have cost Edward a lot of money that he would have preferred to have spent on his legacy, which is what he wants this Cathedral to be."

"So, if we could launch a powerful strike into the Saxon territories in the near future, we would not only delay the building of this huge church, but we would keep the Earl of Wessex occupied."

"I agree." Dafydd noticed that the King was moving their way.

"We will travel to your castle tomorrow, and plan our next move. I have not worried the King with this news; it will be better to tell him when we have worked out our response."

"Nothing is ever certain." Gwriad had a far-away look in his eye. "It is about time that we launched a powerful raid on the Saxons and reminded them that we are not waiting for them to attack us." He clasped his brother's hand. "In the meantime, we'll discuss this in Ceredigion. I know you have a new house, but the castle is as much yours as mine. I know Angharad is very keen to have both you and Teifryn, and especially young Tegwen to stay."

"You two look as though you're plotting something." Gruffydd laughed, but there was a question in his eyes.

"Plotting how best we can serve you, my Lord," Dafydd said smoothly, as he made a deep bow.

Gwriad gave a brief nod of his head. He felt uncomfortable with the manners of the Court. "I think your speech made it clear, my Lord, that you won't tolerate any more insurrections. The death of Iago ap Idwal has proved a strong reminder to the younger nobles that they will get more than a smack on the hand if they disobey you."

Gruffydd's eyes searched the room, as a number of nobles looked away. "I sometimes think I live in a snake pit," he muttered. "However, today went well." He patted Gwriad on the back and marched off towards a group of nobles from Morgannwg.

"He's mercurial," Dafydd observed. "Behind that blunt good humour is a very suspicious man. He trusts few, apart from the Queen, and rarely reveals much of his true self." He frowned. "He was not always like this."

"Is the Queen privy to the affairs of state? I mean, does she influence his decisions?"

"Does Angharad influence you?"

"Not in the military sense. I discuss most things with her, but anything to do with the army is my concern."

"I think the King believes he makes all his own decisions. I present him with facts and suggestions as to how to proceed. He decides on his actions. However, I think Ealdgyth has changed his mind on a number of issues, after he and I have made a decision.

It was she who persuaded Gruffydd to retire her father from his role as Seneschal."

Gwriad raised his eyebrows. "I thought he retired voluntarily because of age and illness?"

"That was the official line." Dafydd moved closer. "Cadell ap Bleddyn is old, but he's still vigorous. He had no intention of resigning from the post. It was Gruffydd who asked if I thought he could still do the job. We agreed, after some discussion, that Cadell was still the best man, especially with his many years of faithful service."

"But?"

"The next day the King appointed a young Northern Lord, Rhys Gwynedd, to the position. He gave Cadell a lavish farewell, which seemed to satisfy the old man, especially as his daughter is Queen and he could spend more time with his grandson, Prince Cydweli."

"Why was Rhys Gwynedd chosen?"

"Why indeed?" Dafydd glanced around stony faced. "I believe he's a friend of Ealdgyth. Recently, whatever the Queen wants, she gets."

"That confirms what Angharad has been saying. There seems to be an increasing coolness between the sisters, and I think..," Gwriad suddenly gave a bellow of a laugh, and clasped his brother's arm. "Tell your lovely wife we look forward to seeing her, and of course your lovely Tegwen!"

From behind Dafydd, the King had appeared as if intent on joining them, but following Gwriad's outburst, his stern face relaxed and he veered off towards another group.

"He's become a different man, Gwriad," Dafydd said quietly. He was never so suspicious of everyone as he is now. I am even beginning to wonder if he still trusts me."

• • •

OCTOBER 1062

THERE HAD BEEN LITTLE RAIN on the West Coast, and the journey from Rhuddlan to Ceredigion had been relatively easy for Gwriad and Dafydd and their families, servants and soldiers. The constant movement of bodies of troops and cavalry in the past few years had established well-used tracks between the main areas of administration. In the North, there was still evidence of some of the Roman roads constructed in the final stages of the Legions' attack on the holy island of Ynys Mon, the last bastion of the Druids. These roads had lasted nearly seven hundred years but, elsewhere, had been replaced with tracks that became quagmires in winter and baked, dusty paths in summer. There was neither the ability, nor the enthusiasm, to build paved roads in Wales. There was certainly no spare money. It has been argued such roads would, in fact, be helpful to invaders.

"Our fall-back position, if we are invaded by superior forces, is to delay the enemy with ambushes and use the difficult terrain to our benefit," Gwriad explained. "If we improved our roads, the enemy could travel faster; we would lose our advantages."

"If we had good roads," Dafydd argued, "we could move our own troops more quickly to where they were needed, and in all weathers."

"You might like to know that many of the long Roman roads still exist in England; I have it on good authority they have proved to be as much help to invaders as to the defending armies." Gwriad enjoyed arguing with his book-loving brother, especially if it concerned anything to do with military matters.

They made their way to the great hall, where the servants, advised of their coming, had prepared a roaring fire and hot wine. Angharad, meanwhile, had quickly stirred up the kitchen staff, moving through the castle like an earthquake, arousing fear and action in servants grown lazy from her long absence. Teifryn, proud mother of the lusty Tegwen, had sought refuge in her usual room with her maids and Alys, her child's nurse.

"Lady Angharad is a fine woman," Alys observed as she changed the protesting child, "but I would hate to work for her. She has such energy, and such a voice!"

"I will tell her you said that," Teifryn said, as her maids helped her to change quickly out of her damp clothes."

"Oh, no!" Alys exclaimed. "It were meant only for your ears m'Lady."

Teifryn patted her cheek. "You're a fine nurse, young Alys, but after more than a year, you still don't know when I'm joking."

"No, Ma'm. I reckon I do better with babies."

Teifryn was pleased with her lot: she was now the wife of an important man, who was also a loving husband. She was a mother of a healthy child and had servants, fine clothes, and was mistress of a large, new house close to Gruffydd's palace in North Wales. Her daughter, Tegwen, had entered into the world with unexpected ease, partly, she suspected, because of a drink Angharad had insisted she take when she was in labour. "This will make you feel good and it will take away the pain," Angharad had passed it under her nose. "Smells good, doesn't it?"

And it did smell good; she drank it with enjoyment. Up until that time, Queen Ealdgyth's midwife had dominated the bedroom, insisting on hot fires, closed shutters, and some vile drafts she said were necessary to purge the body. She was a large, ugly woman who never smiled. She approached childbirth as though preparing for battle. Her hands were large and rough, she terrorized the servants with slaps and threats. Teifryn had felt vulnerable, and rapidly became frightened of this harridan. It did not help that the old woman had come well recommended from the Queen herself. "She has never lost a baby," Ealdgyth said. "She's not the most friendly of people, but she knows her job."

Teifryn took to her bed as soon the first movements in her belly began. When the contractions were becoming more regular, Angharad appeared and dismissed the maids and the midwife. "I need some time with my sister-in-law," she said firmly; all had obeyed, even the harridan. Later, when the baby was close to arriving, Angharad let the midwife and the maids back into the room. "Call me when the baby is born," she announced, and strode off towards the other side of the large house that Dafydd had recently acquired. In the birthing bed, she had left Teifryn with a beneficent smile on her face.

"What was it you gave me?" Teifryn asked, a while after the birth. The baby was snuffling contentedly on her breast, and although her lower regions were feeling vulnerable, Teifryn felt remarkably well.

Angharad smiled wickedly. "I did not give this to Ealdgyth when she was in labour. I thought she needed to experience the whole event with her own much-praised midwife. My sister can be cold and aloof; she needed to suffer. Whereas you, my friend, did not need to go through the usual pain and suffering that most mothers have to accept."

"But what did you give me?"

"A mixture of something to lessen pain, something to stimulate energy, a natural relaxing herb, and of course, honey." Angharad ran her fingers through her thick black hair. "I may not have given birth, but I know a lot of the ancient ways."

"You sound like a witch," Teifryn opened her eyes in mock horror.

"Oh, I am. At least Gwriad thinks so!" Her rich, sexual laugh had filled the room. For a moment Teifryn believed she really was in the presence of a witch.

In the great hall, Gwriad and Dafydd removed their damp cloaks and their wet boots. They settled down comfortably in front of a roaring fire, so fierce it forced them to move back every so often. The servants had served wine and a variety of roasted meats, cheese, and bread. Both brothers relaxed after the journey, while their wives were enjoying each other's company and taking turns to nurse Tegwen.

'We've done well, you know," Gwriad observed contentedly. "We started our childhood with no mother or father, and only our uncle to help us."

"Gomer did a fine job. I loved that man." Dafydd always felt uncontrollably emotional when he thought about Gomer. "To me, he was like a father. It was different for you. You knew Cydweli in a way I never did."

"Our uncle was a good man. I never realized how good until I

grew older." Gwriad grabbed a chicken leg and chewed hard at the flesh. "I think that was why I always rebelled against him. He was not my father, and because I was the first boy he had to deal with, he was hard on me."

"That could be right. I remember I was rarely beaten by him, whereas you seemed always to be getting a hard thrashing."

They laughed and drank, remembering the good times of their youth. "And here we are today," Gwriad observed. "You're the King's right hand man and I'm his chief General."

"And it's all thanks to Gomer."

"And our father," Gwriad said defiantly. "Cydweli is a name that people remember in this country, even if they don't recall Griffith. I'm sure Gruffydd thought of our father when he promoted us. We are the sons of the great Cydweli and, although Gomer was a good uncle to us, I still maintain it's our father's name that carries us forward with this King."

Dafydd turned his head to look at his brother. "You're right, of course," he observed diplomatically. "But if Gomer had not insisted you marry Angharad, then you would not be the man you are today and I would not be married to her friend Teifryn, nor would I be a father."

"That is the one thing I will be grateful to Gomer for: he made me realize what a remarkable woman Angharad is." He drank deeply. "We are blessed, you and I: we have good wives, you have a child, we both have the jobs we enjoy, and which are important to this country. We both serve King Gruffydd ap Llywelyn and we must ensure that he continues to rule this feuding nation of ours."

Dafydd sipped his wine. "I thought you might have started a family by now?"

"Oh, we're not in a hurry. To be honest, I'm happy to enjoy yours."

"Angharad feels the same way?"

"Indeed." He emptied his cup. "I think she fancies herself more as an aunt than a mother." He refilled his wine. "I'm lucky to have a wife who wants what I want. We're both very happy," he said firmly.

Dafydd took the hint.

There was a short silence, as each brother contemplated his life and his future. The alcohol had begun to take an effect; coupled with the food and the exertions of their journey, they began to nod off.

"What do we do about the threat to Gruffydd?" Dafydd suddenly announced.

Gwriad's eyes flashed open. "Duw! That's why we're here." He sat up in his chair and rubbed his eyes. "I can't stay long. Gruffydd's in his palace at Rhuddlan. He's still hoping to travel around the Southern areas before the snows finally set in." He broke some bread and began to eat it with his usual vigor. "I can't imagine the snow on the roads will allow him to travel down to Morgannwg and back before the Christmas celebration. If he thinks of it, I'll remind him of the time he had to languish in a cold castle on the South Coast one winter." He laughed to himself. "Of course, he will remind me that we benefitted from the experience and learned how to attack the Saxons across the Severn."

"We can exclude the chance of an individual Saxon slipping into this country and trying to assassinate Gruffydd," Dafydd said firmly, wishing to divert his brother from further recollections. "I think it's most unlikely. A Saxon would stand out like a fox in a hen coup." As Gwriad poured himself more wine, the younger brother continued, "There is, however, the chance of one of our own people being bribed, or someone might hate Gruffydd enough to try to kill him. This, again, I think is highly unlikely. His personal guard is trained to look out for people who don't fit in."

"So, we are left with an invasion. The Saxons could launch a full-scale attack, or send over a number of smaller groups, who might try to ambush Gruffydd? Let's talk this through." Gwriad helped himself to a chicken leg. "If it was a full scale invasion, where are they most likely to attack?"

"This is not the question," Dafydd said quietly. "If the Saxons want to kill Gruffydd, they know they are not likely to win a major battle on our territory, and on our terms. Even if they did manage to defeat us, their chances of killing Gruffydd are remote. He is too well protected by his personal guard; he knows better than to lead a charge. If ever there was a defeat, it would be up to Gruffydd

to rally the country to repel the invaders." He sat silently, running his fingers through his wiry hair. "If we are to take this information seriously, and I think we should, we must try to envision it as if we were Saxons."

"As if we were Earl Harold," Gwriad said. "I understand he is the most likely Saxon to launch such an attack." He smiled. "I have given Earl Harold enough reasons to hate me, so perhaps we should also think in terms of Harold trying to kill me as well."

"I think we should concentrate only on the King to start with."

"All right," Gwriad conceded, "let's start with him." He sipped his wine, his mind assessing the possibilities. "When do you think is the earliest time the Saxons could launch such an attack?"

"Early springtime?" Dafydd cut himself a small slice of the chicken's breast. "I can't imagine any General trying to launch an attack in winter."

"I agree. This country is difficult terrain for any invading army and almost impossible in winter." He sat up and rested his chin on his hands as he stared into the fire. "Yet, if I was Earl Harold, I would have to do something that was unexpected. Winter would be the best time to catch us unprepared."

"But, he would have to move slowly; we would have ample time to prepare a counter strike." Dafydd also sat forward. The two brothers remained silent while they stared at the glowing logs. "We must always remember that this attack, if the report is correct, is aimed at killing the King. Which would mean knowing where the King was in residence, or creating a situation where he would feel it necessary to lead his forces. Now, at this time of the year, apart from an unlikely visit south, he would always be in his palace at Rhuddlan. He certainly intends to spend Christmas with the Queen and his two sons at his newly improved palace. Could the Saxons attack Rhuddlan, do you think?"

"Most unlikely. The Saxons would have to travel over very difficult country. There is always snow at Christmas and the high ground is usually blocked until February or March. Also, there is General Owain and his Northern Army in the Caernarfon barracks. I think it is more likely that Harold would try an invasion in spring, and attempt to draw Gruffydd to lead a counter-attack."

"I agree," Dafydd said. "Yet, I think we have to be prepared for the unexpected. I have heard enough about the Earl of Wessex to know that he is not a man to be underestimated."

"We know he can't fly," Gwriad said. He raised his eyebrows in a mocking smile. "I suggest we enjoy the winter, as best we can, and get some firm information in the New Year."

"I hope you're right," Dafydd answered. He looked grave and shook his head. "If he caught us off-guard, we might not have a second chance."

"All right. If it will make you feel better, I will post a hundred of my cavalry at Ruthin and they can stay there until spring. It will give them a chance to get to know the area."

"Why Ruthin?

"It's not too close to the border, yet well placed to oppose a thrust from Chester. Also it's not too far from the King's palace at Rhuddlan, so if there were to be a threat, they could quickly reinforce the King's personal guard. Also, I have established some barracks there."

"That's good." Dafydd yawned.

"I think we have worried this one to its conclusion," Gwriad yawned in response. "It's time to see our wives and find out how their day went."

"We know how their day went," Dafydd said. "It's how they want their day to conclude that matters." He raised his eyes in a meaningful way.

"You old ram!" Gwriad exclaimed. "Welcome to the world of men! " He slapped his brother on the back. "There are times when I forget you're married!"

Dafydd pinched Gwriad's nose. "Remember, I'm no longer the ignorant younger brother."

The brothers picked up their cups of wine and, in good humour, made their way to find their respective wives.

CHAPTER THIRTEEN

NOVEMBER 1062

It was a cold November night, and early snow had been falling for
some hours. In his castle at Litchfield, Harold, Earl of Wessex,
waited patiently for his chilled guests to disrobe, warm themselves
by the fire, and fill their bellies with food and drink. He was a large
man in his early middle age, with a reputation for ruthless and
decisive action. His face was notable for the dark piercing eyes
and the thick corn-colored moustache that hung down on either
side of his broad mouth. He was strong, physically impressive,
and used to getting his own way. Eventually, the four Lords he had
invited recovered from their unpleasant journeys, and were ready
to discuss the matter that most concerned him.

"My Lords, I thank you for answering my request for help."
He smiled at each of the local nobility, knowing as he did so, that
none of them would have dared to refuse his invitation to meet at
his castle, no matter how severe the weather. "Our holy King has
asked me to settle the Welsh problem. I have asked you to attend
this meeting to advise me as to the best way of moving against
Gruffydd ap Llewelyn." He nodded to each Saxon Lord in turn.
"You have all suffered from the recent attacks by the new Welsh
armies; I am confident that you will give me your upmost support
in a once-and-for-all invasion that will rid us of the problem of this
Welsh threat to our homes."

There was a quick nodding of heads. Two of the Lords jumped
to their feet, raising their mugs of wine in an impetuous display of
support. One of them only had one arm.

"The question I have to put to you is this: where would you
attack Wales? Would it be in the North, by way of Holywell? In

241

mid-Wales by Offa's Dyke? Further south through Montgomery? Or via the Severn and up through Caerdydd?"

There was a long silence, as each Lord waited for another to commit himself.

"I think the attack on Caerdydd is a good one," suggested Wirt, a young Lord from Deerhurst, in the South. He was a muscular man, who had only recently inherited his family estates. As the youngest of the Lords, he knew the older, more experienced nobles would reject his ideas, but at least he would have made a contribution. Wirt had gained a reputation as a fearless fighter and had a confidence that irritated the senior nobles. He was keen to be recognized by Harold, who could well become the next King; this was the first time he had been included in the Earl's inner circle.

"What about the Welsh fleet?" Harold stared unblinking. "I am told they have many galleys, while we lack ships that can defeat them at sea." He failed to mention that the building of new galleys was well under way.

"I was thinking that we might try to avoid them," Wirt answered. "If we sent some of our older ships to create a diversion, the main fleet could then land soldiers and attack Caerdydd. This might draw Gruffydd down from his mountain lair."

Harold nodded slowly. "A good idea. Thank you, Lord Wirt. Next?"

The young Lord sat down and stretched out his long legs. He felt valued.

"I would speak against an attack through Montgomery, or at the southern end of Offa's Dyke," a tall, elderly Saxon said. He was Lord Alwel, a one-armed man, who in his early days had been a ferocious warrior. "I know the area. We have been defeated often in that land. It is a hard country and favours the Welsh." He paused. "Also, it is easily reached by the army commanded by their General Gwriad ap Griffith. He's a fine officer and has been responsible for many of our defeats in that area."

Harold's face creased with irritation, yet he knew Alwel was correct in his analysis. He turned to the other two. "What about the northern end of Offa's Dyke?"

There was a long pause before Lord Drefan spoke. He was a powerful Saxon warrior in his early forties. "My Lord, there is no easy way to successfully invade Wales. Their borders are well patrolled. They have platoons of professional soldiers trained to respond immediately to an invasion. While they defend their local territory, a second wave of trained soldiers, drawn from their farms and small villages will have time to assemble and counter-attack. All of this I know from spies across the border. It is both King Gruffydd ap Llewelyn, and his General Gwriad Griffith who are responsible for this impregnable defense."

"Impregnable?" Lord Modig queried. He was a heavy man, past middle age, with a huge belly and face dominated by large, disfigured nose, broken in his younger days when he had acquired a reputation for bravery in battle.

"Indeed," Lord Drefan replied. "No longer can we mount an attack on Wales without the knowledge that we will sustain huge losses. They have well-trained soldiers, now. No longer are we facing a mob of farmers. Their soldiers are well armed, well trained, and know how to best use their difficult terrain. Their cavalry, which once was weak and untrained, is now a fine military machine. I believe we have no hope of defeating them in a set battle on their own lands." He locked eyes with Harold. "Our only way, my Lord, is to mount a surprise attack, when they least expect us; when their spies have had no knowledge of our intentions."

Harold sat back in his great chair and gazed up at the blackened beams of his cold hall. "I think that is an idea we will explore." He directed a servant to refill the wine cups. "Where would you suggest we mount this surprise attack, Drefan?"

"In the North, my Lord, and along their coast."

"But, the Northern lands are the most difficult to cross. I'm told there are few places of any importance until we have advanced deep into Wales?" Harold raised his large shaggy eyebrows.

"I agree. Which is why we should choose that area. It is where the Welsh least expect us to invade." Lord Drefan took a long drink of his wine, knowing he had the full attention of everyone. "If it is our intention to kill King Llewelyn, we should launch a surprise attack on his Northern palace, not draw him into a full

243

scale battle. He has proved that if we fight him on his terms, he will win. But, if we do the unexpected, we could destroy him and his personal guard, before his armies can be mobilized."

"We will explore this plan," Harold said, trying not to sound too enthusiastic. "Our spies tell us that Gruffydd has established his winter palace at Rhuddlan; some of his Northern Fleet is based at Conwy." He stood up and addressed the four Lords. "I want you to report back, a week from today, with your plans. I want your assessment of the number of troops I will need, the distance we must travel, anything you can discover about the palace, and how we can hide our preparations and our invasion." He beckoned to his Chamberlain, who was standing at the furthest end of the room.

"Goodnight, my lords. Thank you for your support. My Chamberlain will attend to your needs."

The Lords rose to their feet and gave Harold a deep bow as he marched out of the hall. They sat down and remained silent as the servants filled their cups, brought in roasted meats, and dragged in palliasses, which they arranged close to the fire.

"I hope we're not going to regret this brilliant plan of yours, Drefan," Lord Modig muttered. "I don't fancy a sneak attack across unknown terrain in the dead of winter. It's never been done before and for good reason. Count me out."

Lord Alwel nodded his head, and the young Lord Wirt frowned at the floor. Lord Drefan sniffed loudly. "You have no choice, my Lords. None of you came up with an alternative. I will not be the one to tell Earl Harold that we have changed our minds. You will."

• • •

EARLY DECEMBER 1062

DARKNESS HAD SETTLED WHEN THE King returned from an unsuccessful hunting trip. It had been cold and windy throughout the day and the rain had scythed down, soaking the riders to the skin. The rest of his party had been withdrawn and lacking the good humour and camaraderie that he usually enjoyed. He wondered if he had been partly to blame. He had not been sleeping well and was aware that things he normally disregarded as unimportant were irritating him. Now, as he was dismounting near the stables, the young groom holding the bridle of his horse sneezed loudly. The animal veered suddenly away, causing Gruffydd to stagger, and narrowly avoid falling in the mud.

"Damn you!" he yelled angrily. "Control yourself!"

In the flickering torchlight, he was an imposing and violent figure. The young boy was so frightened by Gruffydd's reaction that he began to shake with fear, and tears streamed down his face.

"Enough, you sniveling idiot. Get out of my way!" He raised his hand and the boy quickly dragged the horse to the side. Around him the nobility, who had hunted with him, watched in silence.

As Gruffydd stamped angrily up the stairs to the main hall, he felt guilty of overreaction; this intensified his black mood. He crossed the hall, nodding briefly to members of his Court, who were sitting on stools at the trestle tables, eating and drinking. The good-natured hubbub ceased as they stood up and bowed. He took a moment to warm himself by the hot fire, conscious of the sudden tension in the room.

"Drink up!" he roared. "It's not a night to be sober." His comments were well received. A number of nobles raised their cups to him. He turned away and quickly entered the short corridor to his bedchamber. As he did so, the door opened and Rhys Gwynedd, his new Seneschal, appeared. He bowed deferentially, carefully closing the door behind him.

"Your Majesty."

"Get me wine and hot food and bring it to my chamber."

"Yes, my Lord." He paused, and seemed awkward. "Is there anything else I can bring your Majesty?"

"No." The man was efficient, but Gruffydd found himself unable to like him. He had a simpering, insincere quality about him that was so unlike Cadell ap Bleddyn, who had seemed, and was, part of the family. He realized he missed Cadell, who had always known what was needed to be done, and had been both a servant and a friend. "That will be all," he said, waving Rhys away from the door.

"Your majesty." He bowed deeply, and finally, after clumsily attempting to open the door with a loud: "Allow me, your Majesty," hurried away towards the kitchen.

Gruffydd snorted with impatience and pushed open the door. Ealdgyth was standing with her back to him, facing towards the fire. She turned with a start, and he noticed how the fire had reddened her cheeks.

"Welcome home, my Lord! I had not expected you until later." She moved away from the heat. "Was the hunt successful?" She kissed him on his cheek.

"No." The black mood began to lift as he warmed himself. "It was wet and cold and the hounds failed to pick up a scent. It's good to be back." He threw off his heavy sheepskin, and sat in a large chair, bending forward to remove his boots.

Ealdgyth kneeled down in front of him. "Let me, my Lord." He relaxed back and watched her with approval. She was an attractive woman. Motherhood had not caused her to gain weight, as it did in many women. She wore a simple dress, yet one that seemed to amplify her breasts and clung to her hips.

"How are the boys?" They never seemed to be around in the evening, and unless he visited the nursery he rarely saw them.

"They are well, my Lord. The nurse has only just returned them to their nursery. They needed feeding." She had employed a wet nurse for both babes, and had told Gruffydd that royal women did not breastfeed, nor did they perform menial tasks. It was for servants to feed, clean them, and wash them.

He leaned forward, and placing his hands on both sides of her face, kissed her with a rousing passion.

"My Lord, forgive me. I'm still unwell." She drew back and removed his hands. "I have a problem caused by the last, lost birth. I'll soon be better, but I cannot share your bed until I have recovered." She stood up, a sad smile on her flawless face. "You're a fine man for understanding."

Gruffydd made a face and sank back into his chair. "Have you seen a wise woman?"

"Yes," she lied. "I'm taking some herbs."

"It's been a while," he grumbled.

"Yes," she said, obliquely. "I'll call a servant to get you wine."

"I've ordered it. I met Rhys Gwynedd on his way out." He stretched, his body reacting to the cooling of his ardour. "What did Rhys want?" He pushed out his legs towards the fire.

"He's been supervising the servants and taking my orders," she said, vaguely.

Gruffydd grunted. "I don't like the man. He fawns about me, and I feel uncomfortable with him. I preferred your father."

Ealdgyth picked up his boots and placed them to one side of the fire. "He's new to the job, my Lord. But, he's doing well. I find him pleasant enough and I'm the one who gives him most of his orders." She smiled, revealing her fine, white teeth. "After all, you're too busy with big issues to worry about the day-to-day running of our palace."

There was a knock at the door. Two servants entered with wine, soup, bread and roasted meats. When they had gone, Gruffydd poured two cups, handed one to Ealdgyth, and proceeded to demolish the food with his customary appetite. The Queen watched him quietly. When he had finished, she replenished his wine and began to pace about the room.

"I think you may be in danger," she said.

He lowered his cup and sat up in his chair. "What makes you say that?" He had received no reports from his Secretary or from his senior officers.

"You remember, I warned you that it was dangerous to keep people in positions of power for too long?"

"You were referring to your father, I believe," Gruffydd drank deeply, preparing to ignore her first comment. "And I wish I'd not listened to you. I was much happier when he was around."

Ealdgyth pursed her lips. "It was not just my father I was referring to, my Lord. You, yourself, must be aware that there are men about you who have become much more powerful than you ever intended. They're ambitious men." She saw Gruffydd frown. "I worry about you, my Lord. You're so trusting. You have such a noble mind; you believe others are the same." She knew he could not resist compliments. "I have heard whispers, from around the Court, that there is a plot against you."

"Who?" He glared at her. "Who plots against me?"

She rubbed her hands together and touched her mouth, as if unable to speak the words. "I'm told it is those closest to you; the ones with the most power."

"Are you meaning Dafydd, my Secretary?" He was almost yelling. "He's my most faithful adviser."

"Then why hasn't he warned you that his brother has brought his army from Deheubarth into Powys? Why has he done this in secret, if not to threaten you, my Lord?"

"Who told you this?" He stood up, his fists clenched at his side.

"It is common knowledge, my Lord. Even the servants know." She rushed to him and threw her arms around his neck. "But you have time to act. Did you know people refer to them as the Great Griffith Brothers? They call them the next Kings." Gruffydd stared at her as if she was mad. "They must be removed before it is too late," she urged. "If you arrest Dafydd, you will cut off the information to his brother Gwriad. Then you can move against him before he's forewarned."

"Enough!" He pushed her away. "Gwriad is married to your sister! He's family. He's my most important General. Why would he plot against me?"

"He's powerful. He leads the strongest army. He's the one most likely to seize your throne." She was desperate. Her plan had gone awry. If only he had not returned so soon, she would have been better prepared. When she discovered from Angharad that Gwriad had moved his soldiers to Powys, she saw her chance to remove both brothers, and her annoying sister at one fell swoop. As she had said to Rhys Gwynedd, "I will not be spied on. I will be Queen on my terms, even if I have to replace every one of my husband's followers."

"Speak no more of this to me!" He thrust his feet into his boots.

"My Lord, I had to tell you."

"Enough!" he roared. He picked up his sheepskin.

"Nobody else dared warn you!" she cried, as he left the room, slamming the door behind him.

Without hesitating, he marched through the main hall, ignoring the nobles who got to their feet. He flung open the door, causing the guards on the steps outside to jump to attention. It was raining hard. He shrugged on his sheepskin as he passed the stables, and stomped towards the main gate, where guards opened a door and stood to attention. Waving a hand to dismiss them, he turned towards the village. He made his way along a narrow, muddy lane, passing a collection of shacks, and came to a small hut, where a candle flickered in the single window. He knocked twice and heard a bolt slide across. A young woman opened the door.

"Welcome, my Lord," she whispered, as she checked the path in both directions. Gruffydd entered; the door was bolted; the candle went out in the window.

. . .

EARLY DECEMBER 1062

EARL HAROLD GODWINSON WAS ALONE in his bedchamber at a large house in Chester. He had been there a week, preparing for his eventual attack on the Welsh King. He had been in close conference for four days with his small group of Saxon Lords. His wife, whom he saw infrequently, had remained in their castle at Litchfield and was unaware of his true reason for moving to this border town before the festival of Christ Mass. She assumed it was one more nail in the coffin of her marriage.

Outside, snow was piling up against his shuttered windows, already knee deep in the courtyard. It was going to be a hard winter. Harold was feeling impatient and confined by the elements. He longed for action and, in his fortieth year, sensed that time was rapidly passing him by. He was certain he was at the tipping point of his career where he could achieve greatness or slip back into a quiet life of hunting and local administration, which others expected, and which he found unacceptable. Although he lived in a luxury that many envied, it was not enough. He wanted to be King.

Harold poured mead into a silver goblet, put on a gauntlet,

withdrew an iron poker from the fire, and dipped it into the liquid. There was a loud hiss and steam rose from the goblet. He replaced the poker, removed the glove, and sipped at the hot drink.

If he could defeat the Welsh King, and preferably kill him, Harold was certain it would be a victory that would echo throughout the Saxon lands. His claim to the throne would have to be acknowledged by the weak King Edward. Harold had a deep respect for the Welsh King, although he would deny it in Court. He recognized that Gruffydd had, against all odds, transformed Wales from a loose alliance of warring princedoms into a unified country. As a younger man, Harold remembered the shockwave that had travelled through the Saxon world when their powerful army had been defeated at the battle of Rhyd-y-Groes. Gruffydd, the new King of Gwynedd, was relatively unknown at that time, but had managed to unite with some of the other Welsh princedoms, and had clearly demonstrated what could be achieved. Since then, he had reinforced his grip on the country, becoming a tangible threat to England.

Across the Channel, he knew that William, Duke of Normandy, known as the Bastard, waited patiently for King Edward to die. It was an open secret that the Confessor, without any direct heirs, had promised the throne to William. Some argued it was a clever move, for there were many powerful Saxon Lords who felt they had strong claims to the throne. By appointing William, it might avoid conflict. Harold scowled. He disliked the idea of a Norman sitting on the throne of England.

In recent years the Norman influence had increased: Saxon Lords drank Norman wines, and their women wore the fashions favoured by Norman royalty. Trade between the two realms continued to expand, the great Cathedral at Westminster was being built to Norman specifications, and even the army was beginning, reluctantly, to adopt the concept of heavy cavalry.

The pious Edward will not live much longer, he thought, as he gazed sleepily into the fire. At that moment, a large ember spilled out onto the stone grate with a crash. He shook himself awake. Recently, he had spoken to Edward's doctor who agreed that the King was always ill during winter; each year he became worse. If

Harold could carry out the defeat of the Welsh before Edward died, he may yet persuade him to abrogate his agreement with William. He muttered his recent mantra: "It is best for England if I prevent the Norman bastard from gaining the crown."

"Brandon!" he called, jumping to his feet. His servant appeared almost immediately. "Get the Lords to attend me!"

The servant seemed confused. "Now, my Lord? It's past midnight."

"I know what time it is!" he bellowed. "Get them here, now!"

Brandon quickly disappeared, leaving Harold to prowl the room like a caged cat. He poured himself more mead. His mind was racing. If I am to defeat Gruffydd, then I must do what he would least expect me to do, and I must act soon, no matter what the cost. He will be at his winter palace. If I attack him now, it will be difficult, but not impossible. If I wait until spring, he will be ready for me. I would need a large army with no certainty of success. He drank deeply. Every passing moment could be Edward's last. If he dies before I have beaten the Welsh, then my hopes are dashed and William will become King.

For four days he had planned and argued with Lord Drefan and the others. The one-armed Lord Alwel and the overweight Lord Modig had favoured caution, while Lord Drefan, supported by the young Lord Wirt, had presented a number of possibilities that might enable a small army to attack Gruffydd's palace before the Welsh could mobilize.

Lord Drefan was the first to arrive. "My Lord," he complained, "I was in bed with a warm woman on this very cold night. I hope your inconvenient invitation is important." He was a blunt man, who possessed great strength and feared nobody. Drefan acknowledged Harold's seniority as the powerful Earl of Wessex, but he spoke as an equal.

"Drefan, I would not have summoned you if it was not important," Harold said. He was always single-minded and unconcerned with the plans of others. "We must agree on our tactics and begin our preparations, immediately. For the next few weeks we can be certain that the Welsh will be keeping inside their homes, celebrating Christ Mass, or one of their pagan festivals, keeping their doors closed to the snow and cold. We have much to do and little time left if we are to catch them off-guard."

Lord Modig entered, followed by Lord Alwel. Both men had been drinking and looked unsteady. Modig belched loudly and sank down on a stool near the fire. He seemed amused as Alwel collapsed on the bed.

"Brandon! Get a bowl of water and a towel and attend to Lord Alwel," Harold said. There was derision in his voice: he had little time for a man who was unable to hold his drink. "Where's the young Wirt?"

"Probably with his boy friend," Drefan replied. He helped himself to mead, and repeated Harold's actions with the poker. "Not that it makes much difference; he's still a dangerous man on the battle field." He glanced at Brandon as he bustled through the door. "Perhaps your servant didn't feel comfortable giving him the message?"

For a moment, Harold stared at Drefan, as though lost for words. "I never guessed," he murmured. Although in truth, he had known for a while. He had thought it might be a useful secret to know, and was disappointed that it was common knowledge.

"He might not be interested in your daughters, but he's very ambitious." Modig clasped his hands over his huge belly. "I wouldn't want him behind me in a fight. He might forget who his enemy is."

"I can use him," Harold said. "Unlike some of you," he looked pointedly at Modig, "he's come up with some ideas. He prefers action to feasting."

"Ah, action. Yes, indeed." Modig smirked and winked at Drefan, who ignored him.

"Brandon." Harold turned to his servant who was attempting to revive the drunken Alwel. "Fetch Lord Wirt. Now!" The servant began to bow his way out of the chamber. "Then, bring some hot food and warm milk," he nodded towards Alwel, who was holding his head.

After a short while, Lord Wirt arrived and gave a small bow to Harold. If he felt awkward, he did not show it. "Forgive my tardiness, my Lord, I did not receive your first urgent message."

He acknowledged Lord Drefan, and pointedly ignored Modig, who blew him a kiss. "I see Lord Alwel has been raising his arm to good effect," he joked.

"He's been drinking with friends," Modig said pointedly. "How have you been spending your time?" There was a hostile silence as the two men faced each other.

"We'll start the meeting," Harold ordered. But at that moment, there was a knock on the door. Brandon entered with a jug of hot milk, and two other servants entered with plates of roasted meats and bread, and jugs of mead. The Lords helped themselves, and it was not until the food was eaten, and Lord Alwel was able to sit upright on a stool, that the meeting began.

"We must agree our plans tonight," Harold said, glaring around the small circle. "Time is not on our side." There was a general nodding of heads. "I am convinced that an attack along the coast is possible, but only with horses."

"Why so?" Modig said. "We have few horses and our soldiers fight best on foot."

"I agree, but we will need to come in from two positions. Some on horse, the most we can muster, and the majority, the foot soldiers, will travel by boat." Harold raised his hand to stop any interruption. "Lord Wirt, I want you to explain your plan for the invasion by boat."

"I hope we're not taking you away from something important?" Modig jested, ignoring Drefan's cold stare.

With barely hidden anger, Wirt explained an idea he had discussed with Harold. "If our foot soldiers tried to cross the border, advancing from Chester, they would quickly be reported. In this weather they would have advanced very few miles before being intercepted by Welsh forces that could be quickly reinforced. It's possible that any large assembly of soldiers in Chester would be reported before they even crossed the border; the Welsh have many spies in the town. However, if we assemble the soldiers to the north, they would not be noticed."

There was a general grunt of agreement.

Wirt began to relax. "There is a large river, some miles north of Chester, that flows into a wide estuary. There is a small port on the other side called Llif Pwll, Welsh for eel pool," he said, proud of his knowledge.

"Get on with it," Lord Alwel muttered. His head was hurting.

"We could assemble the soldiers at this port over a few days and transport them, as soon as the weather allowed, down the estuary and round the headland. Then, it is a fairly short journey across open water to the Welsh coast. I suggest we land a few miles east of Conwy. I have learned there are some suitable beaches north of their village of Rhuddlan, which is where the Welsh King has built a palace. It is almost certain that he will spend his time there for the next few weeks."

"Where did you learn about this?" Drefan asked. He seemed impressed.

"I know a friend from that area," Wirt said, his face suddenly aflame.

"Good," Harold grunted. "We may be able to use fishing boats if there is a suitable wind; but I would prefer galleys. If there are some in the area, we will commandeer them."

"What if there aren't enough boats to carry the men?" Lord Alwel was sobering-up.

"There are a number of small villages along the estuary, and up the river," Wirt said. "There should be enough fishing boats."

Lord Alwel slowly shook his head. "We need galleys, or fair-sized trading vessels. We're asking for trouble if we have to rely on small sailing boats which need a suitable wind and can be affected by the currents and tides. Soldiers don't like travelling on the water. If we use small boats, most of the men will arrive sick or drowned." His words were slurred, but his thoughts were clear.

"That's too extreme," Drefan protested. "If the weather's suitable and the sea is calm, how long do you think it would take to get from Llif Pwll to the Welsh beaches?"

Wirt frowned. "I think we could sail there in four hours, maybe five, depending on the conditions. Perhaps less than three hours by galley."

"Good. We'll send out horsemen to seize all the boats we can in that area." Harold turned to Wirt. "You will be in charge of finding enough boats to carry the soldiers." He rubbed his forehead.

"There'll be at least five hundred men." He stood up and began to pace the room, deep in thought. "I want you to leave tomorrow. I'll arrange for a mounted escort. Get agreements with the local people if possible; I will provide money. Take their boats by force if they are unwilling and set guards on them. Send reports back to me as soon as you have a clear idea if this will work."

He placed a strong arm on the young Lord's shoulders, as he walked him to the door. "You will stay up at Llif Pwll. If this invasion goes ahead, one of us will join you. As you will not be able to return to your lands, send word to your family before you leave, for them to provide armed soldiers. They will muster north of Chester in a week's time. I will decide later as to where that will be." He stared, unblinking into Wirt's eyes, as if trying to read his mind. "We must move quickly; in secret. Do well, and I will not forget."

"I will report back to you as soon as I am able." The young Lord left with a swagger in his step. His new friend, who knew about Rhuddlan, and whom Wirt suspected was a Welsh spy, would be fed some false information. It pleased him to think the fisherman had become the fish. His friend, who went under the name of Egbert, pretended to be a travelling troubadour, which enabled him to enter the houses of the rich and the important. He was a pleasant man, but he had not deceived Wilt, who throughout his mature life had grown skilled at deception. He could quickly recognize it in others. Yes, he thought, Egbert could be useful to him and he would inform the Earl of what he had done if the invasion was a success. It would be good to have such a powerful ally, for he was well aware that Lords, such as Modig, would seize any opportunity to bring him down.

• • •

THE MORNING AFTER GRUFFYDD'S ARGUMENT with Ealdgyth, at the end of one of their regular meetings, Dafydd stood up and began to gather together the numerous reports that he had dealt with. They ranged from the launch of another galley for the Southern Fleet, to an analysis of the increasing trade with Ireland. Apart from the positive news, there had been reports of further unrest in some mountain villages, following the defeat of Iago ap Idwal. There had also been a rejection by King Mark of the Camori Tribe of a formal alliance between Wales and Cornweal, a clear challenge to Gruffydd's wish to be King of the Britons. It had been a difficult meeting, and Gruffydd had seemed unhappy throughout. He was a man of enormous energy, capable of absorbing a wealth of information, and often witty and perceptive in his responses. Yet, three times he had asked Dafydd to repeat a report, and had ignored his Secretary's attempts at droll humour.

An ominous silence hung in the room after Dafydd had concluded his final report. He observed the King with increasing unease. Gruffydd had arrived late, dressed in body armor and wearing a sword, as though going hunting or preparing for some sword fighting in the exercise yard. He seemed gripped with some deep worry.

"Is there anything more I should know?"

"No, my Lord. Those were the important issues."

"Think carefully, Dafydd. Is there anything more I should know?" Gruffydd's voice shook with emotion. "Do you know of some conspiracy against me, perhaps?"

"Apart from the pathetic ranting of Iago ap Idwal's son, Cynan, I know of nothing that I need to bring to your attention, my Lord."

Gruffydd leapt to his feet. Although built like an ox, he was shorter than Dafydd, and was forced to look up at him. "Which of you wants my throne?" he bellowed. He pushed Dafydd back into his seat and stood over him, a blue vein pulsing on his forehead. "Tell me! Is it you, or Gwriad? He has the military power, but you have the brains. And to think I trusted you both!" He moved back and sat on the edge of the oak table, his hand resting on the pommel of his sword. His eyes staring at his Secretary with unconcealed loathing.

Over the past years, Dafydd had come to know the King like a brother, and had always been comfortable in his company. He had served as Secretary to the best of his ability and had, until very recently, been confident in Gruffydd's unconditional approval of his work. But, in the past few weeks there had been a subtle change in their relationship. First, Gruffydd had appeared awkward at any mention of the Queen. Then, he had begun to ask unexpected questions, hinting at issues not revealed, yet not pertinent to the subjects they were dealing with. Now, it was as if a mist had blown away, revealing a deep crevasse between them.

Dafydd rose slowly to his feet, and bowed deeply. "My Lord, I have always been your true servant and friend; I always will be." He spoke quietly, but with undeniable passion. "I have no idea who has poisoned your mind with these lies," he paused, noting the guilt that crossed Gruffydd's face. "But, I swear that my brother and I would lay down our lives for you." He waited while the King absorbed his words. "Furthermore, my Lord, you know this to be true. Who has turned you against us? And what lies have they used to destroy your trust in us?"

"You have been plotting to assassinate me at my palace this winter!" He clenched his left hand. "You can't deny that your brother has been increasing the number of his soldiers in this area!"

Dafydd nodded in agreement. "That is true, my Lord. He did the same last winter, as well you know." Gruffydd glared, but said nothing. "Every time he gets a rumour of a possible invasion, or I get word from my spies of another attempt on your life, General Gwriad always reinforces your Majesty's army."

"He did not have to bring up his own forces from Deheubarth to reinforce my safety. I have a Northern Army for that."

"Indeed, my Lord. But, you will remember you ordered General Owain ap Pasgen to winter the Northern Army in Caernarfon, to prevent any further insurrection from the local tribes, both there and on Ynys Mon." Dafydd was puzzled: the King had discussed this issue some weeks ago. Caernarfon had been chosen as a logical place to house the soldiers before the snows made travel difficult. The old Roman fort of Segontium was the major reason that Caernarfon had been chosen. In the past few years it had been partially restored. It provided a strong defensive position in which to accommodate the officers and the small standing army that provided security from Irish barbarians, whom the Welsh called *anwariads*. Having a well-armed permanent army, was also a powerful deterrent to local insurrections.

"Are you saying there is some new report of a threat to my life from the Saxons? If so, why am I unaware of it?"

"My Lord, I receive many reports of plots and possible incursions by the Saxons. But, as your Secretary it is my job to try not to burden you with unnecessary detail."

"Yet, you encouraged your brother to bring his troops to Ruthin before the heavy snow arrived. For what reason?"

"My Lord, General Gwriad has billeted a mere hundred horsemen at Ruthin, certainly not his whole army. He has done so because I received a report that I am still investigating. It could be nothing, but if there was a move against your Majesty's palace during the winter, then General Gwriad is well placed to intercept the enemy." He watched the tension ease on the King's face. "Your Majesty has been troubled for the past few weeks; I was loath to add to your burdens with warnings that might be mere gossip."

There was a silence as Gruffydd scratched his beard, which he often did when he was deep in thought. Dafydd decided to risk his anger. "My Lord, the only person who could know of this troop movement is your wife, the Queen..." Gruffydd's eyes flashed, "... who would have learned of it from her sister."

"My wife keeps me better informed than you do!"

Dafydd winced. "Angharad and her servants arrived at my house, yesterday, when you were out hunting, my Lord. She visited your wife last night, while you were still away. I imagine Angharad would have explained why she had arrived without her husband. I am expecting General Gwriad to arrive sometime tomorrow, at which point we were going to review this latest report and bring it to your Majesty's attention, if we thought it important. He's been inspecting his troops at Ruthin and gathering local reports. We have both been doing our jobs, as we thought best, on behalf of your Majesty." He dropped to one knee. "We are loyal, my Lord, we always have been." He took a deep breath as he stood up. "I wonder why, in the past weeks, her Majesty has ceased to trust us? We are all family. We are devoted to helping you, as our King, to rule a united Wales. Why has the Queen turned you against us?"

Gruffydd twisted his head from side to side, as if releasing a crick in his neck. He felt outraged that Dafydd had dared to mention the Queen. But there was some truth in what he said. Something had changed between himself and Ealdgyth in the past few weeks. She was less amorous and more demanding. Perhaps he had been away too often? Yet, she was the one who worried about his safety; she had passed on the news of the troop movements. "Ealdgyth alerted me to information I should have been told."

"Your sister-in-law, General Gwriad's wife, told her! Where is the plot in that, my Lord?"

He chewed his lower lip. He had not been sleeping well since his return to the palace, partly because he had been denied his marital rights as Ealdgyth was suffering from some female complaint, partly because of his growing conviction that there was a conspiracy to kill him. Gruffydd knew he had no evidence of any such plot, but the thought had gradually intensified. He was convinced it had some foundation. If it was not Dafydd, then it must be his brother. But again, he had no proof of his treachery either, only a growing, nagging doubt. The brothers were too close to the throne, too powerful. Other members of the nobility had hinted at the Griffith family's control over the running of the country. Now Ealdgyth was concerned.

"We will say no more," he muttered. More than anything, he wanted to return to the jovial, light-hearted days when he and his Secretary would plan a new future for Wales. But somehow those days had faded away to be replaced by tension and suspicion on his part and a cautious restraint by Dafydd. Even the nobles in Court had become less spirited and engaging. "When General Gwriad arrives, send him to me."

Dafydd watched him stride out of the room and wondered, sadly, if the King had worn his sword for a reason. Could it be that he felt the need to protect himself from his closest advisers? He would consult Teifryn and get her to speak with Angharad. If anyone could discover what Ealdgyth was up to, her elder sister could.

· · ·

It was later in the morning when Angharad, having recovered from her journey of the night before, joined Teifryn, who was rocking her baby in a crib. It was warm and welcoming in the main room of the house. But, her joy at seeing Tegwen quickly vanished when she heard the news.

"He accuses my husband of disloyalty?" Angharad was outraged when Teifryn described her husband's interview with the King. "Gwriad, whose life is focused on that man's safety, is accused of plotting against him!"

"I'm as upset as you are," Teifryn said. Her anger had subsided after a long discussion with Dafydd, who, in his usual calm way, had explained what he suspected had led to Gruffydd's accusations. "Dafydd, like Gwriad, is the epitome of loyalty. For both of them their ambitions rest and fall on preserving the King and advancing the security and wealth of Wales. We both know that."

"I knew my damnable sister would not be happy with being Queen." Angharad's eyes flashed. "She has never been content. Throughout our childhood, she always had to have the best of everything, only to toss it aside once she had gained it: the most expensive gowns, worn once only; the best horse, which she neglected and mal-treated. She always had to win over any man I was interested in, only to pass him over once she had his attention."

"I know about your previous men," Teifryn smiled. She was keen to calm the situation.

"Yes, indeed. But she never understood that they meant nothing to me. She's like a viper: she needs her place in the sun, she will lash out at anyone or anything that threatens her. Ealdgyth has always had everything she wanted; my father worshipped her, and still does; although, she never cared for him. He will not believe that she was responsible for his recent demotion."

"Why did she have him removed?"

"I imagine he was becoming a nuisance; perhaps, he was still acting as her father, rather than her servant. She's willful and will scheme to get her own way." Angharad smacked her fist in her palm. "Listen to me! Hardly the loving statements of a sister."

"You went to see her yesterday. Did she say nothing about accusing our husbands?"

"I was tired from the journey and simply called to announce my arrival. We had a brief, and unfriendly conversation." She carefully picked up Tegwen, who began to giggle, and rocked her in her strong arms. "She accused me of spying on her and of failing to remember that she was the Queen. I had the impression I had called at the wrong time."

"Oh?"

"The new Seneschal was with her. What's his name?"

"Rhys Gwynedd. Did you like him?"

"He's young and good looking, but he wouldn't make eye contact. There's something slimy about him. I have a suspicion she's having an affair with him."

Teifryn gasped. "But she's the Queen. Why would she risk upsetting Gruffydd?"

"Perhaps, because she's bored." She handed the baby back to Teifryn. "Ealdgyth's not very bright, you know. That beautiful face hides a dull mind. She has no idea how a queen should behave, apart from wearing expensive clothes and jewels, and enjoying being looked at, of course. She has no interest in politics, trade or even how her subjects live. She does not sing or play an instrument, and hates weaving."

"She has children: two lovely boys; they must keep her busy?"

Angharad shook her head. "Once she had proved to Gruffydd that she could give birth to two healthy heirs, she lost interest in them, too. I understand her wet nurses and her servants do the mothering, except when Gruffydd is around. Then, she pretends to be the perfect mother. I have my suspicions that she did not want the third child."

"Why would she not?"

"She dislikes the process: the loss of her fine figure and the pain of childbirth. When you couple this with her dislike of babies, I would not be surprised if she brought on her own miscarriage."

Teifryn was aghast. "I can't believe that." She had no idea how a woman could cause such an outcome and the mere suggestion was beyond her comprehension.

Angharad smiled at her innocent friend. "She's my sister. Nothing that she does, or may do, surprises me. I'm just sorry she's the Queen. She's too willful and untrustworthy to be in a position of such power." She looked longingly at Tegwen. "When I arrived without Gwriad, she wanted to know where he was. She thought he'd left me."

"How absurd," Teifryn said. "Why would she think that?"

"Because she understands nothing! She thinks that all men require sons and, because I have none, unlike her, she assumes Gwriad will toss me aside." She stood looking into the fire, as if expecting a revelation. After a moment she passed her hand over her face. "Her children mean nothing to her, they are mere ornaments that give her distinction. Motherhood, like true love, is something she doesn't understand."

Teifryn placed her baby back in its crib, and thoughtfully changed the direction of the conversation. "Why do you think she's trying to destroy our husbands? Is she jealous of us?"

"Perhaps, or it could be she sees them, and us, as a threat to her freedom of action. If Dafydd and Gwriad were dismissed, or worse, she would have a big say in deciding who would replace them. I think, in her limited imagination, she dreams of being more important than the King. Her perfect world would be where she was free to behave as she wishes, with nobody to control or question her."

"Can you imagine what would happen to Wales if Gruffydd was not well supported. No man can run a country as volatile as this one by himself." Teifryn nodded to a servant who entered the room carrying a tray of milk, cakes and honey. "This is Alys, my good friend and servant."

Alys put down the tray and curtsied. "My Lady Angharad," she said. She smiled down at the sleeping Tegwen, and quietly withdrew.

"I wonder how many friends Ealdgyth has among her women servants?" Angharad said thoughtfully, as she drank some milk and nibbled on a cake.

"I could ask Alys if she knows of any particularly discontented ones," Teifryn said, understanding immediately how her friend was thinking.

"Thank you. I would like some confirmation of the relationship between Rhys and my sister. It could be useful information if we are forced to defend ourselves. Has the King gone hunting again?"

"He left at first light with some of his Northern friends. He spends little time with the Queen, which might be part of the problem?"

Angharad gave a dismissive snort. "I truly believe if the King was the most thoughtful of husbands, she would still be discontented." She hugged Teifryn. "I am hoping Gwriad will arrive here before the King returns. I need to prepare him for Gruffydd's accusations, or I can see a difficult situation developing. Just what my dear sister desires." She turned back at the door. "Gwriad does not possess Dafydd's gentle personality. It's like comparing a raging winter storm to a summer breeze. Wish me luck."

• • •

THE KING AND HIS NOBLES did not return that night and it was rumoured that he had travelled to Caernarfon. The weather was cold and dry; there was minimal snow on both the low ground and near the coast along by Ynys Mon. In the royal chamber in Gruffydd's palace, a fire was roaring and the room was warm.

"Why would he do that?" Ealdgyth demanded. "Why would he go to Caernarfon without telling me?" She advanced towards where her green woven dress lay bunched on the floor near the fire. She fastened a necklace of Welsh gold, inset with a large topaz, around her slim neck. Having fixed the clasp, she picked up a cup of wine imported from Brittany, a favourite of hers for the last two years. Standing naked by the window, she repeated her question.

The new Seneschal, Rhys Gwynedd, was lying in her bed. He seemed asleep. One arm hung listlessly over the side of the quilt. "Come back to bed, my Queen," he murmured.

"Did you hear my question?" She spoke sharply, unlike the coaxing, wheedling voice she had used a short time before. He did not respond. "Wake up!" she hissed, pulling the coverings off the bed. He did not react immediately and she noted his fine, muscular body with greatly diminished interest. She had been serviced. He had done his part, and now she wanted to move on.

"Wake up!" she shouted. Immediately, she cursed herself: there were always servants listening outside the door. She grabbed his arm and pulled him off the bed.

"My Lady?" He raised his arms, his eyes still closed, inviting her to join him.

She kicked him forcefully in his chest and his eyes opened wide with surprise. "Can't we go back to bed?" he whined, and closed his eyes.

"Get up!" she ordered. "Get up!" She knew it was her own fault for encouraging him to drink too much wine. It was meant to relax him, as he seemed unable to forget that she was the Queen. Unfortunately, he had drunk too much, and his performance had been disappointing. Her obsession with him was over, and she wanted Rhys to become her obedient servant again. As she stared down at his limp body, she wondered how she could have chosen him as her illicit lover. "You're pathetic," she said, and kicked him again.

It was at this moment that there was a loud knocking at the door. "Go away!" she yelled, no longer the Queen, but a silly girl caught sinning.

"My Lady?" It was the agitated voice of Blodwin, her least able servant. "Your Highness, your sister, the Lady Angharad, wishes to speak to you."

"I'm not able to see her at this moment!" Ealdgyth shouted, as she quickly pulled on her dress and hunted for her slippers. All her life, her elder sister had dominated her. But now she was the Queen and should be free of her infernal sister. All she wanted was to be able to live her own life without people constantly making her feel guilty. "Tell her to meet me in the garden in an hour," she called. "Tell her I've been taken up with the children." She had forgotten that the garden was covered in snow, and that her sister had already remarked on how infrequently she saw her children.

Rhys jumped to his feet and reeled from side to side as he tried to focus his eyes. His head hurt and he felt nauseous.

"Hurry up, you fool!" she hissed. "Quickly, get dressed." There was a note of panic in her voice. She bit her lower lip as she rapidly brushed her long, tangled hair.

Rhys slipped on his rich blouse and doublet. He had trouble

getting his feet into his hose while standing on one foot. He hopped about awkwardly, as he tried to get the second foot in, a display that would have been amusing at any other time, and fell backwards onto the bed in a heap.

It was then that they heard an anxious cry from Blodwin. The door burst open and Angharad stormed into the room. She stared in horror at Rhys' partially naked body on the bed and exploded with anger. She was always an imposing woman, strong and full-bodied. But, at that moment she was like one of the ancient Furies. "Get out of here!" she roared, advancing on the terrified Rhys, who was trying to cover himself.

"You can't give orders!" Ealdgyth said, trying desperately to regain some sense of control. "I'm the Queen, I..." Angharad smacked her hard on the cheek with the back of her hand and she collapsed, sobbing, into a chair.

The enraged Angharad dragged Rhys up from the bed, propelled him across the floor, and literally threw him out of the chamber into the corridor, where he crashed down in an undignified heap at Blodwin's feet. She began to scream in an hysterical manner, just as the door to the Main Hall opened and a crowd of guards and nobles appeared. Angharad slammed the chamber door shut. She stood with her back against it, shaking with rage.

Outside the chamber there were muffled hoots of laughter, and an animated, muted discussion. After a short while, there was the sound of shushing. Blodwin stopped crying, and a male voice spoke up: "Is everything well, your Majesty?"

This was greeted with more spluttering of mirth, and more shushing.

Angharad pointed at her sister, and nodded at the door. Ealdgyth got unsteadily to her feet, sniffed and took in a deep breath. "Go away," she ordered, with as much dignity as she could muster. "I will call you if I need you."

They listened, as the crowd moved back down the corridor. They heard an eruption of laughter before the door to the Main Hall closed, and silence returned.

"You have always been stupid," Angharad said. Her voice was steely hard. She stared, unblinking, into Ealdgyth's red-rimmed eyes. "But even I could not imagine that you would be so stupid as to commit adultery with such a pathetic creature. Don't you realize that this will get back to Gruffydd? You have made him a cuckold: a laughing stock among his courtiers. Have you thought what will happen when he returns?"

"It was your fault. If you hadn't barged in, nothing would have happened."

"Everyone knew what was going on! Your servants talked about it. Did you think you could appoint such a wretch as Rhys Gwynedd and not have people wonder why he was chosen?"

"I'm the Queen. I can do what I like. You had no right to burst into my chamber. You can't hit the Queen and get away with it." Ealdgyth backed away as her sister advanced on her. "You touch me again, and I'll have you locked up." She looked and sounded like a frightened girl. There was no hint of majesty about her.

Angharad stopped, her anger giving way to the reality of the situation. "I dread to think what Gruffydd will do when he gets to hear about Rhys. You have endangered your marriage and the reputation of the King." She began to smack the back of her right hand into the palm of her left. "Have you lost your wits? You try to discredit my husband, who is the most loyal of Gruffydd's Generals. Not satisfied with that, you poison the King's friendship with Dafydd, who has been, and is, his right hand adviser. You even plotted against your own father, in order to have a sordid affair in your own palace. Have you lost all sense?"

"I'm the Queen. I will not be spied on." Her lower lip began to shake, and tears streamed down her face. "Gruffydd will understand when I tell him."

"Tell him what? That Rhys is your lover?"

"No. It was just a mistake..." her voice trailed off, and she sat back on the chair, her confidence rapidly waning. "What can we do?"

"We?" Angharad's eyes opened wide. "I should leave you now, and let your husband deal with you. Ha!" She paced around the room. "Before I try to help you, I have some demands to make."

"Yes," Ealdgyth nodded.

"You will tell the King that you have made a mistake. There

is no plot against him from Gwriad or Dafydd. You have come to realize that they are devoted servants of the King."

"Yes. I agree."

"You will tell the King that with the disappearance of Rhys Gwynedd, he should reappoint our father as Seneschal, until a more suitable person can be found."

"Disappeared?"

"If he's still in this castle when Gruffydd returns, the Lords will enjoy watching him die." Angharad gasped in frustration. "Everyone knows! He's probably fled the Palace by now. But, if he hasn't, you must arrange for him to leave immediately, never to return."

"Yes." This was not a queen speaking, merely a younger sister.

"Which is why you will arrange for your father to offer his services to the King."

"All right."

"Now, this is the story for Gruffydd and the Court, and for the servants." Angharad stared at the fire. "You had not realized that Rhys had fallen in love with you and were unaware that he had mistaken your kindness for encouragement. He tried to force himself on you. As you were resisting, I entered having heard you cry out. We threw him out of the door and Blodwin and the nobles witnessed this. You will tell Gruffydd you had Rhys expelled from the Palace, which is why you have asked your father to return."

"What about Blodwin? What did she see?"

"The girl is a half-wit. You will tell her what she saw. She will not dare to contradict you." Angharad moved towards the door. "I'm leaving. I will send a manservant to you, so he can find Rhys or confirm his departure. Either way, let it be known he's a lecher. When Gruffydd returns, send for me. I will confirm your story." She looked at her sister's red eyes, and the red mark on her cheek. "You look as though you have been assaulted. You need to be convincing; your future and mine are at stake."

• • •

GWRIAD AND A SMALL GUARD arrived at the Palace later that evening. He was told the King was not in residence and was believed to have travelled to Caernarfon. He headed immediately for his brother's house, where Angharad and Dafydd told him what had occurred.

"I've been worried about Gruffydd's behaviour for some months now," Dafydd said. "He's become morose, suspicious and lacks the enthusiasm he used to show."

"Why do you think he's gone to Caernarfon?" Gwriad sat hunched around the fire. He had arrived tired after his journey. The weather was cold and the previous rains had reduced much of the valleys into mud and bog, making travelling difficult. He had devoured a vegetable soup with lava bread, a favourite of his since childhood and was now working his way through a dish of ham, pickled onions and cheese, with his customary zest for life. He emptied a second mug of ale.

"There's only one reason," Dafydd said grimly. "He's gone to collect General Owain ap Pasgen and his Northern Army."

"Surely, he doesn't really think I'm a threat to him?"

"There's no other reason for him to go there at this time." Dafydd stared into his mug. "I believe he will return with the Northern Army and with Owain's support will order you to take your soldiers back south."

"He had only to speak to me!" Gwriad said, angered by the insult to his reputation. "He's my King and my friend, or so I thought. He had only to order me to do something. He should know I would do it. How has he lost his trust in me so quickly?"

"Gruffydd has changed," Dafydd said. "He's not the man I worked for only a few months ago. It is as though Ealdgyth has undermined our reputations to such an extent he is convinced we are reaching for his crown."

Gwriad rubbed the back of his neck and eased away from the hot fire. "Your sister is obviously very persuasive," he said bitterly, turning to Angharad. "I'd no idea Gruffydd was so influenced by her."

"It would be helpful to the situation if she was more than just a pretty butterfly. But, she thinks only of herself and has not the wit to see the consequences of her actions." Angharad poured herself some ale. "I thought with the birth of her two sons, she would enjoy motherhood, be a support to Gruffydd, and become a popular Queen. None of these things has happened. She positively dislikes babies; she has undermined her husband, and she has made no friends among the women of the Court."

Gwriad turned to his brother. "What do you think will happen when he returns?"

"There are two issues here," Dafydd said, assuming his role as adviser. "First, there will be the confrontation between you and the King. I would like to hope you could persuade him of his error. But I think if he returns with General Owain and the Northern Army, he will have committed himself to such a degree that he will not back down. It will be up to you to extricate yourself with as much diplomacy as you can muster. Perhaps, the best way forward is for you to suggest that your one hundred men be replaced by some of Owen's men and that you will send them south under your second-in-command, um...what's his name?"

"Alun ap Iwan. A good man. Utterly trustworthy. He returned with me tonight. He's sleeping in the main hall at the Palace."

"My suggestion is that you remain and plead your case over a day or so, as things settle down. If you depart with your army, he will almost certainly jump to the conclusion you are returning to gather more men. If you stay, you'll be more aware of how things are developing." He paused. "I don't think he will dare arrest you, although in his present mood anything is possible."

"I'll stay. I can't believe he won't listen to me."

"You will have noticed, that although Gruffydd speaks passionately about the Welsh being one people, he always favours his friends of the North, especially those from Gwynedd. A while ago I warned him about General Owain, and told him how the man murders his soldiers and terrorizes their families. Gruffydd promised to keep an eye on him, but nothing was done. He feels safer with his long-time friends, even though he knows their crimes. You and I, for all that we have achieved, are still Southerners. His wife has merely fanned an ember that has become a fire. He does not trust us."

Gwriad nodded. He knew it was true.

The second issue," Dafydd looked up at Angharad, "is how he

will receive the news of Rhys Gwynedd's attempted assault on the Queen." He had no time for Rhys, but he found the lie both awkward and unpalatable. He understood it was necessary if they were to save Ealdgyth, and to a certain extent Angharad, but it went against his moral code. "We have to assume that your sister will stick to the story you agreed, but you should be prepared for anything. Even if the King accepts the story, he will find it strange. After all, Angharad saves her sister, his wife, even though Ealdgyth accused Gwriad, Angharad's husband, of treachery. I think one reason that Gruffydd was able to believe in Ealdgyth's earlier accusations was that she was apparently standing up for her husband against her own family. If I was Gruffydd, I would find the story hard to accept, especially in his present mood."

"So, what should I do?" Angharad was angry with her sister, unhappy about the lie that might result in Rhys' death, and concerned about her husband.

Dafydd frowned. "I think the only thing we can do is to wait and see what happens when Gruffydd returns. Let Ealdgyth get to him first; hopefully before his friends in Court. We shall see what results. I will do my usual job. I may be able to gauge what is happening. I suggest, Gwriad, you call on him before he sends for you. This is going to be a difficult day."

"Well done, brother. A wonderful understatement." In spite of the tension, Gwriad toasted his brother. "Let's get some sleep," he said to Angharad. He raised his eyebrows in a meaningful way, and they both left the room giggling like children.

CHAPTER FOURTEEN

As Dafydd had predicted, the King returned later that day with a strong force of cavalry, and with General Owain ap Pasgen in tow. The horsemen formed up in ordered ranks in front of the Palace. Gruffydd advanced into the courtyard on his huge warhorse, followed by General Owain and a cluster of officers. Everyone was wearing armor. The King entered his grounds with his hand on his sword, as though expecting opposition. He looked anxiously around, but apart from his usual Palace guards, he saw nothing to cause alarm. He rode up to the steps, where Ealdgyth waited, wrapped in a long cloak with a fur collar. Behind her stood Dafydd in his usual drab uniform. Nobody cheered his entry, and he was conscious of his own lack of humour. Somewhere at the back of his mind was almost disappointment at the lack of any threat.

Gruffydd looked impressive on his high saddle. Having assured himself that he was not going to be attacked, he finally looked down on his wife. His grim expression turned to concern, as he saw that Ealdgyth was red eyed and weeping. Her face, thanks to some clever makeup by Angharad, showed clear signs of injury. He dismounted quickly, and taking her in his arms, attempted to comfort her. "What has happened?" he asked, and failing to get an answer, glared at Dafydd.

"My Lord, the Queen was assaulted last night in her chamber," Dafydd said, choosing his words carefully. "Your Seneschal, Rhys Gwynedd was, I understand, involved."

"What!" Gruffydd exploded. "Is this true?" He was unable to get more than a nod from his sobbing wife. His eyes opened wide as he looked about the courtyard, as though expecting to see the villain in chains. "Where is he?"

"He's fled, my Lord." Dafydd bowed to enable him to regain his composure. "The Queen has not been violated my Lord, but she is deeply shocked by the event. Perhaps, we should get her Majesty back into the warmth?"

"Yes, of course." He took a deep breath, rapidly digesting the good news with the bad. "Dafydd, take care of the Queen." He passed her over to his tall Secretary, and it was then he noticed Cadell ap Bleddyn, his former Seneschal, standing slightly apart. "Cadell, my old friend. What bad news, indeed?" He patted the old man's hand. "But, I understand it could have been worse?"

"Indeed, your Majesty. I'm sure she'll soon recover." He bowed his head. "If your Majesty pleases, I could take back my old position, until such time as you can appoint another Seneschal?" The old man was almost smiling.

"I would like that. I need some good men about me at this dark time." He seemed to remember the soldiers behind him who sat quietly on their horses. "Owain, get down, man. Tell your officers to get some food and drink. Cadell, here, will look after them." He seemed at a loss to know how to proceed. "Owain, tell the officers to find your men some cover in the barns, and arrange for them to be fed and their horses to be provided for. We will send them on to their positions tomorrow." He looked angrily about, and stamped up the stairs to the hall.

It was certain that some of his Northern Lords would have been delighted to recount their version of what happened between the young Seneschal and the Queen, but the look on Gruffydd's face changed their minds. They merely bowed as he stalked through the hall.

In his chamber, he eventually understood from his distraught wife, the story of Rhys Gwynedd's assault on her, and the way that her sister, General Gwriad's wife, had stood up to the villain. Eventually, he removed his travel clothes, discarded his armor, and relaxed in a chair before the fire with a cup of wine and some warm food. "We should never have appointed him," he said. "Although, I remember it was your choice."

"It was, my dear Lord," she sniffed, "and I admit to the error. He had seemed such a fine man and he was, as you know, from one of the important families of the North."

'Indeed." Gruffydd flinched at the reminder. What was he to think? Dafydd had warned him about giving too many appointments to Northern nobility. "You are King of All Wales, my Lord," he had said, "and people will expect you to spread your largess throughout the whole country, not merely among your Northern friends." He turned his attention to the silent man who stood by the door.

"Dafydd, do you have anything to add to this?"

"No, my Lord. Your Queen has adequately covered the situation, to the best of my knowledge."

Ealdgyth gave him one of her rare smiles.

"Good." He took Dafydd by the arm, and led him to the other end of the chamber. "Do you have any idea where Rhys has gone?"

"No, my Lord. I sent for him once this tragedy had come to my attention, but he had already left the Palace. None of the guards could give me any information that agreed with any other. After such a crime, my Lord, I suspect he will seek sanctuary in the Saxon lands."

"Surely, he'll be killed by them?"

"Not if he's able to convince them of his previous position in your Palace. He could be a valuable informant." Dafydd had no conviction in his assertion, but he knew it would divert the King's thoughts.

'Where's your brother, General Gwriad?"

The question was so sudden that Dafydd had to take a breath. "He's residing in my house, my Lord. Awaiting your Majesty's command. He arrived a few hours before your Majesty."

"Does he have troops with him?"

"My Lord, my brother, like I am, is loyal to you. He arrived with a handful of guards, as you would expect a General to travel. They are somewhere in the local taverns, preparing to spend the next cold weeks guarding the frontier, in order to protect your life and that of Wales."

There was a long silence.

"Tell General Gwriad to meet me tomorrow in the Small Room."

It was a name given to the room where Dafydd and the King met most days. "I will meet him at noon." He nodded to Dafydd, who hurried towards the door.

"Your Majesty," he said, as he bowed towards Ealdgyth. "May you make a quick recovery." He turned quickly, before she could see the anger on his face. With a last bow to the King, he closed the door behind him.

"You must be wrong about Dafydd," Gruffydd said to his wife. "I would know if a man was untrustworthy. I would bet my life on his loyalty."

Ealdgyth said nothing. Now that the worst was over, she was beginning to think that perhaps she did not owe her sister anything. After all, if Angharad had not interfered, then Rhys would not have been discredited, and she would not have suffered the indignity of the past few hours. "Yes, but what about his brother? Do you trust him?"

"Perhaps I misjudged him too," he said. "If so, I have acted precipitously." He sat down on a chair facing the fire. Ealdgyth, sitting to his left, studied his face, waiting for a clue as to how to safely proceed. He looked tired, and there was a twitch in his left eye. "He's always served me well, I can't think why I suddenly distrusted him."

"I think it was because he and his brother wield so much power these days?" she suggested softly. "I think it was because you discovered he had moved his troops without your knowledge?" She could not resist the temptation of getting back at her sister.

"He always moves troops around the country, that's why he's a General," Gruffydd muttered. "Yet, suddenly I didn't trust him. Why did I behave so?" He gave a humorless laugh. "To think, I actually believed he might have taken over my Palace when I returned. It was why I brought General Owain ap Pasgen and his Northern Army with me. What was I thinking? I left you alone. If it had not been for your sister, you could have been raped, and even murdered. "

This was not the way Ealdgyth had anticipated the conversation would go. "My sister is a fine woman," she agreed, "but it is her husband who wields the power. It is he who is the most popular of your Generals. I'm sure you did right to bring General Owain with you. It demonstrates your power."

There was a knock at the door, and Cadell entered. He bowed, and snapped his fingers to usher in two servants who brought wine and food, and more wood for the fire. They bowed and he followed them, a big smile on his face, glorying in his re-established position. He did not need to be told what had to be done.

Gruffydd nodded his satisfaction, grunted, and rubbed his tired eyes. The journey had been long and cold. There had been heavy snow on the high grounds. A soldier had died on one of the passes, when his horse had lost its footing and fallen from the narrow path to the valley below. They had left five men to recover the body. The King had pressed on as progress was slow, and the paths were even more dangerous at night.

He felt exhausted. Gruffydd realized he was beginning to feel his age. In his younger days he could have travelled all day and then be ready to womanize at night. He looked cautiously at his wife as she poured his wine; she would not be in need of him tonight, not with her recent trauma, although her face did not seem as battered as when he first saw her. That was some compensation.

"Now what am I to do?" he mused as he sipped his wine. "I don't need two Generals in the same place, and Owain and his men will not be wanting to travel back until they have rested. A man died on the journey, and for what?" He began to eat with the steady single-mindedness of a man who has not had food for many hours.

"You're their King," Ealdgyth said, as she refilled his cup. "You travelled with them and shared their suffering. You showed your nobles that you have the power to appear anywhere, even in the dead of winter." Her eyes flashed as a thought came to her. "I understand that General Gwriad has installed a hundred men in Ruthin? It would be easier for him to withdraw his men back to their barracks at Ceredigion, than for General Owain to retreat back to Caernarfon." She knew the word 'retreat' would grate with Gruffydd. "There was no reason for you to know that General Gwriad would move his troops up into this area. Why should he, unless he was testing your strength and determination?" She refilled his cup. "It would defuse the situation if you ordered General Gwriad to remove his troops. You would sleep easier in your bed knowing you had General Owain to call on."

The wine was beginning to have an effect on the tired Gruffydd. He had to make an effort to respond. "I am seeing Gwriad tomorrow. We will discuss the matter."

"As you will, my Lord." Ealdgyth smiled. If Gwriad were ordered to return to Ceredigion, it would mean her sister would leave as well. Ealdgyth would be free of her interference for the whole of the winter months.

• • •

AT NOON, GWRIAD ATTENDED THE meeting at the Small Room in his best robes, without body armor, and without his sword. It was Angharad who had persuaded him to appear without any semblance of a threat. Two guards stood to attention at the door, preventing his entry. "We are ordered to search you, my Lord," the sergeant said, avoiding Gwriad's glare.

With great reluctance Gwriad allowed the two guards to check that he carried no weapons.

"Thank you, my Lord." The sergeant knocked loudly on the door.

A Northern officer opened the door, nodded to Gwriad, and allowed him entry. Inside, the King was sitting behind a table with a number of maps and scrolls in front of him. Beside him stood General Owain ap Pasgen wearing body armor and a sword. Lining the wall behind them was a row of five soldiers standing to attention, each carried a spear and was in full armor. Dafydd was not present, which was very unusual as he took notes of all meetings.

Gwriad bowed slowly. "You called for me, your Highness?"

Gruffydd looked up as though surprised to see Gwriad. "Ah! General Gwriad. I'm pleased to see you." His voice and disposition indicated otherwise. "There seems to have been some misunderstanding. I did not order you to bring your troops up to Ruthin. Why did you do that?"

"Your Majesty," Gwriad spoke slowly with great emphasis,

"when you made me General of the Central Army, you made me responsible for the defense of mid-Wales. Last winter, I moved troops to Ruthin to enable a quick response to any border incursions. To this end, and with your agreement, I built permanent barracks for a cavalry detachment. I have done the same this year. The men are engaged in expanding the barracks while they patrol the area."

"You did not inform me that you were bringing up your forces. I should have been warned."

"Warned, my Lord? There is no threat. I moved but one hundred of my cavalry into the barracks they occupied last year. I am constantly moving detachments around the country. You have never questioned my judgement before."

Gruffydd looked uncomfortable. He turned and beckoned to General Owain, who bent close to the King. They had a whispered conversation. After a few moments, Owain stood up and took two paces back.

"Was there any reason why you felt the need to double the number of men that you brought last year?"

"My Lord, your Secretary, my brother, received a report from one of his spies in Chester, that Harold, the Earl of Wessex had been ordered by the Saxon King to attack Wales, and in particular to capture or kill you."

Owain let out a gasp of surprise; his left hand gripped his sword. Gruffydd did not move or show any reaction.

"He often gets such reports, most of which he does not pass on to your Highness, as they are mere gossip. This report seemed most unlikely, especially during the winter, but as it involved Earl Harold I thought it best to double the usual garrison in Ruthin."

"I was not told of this report."

"My Lord, it is the responsibility of your closest advisers and friends to give you advice and to make reports on those things that are deemed important and reasonable. We did not consider this a realistic threat and did not wish to concern your Majesty with it."

"Yet you moved more troops?"

"Yes, my Lord," Gwriad sounded almost tired of the subject. "I wanted to be doubly sure that we were prepared for the most unlikely of threats. Yet, I did not wish to waste our limited funds, which is why I limited the garrison to one hundred."

"Ruthin should be the responsibility of the Northern Army. If you had warned me of this threat, I would have stationed General Owain's men there."

Gwriad took a deep breath, fighting to keep his temper under control. "For a number of years, my Lord, I have taken responsibility for this area, to allow General Owain greater flexibility in defending the coastal towns of the North, including the ports used by the Northern Fleet, and keeping control of the dissident mountain tribes. You were in agreement with this, my Lord."

There was a long pause as Gruffydd examined his hands. Owain took a step forward and changed his mind. He stared coldly at Gwriad as if looking at an enemy and not at a fellow General. Gwriad stared back, noting his cruel face and his powerful physique. He wondered if they would come to blows one day.

"There is no threat to the coastal towns at this time of the year. Since the defeat of Iago ap Idwal, the self-styled King of Gwynedd, there have been no real problems." Gruffydd gave a slight smile; he remembered the enjoyment of defeating Iago's rag tag army. Then, he remembered that Gwriad had closed the trap, and helped to defeat the mutinous Lord. His expression changed.

"My King," Gwriad bowed. "Perhaps, if I ordered Alun ap Iwan, my chief officer, to return the men to their winter barracks in Ceredigion, then General Owain's men could occupy those barracks, and provide the defense for the area." He could see the idea was not acceptable to Owain, who had come with Gruffydd in the expectation of a fight.

Gruffydd stood up and glanced back at Owain.

"I could stay for as long as Your Majesty wishes and help you prepare for the spring offensive," Gwriad said. He was pleased to see that Owain was barely containing his anger.

Gruffydd stood up and walked towards the single window. He stood there for a few moments in deep thought. "General Gwriad," he said turning to face him, "I do not need two Generals in one place. I want you to take your men and return them to their winter barracks, where you can guard the heartland of Wales."

His use of the term heartland did not escape Gwriad, who realized it had more to do with geographic position than importance. In the King's mind, Gwynedd was the most important part of Wales and always would be.

"I will obey your orders immediately, my Lord." He stood to attention and gave a formal bow.

"I will send for you in the spring, General Gwriad," Gruffydd sounded almost friendly. "In the meantime, during these winter months, you may allow your men to stand down. Let them get back to their farms." He gave a satisfied smirk. "It will save our limited funds." Owain grunted in amusement.

Gwriad remained silent, grateful for his brother's advice to remain on cordial terms with the King, whatever the provocation. He was delighted to be leaving the Palace. He knew that Angharad would be glad to join him.

"Thank you, General Gwriad, you may go." As he left the room he heard the King say, "Owain, I'm glad you're here, man. We'll have a good celebration."

• • •

BY THE NEXT MORNING, GWRIAD had made the arrangements for his senior officer Alun ap Iwan to return to Ruthin and oversee the return of the cavalry to Ceredigion. The King had gone hunting with Owain, and some Northern friends, whilehe Northern Army was still camped around the Palace. "I wonder if those troops will be sent to Ruthin, or whether the King will be happier to have them around him," Gwriad remarked as he and Angharad prepared to leave Rhuddlan.

They had spent the previous evening in close family discussions. It had not come as a surprise when Dafydd had suggested that his wife and daughter spend Christ Mass at Ceredigion. "The Queen knows Teifryn is a friend of yours," he said to Angharad, "and I would feel happier if she and Tegwen were with you."

Teifryn nodded. "We have talked about it, and although we will miss each other," she clasped Dafydd's hand, "we think it is safer for Tegwen." She turned to Angharad. "I don't trust your sister any more. Who knows what other lies she might spew into the King's ears."

"We hoped you would come," Angharad said. "My sister is not a safe person to be around." She gazed at Tegwen. "However, I hope the journey will not be too much for your baby?"

"Tegwen will be fine," Teifryn said firmly. "Anyway, we don't really have a choice." She smiled at her husband. "I've arranged for Alys to stay and look after you."

"I am determined to stay," Dafydd said. "I'm his Secretary, and until he dismisses me I will do my job. Anyway," he smiled sadly, "if I left, he would brand me as a traitor." He embraced Teifryn. "Perhaps I do need a child's nurse to look after me."

The Queen had bid her sister a frosty farewell. She had been secretly delighted to see the first flurries of snow begin to settle around the courtyard. It had not snowed for a while and the recent heavy rains had melted the early falls and made the paths in the valleys into muddy quagmires. With luck, her sister would have a torturous journey and would be unable to revisit the Palace before spring. By then, she and Gruffydd would be starting their tour of the princedoms. She was equally pleased to learn that Teifryn and her beloved child were leaving. Ealdgyth was convinced that Angharad's friend's obsession with motherhood was designed to make her feel guilty. What a pity that Dafydd had not gone with her.

"It's going to be a difficult journey," Gwriad murmured to his wife as they formed up in the courtyard. "I hope their baby's not going to suffer?"

"She'll be fine," Angharad said, echoing her friend. "Babies are much tougher than men think and the same applies to Teifryn. There's not a lot of body to her, but she's very determined." She walked her horse over to where Dafydd and his wife were having a tearful leave-taking, while Tegwen happily sucked her fingers. "You're not to worry about your family, Dafydd. They're in good hands and we will soon have them safe and warm in our castle."

"Take care, brother," Gwriad said, as he embraced Dafydd. "Stay out of trouble with the King, which means don't upset Ealdgyth." He laughed, but then became serious. "If you hear any more about that threat to the King, send a messenger to me, whatever the weather. Tell the man I will reward him for his trouble."

Dafydd looked at Tegwen, sniffed and wiped his eyes, "I seem to get more emotional as I get older," he muttered.

"There's a gwirion man," Teifryn said, as she hugged him, tears rolling down her cheeks. Angharad took hold of Tegwen, who gurgled with delight, seemingly oblivious to the cold weather. Teifryn mounted her horse, Angharad gave the baby to Dafydd for a final cuddle, and he handed the child up to his wife who wrapped the baby in her fur-lined cloak. All three were wearing thick woolen garments and fur-lined boots.

Gwriad had insisted that the soldiers wore leather body armor under their thick cloaks, and that each man wore mittens or leather gauntlets. "You may have to fight outlaws or defend us from wolves. You can't do that if you have frostbite," he said.

As they left the courtyard, the three riders were joined by their small troop of well-armed cavalry. A sergeant and two soldiers rode in front, and the rest formed up behind. "Keep up a good pace now, I'll tell you when to slow down," Gwriad ordered. "When we get home, you'll all get a silver piece, provided of course I'm still in one piece," he joked.

The men grinned. They liked General Gwriad.

Dafydd stood at the main gate, watching the small party as they made their way along the snow-clad path leading south. The countryside was slowly turning white around them. Soon, they disappeared from sight. He remained in the same spot, staring into the fading landscape, until a guard enquired if he could help. He shook his head and made his way to the cold room he called his office. It was going to be a lonely winter.

The sergeant was an experienced traveler, and had made the journey from the King's palace to Ceredigion on many occasions. He led the group at a brisk pace, determined to reach the village of Ffestiniog before darkness. The village was on the edge of the mountain range, the other side of the Cambrian mountains, and boasted three inns. However, the snow increased, and by mid-day a wind had arisen, causing blizzard conditions that forced the riders to slow to a walking pace. The wind was mainly behind them, and they travelled in close formation in a white world. The travelers wore hoods with fur or woolen scarves around their mouths, grateful that the snow was not coming in their faces. They travelled in silence, the roar of the wind preventing conversation. Around them, the high mountains faded into obscurity; the narrow paths through the twisting valleys were soon covered in thick snow. It was well past mid-day when the sergeant called a halt.

"There's a small village up ahead!" he bellowed.

"We'll stop there!" Gwriad yelled back.

After a few hundred paces they came to a huddle of small, drab buildings. Smoke leaked out of the holes in the roofs, before being snatched away by the gusts of wind. They stopped in the center of the clustered houses; some had no windows, and those that did were firmly shuttered. There was no sign of life.

The sergeant dismounted and marched quickly towards one of the larger hovels. He battered at the door, but it remained firmly closed. "Merfyn!" he called. "Merfyn! It's Iago! Open this door before I break it down!"

The door opened a crack, and a cautious voice demanded to know who it was. After a brief conversation, the door opened. A tall bearded man dressed in sheepskins and carrying an axe stood in the doorway. Behind him the riders could see a cramped, bare room with a roaring fire, and a thin woman with a group of small children.

"My Lord," the sergeant said to Gwriad, "this is Merfyn, he's the village chief. He'll give you and your two women shelter until the storm blows over. I'll get the men lodged with the other families; there are barns at the back for the horses."

Merfyn stood aside while Angharad guided the exhausted Teifryn into the hot room, which smelled of unwashed bodies. Tegwen was crying loudly. It was clear to Gwriad that they had found shelter just in time to avert a crisis. As soon as the door was closed, the poverty of the room was evident. The wife, a haggard woman dressed in rough sheep skins, stood awkwardly against a wall, unable to bring herself to say anything. The ragged children stared wide-eyed at the well-dressed strangers, who had appeared from nowhere.

"We have food," Gwriad said, as he guided the women towards the fire. He understood immediately the importance of food to this hungry family. He slipped two saddlebags from his shoulder and opened them up. The family stood transfixed as he produced bread, cheeses and cold cooked meats; even a bag of wine. On the fire was a large iron pot that held a thin, mainly vegetable stew, to which Gwriad added chicken legs, cooked bacon and onions. He always carried onions when he travelled, as he believed that they reinforced his sex drive.

The family stared in amazement at the meat that disappeared into their normal gruel. The wife came alive, and with few words helped Teifryn with her baby. Angharad soaked in the heat from the fire, smiled at the small children, and eased herself onto a stool. "Now, you're fine looking children. Come here, now, and tell me your names." The effect was almost magical. The children were soon gathered around her offering their names and diffidently touching her rich clothes.

Gwriad, sincerely grateful to have a warm refuge for the women for whom he was responsible, embraced Merfyn as an equal and insisted that he fetch two cups. Gwriad did not care to appreciate the huge social gap that separated him from Merfyn, as he, a Lord, poured wine into the badly glazed clay cups and encouraged a peasant to drink. It was the first time in his life that Merfyn had seen wine, let alone drink it, but in a short time everyone was relaxed and enjoying the fortified stew, taking turns to use the few spoons, and the limited number of bowls.

They all slept on the floor in front of the fire, which was not allowed to die down. By the next morning, the storm had passed; the white world was illuminated by a brilliant sunrise and a clear sky.

Gwriad gathered his soldiers together and invited the peasants, who had given them refuge, to report any grievances. There were none. It gave Gwriad a great sense of pride in the behaviour of his men. "The best soldiers in Wales," he said to his sergeant.

"Indeed, my Lord, although I had threatened to cut off their balls if they took advantage of any woman."

"I see," said Gwriad, keeping a straight face. "What if they had taken advantage of any of the sons and the fathers?"

The sergeant looked shocked. "These are Welshmen my Lord, not Saxons."

When the time for departure arrived, the whole village turned out to see them off. Some young women were in tears, having met men who had enjoyed their company and not taken advantage of them. Most of the young men were exhilarated, having met soldiers who had travelled throughout Wales. They had seen something of the world. Many fathers, however, were fearful of the future and the loss of their sons now that a wider world had opened up to them. Unaware of the social chaos he had caused, Gwyriad gave coins to each household that had sheltered a soldier, and a handful of coins to Merfyn.

"You're a good man, Merfyn," Gwriad said as he climbed onto his horse. "King Gruffydd ap Llewelyn will hear of you. We will be looking to your young men to train as soldiers." As he rode off with his small company, he did not see in the faces of the fathers, the misery that his statement had caused.

• • •

JANUARY 1063

It took three weeks to assemble over five hundred foot soldiers in the makeshift camp near Llif Pwll, which the Saxon soldiers called Liva Pool, or eel pool. After the main muster north of Chester, they had moved in companies to a cleared area behind the village. The weather had been unpleasant, with bitterly cold winds and deep snow that had blocked the road from Chester. There had been problems with the food supplies. Many local farms had reported the loss of cattle and food stocks as the hungry soldiers stole at will. In Liva Pool, the only inn had been ransacked.; there had been complaints of rape.

Lord Wirt, although fierce in battle, had not impressed his officers with his organization. They blamed him for the poor accommodation, the feeding of his army, and the subsequent mutinous behaviour of the men. The weather compounded the problems. It was not until Lord Drefan and his personal guard arrived that any sense of discipline was achieved.

He began by ordering the officers to form up the army to witness the hanging of three soldiers accused of rape. Soldiers who defied their officers were publicly whipped and made to dig latrines. Weapons training was established: all soldiers were made to spend each day exercising in platoons or labouring in work groups; idleness became a thing of the past. Within a short time, logging parties had assembled huge piles of fuel for the dozens of fires needed to cook on. The warmth and hot food gradually restored the morale of the men, while they endured the extreme winter conditions. Payments to local farmers replaced pillaging and quelled the discontent that was likely to have become a local war. However, many farmers complained they could not eat money, or replace the loss of their livestock in mid-winter.

"This cursed weather," Wirt complained as he stood at the entry of his tent, looking out at the dismal scene. Around him stretched a huge jumble of tents and poorly constructed wooden bivouacs. He noted how the men, who had returned exhausted from their training and labouring, sat in sullen groups around smoky fires, awaiting the call to their evening meal. It was late afternoon. The snow had returned as the light faded. A gust of wind blew the flakes into his face and he reluctantly closed the flap of his oiled skin tent. Inside, Lord Drefan sat staring into the glowing brazier in the centre of their spacious quarters, deep in thought.

Wirt sat on a stool opposite him, and warmed his hands. "What do we do if the weather doesn't change?"

"Do?" Drefan studied the young Lord in front of him. "We wait." He had taken part in many battles, not only in Wales but also against the ferocious Scots in the north. He was used to living with an army; he considered bad weather and long periods of waiting to be part of any campaign.

"The men are rebellious. They want to go home."

"The men were rebellious, but now they'll do as they're told." He was aware that he had arrived with his personal guard in the nick of time. Another few days and there would not have been an army. "How many times have you led a campaign?"

"I've fought in many battles," Wirt said, defensively.

"That wasn't what I asked. Your reputation as a formidable fighter is unquestioned."

"None. I have always served under other Lords, including Earl Harold."

Drefan sniffed. "You can't be popular with the men by trying to understand them. They admire ruthlessness and an ability to win battles. If you try to bring your civilized, humane behaviour, that you exhibit in your daily life, to the ferocity and barbarism of the battlefield, you will be snuffed out like a candle in a storm. Heroism is only for stories, where good men, behaving with courage and skill, overwhelm the forces of evil and come through the experience unscathed. It's all make-believe; the stories old men tell little boys. Actual war is about marching, finding food, avoiding illness, weeks of boredom and waiting, followed by a short and bloody confrontation."

"But, surely we must set an example as to how to behave? There must be an understood code of behaviour." In all his previous campaigns, he had turned up when the battle was about to start. He had led men, commanded by officers he liked and trusted. Whatever the result of the battle, he had returned uninjured, and with his reputation for fighting intact. The past few weeks had, in contrast, been an unending nightmare.

"In time of war, you must set a strict code of discipline. If you are thought to be decent, generous and forgiving, your officers will not trust you and the men will take advantage. Always punish any transgression with extreme brutality. Soldiers are like dogs, they serve and respect the alpha male, but will, like a pack of wolves, hunt you down and slaughter you if you are seen to be weak."

Wirt sat staring at his hands. He knew Drefan was right, although it went against everything he believed in. To him, war was a time for heroism, when courage in battle was linked with nobility, honour and a skill with weapons. Since he had arrived in Llif Pwll, his enthusiasm for his plan to attack the Welsh had evaporated. Stuck in this wilderness of snow and biting cold, where his reputation had been severely tarnished amid a seemingly unending list of grievances and misjudgments, Wirt had come close to deserting. Before Drefan arrived, he had thought to return to Earl Harold with the excuse of seeking assistance and leaving his officers to cope as best they could. Now, he realized the stupidity of his intention. "How long do you think we can exist here?"

"Now that the men are occupied and we have plenty of fuel and food, we can continue to wait until spring if necessary." He frowned. "But the weather will improve before then, it always does. What's the situation with the boats?"

"My one good achievement," Wirt joked. He helped himself to a cup of mead; he looked towards Drefan, who shook his head. "I have assembled a small fleet, anchored around Llif Pwll, consisting mainly of fishing smacks, but I have also requisitioned eight strong galleys. As we are not intending to take many horses, we should be able to transport the majority of the men in one trip." Drefan raised an eyebrow, but let Wirt continue. "I've been thinking. If we divide the fleet into two parts, it means the galleys can travel ahead of the smaller sailboats, especially if the wind drops. Their soldiers can establish a beachhead, and await the rest of the army. Meanwhile, some of the galleys could return for those we've left behind."

"That makes sense," Drefan said. He tried to imagine the condition of the men when they finally reached the Welsh beaches.

"We'll place our best troops in the galleys. They'll be responsible for establishing strong defensive positions in case the Welsh forces have been alerted." He finished his drink in a gulp. "It could take longer than I first imagined," he admitted.

"No doubt," said Drefan. He did not seem surprised. "You and I should be in the largest galleys, to direct the defenses and lead the attack when the majority of the army has arrived. Remember, most of the soldiers have never been on the sea before. If it gets rough, there will be panic and sickness. We may be lucky to have half the army ready to fight." He did not reveal his own lack of experience on the water, or that he feared the crossing as much as he feared the bloody flux. He had noticed in his campaigns that the flux, which could decimate an army, was worse in summer; so far, there had been no reports. Likewise, he had heard that the sea could be calm for days on end. He was prepared to wait. What he was not prepared to do was to admit to his own fears.

"How were Alwel and Modig doing when you left?" Wirt said, with a hint of sarcasm.

"Unlike you, they have lived comfortably. When the weather allowed, they travelled to the east of Chester to inspect the semi-permanent barracks and stables the Earl has ordered to be built. The officer corps is well accommodated and the Earl is happy with their performance. He will arrive here as soon as his local conscription is complete." He grunted. "If the weather allows."

"It will be difficult to coordinate the two forces," Wirt said. Problems that he had dismissed or not considered were beginning to unnerve him.

"Indeed," Drefan stretched his compact body. He remained strong and athletic despite being in his early forties, and never gave way to anger. "Now, you can see why armies rarely try to fight in winter. Your idea appealed to Harold, although he is shrewd enough to foresee the problems. The fact that he has proceeded with the plan, despite the risks, indicates the importance he attaches to defeating Gruffydd."

"We will all benefit from a Welsh defeat."

"Perhaps. But supposing the fleet sinks and the cavalry is ambushed?" His blue eyes looked thoughtfully at the young noble. "None of us will benefit, some of us may die. Why would he take such a risk, and particularly at this time of the year?"

"We've discussed this. Harold thinks this is the only way to defeat Gruffydd, now that he has such powerful armies."

"Why try at all? It's easier to defend our lands than attack the Welsh. No, there's more to this," Drefan said, his deep voice barely above a whisper. "Harold has his eyes on the crown. He wants to be King of England, and the only way he can achieve it is to present himself to our pious King Edward as an alternative to William the Bastard of Normandy. At the moment, this is unlikely.

However, if Harold defeats Gruffydd, he will become a legend in his time, popular beyond belief, and Edward will be forced to take note."

• • •

FEBRUARY 1063

THE HEAVY SNOWS HAD GIVEN way to fine, dry weather, but the clear skies had produced bitterly cold nights with no chance of a thaw during the day. In spite of the thick snow that blanketed the land, life was slowly getting back to normal at Ceredigion. There was great relief and anticipation at Aberteifi when a letter arrived from Dafydd, brought by a messenger who claimed he had been pursued by wolves. Gwriad felt it was merely a ploy by the exhausted man to get a good reward, but he still paid him handsomely for his efforts.

Gwriad scanned the letter, written on the expensive French paper that Dafydd had imported for King Gruffydd's personal use. "Dafydd must have got back in favour," he quipped.

"Read it out to us," Angharad insisted, "then we can all hear it at the same time." She and Teifryn sat around the fire, Tegwen slept in her cradle, and Gwriad, with a large candle behind him, began to read out aloud. It was something he enjoyed doing.

> *My dear wife, brother and sister-in-law, and of course, my lovely Tegwen. I miss you all. Life here, as you can imagine, has been lonely, but never boring. In the weeks since you left, there have been some considerable changes and I will try to outline the main ones.*
>
> *First, I have regained the King's trust, which is a great blessing. This is almost certainly because he no longer listens to Ealdgyth. Shortly after your departure, the King began to receive hints from some of his Northern friends concerning Ealdgyth's true behaviour with Rhys Gwynedd. This came at a time when a message*

arrived from Rhys' father, pleading his innocence and indicating his son had sought refuge with them. As you will remember, Rhys comes from a powerful family from Powys and his father, Gwynedd, was a childhood friend of Gruffydd's. As a result, the Queen is in disgrace, and her influence over the King is greatly diminished.

Angharad will be interested to know that her father, Cadell ap Bleddyn, is securely entrenched in his former role as Seneschal. As a part of his revenge, Gruffydd has appointed Cadell to be the Queen's protector, whenever he is away. As you can imagine this does not please Ealdgyth who is, once again, answerable to her father. To add to this indignity, Gruffydd has insisted that she spend her days with her children. He has banned her from taking part in any activities without his consent. I believe it will be a long time before she regains her power over him. Finally, he was heard to remark that the Queen has recovered, at last, from her 'woman's sickness'. I can vouch for the fact that he seems more relaxed and even somewhat happier!

Another unexpected development concerns our 'friend' General Owain ap Pasgen. As you suspected, Owain did not depart to Ruthin, but became Gruffydd's constant companion. Eventually, when the King was convinced that there was no threat to his life, he allowed a strong contingent of cavalry to move to Ruthin, sent some back to Caernarfon, and kept at least fifty soldiers to augment his personal guard. I thought this would have been the final troop movement this winter, for the weather has made such deployments difficult; however, after a heavy bout of drinking, Owain picked a fight with a Northern Lord, and killed him with a knife. It did not help that the victim was a noble

from Conwy and distantly related to the King. After an
angry exchange, Gruffydd banned Owain from Court
and ordered that he spend the winter in the barracks at
Ruthin.

I think it possible that you will all be welcomed
back to Court in the spring!

The letter was then addressed to Teifryn, and Gwriad handed it to her with a broad smile. "I think he misses you." He winked at Angharad.

· · ·

HAROLD ARRIVED AT LLIF PWLL in the first week of February, accompanied by the Lords Alwel and Modig. He inspected the camp, checked on the boats, and called a meeting of the senior officers. He had heard rumours of desertion, mutiny and poor living conditions, but was favourably impressed by what he saw. The camp was no worse than others he had experienced, and there were no outwards signs of mutiny.

"Have you had many desertions?" he asked Drefan.

"There were some to begin with. But it's hard to run away in these conditions. Deserters leave tracks in the snow and travel slowly. Those we have recaptured have been publicly hanged. There have been no reports of any recent desertions."

Harold nodded his agreement. He liked Drefan who thought and behaved as he did. An army had to be well led; discipline and punishment were essential. "Good man." He leaned forward, "I gather you arrived just in time to save Wirt's neck?"

"He'd done his best," Drefan said, coolly. "You can't expect to establish a military camp in the middle of nowhere in the dead of winter, with untried troops, and dysfunctional officers, and expect everything to work smoothly." He smiled at Harold. "Wirt has imagination, coupled with bravery and nobility. He lacks experience in such conditions, but so did we, at one time."

Harold stared out at the sea, his mind had moved on. "When do you think we can invade?"

"As soon as the sea calms down," Drefan replied, conscious of his own prejudice. "How will we co-ordinate the attacks?"

"That is the unsolved question," Harold admitted. "I have two choices: to wait for you to tell me the sea is calm and a light wind blows: the perfect conditions. At which point I begin the advance from Chester, and you release your armada." He stifled an ironic laugh. "We both know this may not happen for weeks, and we cannot afford for the weather to improve so much that the Welsh army is back in the field."

Drefan nodded sagely. He knew the alternative. Harold glared out at the white flecked ocean, as though at an enemy. "Or, we agree a date and, no matter what the conditions, we launch our attack." Drefan remained silent. "You have some large galleys. They should be able to transport the best of your soldiers, no matter what the weather." He cleared his throat. "We cannot expect the whole army to arrive safely by sea. But, if a good number arrive on the Welsh coast, they will be able to mount an attack on Gruffydd's Palace; that will divert the attention of the Welsh King." He walked slowly around the brazier. "I will lead the cavalry in an attack on Rhuddlan. If you can manage to get even a few hundred of your men to attack from the north, then we will have him in a trap." He noticed the young Lord Wirt approaching and beckoned him forward. "I have been hearing good things about you, Lord Wirt. You appear to have created a formidable army here and one that I will soon be using for our attack on the Welsh."

Wirt gave Drefan a grateful look and bowed to Harold. "With Lord Drefan's help, my Lord."

"Yes, of course," Harold barreled on. "We have decided," he raised an eye in Drefan's direction, "to attack the Welsh in three days, no matter what the conditions. Understood?"

'But, what if there's a storm?"

"No matter what the conditions!" Harold yelled. "You will place your best soldiers on the galleys and make sure they are landed on the Welsh coast north of Rhuddlan. Then, you will march on Gruffydd's Palace. Is that understood?"

Wirt stared wide-eyed at the Earl. "Yes, my Lord."

"You will find the best local sailors and order them to sail their little boats, with the remainder of our army, over to the Welsh coast. Once landed, the soldiers will march on Rhuddlan in a second wave. No matter how many hours later. Understood?"

"My Lord, this could be a disaster," Wirt protested.

"I'm taking responsibility for this!" Harold roared. "Not you!" He walked to the opening of the tent and stood staring out at the wild sea; its unrelenting roar was audible a half mile away.

"What time of the day do you want us to embark?" Drefan asked, refusing to imagine how this could be achieved if the storm persisted.

"In three days time, before first light. Make sure the men are formed up in companies during the night and are embarked before sunrise. The galleys must be ready to depart as soon as the Captains are able. You have two days to build enough embarkation platforms on both sides of Llif Pwll." He handed a leather map to Drefan. "This will give you some idea of where to go once you are disembarked. It is vital that you reach Rhuddlan and the King's Palace by early afternoon. It gets dark early." The Earl's eyes were alive with enthusiasm.

"I will begin my advance from the eastern side of Chester and move south, to avoid their spies." Harold sounded confident, though this was the first time he had formulated his plan. "Within two hours, or maybe three, we will be at the Welsh border, where we will arrange our final approach. With luck, we will cross the border without too much opposition. Then, it is only a few hours or so before we reach Rhuddlan." He wiped a hand over his mouth. "Your galleys should have off-loaded their soldiers within three hours of dawn." Wirt looked as though he was about to protest, but Drefan shook his head. Harold continued to stare at the map. "If they're landed at the right spot, it should be less than a two hour march to Rhuddlan. If all goes well, I will catch Gruffydd in a trap. I will kill the so-called King of the Britons!"

Drefan looked pointedly at Wirt. "Let us pray that the Gods are kind to us, my Lord."

"You have to believe that, my Lord Drefan," Harold growled. "There is no turning back."

• • •

"So, TELL ME WHAT YOU'VE heard," Gruffydd said. He was sitting at the table in the Small Room, and Dafydd was standing next to him. They were looking at a map of Wales painted on fine leather, and Dafydd was using a thin, wooden rod to point out the features. Since the Queen's disgrace, and the removal of Owain, the relationship between the two men had improved, but was still a long way from the amity that had previously existed.

"After many weeks, I have finally heard from my spy in Chester," Dafydd explained. "He tells me there is a build-up of cavalry to the east of the town; his sources tell him that Earl Harold is in charge. However, the men are quartered in barracks. There are too few to be an invasion force. He suspects that they will be part of a spring offensive."

"Was this the threat that caused General Gwriad to bring up some of his cavalry?"

"It was, my Lord." He pointed with the rod. "Which is why we decided not to concern your Highness until we had more information, and why General Gwriad moved a small detachment to Ruthin, where he could assess the threat first hand."

The King grunted and rubbed his beard thoughtfully. "So, your spy thinks it's not a present threat? At least, not until the winter's over?"

"That is the report I've received. However, I'm still concerned. It is most unusual for the enemy to concentrate fresh forces near the border at this time of the year. It presents him with problems of supply, accommodation and maintenance of discipline. It's too early in the year for maneuvers. But, Harold must have some idea in mind, if these reports are to be believed. It's why General Gwriad wanted to be at Ruthin, where he could send out patrols to check the situation."

"Yes, so you said." He yawned. "What can Earl Harold hope to achieve?" Gruffydd was beginning to lose interest. "The Saxons have never risked an invasion at this time of the year. It's difficult to move soldiers in large numbers in these conditions. They don't know the area as we do, and their supply lines would soon be destroyed. I think we will review this matter in a month or two."

"Will the Northern Army remain in barracks?" Dafydd asked cautiously, knowing he was treading on thin ice. "Or would it be wise to increase patrols? Just in case Harold does something unexpected?"

Gruffydd groaned. "All right, I can see this disturbs your cautious nature." He stood up and stretched. A wry smile crossed his face. "I'll order General Owain to increase patrols along the border and to give you regular reports." He swept towards the door. "That will please him."

Dafydd immediately wrote out the order to General Owain for the King's signature and seal, and was preparing to leave the Small Room when a servant knocked, entered and handed him a report. "Where is this from?"

"From Prince Anarwd ap Tewdwr of Morgannwg, my Lord, General of the Southern Army." The servant looked pleased with his introduction.

"Make sure the messenger is well fed and given fresh clothing," Dafydd said carefully breaking the seal. "Tell him to report to me as soon as he has rested."

The servant bowed his way out of the room, blowing out his cheeks with relief. Although quiet and thoughtful, Dafydd commanded respect. In spite of his tall, lanky appearance and his mop of unruly hair, he was never an object of ridicule. He had a reputation among the servants as humourless but even-handed. Even Gruffydd's Northern friends recognized his intelligence and his efficiency. He worked long hours, rarely spent time with courtiers, and seemed indifferent to the wines, rich foods and costly clothing that were seen as the prerogatives of the Court. Dafydd read the message carefully. With a deep frown, he read it again.

Prince Anarwd reported a sudden and unexpected series of attacks on villages along the South Coast by large Saxon galleys. Prince Rhodri, the Admiral of the Southern Fleet, had engaged them off the village of Margam and there had been heavy losses on both sides. Anarwd was convinced that the Saxons were testing the strength of the Welsh fleet, in preparation for a spring attack by land and sea. He had sent a similar report to General Gwriad.

When Gruffydd read it, he looked up at Dafydd, and banged his fist on the table. "So, that's it! Now, I see what Earl Harold's up to. He knew we had spies in Chester. He hoped his troop movements in the area would be noted, and that we would respond by moving the Central Army up north before the snows set in. Then, as soon as conditions improved and he was able to move his army, he'd attack the South, hoping to have defeated Anarwd's forces before General Gwriad could march back." He leaned into his chair and stared up at the oak ceiling. "But he didn't succeed! And the irony of it is that my scheming wife, of all people, is responsible for General Gwriad being in the right place with all his army." He bellowed with laughter, poured himself a celebratory cup of wine, and then poured another and handed it to Dafydd. "To Wales, and the defeat of the Saxons!"

He was in such good spirits that Dafydd stoically accepted the wine and sipped it as Gruffydd elaborated on his theory. "It stands to reason," he explained enthusiastically. "It's much easier to invade the South than the North: it has more hills than mountains; it produces more food, which would enable an invading force to feed itself, and…" he paused for effect, "spring comes earlier."

"There is another way of looking at it, my Lord," Dafydd suggested hesitantly.

"Oh, indeed!" Gruffydd exclaimed. "There's always another way with you. Nothing is ever what it seems." He spoke, however, without anger and refilled his cup. "Go on then, tell me."

"My Lord. Could it not be argued in reverse? Suppose the attacks on the South were to distract us from a potential invasion of the North?"

"I have given you my reasons why I think the Saxons will attack the South."

"Indeed, my Lord. But supposing Earl Harold has only one real aim; to kill or capture you. He might guess you will spend the winter at your Palace. Rhuddlan is not so far from the border. He could attack with a small army, even in this weather, in the hope of catching you unawares."

"There are more than two hundred cavalry at Ruthin, conducting regular patrols. I would know if there was any incursion."

"The patrols have not yet begun, my Lord. You only signed the order this morning."

Gruffydd sighed deeply. "I am surrounded by my personal guard. There are at least another hundred men of the Northern Army in and around Rhuddlan." He began to point to his fingers. "It is very expensive to keep a large army during the winter. It is difficult to keep them occupied. It is very difficult to move a large body of men across our country, even in summer, let alone winter, which is why we have never been invaded when the snow is on the ground!" He was beginning to sound like a father explaining a simple piece of logic to an inattentive son. "In the snow, cavalry move slowly, marching troops soon become exhausted, and scouts have nowhere to hide. Supply wagons get bogged down; there is nothing to forage in our bleak Northern landscape, even supplying water is difficult. Soldiers get cold, get frostbite, and become ill. Many desert. Generals have difficulty identifying the best places to fight battles. Laying siege to fortified buildings is almost impossible in these conditions. That is why we fight when the snow is gone and not before. And that is why I am convinced that the Saxons will invade the South. I agree with General Anarwd." As a final thrust, he gave Dafydd a humourless smile. "You might be a good Secretary, but you're not a military man. I will speak with General Gwriad as soon as the weather improves."

"As you wish, my Lord." Dafydd risked one more suggestion. "Would it be a good idea to move the Court to Conwy, just for a few weeks?"

"Why in God's name would I do that?" Gruffydd had begun to shout.

"My Lord, Wales cannot do without you," Dafydd persisted. "You would be safer in Conwy."

"To move the Court in this weather?" He rolled his eyes. "Do you have any idea how difficult that would be? I am perfectly safe here, I tell you. I have nearly five hundred soldiers in this area!" He slammed down his empty cup and stalked towards the door. "We will not discuss this again!"

CHAPTER FIFTEEN

"This is lunacy!" Lord Wirt protested. He was standing with Lord Drefan near their command tent, gazing out at a tempestuous sea. Light was fading, the white landscape around them was dotted with the flickering glow of campfires. It was not snowing, but a strong wind was buffeting the tent and the brazier was roaring. "We can't possibly cross the sea in this weather. The whole army will drown."

Drefan did not reply immediately. He was enjoying a haunch of venison. He had caught the deer that morning, when hunting with other officers. It was the first animal he had caught for weeks; it was a small celebration in an otherwise cheerless existence. "It might be calmer in the morning. It often is." He took another bite, chewed thoughtfully, and after rubbing his tongue around his teeth, continued. "You were the one we have to thank for this idea." He saw the pained look on Wirt's face and raised an apologetic hand. "It was a good idea, and most likely to succeed, as long as the weather gods are on our side." He tossed the half-eaten bone into a snowdrift. "The one thing that is certain, my friend, is that we will be assembling the troops in the early hours, forcing most of them onto the galleys, and the others onto those small fishing smacks. At first light, no matter what the weather, we must attempt to reach the coast of Wales."

"But, none of us might survive on that sea!" Wirt was gripped with fear. Throughout his career as a soldier, he had understood the risks of fighting a pitched battle on land. He had never balked in a fight. But, he had never travelled by sea and the powerful, seemingly unrelenting nature of the waves terrified him.

"That is true. However, you and I are soldiers. We take orders, we give orders, and we set an example." Drefan walked slowly over and put his arm around Wirt. "Like you, I have never been in a boat. But, think on the bright side: we will be leading this small army. So, we will be travelling in galleys. These are, I understand, immensely stable boats. People travel the known world in these, and we are only going on a short trip across the bay. Have hope, my friend. Never let the men think you're afraid."

And so it was, in the early hours of the next day, that Wirt and Drefan supervised the embarkation of the soldiers. The rowers went first, led by local men who had agreed, for a payment, to man the oars and supervise the others in their row. Next, came the prisoners: soldiers who had committed crimes in the camp. They were already manacled; each man was chained into his position, knowing that if the vessel capsized, he would drown at his post. Once the rowers were seated, the heavily armed soldiers came aboard. They were forced to sit in lines down the centre of the broad galleys, sitting shoulder-to-shoulder, in silent, subdued rows, knowing they would be unable to move until their boat reached its destination.

The eight galleys were of different sizes; they carried between thirty and fifty fighting men. Wirt had agreed to be in the first galley, which was the largest, and Drefan travelled in the fifth; both were of similar design. They had been modified to carry a single warhorse, which was tethered within a wooden cage-like structure. Near the centre of each boat was a single mast, with a large, heavy sail; at the back, was a small raised platform where the Captain stood with a crew of four. Two operated the large tiller connected to the heavy rudder, while the other two controlled the sail.

Just before dawn, the officers climbed aboard and took up their positions on the cramped raised decks. Junior officers, with a core of sergeants, supervised the loading of the smaller boats, which had a crew of three and transported between ten and fifteen soldiers. The wind had dropped and the waves, although terrifyingly large to the soldiers, were of no apparent concern to the seamen. As darkness gave way to a steely grey dawn, the sleek galleys moved out into the wide estuary. Each Captain shouted out his orders. The lines of oars struck the water in unison. The sails were raised as the galleys creamed through the water, heading into the breaking waves. They were followed, at intervals, by a rag tag of small fishing vessels, which were soon separated from them.

The armada headed west along the wide estuary, keeping the north shore in sight. As they approached the opening to the Irish Sea, the galleys began to encounter larger waves. They rose and dipped with increasing violence, causing many of the soldiers to vomit, and the horses to panic. The estuary narrowed; for a while they could see both shores. Then, the north side began to fade away and, having reached the open sea, the Captains turned their vessels to the south, intending to follow the coastline.

Wirt's galley was the first to turn. He was suddenly conscious of an enormous change in the way the vessel behaved. Up until then, the galley had faced into the white-topped waves, its bows rising and falling and the oars maintaining a comforting stability as the boat pushed forward, aided by the wind in the sail. But, as they turned south, the waves immediately began to pound against their starboard side. The two men on the tiller fought to control the heavy rudder. Icy waves broke over the rowers on the right, soaking those soldiers closest to them, and adding to their ordeal. With each large wave the galley performed a corkscrew movement, seeming to fall sideways into a trough, before fighting its way up with one set of its oars biting into the departing wave, while the other side waved helplessly in the air. The oarsmen lost their balance. They were only held in position by the proximity of other bodies, and by those chained to their oars. The heavy sail began to flap above their heads like a demented fiend and the confined soldiers screamed in terror.

The Captain issued frantic orders to the two men on the tiller. The galley lurched to the right as the agile crew fought to lower the sail. There was a moment when it seemed that all was lost and the vessel would flounder, as a huge wave broke over the right bow, filling the boat to knee depth. The vessel shuddered. The oarsmen put a mighty effort into what might have been their final pull and, as though by magic, the bows lifted up, the sail came down, and they were back on course, facing into the waves.

"Order your soldiers to use their helmets to bail out the boat!" the Captain bellowed. Lord Wirt, who had been gripping a rail with both hands, with his eyes tight shut, responded like a man released from a bad dream. He sprang into action, lost his balance, and tumbled down the three stairs to the deck, falling among the sergeants who were grouped there. Some of the rowers laughed, in spite of their peril; they despised soldiers. The message was passed down the boat; the soldiers were quick to react, grateful for an excuse to move. But, as they struggled to their feet, they were unprepared for the violent upset caused by each wave. Many fell down and others collapsed on top of them. Those at the bottom of the pile, were weighed down by thick leather armor. They were unable to fight their way up and some drowned in the knee-deep water that washed around the deck of the boat. In the nightmare situation, the sergeants fought to restore order and slowly the chaos subsided.

Eventually, they established teams of soldiers who formed up on either side of the bows and stern, having found it was impossible to bail over people who were rowing. Helmets, full of water, were passed to those nearest the sides, who tossed the liquid overboard and returned the empty containers to the second line. As men tired at their posts, other soldiers replaced them, keen both to help and to bring heat back to their frozen limbs.

Slowly the boat became lighter in the turbulent sea, but the situation remained dangerous. Four of the soldiers had drowned, and their bodies, stripped of armor, had been thrown over the stern. Others, who had narrowly escaped death, sat coughing and nursing broken bones.

Wirt had cut his lip and lost a tooth when he fell down the stairs. He was suffering from extreme seasickness. He felt dizzy, his stomach ached and he could hardly stand. Dimly, he was aware of the Captain yelling at him above the roar of the storm.

"We're going west for a while, facing into the waves! Eventually, I'll turn due south-east. We'll have a following sea. It's the least dangerous course. It's impossible to turn back!"

"Will we land in the agreed place?" Wirt called back hopefully, trying to make his damaged mouth form intelligible words. He was gripping a rail above his terrified horse. The animal had been securely tethered in its cage, but this had not prevented it from kicking out the back frame. Its head was a few feet from where Wirt stood, and the animal's huge terrified eyes stared up at him, as if blaming him for its ordeal.

"Idiot!" the Captain screamed. "We'll be lucky to reach the Welsh shore at all!"

Wirt waved a hand of acknowledgement, silently vowing never to board another boat. He sucked on his bleeding gum as he reviewed the situation. There was no other galley in sight. He had no way of knowing if any of them had survived. When his galley approached the Welsh coast, if it survived, the Captain would have to beach the vessel; everyone would have to wade ashore as best they could. It was clear that there would be no way the boat could anchor off shore, as first planned. Once the initial force had been deposited on Welsh soil, he had intended for the galleys to return for a second delivery and, on the way, to encourage the smaller boats. But, the weather had made it impossible.

"Oh shit," he murmured. It was likely that they would end up on an unknown beach, perhaps with dangerous rocks, unable to get reinforcements, or even preserve a way of escape. If he were lucky, he would be leading a small, depleted invading force of exhausted men, into hostile country, without having a clue where he was. And to make it worse, it had been his idea.

• • •

HAROLD HAD FARED ONLY MARGINALLY better. At first light he had led some two hundred and fifty cavalry around the south side of Chester. They crossed over the bridge that spanned the raging River Dee, to the cheers of those who were nearby. They had moved as quickly as possible towards the Welsh border, knowing that Welsh spies would have been alerted. Harold rode at the front of the squadron with Lords Alwel and Modig, and his senior officers, setting the fastest pace that was physically possible. The snow was deep. There were no identifiable roads to follow, and the cavalry moved in a broad swath across the fields, coming together when passing through forested areas. Saxon peasants, who observed their passing gave thanks that the troops had moved through; from their perspective all soldiers were trouble.

After a series of delays caused by swollen streams making the fords deep and dangerous, and by narrow forest paths clogged with snowdrifts, the small army came to the north end of Offa's Dyke. Scouts had surveyed the area. They had advised the Earl to make a diversion to the south to find a safe way through. Harold had become increasingly agitated at the delays, many of them unexpected. He urged his soldiers to increase the speed of their advance. Towards mid-morning, they approached a gap in the Dyke. Lord Modig demanded that they rest the horses. "You may be able to travel all day in these conditions, my Lord, but we mere mortals and our horses can't, and won't."

"Take a short rest!" Harold ordered peevishly. "We're about to cross into Wales. We may already have been noticed." He turned to Alwel. "I want more scouts from now on. Position them in pairs in all directions, so we're not caught in an ambush."

"My Lord, I think there's little chance of that," Lord Modig sneered. "No one in their right senses would be preparing for an attack in this weather." He climbed slowly off his horse, wishing he had stayed in Chester.

"You're so right, Modig, " Harold responded acidly, "which is why I am leading this attack at this time. But, although these conditions will hide our advance, we can never assume the enemy is sleeping." He called to a Sergeant. "Make sure the men check their animals. We'll need to move quickly from now on."

The Sergeant saluted and passed on the message, but was unconvinced. "He thinks we'll move faster once we're over the border," he said to his friend. "You can tell he ain't been campaigning in this area before."

"Yea," his friend agreed. "There's nothin' around 'ere but steep hills and mountains, fast-flowing rivers and miles of bloody bog. We won't get to Rhuddlan before nightfall."

"'Ow far is it, then, d'ye think?"

"Well I reckons we've only done 'bout a quarter of the way."

Other soldiers, who had taken part in raids in this area, nodded their heads in agreement. It was going to be a long, hard ride.

At midday, they approached the village of Mold, known to the Welsh as Yr Wyddgrug. It was a large village standing on a hill above the far bank of a fast-flowing river. It boasted a defensive earthen rampart with a ditch on three sides. There was one main entrance to the village, and a crowd of armed men stood on the ramparts on either side of the closed gate, beating their shields with their swords and shouting insults. The scouts reported that riders had been seen galloping off in a number of directions.

"You should have stopped them!" Harold roared. "That was your job!"

"My Lord," a sergeant spoke up, braving the Earl's anger. "They'd known we were coming. They crossed the river before we could descend from the high ground."

"We never thought we'd get to Rhuddlan without being reported, my Lord," Alwel said, calmly. "In fact, we hoped to draw Gruffydd's forces away from his Palace to enable the main attack from our foot soldiers to succeed. Was that not the plan?"

"Of course it was the plan," Harold snapped, "but I had hoped to be much closer to Rhuddlan before they had news of us." He glared down at the jeering Welsh defenders. "Perhaps we'll deal with them on the way back."

Lord Modig winked at Alwel and quietly shook his head.

For the next hours, they struggled to keep together and maintain the pace that Harold was determined to set. The weather had turned against them, and snow began to fall on the higher ground. As they descended, a gathering wind lashed at them from the north, punishing both men and horses. The icy streams were difficult to cross, and it was mid-afternoon when the damp and tired men came over the brow of a hill and saw a fortified village far to their left. The settlement had an earthen rampart, surrounding a rocky promontory on which was perched a well-designed fort. It was a dark blob on a white landscape.

"That's not Rhuddlan, is it?" Harold demanded hopefully. Although prepared to ride further, he was beginning to realize that many of the horses could not continue unless they were given a chance to recover. It had been a grueling advance, much longer than he had imagined.

"No, my Lord," a Sergeant of the scouts replied. "This is Denbigh. The Welsh call it Dinbych, which means a small fortress. Rhuddlan is about another five leagues to the north."

"They have an imaginative way of naming their cursed villages," Lord Modig observed. He was breathing heavily, grateful for the temporary stop. His bones ached. A river crossing had soaked him from the waist downwards; he and the horse were still steaming from their exertions. He was a strong man, but overweight and no longer in his prime. He edged his horse towards Alwel, who sat bolt upright in his saddle with his head down, as though in deep concentration. Although older than Modig, Alwel was a seasoned campaigner who seemed unaffected by the demands of the journey. He had no difficulty riding with one hand. In battle, he fought with a heavy axe, while controlling his horse with pressure from his long legs.

"I could do with a sleep and a good meal before we attack these half-naked barbarians," Modig muttered.

"You always fight best on an empty stomach, my friend," Alwel grinned. He had known Modig for years. "And give thanks it's winter. In summer many of them fight dressed only in blue woad." He paused, "Let's hope Wirt doesn't come across any!"

Modig gurgled with delight, and rubbed his belly.

Ignoring them, Harold pondered the situation. "Five leagues?" Behind him was a suitable site to camp for a while where he could observe Denbigh, yet not be seen. "We'll take time to rest the horses," he said to the Sergeant. "Pass the word that the men should eat their rations. This could be their last chance before we meet the enemy."

He gathered the junior officers around him. "Keep the men away from the brow of the hill. Tell your scouts to keep a firm eye on the settlement, just in case they decide to attack us, which I think is most unlikely. The Welsh soldiers down there will, almost certainly, know of our approach. I don't want them to know we have arrived. They may think that their village is the object of our invasion. I doubt it. What I don't want is to advance on Rhuddlan and find the soldiers of Denbigh behind me. Watch them carefully, and report any unusual activity."

. . .

IN RUTHIN, GENERAL OWAIN WAS asleep, having drunk himself stupid as he did every night since he had arrived at what he considered to be the 'arse hole of Wales.' He was a man given to huge anger. His sudden demotion from being General of the Northern Army, and close friend of the King, to being merely the commander of a border post, was beyond his comprehension. He had been allowed to keep the title of General, but Gruffydd had made it clear that he would serve out the winter in, what was in Owain's mind, a jail. He remembered he had killed an arrogant Lord, who happened to be related to the King. He had considered it a minor accident; he had not been prepared for Gruffydd's convulsive reaction. Owain's anger and violence was such that, since arriving in Ruthin, no officer had dared approach him when he was drunk. He had been drunk for days.

"My Lord!" A voice cut through his sleep. "My Lord! I have grave news, which you must hear!" Owain screwed up his eyes as he tried to focus on the person who had dared to awake him. Slowly, he sat up on his bunk and rubbed his face. "This had better be worth waking me," he threatened, his speech blurred and almost inaudible. The soldier continued to speak in an excited tone, battering at his befuddled mind.

"Enough!" Owain shouted. There was a long silence. He raised his head to find the officer still standing in front of him. He noted the man was fully armed and wore the insignia of a cavalry officer. Owain rubbed his eyes, unable to remember the name of the man. He was surprised when the officer handed him a cup of wine. He drank the wine, felt slightly more alert, and tried to stand up. He felt the room begin to spin and sat back heavily on his bed. "Give me the news," he murmured.

"My Lord, the Saxons have invadedus from Chester!" He was unsure he was getting his message through to the drunken lout who was supposed to be his commander. The news of Owain's murder of a fellow cavalry officer, who was related to the King, had preceded him; his arrival had been greeted with contempt and outrage by the officer core of the army he was supposed to command.

"What d'you mean?" Owain said, seeking some sense of reality. It was winter. There was deep snow everywhere. Armies did not invade in these conditions.

"My Lord, Saxon cavalry, a large force, is reported to have passed Mold, heading north towards the King's Palace." The officer could barely hold back the contempt in his voice. "Is it your command that we should attempt to engage them?" He could not control his anger. "Immediately, I suggest, my Lord?"

Owain was not in full control of his reactions, but he understood when he was being sneered at. "You bastard!" he yelled. He reached for his dagger. Before the surprised officer could take full avoiding action, Owain stabbed him in the neck. The officer, however, was a man of considerable experience and managed to draw his sword in a reflex action. He was unable to stop Owain's knife, but, as the life drained out of him, he thrust his blade into Owain's unprotected belly.

The officer collapsed, blood trickling from his mouth, as Owain staggered towards the door of his barracks, holding his stomach. He dragged open the door and stared out at the rows of horsemen formed up in the training yard. This was not how it was meant to be, he thought, as he collapsed in the doorway.

The chaos that followed these deaths delayed the departure of the cavalry for a long time, as the competing officers decided on their action. By the time the cavalry of the Northern Army was ready to leave the barracks at Ruthin, Harold's small invading force was approaching Rhuddlan. The light was beginning to fade.

• • •

THE MESSENGERS BEGAN ARRIVING AT the Palace in mid-afternoon, each with his report of a Saxon cavalry incursion. Dafydd sent out patrols to locate the King, who was hunting in the nearby woods with some Northern friends. It was an hour before he finally returned to the Palace. The condition of his sweating horse and the mud splattering of his clothes spoke of a rapid journey back from the hunt.

"Your Highness," Dafydd said, calmly, "there is no doubt the Saxons are trying an unexpected attack in the hope that we will be unprepared for such an action. We have no real idea of how strong they are. We do not know for certain if this is their only form of invasion. I suggest two possible courses of action. One, we prepare your Palace for an immediate attack, and await the response from the Northern Army in Ruthin. Or two, we make a rapid retreat to Conwy, where you board your fleet to await reports."

"Are you saying I should retreat and leave my people to suffer?" He shook his head in bewilderment. "If the reports are true, we have been caught off balance. But, we have not lost the war. I will not retreat at such a time. Call my Lords and officers to the main hall at once."

"My Lord, you are our King. We need you to help us fight back, once we know what is happening. In the meantime, you must not get caught in a situation over which we have no control."

"At once!" Gruffydd bellowed. "Don't argue with me. Assemble the Lords and officers!"

The meeting was brief and to the point. Gruffydd ordered his personal guard with the hundred or so cavalry from the Northern Army to assemble, in full armor, outside the palace. Scouts had gone ahead to establish the number and direction of the enemy, and to discover the position of General Owain and the main body of the Northern Army. Messengers were sent to alert General Gwriad and the Central Army, and to Elwyn Davies, Admiral of the Northern Fleet, which was reported to be along the coast at anchor in the Bay of Conwy, riding out the winter storms.

The day was well advanced. With the deep snow preventing fast travel, Dafydd was doubtful if the messengers would reach their destinations in time to provide reinforcements for Gruffydd's small army. The King had sent out word for a general muster of foot soldiers, which had never been tried in winter. From spring until autumn, the peasants would have been in the fields, and word would have spread quickly. But, with deep snow and a cruel wind, the people were shut tight in their homes.

"General Owain will certainly have been informed of the Saxon advance," Gruffydd said to his assembled officers, "and most likely before we were." He pointed to the map on the table. "The enemy's cavalry was reported to have passed Mold. It was seen to the east of Dinbych. In neither case did they attempt to attack the settlements. This suggests they intend to attack my Palace, which means their forces will almost certainly advance along the vale of the River Elwy. If we travel fast, we could stop them at St. Asaph's Monastery. If we arrive before them, it's there we'll make our stand." He frowned at the map. "We have had no reports of any other Saxon forces crossing our border; without foot soldiers, they cannot be intending more than a surprise raid." He scratched his beard meditatively. "What can they hope to achieve with just cavalry?"

"The Northern Army might already have intercepted them," a young officer remarked. He sounded like a boy who had been denied a treat.

"That is my hope," the King said, gravely. "But, don't worry, I'm sure you'll get a chance to kill a Saxon or two." His face lit up, "Come on, my boys! Let's show them what happens to Saxons who invade Wales!"

The officers were in high spirits as they followed the King out to their horses. It was a cold, dull afternoon, with a sharp wind blowing from the north.

Dafydd stood on the steps. He bowed to Gruffydd as the King walked his destrier towards him. "I have left only a few soldiers. You should be reinforced throughout the day, as the word gets around." He paused, and looked into Dafydd's eyes. "I trust you with the safety of my family, as you would protect yours." He gave a sardonic smile. "You'd better keep an eye on the Seneschal as well."

Dafydd did not respond.

I know what you're thinking, Dafydd, and you were right: Earl Harold has done something unexpected. But, if he is among these Saxon invaders, I will kill him." He turned his huge horse and with a yell of encouragement, led his small army out into the white landscape.

The Celtic monastery of St. Asalph, built in the sixth century, was situated near the banks of the River Elwy. It was named after a boy who had lived in the community and was believed to have had saintly qualities. It was surrounded by gentle rolling hills and from the vantage point that Gruffydd had chosen, the vale spread out before him.

The grey sky was darkening and the temperature was dropping.

"Are we to remain here, my Lord?" one of his Northern lords asked.

"We will remain until we are certain they'll not be attacking us tonight. I hope to have news of their positions as soon as the scouts return." He scowled. "We should have heard from General Owain by now." His face relaxed. "Perhaps, he has already defeated them, think you?"

The Welsh cavalry remained in position as darkness blotted out their view of the valley. The wind moaned, and men and horses suffered in the cold air.

• • •

As the wind lessened, the galley had been partially bailed out. The Captain had finally turned towards Wales after what had seemed, to Lord Wirt, to be an eternity. He had been sick until there was nothing more to puke up; he sat, half asleep, on the raised deck, his feet hanging over the side above the heads of his officers. He could not remember ever feeling so ill. But, even in his jaundiced state, he was aware that the waves were no longer bursting over the bows.

He staggered to his feet. He was amazed to see a distant coastline stretching from one side to the other, with a diminished sea following the galley. The crew had hauled up the sail and the rowers were beating the water with a relaxed and disciplined stroke, so different from their earlier performance.

"Wales!" the Captain said proudly. "We have survived."

"Well done," Wirt muttered. His mouth throbbed and his stomach ached. He hesitated to ask: "Are we near where we hoped to land?"

The Captain stared at him as though talking to an imbecile.

"My Lord, we are lucky to be alive. If I have calculated our position correctly, we are far to the west. Perhaps near the furthest point of the northern Welsh coastline, before it dips south."

"What's the nearest Welsh port do you think?"

"I believe it would be Conwy." He saw the lack of recognition in Wirt's face. "It's a port tucked in to this promontory." He pointed to his right, where Wirt could see the coastline ended. As an afterthought, the Captain added: "It's one of the ports they use for their fleet of warships that have recently started to patrol this coast."

For a moment Wirt did not react as he assessed this information. It would seem that the weather was such that it would be difficult, if not insane, to try to head east, back to the beaches they should have landed on. But, if they headed slightly west, they could pass this promontory and seek shelter in Conwy. If the Welsh fleet were anchored there, they would be able to catch them unawares and perhaps sink many of them. Suddenly, he felt much better. "I want you to take this galley to Conwy," he announced to the truculent Captain. "If the Welsh fleet is anchored there, I want you to get close to each vessel." His face lit up with enthusiasm. "I will need to have fire!"

• • •

THE OFFICERS OF THE NORTHERN Army were divided as to the best action to take. Some were convinced that they should ride towards the hills north-east of Mold, in the hope of intercepting the Saxons, as this was the most direct route to Rhuddlan. Another group argued that they should head for Dinbych, which, although longer, was an easier route and one the invaders were most likely to take in the winter conditions. The passions on both sides were inflamed by the urgency of the situation. The argument was only resolved when the leading officers agreed to divide the cavalry: one squadron would cut across country to the north of Mold; the other would head directly for Dinbych. It was acknowledged by many that this plan might provide the opportunity to attack the enemy from two sides.

Hwyel ap Morgan, a senior officer, was convinced that, because of the snowy conditions, the Saxon cavalry would take the easier route, even if it were longer. "It makes sense to aim for Dinbych," he argued. "If we were attacking the Saxons at this time of the year, we would travel by the easier route to save the horses. But, I'm equally certain we should not divide our forces. They could have superior numbers to us."

"We could catch them in a trap!" a young officer exclaimed, waving his fist in the air. "We could destroy them!"

"We won't catch them if we stay here arguing," another protested.

While the death of General Owain was cause for celebration, the death of a popular officer had shaken the confidence of the remaining senior men. There was a void in the order of command. Unable to get any consensus, they agreed to divide the counter-attack. Hwyel ap Morgan would lead his squadron towards Dinbych. If he failed to locate the enemy, he would ride on to Rhuddlan. Dafydd Davies, the second most senior officer, but lacking combat experience, would ride to the north of Mold and come round in a circle to approach Rhuddlan from the east.

For many of the cavalry, this was their first real action since becoming part of the new standing Army of the North. All of them had taken part in maneuvers, but the majority had never been involved in a battle. They were well equipped; their horses were in top condition, and the men left Ruthin in high spirits, even though the country before them was unforgiving and the weather was harsh.

The two commanders saluted each other. "I wish we were travelling together," Hwyel said.

"We'll meet again on the battlefield, or at Rhuddlan!" Dafydd Davies was excited; he stood up in his saddle. "For Wales, boys! Let's find those Saxons!" He led his men at a fast trot, the most he could achieve on the flat, snow-covered field, and headed for the high ground. Hwyel, with considerably less enthusiasm, led his men towards the valley that would eventually lead to Dinbych and on to Rhuddlan.

· · ·

THE MEN HAD EATEN THEIR rations, the horses had been fed and rested, and although cold, Harold's troops were ready for action. He had moved his army past Denbigh, keeping to the high ground, and getting frequent reports from his scouts. It was just before twilight when an exhausted scout brought news of a Welsh column moving quickly along the valley beneath them.

" My Lord, these are not the men from Denbigh. They are well-armed and travelling in formation."

"How many?"

"I estimate fewer than one hundred and fifty, my Lord."

Harold dismissed the man, and pondered his next move. "Lord Alwel. Take fifty of the troops. Move along this high ground for about a mile. Take up a position along the valley floor and wait until you see them. Charge in a tight formation. If you hear fighting, come as quickly as you can."

Alwel nodded enthusiastically; he was pleased to be in charge. He turned to a junior officer and passed on the order. As he moved off, Harold developed his battle plan with his other senior officers. "Lord Modig, take fifty of the troops, and move south. Keep hidden. Stop as soon as the scouts tell you the Welsh are below. Wait until they are well past, then descend to the valley and advance quickly on their rear."

"I shall look forward to it, my Lord," he said ponderously. He always enjoyed a good fight. Modig patted his white warhorse, the envy of the other officers, and moved into position.

Harold divided the main body of the cavalry among the junior officers. After a brief word of encouragement, they began the descent. They travelled in broad lines, riding slowly and carefully down through the pine forest that clothed the hillside. From the brow of the hill, there had been no sign of the expected riders; Harold was able to complete the positioning of his men without hindrance. There was a clearing sky and a three-quarter moon; with the brightness of the white of the snow, there had been no problems. He was tempted to have men on both sides of the ambush, but caution prevented him: the valley path was covered with unmarked snow, and he wanted to maintain that pristine effect to encourage confidence in the Welsh cavalry.

They waited among the trees like statues, each man calming his horse, willing it not to whinny or shake its head. After a short while, the long column of Welsh cavalry appeared, travelling in rows of three. Harold waited until two-thirds of the riders were passed before he launched his attack. At the same moment, Modig charged into the fray. When some of the Welsh tried to gallop on, they were met with Alwel's soldiers.

It was a brief and bitter fight. The Welsh had not expected an ambush, convinced that the Saxons would be far ahead of them. Hwyel ap Morgan, unable to assess the number of their attackers, urged his men to break out of the valley, where they collided with Alwel's cavalry. Alwal was wielding his axe, and urging his men forward, and so identified himself to Hwyel, who knew the importance of killing the commanding officer.

Hwyel used his long sword and round shield to fight his way through the Saxon horsemen until he reached Alwel. Both men recognized a worthy foe. Each man slowed his horse before moving in to fight. Alwel's right arm was immensely strong; he wielded his axe with supreme confidence, distaining the need for a shield. Hwyel did not underestimate the one-armed man, and used his own shield to good effect. After a brief sparing, Alwel urged his horse forward, bringing his double-edged axe down on Hwyel, who deflected the stroke with his shield, and thrust forward with his sword. Alwel was well armored, and the force of the blade stroke was resisted, but its power forced him back, almost off his saddle. He tried to regain his balance, swinging his axe at Hwyel's head, but the movement of his horse allowed Hwyel to bring his sword round in a slashing move that almost decapitated the Saxon. Alwel dropped his sword, and fell slowly from his horse, unaware that the Saxons had won a decisive victory.

Hwyel became suddenly aware that the battle had already been decided; only a few of his men were still fighting. "To me!" he yelled, as he forced his way through the thin Saxon line, hoping some of his young soldiers might escape. At the top of the valley, he turned to face any Saxons who were following him, and was dismayed to find only one injured Welsh soldier had escaped the mayhem.

CHAPTER SIXTEEN

It was dark. Although the clear sky and the bright moonlight illuminated the white landscape, there was no sign of the enemy. Gruffydd knew it was time to return to the Palace. The Vale of Elwy stretched before him; below was the Monastery of St. Asaph. "We'll go back, rest our horses, feed ourselves and get some sleep," he ordered. "Tomorrow, we will find those Saxon scum!"

There was a half-hearted cheer from the suffering soldiers. Their hands were frozen, many shivered with the cold, and the thought of warmth and food was uppermost in their minds. The excitement of fighting the Saxons had waned, and most thought only of hot food, beer, sleep, and in some minds, the warm body of a woman.

"What if they're still advancing, my Lord?" A Northern noble queried.

"If we'd caught them in daylight, that would have been different. But, there's no sense in waiting here when we could be preparing for tomorrow, safe behind our walls." He laughed. "I have yet to see cavalry jump over walls!"

The King turned his horse. With his lords and chief officers, he led the way back to his Palace at Rhuddlan. The squadrons of cavalry formed up behind; they moved at walking pace, threading their way through trees made spectral by the moonlight. As they reached the top of a small hill, a mile from Rhuddlan, the darkness suddenly gave way to a vision of an inferno. In front of them, the Palace and the village of Rhuddlan were a fiery holocaust, and amid the red light of the consuming flames, tiny figures could be seen rushing about like ants.

"My Palace!" The King gasped. "My wife! My children! Oh, my God what have I done?"

Other officers rallied around him. "We must see what we can salvage," one cried.

"Lead us forward, King Gruffydd!" another urged.

But, for a short while, Gruffydd stared at the blaze, dumbfounded. Never in his worst dreams had he considered that the enemy might attack him from behind.

· · ·

By MORE LUCK THAN JUDGEMENT, Lord Drefan's galley had kept in sight of the smaller galleys, as they struggled to survive the storm. And whether by good fortune or remarkable seamanship, all of the vessels had survived and ended up on a long beach close to the village of Dyserth, which was just inland and near to Rhuddlan.

The Captains were relieved to beach their galleys at flood tide, which meant their vessels remained high up on the shingle beach until the next full tide. The exhausted men collapsed on the ground, grateful for their deliverance from almost certain death. There was huge rejoicing along the beach. Slowly, the junior officers took control. Fires were lit, food was cooked, and the single horse was finally released, unhurt, from Drefan's galley.

It was mid-afternoon. Drefan had consulted with the Captains and agreed that there was no way they could return to bring over the remaining soldiers. "You must be back here tomorrow before mid-day, if you want to return with us," the Captain of Drefan's galley warned. "I will not risk my ship any further."

Drefan patted the Captain on the shoulder. "If we haven't completed our raid by then, we'll have failed, and are probably dead. You have my permission to leave on the full tide."

The Captain smiled. Whether the soldiers were back or not, he and his crew would be leaving.

After a short period of recovery, Drefan ordered the officers to assemble the men on the beach. He stood on the bows of one of the smaller galleys, where he could be seen and gave one of the few speeches in his life.

"You could have died out there!" he yelled. Many nodded their heads in agreement. "We knew it would be a difficult crossing, but not that difficult!!" There was a ripple of laughter. "But, we're here now. And we have a job to do. We're close to the Palace of the Welsh King. I want you to help me destroy it!" There was a roar of agreement. "There will be lots of plunder for those who march with me." He heard more enthusiastic cheering. "We leave now. We fight our way to Rhuddlan. There is a pot of gold for anyone who kills or captures the Welsh King!" The roar of approval was matched only by the sound of hundreds of seagulls, hovering in the billowing wind.

Before dusk, the foot soldiers marched off the beach, heading south. A scout, using Drefan's horse, had established the route towards Rhuddlan. They advanced across the snow-covered heath without meeting any opposition. Soon, they reached the village of Dyserth on their left. It was a small habitation, but one that had a formidable earthen rampart with a deep trench around it. Drefan decided it was not worth the effort of subduing.

"There are very few guards that I could see, my Lord," the scout reported. "But there are numerous cooking fires. I think many of their men have marched towards the Palace. There is a fresh, well trodden path in the snow, leading south-west."

"We will pass by," Drefan ordered. "I think it unlikely that any of the men left to guard their homes will leave the safety of their fort to attack us." He turned to the scout. "Ride on ahead and see if you can catch up with these villagers. If you do, assess their numbers and report back immediately."

The scout trotted off into the twilight. Drefan followed, leading his men at a half run. They were unable to keep going for long, and soon reduced their speed to a fast march. But Drefan knew they had travelled faster than the men in front of them; he was fairly certain that his trained soldiers were still moving at a quicker pace than the local Welsh. The power of the wind was gradually subsiding; a silence began to settle on the encroaching forest. In front was the clear, dark trail of many feet. Overhead, as darkness descended, the unnumbered stars filled the heavens.

It was only moments before the scout returned. "My Lord," he gasped, "there's about forty armed men ahead. They're moving towards the direction of the Palace at a slow march. They're talking loudly and seem unaware of us."

"Well done," Drefan said. "Keep the horse, and try to circle round them. I want to know how far away the Palace is, and what we will encounter." Once again, the scout trotted off on Drefan's horse; he turned off the path to the south.

"We will advance at double pace," he said to his officers. "No man is to speak. When we come across the villagers, slow the front line. Allow our men to bunch up and make a running attack."

The soldiers marched quickly, each man dreaming of an easy kill with the chance to plunder the enemy's homes.

They moved quickly and in silence, their weeks of training bearing fruit. The only sounds were the gasps of the soldiers and the clink of metal. As they came over the brow of a small hill, they could see the outline of Rhuddlan less than a mile ahead with the imposing wooden walls of Gruffydd's Palace. The glow of cooking fires could be glimpsed around the village, and from inside the fortified walls. Below them, only an arrow's length away, was a group of armed men. They were descending the slope quickly, and had suddenly become aware of their enemy above them.

A roar of defiance went up from the Welsh, who realized their dangerous position. They quickly formed up in a semi-circle facing up the hill. There were sturdy trees around and many of the villagers positioned themselves with oaks and elms behind them. Some carried bows, a few had swords, but most held a mixture of agricultural tools including scythes, pitchforks and gutting knives. Very few wore armor. One man began blowing a horn, its eerie sound echoing out over the still countryside.

The Saxons rushed down the hill in compact formations, screaming their battle cries. They were well equipped with hardened leather body armor, metal helmets, long swords, embossed shields and huge double-edged axes. They expected to over-run the villagers in a single onslaught, but a small volley of

Welsh arrows felled a number of warriors in the front row, causing others behind to fall, stop or crash into those on either side. The power of the charge was deflected, like a wave hitting a rock. It gave the villagers a brief chance to prepare themselves. For, unlike peasants of former times, these had received some military training.

The Saxons' overwhelming numbers, coupled with their superior armament and experience, made the result of the violent engagement a foregone conclusion. However, before the protracted resistance of the forty or so villagers was finally broken, more than a dozen Saxons were killed and many more severely injured. "That was unexpected," Drefan observed, as he gazed critically at the carnage around him. "They fought like soldiers, not peasants." He watched dispassionately as his troops wreaked revenge on the injured. The blood lust was in them. "I want a report of our numbers: killed and seriously injured. Those who are unable to walk must stay here until we return."

An officer saluted and began to shout orders.

"My Lord! They're fleeing the Palace!" a young officer was pointing at the distant outline of Rhuddlan. The main gate of the Palace had opened. A line of riders was silhouetted against the background of the cooking fires, before they disappeared towards the west.

"Quickly!" Drefan yelled. "We must stop any others escaping."

The officers rushed about marshaling the soldiers, many of whom were still recovering from the fight. They led them at a fast march towards the Palace gates that, for some inexplicable reason, still remained open. As they came closer, they could see a mass of people struggling to get into the Palace, preventing the gates from being closed. They could hear the terrified screaming and wailing as the crowd, mainly women and children, fought to keep the gates open. Some older men and women were trying to save their animals, adding to the confusion, while others were attempting to carry sick or elderly members of the village.

Suddenly, a small group of armed men forced their way out of the Palace, and formed up as a protective shield in front of the struggling crowd. They faced the advancing Saxons with grim determination, in a suicide attempt to save their relatives. Above them, on the parapet overlooking the gates, fewer than a dozen archers began to unloose arrows at the nearest invaders, who were running towards them like men possessed. Around the gates, peasants were drowning in a sea of panic.

Drefan led the attack on the thin line of guards, who fought back defiantly. Meanwhile, other officers led their men around both sides, outflanking the Welsh defense, and hacking their way through the mass of terrified humanity that was still preventing the gates from closing. Women and children were forced aside, trampled under foot and slaughtered as they tried to escape. The first Saxons to break through to the courtyard were huge men. In their armor and helmets, they towered over the smaller Celts. The invaders fought their way like demons towards the small group of guards, who had been trying to close the gates, quickly dispatching them. Other Saxons poured through the gateway, killing any peasants in their path and raced up to the ramparts to destroy the last remains of military opposition.

In a short while, the fighting was over. The victorious troops surged through the Palace, seeking plunder and exacting terrible revenge on anyone found alive. Others raced around the village, searching for anything of value, setting light to the thatched roofs as they left. They killed chickens to eat later and destroyed all other animals. They looted the Palace and, urged on by the officers, systematically set fires throughout the buildings. They piled straw from the stables at key points in the timber walls, setting raging fires going as they retreated out beyond the walls. Their final gesture was to pour pots of cooking oils, taken from the Palace's kitchens, over the heavy wooden gates, before setting them ablaze.

The victorious army rested outside the burning Palace, staring up in wonder at the wild conflagration they had created. Fierce flames roared above the doomed building, its roofs and walls slowly collapsing, causing sudden explosions that lit up the night sky. Drunken and exhausted men slept on the snow, while others quarreled over their plunder. It had been impossible to set sentries; the organization for the retreat back to the boats was in chaos. Most of the soldiers were in various stages of intoxication after looting the Palace stores of wine and beer. All of them were in celebratory mood, yet for some, the blood lust was still raging inside them. They roamed the burning village in drunken packs, killing any survivors, fighting each other for small items. The officers trod carefully, concentrating only on those soldiers who were still able or willing to take orders, avoiding dangerous confrontations with those men who had lost all sense of discipline.

Drefan had regained his horse and rode urgently among the flotsam and jetsam of his wrecked army. "We'll march to the boats, now!" he ordered, yelling down at the hostile faces. He knew that after battles men behaved like this. Usually there was no urgency to reestablish discipline. Soldiers who fought and survived needed to release their pent up emotions. But this time it was different. "Those of you who refuse to march can stay behind! If you are not on the beach by mid-day tomorrow, the boats will leave. You will be left as a sacrifice for the Welsh!"

Barely a hundred men formed up, far fewer than half of his original army. Many had died or were injured; others lay unconscious on the snow, or were openly rebellious. Some had still to return from the ruins of the village, where they continued to hunt for peasants, especially women. Eventually, his officers had rounded up all of those who were fit or willing to travel. Disheartened, he led the assembled men away from the fire, the smoke, and the dead. They marched behind him in ragged rows, carrying food, clothes, weapons, and any gold or silver ornaments they had found. A group of soldiers at the back of the army pulled a two-wheeled cart laden with furniture and kitchen utensils. Some of the more inebriated had discarded their heavy armor in order to carry more loot.

"Tomorrow, we'll knock some sense into them," Drefan promised.

The officer who marched next to him, nodded wearily. It had been a long time since he had slept. The voyage had been exhausting and he had survived two battles. If the men did not wish to obey orders, he was too tired to insist. "It was a victory, my Lord."

"Yes. At least, a partial victory," he agreed. "I wonder if Earl Harold was successful in engaging the Welsh King? If so, then we won't worry about the fate of a few mutinous soldiers."

They continued at a slow trudge, their breaths steaming in the cold night air. The men had stopped talking, exhausted now that the excitement was past. The wind had dropped; the only sound was the squelch of marching boots in the snow, and the puffing and grunting of the men who wore them.

The return journey seemed longer, although they were following their earlier route, retracing their steps along the clear path they had previously trod in the smooth snow. Eventually, they came to a smaller path to their right, leading back to the village of Dyserth, which was soon to learn it had lost most of its men folk. Drefan noticed the path. He glanced up at the distant glow of the village's fires. Now, only boys and old men would be manning the defenses, and it would be easy to overrun the settlement. Nevertheless, he continued on towards the sea; the time for killing had passed. His eyes began to close as the regular rhythm of the horse induced sleep.

It seemed only moments later when the soldiers at the back of the column began to scream their warning. He awoke to a silent night that had suddenly become a murderous cacophony.

• • •

THE EXPECTED LARGE MUSTER DID not materialize. Instead of a wave of soldiers, only a trickle of armed peasants appeared at the Palace, arriving just before darkness, in ones and twos. Most were bowmen, a few had swords or spears, but the majority carried knives and farming tools. Gruffydd had left only five of his personal guards to defend the Palace, confident that the muster would bring in dozens of men from the local villages. He was equally certain that his cavalry would contain the threat from the south-east.

Dafydd had always been a worrier, and he was dismayed when he realized how few men had arrived to guard the Palace. "What will we do if we are attacked?" he asked the elderly officer in charge. "We need more men, surely?"

"Indeed, my Lord," the officer agreed amiably. He did not consider an attack on the Palace at all likely. "I've heard that Dyserth are sending a strong force to help out." He gave an encouraging smile. "They're good men, my Lord. They should be here before long."

"But, if we were attacked," Dafydd persisted, "what would happen to the villagers?"

"Oh, they'd be fine, my Lord. We'd have them inside these walls at the first sign of danger." He liked the King's Secretary, but the man was certainly not a soldier.

"Am I right in thinking that all the able-bodied men went off with the King?"

"Just about, my Lord."

"So, wouldn't it be better to gather in the women and children, and the elderly, now, while there's still time?" Dafydd could not hide the concern in his voice.

"Oh, I don't think so, my Lord. They'll want to be close to their fires on such a cold night." He glanced around and lowered his voice. "Also, the Queen doesn't want her Palace full of peasants, when it's not necessary." He gave a complacent little laugh. "All those crying children, and all those old people who will need somewhere warm and dry. And they'll want to bring their animals, and they'll all need feeding. The Queen would not be pleased, my Lord, nor would the old Seneschal." He bowed. As he walked away to check the latest situation, he could not resist flexing his shoulders.

Dafydd stared after him with rising consternation. He was convinced that Earl Harold would not have committed himself to a single raid, and at this time of the year. Something was not right. He made his way to the Small Room, where he lit a candle and studied the map laid out on the table. There had been no reports of any incursions along the border, other than the one that Earl Harold was thought to lead. Yet what could he achieve? In the ideal situation he would hope to confront King Gruffydd, and kill or capture him. But if Gruffydd had remained behind his Palace walls, what could Harold have accomplished without a proper army? He studied the border closely. Then, his attention focused on the coastline. Could the main army be coming by sea? He shook his head. It was impossible. There had been ferocious storms, even their own fleet had not ventured out and was, he knew, anchored at Conwy. But, if the Saxons had come by sea, what better way to catch Gruffydd off balance? Dafydd admitted to himself that he was not a sailor. He could not guess at the chances of a sea invasion during winter storms. If they were too strong for the Welsh fleet, then the same would surely apply to the Saxons'?

The feeling of disquiet was enhanced when he passed through the main hall. Instead of the usual buzz of activity, only two ancient nobles sat hunched around the fire drinking in silence. Behind them, the rows of bare trestle tables with their long benches emphasized the emptiness. He guessed the Queen was eating in her room and the servants were keeping warm in the kitchens. Dafydd went quickly to the Small Room. He wrote a message, sealed it and handed it to the soldier at the main door.

"This is from the King. Find a messenger. It must be sent to General Gwriad immediately." The soldier checked the royal seal, saluted and hurried away to the stables.

Dafydd closed the Palace door. With the aid of a flaring torch, he crossed the courtyard, making his way to a small door in the thick timber walls. He produced a key, unlocked the door, and walked through into a small snow-covered garden that led to his large house. Normally, there would have been a guard outside, but today was anything but normal. As he approached his front door, he was gripped with an undeniable sense of dread. He knew he must act.

"I want you to dress for a long journey," he said to Alys decisively as he walked into the main room of his house. Teifryn had insisted she stay to look after Dafydd, and she was in the act of placing food on the table.

"When?" she asked, realizing immediately that something was wrong.

"Now. This very moment." He quickly explained the situation. "I may be wrong, but I want to prepare for the worst."

"Of course, my Lord. I haven't left the house today. I had no idea." She was speaking fast. In all her time with Dafydd and Teifryn, she had never known him to panic. If he said they were in danger, she believed him.

They bolted down some food, changed into winter travelling clothes, before rushing to their stables. A youth helped to saddle up their horses and handed Alys up into her saddle. "Good lad," Dafydd said. He gave the boy a silver coin. "Now run back to your mother, put on your warmest clothes, grab some food and hide in the forest until tomorrow." The youth looked amazed. "Now trust me. Something bad could happen tonight. Hurry!"

The youth ran off. Dafydd mounted his horse and taking Alys' reins walked the animals out of the stables. He reached for a torch on the way past his house, holding it up high he led the way around the Palace walls towards the open gates. Everything was very quiet, the sort of silence that comes at night after heavy snow, when the wind has dropped. Even the wolves were silent. Two guards stood to attention as the horses approached; the elderly officer hurried from the guardhouse.

"My Lord?" He stared in amazement. "You're leaving, at this time of night?"

"Yes." He climbed down from his saddle and handed the reins to a stable lad. "I believe the Palace will soon be attacked. I have come to advise the Queen to travel with me."

"My Lord," the officer was clearly trying to control his anger, "I have received no reports of any enemy activity. None. The King gave me command of the Palace. It is my duty to defend the Queen."

"He made me responsible for her safety," Dafydd said firmly. He was taller than the officer, and stared down into his eyes. "You will guard my maid while I fetch the Queen." Dafydd beckoned to some servants. "Quickly! Get the horses in the stables saddled up."

"All of them, My Lord?"

"How many are left?"

"Four, my Lord." The servant was looking anxiously between Dafydd and the officer.

"All four. Yes." He waved the servants away. "You must warn the villagers and then lock the gates," he ordered, marching towards the Palace steps.

"I will remind you, my Lord, that I'm in charge of the defense of the Palace. I will not cause panic in the village without a reason!" the officer called after him.

Dafydd raced up the stairs, where a single guard opened the door; he rushed through the dimly lit hall and down the narrow corridor to the royal chamber. A maid was sitting on a stool outside, illuminated by a single candle. She jumped to her feet, her eyes wide with surprise. "My Lord, the Queen is eating…"

Dafydd pushed past her and threw open the door. Inside, Ealdgyth and her father, the Seneschal, were dining at a rich table, while two of her maids were caring for the two Princes at the other end of the room.

"Quickly!" Dafydd yelled. "We must all leave now!"

Ealdgyth rose instantly from her chair, her face flushed with rage. "Are you mad! How dare you break in like this?"

The old Seneschal had knocked over his wine and lurched uncertainly to his feet. "Dafydd?" he queried in a slurred voice, "What's wrong?"

"The Saxons are coming! Their main army will attack the Palace tonight."

"How dare you burst into my room, without my permission!" Ealdgyth screamed. "I'm still the Queen and don't you forget it!"

"Are you not listening to me?" Dafydd roared, forgetting any form of courtly address. "You're in great danger. I've got horses ready. Get into warm clothing. I'm taking you to Conwy."

"Now, listen…" Cadell began, staggering slightly. His daughter pushed him out of the way.

"Get out!" she stormed. "Conwy? At this time of night and in this weather? This is another of your tricks." She snatched up a carving knife from the table, and advanced on him, her face twisted in hate. "I blame you and your interfering family…"

"You and your family are in danger," Dafydd insisted, backing towards the open door.

"Saxons!" the cry was behind him. Dafydd turned to see a servant running down the corridor. Everyone in the room froze, as the servant yelling the same word, halted at the open doorway. "Your Highness, the Saxons are coming!" Without another word, he turned and ran back towards the hall.

"Now, do you believe me?"

In the blink of an eye, Ealdgyth passed from anger to terror. Although not intellectually bright, she possessed a well-honed sense of survival. "Why Conwy? Why not stay here?

"There are too few soldiers to defend the Palace."

She understood the logic, and realizing that Dafydd intended to flee was instantly persuaded. Outside she could hear people yelling orders; she began to give her own.

Dafydd ran back to the courtyard as frightened servants appeared with the four extra horses. Alys gave a cry of relief as he reached her. "The Queen is coming with Cadell," he said, patting her hand. "Two maids are looking after the princes." He noticed the officer was on the parapet above the gates, pointing and waving his arms at the crowd of peasants who were pushing through the half-closed gates; on either side, soldiers were desperately trying to close them.

Ealdgyth and her maids were hustled down the steps by Cadell, who had somehow sobered up and had taken charge of them. He and Dafydd helped the women into their saddles, then passed the frightened children to the maids. The old Seneschal was wearing a long sword and a helmet. He led the small column of horses towards the gates, trying to force his way through the struggling mass of villagers.

The officer ran up to them. "Your Highness, I should come with you," he pleaded. He did not look like the confident commander of the palace, just a frightened man.

"Your job is to defend this Palace!" Ealdgyth yelled at him. "Get your soldiers to clear a way through those peasants! Now!"

For a brief moment, Dafydd had to admire her. For a brief moment she was a Queen who meant to be obeyed.

Rebuffed, the officer quickly rounded up some soldiers who began to force their way through the crowd. "Make way for the Queen!" he yelled. The frightened peasants squeezed themselves to the sides, as the six horses moved slowly through the gates.

When the Queen and her party were outside, the soldiers had to force their way back towards the courtyard, while the crowd of terrified people and animals surged around them.

Cadell led the small party around the walls of the palace and headed off towards the north-west at a careful trot. Dafydd brought up the rear. Staring into the night, he could see that the hill to the east was alive with movement and the sound of battle; his final memory, before he turned to follow the others, was of a dark wave moving inexorably across the white fields.

•   •   •

AT HIS HOME IN CEREDIGION, Gwriad received a tired messenger from Ruthin, a young man from the village whom he had befriended when he had established the barracks. It was mid-morning, and a cool breeze forced them inside. "So, Owain is dead?" he murmured.

"Yes, my Lord. I'm told he was always drunk. He killed the senior officer of the force when he was told of the invasion. General Owain died shortly afterwards."

"They divided their forces, you say?" Gwriad could hardly believe such foolishness.

"Yes, my Lord. With no commander, the officers could not agree. The Northern Army went in two directions, hoping to trap the Saxons between them."

Gwriad shook his head. If it had not been for Gruffydd's ambitious wife, he would have been in charge of the Ruthin barracks. He would have acted quite differently.

"Have you heard anything else?"

"I heard Earl Harold was supposed to be leading the Saxons."

"That doesn't surprise me," Gwriad muttered. He ushered the young man towards the warmth of the kitchen.

'What do you think I should do?" he said to Angharad, who had been listening from outside the room. "I can call the Central Army to muster. That could take at least two days in this weather, perhaps more, and it would be a slow march up north. Or, I could take my small personal guard, all cavalry, to Ruthin, in the hope of catching the Saxons as they withdraw back across the border. Or,

I could make directly for Gruffydd's Palace at Rhuddlan, where the fight, if there ever was one, will almost certainly be over." He sighed deeply and began to pace around the room.

"What's your gut feeling?" Angharad said. She threw a log on the glowing fire.

"Dafydd was certain that his spy had good information. He reported that the Saxons were going to do something unexpected during the winter." He gave a humourless laugh. "Well, he was right about that."

"But, why would Earl Harold lead a cavalry attack against Wales in this weather?" Angharad poured two cups of wine. "Surely, he would need foot soldiers and supplies to attack fortifications? Am I not right?"

" Yes," Gwriad agreed, thoughtfully sipping his wine, "You're quite right. So, the question is: where are his foot soldiers?"

"My Lord," a servant appeared in the room, "a messenger from the King has arrived."

They both listened carefully to the messenger, who was barely able to speak. He trembled with cold, as he stood near the fire in his sodden clothes, but was determined to give his message. He confirmed he had been sent from the Palace as soon as the King heard of the invasion. "The King has his personal guard and a hundred cavalry from the Northern Army. He intends to set out for St. Asaph's Monastery, to block the enemy's advance. The King hopes the invaders will have already been defeated by the Northern Army." The messenger gave a brave smile, but seeing Gwriad's grim face, hurried on with his message. "My Lord General, the King orders you to bring your full army up to the Palace, to help restore confidence, and to maintain the peace."

"Those were his words?" Gwriad demanded. It sounded so unlike the King. "Did he not want me to come as quickly as possible with my cavalry?"

"Those were his words, my Lord." The messenger rubbed his frozen hands together. "His exact words, my Lord." He handed over his badge of identity with the King's seal.

"You've done well. The servants will find you dry clothes and give you a hot meal."

Angharad showed the grateful man to the kitchen. She returned to find Gwriad staring out of the glass window, a very new addition to the castle. "If there is something happening that we know can't be right, what do we do?" He rubbed the glass to clear away his breath. "I think I should go quickly with as many men as I can gather, yet the King orders me to bring my whole army, which could take days. What do you think?"

"I think you should do what you feel is right," Angharad said.

"Thank you," he kissed her gently. "You never fail me." He immediately left the room, and began to issue orders to the servants, while Angharad went to find Teifryn.

As night fell, Alun ap Iwan, Second Officer of the Central Army, reported for duty. He owned a large farm north of the village of Aberteifi, and had only recently returned to his family after his recall from Ruthin. He was a young, enthusiastic officer, popular with his troops, but lacking experience in battle.

"I want you to organize the cavalry to leave by mid-day tomorrow. I will lead them and you will stay behind to complete the muster." He saw the look of disappointment on Alun's face. "I'm leaving you with a big job, Alun." He began to count on his fingers. First, rely on the older officers to arrange for supplies; next, it will be your responsibility to ensure that every able-bodied man responds to the call. Then, you will lead the army directly to Ruthin, and if all is well with the Northern Army, you will continue to the King's Palace at Rhuddlan. If, for some reason, the Northern Army is in disarray, you will stay at Ruthin and combine the armies."

"Disarray, my Lord?"

"I have heard that General Owain and his Second-in-Command are both dead. It is possible the army has made contact with the enemy. They may have been defeated. You will make your decisions based on what you find, and I will support you."

"Thank you, my Lord." He was suddenly aware of the immense trust General Gwriad was placing in him. He stood to attention. "I won't let you down, my Lord."

"No, I know you won't." He paused. "We live in dangerous times. Our worst problem at this time of the year, is our lack of information. It's our great weakness. I'm starved of news and must rely on guesswork. Both of us must use our common sense and react to situations as we find them."

Alun ap Iwan nodded furiously, anxious to get started with organizing the cavalry.

"When I leave tomorrow," Gwriad said, "I will head straight for Rhuddlan. Send me reports as soon as you can." He shook hands with Alun. "Good luck. Remember, when you have no clear information, trust your instincts."

At first light, Gwriad was working with a stable boy to prepare his warhorse for the journey. It was bitterly cold and occasional snow flurries sent the yard's chickens seeking cover. "A rider, my Lord!" the boy pointed to where a snow-covered figure urged his tired horse towards the castle.

He was a messenger and, like those before him, was exhausted by the weather and the difficult terrain. "A message from your brother, the King's Secretary, my Lord." He handed down a scroll, with the royal seal, and staggered as he dismounted.

"Help him inside," Gwriad ordered. "See he's well looked after."

The stable boy ran forward to help, but the messenger stood his ground. "I'm sorry to have taken so long, my Lord," the man said. "My horse stumbled and broke a leg. The wolves took the horse. I walked all night. Eventually, I found a family who sold me this horse. I'm sorry I'm late."

"You're not late," Gwriad said. He embraced the man, before passing him on to the stable boy. "You're a good man, and I'll reward you."

Gwriad walked inside and read the contents to Angharad, who had been brushing out her long, lustrous black hair, which had recently shown its first glimmers of grey. She stopped brushing. Teifryn entered quietly, her baby asleep in her arms. They both listened intently.

> *"My dear brother,*
> *The news is not good. Gruffydd has received reports of*
> *an invasion by a large army of Saxon cavalry. The army*
> *has bypassed Mold and Dinbych and is believed to be*

*heading for Rhuddlan. The King has insisted on taking
all his available troops and intends to make a stand at
the Vale of Elwy. There are only a few soldiers left to
guard the palace, and I am convinced the Saxon cavalry
is only a diversion. There have been no other reports
of Saxon forces, yet I am gripped with forebodings. If
things go badly, I will try and escape to Conwy with
the Queen.
Come quickly.
Dafydd"*

"Are you ready to go?" Angharad whispered, hugging him tightly.

"Yes. I will take what men I can. Those who arrive later can travel with Alun's forces."

"Give him my love," Teifryn said bravely. She wiped a tear from her face as she left the room.

"I am certain your brother's fears are real," Angharad said. "He's like you, he knows when things are wrong." She kissed him passionately. "Send me a message as soon as you can, and come back safely."

• • •

GRUFFYDD LED HIS CAVALRY IN a thunderous charge down the hill and across the snow-covered fields, which were criss-crossed by the footprints of the Saxon army. When he reached his burning palace, it was impossible to force an entrance into the inferno. There was no way of knowing if his wife and family had perished inside, or had escaped. He stared dumbfounded at the destruction of his home, while his men made short work of the drunken Saxons. Many died under the hooves of the cavalry; others were hunted down, unable to hide in the burning village. The Welsh troops had known friends among the inhabitants of the village, in some cases were related to those whose bodies lay bleeding in the snow; there were no thoughts of taking prisoners. The horsemen spread out beyond the fiery buildings, determined to find any Saxons who had sought refuge in the surrounding woods.

"My Lord!" the officer said, raising his voice above the roar of the fire. "My Lord!"

The King glared at him, unable to draw his eyes from the conflagration. "What now?"

The officer pressed on, knowing his message was important. "The Saxons have retreated towards Dyserth, my Lord. We think they are moving towards the coast."

Gruffydd breathed in deeply. His sons could be dead, his wife also, and he was desperate for revenge. "Form up!" he yelled. "Form up! Send out scouts!" He ground his teeth in frustration as the officers began the long task of rounding up the disparate horsemen. But he refused to allow the officers to use their trumpets. "We must not give them warning. We might yet catch them unprepared."

Eventually, the excited horsemen were recalled and forced into recognizable formations. Gruffydd raised his sword above his head. He led his cavalry at a dangerous speed across the fields towards the hills, in the direction of Dyserth. The packed path that the retreating Saxons had taken was clearly etched like a black scar in the white landscape; the scouts soon reported a long, slow-moving column of soldiers a mile ahead. Gruffydd paused to take breath.

"We will attack from the rear and sweep up both sides of the column," he instructed his officers. He turned to face the waiting soldiers. "These men ahead of us have killed our friends and family. We give them no quarter. We take no prisoners!" The men raised their weapons in a silent salute.

The cavalry raced up to the top of the hill overlooking Dyserth. To the left of the village, they could see, in the moonlight, the dark line of the Saxon army weaving its way through the trampled snow. Many were burdened down with their loot and others marched as if asleep.

"We'll kill them all!" Gruffydd snarled.

The cavalry moved forward in two formations. The Northern Army troops on the left, and Gruffydd, with his personal guard, on the right. They careered down the hill, their horses bunching up; each man driven by a need for personal glory. Those in the front carried spears; those behind had drawn swords; all carried small round shields and wore body armor. Gruffydd's personal guard considered themselves the cream of the Welsh soldiers; each man was determined to prove himself in the coming battle.

They were within two hundred paces of the rear of the Saxon column, before the alarm was raised. The rear guards, many of whom were drunk, had barely time to draw their weapons before the Welsh were upon them. In the initial contact, the Saxons at the rear were knocked down and trampled underfoot by the galloping horses. The momentum of the charge was slowed as falling men became entangled in the horses' legs, and individual battles were established. Many of the cavalry rode around the increasing circle of combat. They raced down towards the front of the Saxon column, finding the invaders had formed a long shield wall, and were prepared to fight. The Welsh cavalry raced along the sides of the hastily-formed shield wall, seeking weaknesses and forcing their horses into the spaces, creating havoc, but also losing animals and men in the intense fighting.

Lord Drefan, the only Saxon on a horse, moved to his right. He galloped forward to oppose the Welsh officers leading the charge on that side. His heavy axe destroyed the shield of the front horseman, knocking the man off his saddle. Drefan turned quickly, easily deflecting the sword of a second soldier. But, as he turned his horse to protect his back, a spear was thrust into his thigh. He bent forward with the shock. Instantly, a sword bit into his neck. He dropped his axe, and fell to the ground. A cheer went up from the circling cavalry; they knew they had killed the leader. They turned to face the remains of the shield wall; reformed for a second attack, confident that the Saxons would soon be decimated.

Suddenly, the moonlight revealed a huge wave of Saxon horsemen sweeping down from the east, their metal helmets gleaming in the spectral light, catching the Welsh cavalry completely unprepared. In a trice, the balance of the battle shifted. The remnant of Saxon foot soldiers, bunched up in a tight wall, were on the point of being overwhelmed, when suddenly the pressure was relaxed as the Welsh cavalry turned to face its new foe.

Gruffydd realized his mistake. This was the long-reported Saxon cavalry, led by Earl Harold. He yelled for support and galloped towards the centre point of the line of horses that raced towards him. A large Saxon was in the centre of the cavalry charge. He was seated on an immense horse and was clearly heading the attack. Gruffydd recognized leadership, even in the strange moonlight, and forced his way towards him. He was conscious of other Welsh riders defending his flanks. Wielding his long sword, he rode directly towards the man he assumed to be the Saxon Earl Harold. The lines of horsemen clashed in a violent impact. Horsemen of both sides blocked the advance of the two leaders. The air was rent with the screams of horses, the clash of metal, and the insane roar of battle.

Even in the moonlight, King Gruffydd ap Llewellyn was easily recognizable among the advancing fighters. Apart from his massive horse, he carried a long shield and two of his guards carried royal pennants on their spears. Harold knew this was the critical point of his life. He must kill this Welsh King, or die in the attempt; for his future depended on this single event. Both men urged their horses towards each other, lashing out at anyone in their way, both friend and foe. This was the moment of destiny for each man; the time when history would be established and when their fortunes would rise, or be forever destroyed.

Harold was armed with a great double-edged axe, which he wielded in his right hand; he carried a heavy leather shield. Gruffydd clutched his traditional long sword and his large shield was decorated with a red dragon. Soldiers, on both sides, were brushed aside, as the two most powerful leaders in the British Isles prepared to do battle.

Without warning, Gruffydd's horse staggered and fell forward, victim of an axe blow from a Saxon foot soldier, who was, himself, killed a moment later. The King jumped free of his huge animal as it collapsed in its death throes, throwing away his shield as he rolled to the side. Meanwhile, other cavalrymen had ensnared Harold in a tight position, and he lost sight of his opponent as the battle intensified. He was soon fighting for his life against a determined Welsh attack, no longer able to locate the Welsh King.

A large bearded warrior with a huge belly attacked Gruffydd as he struggled to his feet. The man was finely armored, and was mounted on a white warhorse. He was clearly a Saxon Lord, and one who was seeking glory, no matter what the cost. The warrior gambled on a single blow and aimed his long sword in a powerful slashing movement, as his horse careered forward. Gruffydd stood his ground, dodging at the last second and deflecting the downward blow. As the horse charged past, the King used both hands to reverse the direction of his own sword. With an upward swing, putting all his weight on one foot, he cut up under the man's armpit, inflicting a mortal wound. Before Lord Modig's eyes had glazed over, Gruffydd was retreating back towards his own men, trying to extract himself from the melee.

"My Lord King!" a young Welsh officer shouted. "Behind you!"

Gruffydd risked a quick glance back to see the young cavalry man jump from his horse and rush forward to cover his withdrawal. "My thanks!" Gruffydd roared, as he swung into the vacant saddle. Around him a strong force of Welsh cavalry moved forward to protect him, as the young officer climbed on the back of another horse.

The King looked around quickly, searching for the Saxon Earl. But, in the shadowy light, he was nowhere to be seen. From his horse, it was clear to Gruffydd that the Welsh situation was rapidly deteriorating. Fresh Saxon cavalry were joining from the right, using their superior numbers to encircle his embattled horsemen, who were soon engaged in a disorganized defense. Meanwhile on the left of the heaving mass of men and horses, the exposed left flank of the Welsh squadron was under sustained attack by the remnants of the Saxon foot soldiers. The battle had become a static struggle, and the advantages that Gruffydd's cavalry had previously enjoyed had become negated as foot soldiers demonstrated their ability to hem in the horsemen and attack from all sides.

"Withdraw!" Gruffydd yelled to his officers. "Regroup!" Trumpets sounded. The Welsh tried to disengage, leaving many of their companions to fight lone battles before a quick death. The officers tried to keep the men together as they attempted to withdraw, but the superior numbers of the Saxons turned an organized retreat into a rout.

To the east of the pitched battle, Harold lay unconscious on the ground having fallen from his injured horse. Members of his personal guard had surrounded him, prepared to defend him, no matter what the odds. "We cannot leave with him," an officer insisted, "or the soldiers will lose heart."

As the course of the battle unfolded, and the Welsh cavalry attempted to regroup, the Saxons were able to utilize their superior numbers. They charged from two sides. Gruffydd, meanwhile, had retreated to a small hill to the west with a handful of officers. In the strange moonlight, he watched in dismay as his fractured cavalry was forced into a constant retreat. "Where is the Northern Army?" he muttered. "Surely, they can't have been defeated?"

"My Lord King, we must leave now!" an officer implored him. "You must survive for us to fight another day!"

"I won't leave my men to die like this." Gruffydd wiped tears of anger from his face.

"You have no choice, my Lord King. Or your men will have died in vain."

Gruffydd stared down at the battle, which was fast becoming a massacre. He breathed out, trying to overcome his emotions. Reluctantly, he turned his horse towards the west, his dreams in tatters. "We ride for Conwy!" he shouted. "Pass the word."

The survivors fought their way from the chaos of the battlefield, where exhausted men were barely able to lift their weapons. Both sides had been in the saddle for hours, with minimal rations and, prior to the fighting, had endured freezing conditions. It had been difficult for both sides to clearly identify the enemy once the combat had started. Finally, as the Welsh soldiers fled in ones and twos, small groups of Saxons, whose anger had not abated, pursued them relentlessly. Throughout the area, the hunters and the hunted played out their deadly games. Groups of Welsh villagers, incensed by the burning of their King's Palace, ambushed Saxons who had thought the day was theirs and, back on the battlefield, the remaining Saxon foot soldiers wreaked their revenge on any injured enemy they could find.

Eventually, as a grey dawn began to break, the carnage of the battlefield was slowly revealed. The Saxons burnt their dead and began a slow retreat towards the border. Harold had made only a partial recovery. He was barely able to sit in a saddle. His men and their horses were at the limit of their endurance, and the depleted army dragged itself home at the speed of the remaining foot soldiers, who had determined to march home rather than risk a further sea crossing. It had been a costly victory, with the confirmed deaths of Lords Alwel and Modig, and the presumed death of Lord Wirt. Harold glared at all around him. "We have only punished the Welsh King, not chained him. He will return to plague us." He wondered if his victory would be enough to satisfy King Edward and whether he would pay for the cost.

To the west, Gruffydd and a small remnant of his broken army rode slowly towards Conwy. "We'll rouse the fleet," he said confidently, "and destroy the boats that brought the Saxons to our shore." The officers nodded, fighting to keep awake. "They'll flee for the border now. With luck the Northern Army will destroy them." He was beginning to feel optimistic again. He was a man of action and already he could imagine getting his revenge on Earl Harold.

Gruffydd would have been outraged, and in disbelief, to know that his Northern Army had divided its forces, and that Hwyel ap Morgan's men were dead. Or, that Hwyel and the one surviving soldier, had been tracked by Saxon scouts and killed in an ambush, while the company under Dafydd Davies had returned to the barracks at Ruthin, having failed to make contact with the enemy. But this was for another day.

CHAPTER SEVENTEEN

As Dafydd had expected, the Saxon foot soldiers did not try to follow them. He led his small party at a safe pace through familiar valleys, while behind him Alys, Teifryn's faithful maid and friend, rode a quiet horse, followed by one of the Queen's maids with Prince Cydweli. Ealdgyth, very much the angry Queen, rode in bitter silence. She was followed by her other maid, cradling the youngest Prince, who cried incessantly. Cadell, dressed in heavy armor, and feeling his age, brought up the rear. He peered slowly round at regular intervals to make sure they weren't being followed. He would have given a great deal to be in a warm bed.

It was cold, and a sharp breeze blew in their faces. In the distance, the howling of wolves reminded them of the wildness of the country through which they were passing. When the snow-covered path allowed, the travelers bunched up for comfort and support, but often were forced to travel in single file through a desolate landscape.

"How much further?" one of the maids asked. She was tired, and the only warm part of her body was where the baby was snug against her.

"We should be there before dawn," Dafydd said, reassuringly, his hand resting on his sword. The sound of the wolves was closer.

After a while they halted near a rushing stream. "The wolves are getting bolder," Cadell said, stifling a yawn. "They're after our horses."

Dafydd glared at him. "Wolves don't attack people. It's an old wives' tale."

"But they do attack horses," Cadell said defiantly. "We had best keep close together. If they come too near, one of us will have to attack them, while the other defends the women and horses."

"Agreed," Dafydd said reluctantly. He did not wish to scare the women.

They were close to Conwy, moving through a wooded valley, when wolves appeared behind them on the trail.

"Dafydd!" Cadell called. "Look behind!"

A pack of wolves, numbering at least ten, were advancing at a fast lope. Dafydd stopped the group and insisted that they kept close together. He drew his sword, and his eyes searched the path in front and to the sides for any sign of other wolves. Seeing none, he moved back to support Cadell, who had drawn his sword, but was breathing as though he had run a race.

"Are you well?" Dafydd asked. He saw the wolves had gathered a hundred paces away. They were padding around, yelping in anticipation, drawing closer.

"Yes," Cadell wheezed. "I'll stay with the women, you chase them off."

"No," Dafydd said cautiously. "We'll keep together." He had no experience of wolves; there were very few around Ceredigion, but he had identified the alpha male of the pack. It was a large beast that moved quickly from one side of the path to the other, as if testing them, looking for a weakness. "We're not in a good place to defend ourselves, so keep moving. But don't hurry. If we do anything differently, I'm sure they'll attack."

He moved up besides Alys, who was leading the group. "The horses are afraid, but keep a tight rein. They must not be allowed to bolt."

"Don't worry, my Lord." She smiled reassuringly. "I've ridden horses all my life."

Their animals were anxious, made worse by the Queen's maids who were twisting nervously from side to side. The women's faces glowed pale in the moonlight, and their eyes were wide with fear. Ealdgyth dropped back beside her father. "Give me your spare weapon?" she demanded. He nodded and handed her his dagger; his hands were shaking.

"Are you ill?" she asked. There was no warmth in her voice, merely disgust. It was his duty to defend her, not cause problems.

"No," he gasped. The sword in his right hand felt unnaturally heavy. In the cold air his face was wet with sweat. Out of the corner of his eye he saw the wolves moving closer. He rose in his saddle, and lashed out at them with his sword, although the nearest wolves were at least thirty paces away. A jarring pain gripped his chest; he dropped his sword and, with a gurgling moan, fell sideways out of his saddle. Ealdgyth screamed. Cadell's horse reared up and galloped off, closely pursued by the wolves.

They all dismounted, standing silently around the body, while Dafydd confirmed he was dead.

"We must move on," Ealdgyth said. She showed no emotion.

"Help me get your father on a horse." He deliberately omitted any words of deference, and was finding it difficult to hide his contempt.

"Leave him! He's dead. We can't take him!" Ealdgyth shouted. Her eyes darted around, checking for any sign of the wolves.

Dafydd unbuckled Cadell's heavy body armor and his helmet. He stood up, removed the screaming baby from the maid, and thrust him into the Queen's reluctant arms. The maid was a strong girl of farming background, and had no difficulty helping Dafydd lift the body onto his horse.

He helped Alys into her saddle.

Ealdgyth waited impatiently for her maid to regain her saddle, and hurriedly transferred her distraught son. She turned to see that Dafydd was back on his horse, with the limp body of her father hanging over the front of the saddle. "Help me up!" she ordered, her eyes flashing with anger.

Dafydd walked his horse towards her and the confident look on her face faded as she realized he was not intending to dismount. "If I could believe in you as a queen, as a mother, or even as a daughter, I would help you. But you are beneath my contempt." He returned slowly to the front of the group and continued the journey, leaving Ealdgyth to yell her threats to a sky that was beginning to lighten behind them.

As they reached the brow of a ridge, before the final descent to Conwy, they looked down in horror. Below them, the bay was aglow with the fiery hulks that had once been King Gruffydd's Northern Fleet.

· · ·

THE KING ARRIVED AT CONWY before mid-day, almost too tired to get off his horse. Later, he sat on a bench by the waterfront in numbed silence, while local people served beer and food to the disheartened remnants of his once proud army. "Are they all destroyed?" he asked sadly. He could not draw his eyes away from the devastation.

"Not all, my Lord," replied Elwyn Davies. His title of Admiral seemed out of place. His family had chosen to keep the name Davies, and his son Jon would be also be a Davies, not Jon Elwyn. He looked grim, but spoke with energy. "We managed to save two, and with them we were able to destroy the Saxon galley that was responsible."

"Only one Saxon galley?" Gruffydd shook his head in disbelief.

"The conditions had been extreme, my Lord. It was impossible to imagine we might be attacked. The ships were well anchored to withstand the storm, and the weather was so bad, I'd ordered all crews to come ashore. When the alarm was raised, a number of ships were already alight. Immediately, every rowboat was commandeered. I managed to cut the anchors of two of our smaller galleys. Fully manned and, with many of our bowmen aboard, we finally disabled the Saxon vessel and were able to board it." He paused. "They fought bravely to the end, causing us to lose some good men." He pointed down the bay, where a large galley lay beached; a crowd of Welsh sailors was inspecting it, swarming around its deck like ants. "It's a big galley, indeed," he mused. "I imagine, my Lord, the rest of the Saxon fleet sank?"

"No," Gruffydd rubbed his face. "Their crews destroyed my Palace."

The Admiral, a childhood friend of Gruffydd's, bowed silently. There was nothing more to say.

Eventually, when he had gathered his strength, the King

went to the nearest inn, where the Queen and her maids were staying. He checked on his two sons who were sleeping, congratulated the weary maids, and avoided his wife. "What is your advice?" he asked Dafydd, who was sitting by a fire, fighting to stay awake.

"My Lord King, I'm certain General Gwriad and his Central Army will march to Ruthin. Once they have recaptured our borders, they'll march to Rhuddlan. I sent him a message before the Palace was attacked. I told him we would head for Conwy if the Palace was attacked."

Gruffydd stared into space, as though unable to grasp the situation. "I sent a messenger to him ordering him to come directly to the Palace with the Central Army. It will take him at least two days to muster the men at this time of the year," he said in a dead voice, "and it should be possible to intercept him. With the help of the Northern Army, I should soon be able to reestablish order."

"Why do you think we have heard nothing from the Northern Army, my Lord?"

"My hope is that they are still chasing the Saxons off our lands." The King ran his hands through his beard. Dafydd knew better than to dispute this hope. "We will rest today, and tomorrow I will lead my men through the mountain passes to the village of Ffestiniog. I will send scouts ahead. We should meet General Gwriad on the third day."

"My Lord King, you and your men need time to recover. General Gwriad will come here with his army as soon as he sees your ruined Palace." Gruffydd did not reply. "My Lord King, there is little to be gained by risking

such a march through the passes in this weather."

"Admiral Elwyn Davies will be in charge of the security of Conwy. You will stay to look after my family. Is that understood?" He glared at Dafydd. "I am still King of All Wales! I am King of the Britons! I will not be opposed in this matter." He stormed out of the inn and began to give orders for his proposed departure.

Dafydd knew it was Gruffydd's pride that drove him to make

bad decisions. With sense of foreboding he paced about the room, before fatigue overwhelmed him and he curled up on a blanket in front of the fire.

• • •

THE KING LEFT AT FIRST light with a guard of only twenty soldiers. The villagers and the seamen turned out to cheer him off. He rode out of Conwy with a smile, gratefully acknowledging their support. The Queen was not in evidence.

Scouts had gone ahead, but had not reported back by the time Gruffydd and his men reached the impressive Llanberis Pass. Around him, high white peaks reached to the sky and the valley was strewn with huge boulders. They travelled carefully along a high narrow path that followed the course of a thundering river far below them. A light powdering of snow was blowing into their faces, made worse by a gusting wind, which obliterated the path ahead.

"My Lord, we're not the first," an officer said, pointing to a web of footprints in the snow. "A number of people came this way recently and then turned around." He ordered two of the soldiers to ride ahead. "Find out who they are, and report back." The men moved off in single file, soon disappearing in the swirling snow.

"They're probably local villagers, my Lord," a soldier suggested. "They saw our horses and moved back to a safer place to pass."

Gruffydd nodded his agreement. His mind was focused on how he would revenge himself on Earl Harold. 'I have suffered a lot,' he said to himself, 'and I will make him suffer in return. He, too, has buildings that will burn and soldiers who will die.' He rode slowly forward, his head down, avoiding the snow from getting in his eyes. When the first arrows struck, it was as though he was in a bad dream. The soldiers in front of him collapsed in their saddles; one jerked backwards with an arrow protruding from his forehead. There were angry yells, men were screaming in agony, horses reared up, and arrows streaked through the snow-blinding air. Gruffydd realized the narrow path had widened and archers were firing from behind a pile of rocks to his left.

An officer led a charge of about ten men against the attackers, but things were happening too quickly. Before the men could reach their enemy, they and their horses were mowed down in a withering hail of arrows.

Gruffydd drew his sword, encouraging the few survivors. He raced towards the archers, reached the rocks, but the enemy was well positioned and he could not attack them on his horse. He jumped from his saddle, as an arrow struck the animal in the neck. It reared up and fell sideways against one of the few surviving horsemen, knocking him to the ground. Gruffydd lunged forward. He dismembered an archer before he could fire. Other archers appeared. He was able to cut down two of them before an arrow lodged itself in his right shoulder; he dropped his sword and other arrows pummeled him to the ground. He lay on his back, knowing he was dying, and unable to move. His eyes began to blur, but he was aware of a face up close.

"Remember me?" a rough voice screamed. Gruffydd was unable to see clearly, and the voice was unrecognizable. "You killed my father, you bastard. Now I'm going to kill you!" In his last moments, he wondered whom he had killed, but somehow it didn't seem to matter.

Cynan ap Iago, son of the rebel chieftain Iago ap Idwal, drew a knife across Gruffydd's throat, bellowing his victory over the dead King. Cynan did not consider whether Gruffydd had been a great King for Wales, he was merely the man who had killed his father.

• • •

THE SUN WAS SHINING WHEN General Gwriad and his army rode into Conwy. The villagers welcomed him, and made a fuss of the weary soldiers; even the sailors were pleased to see them.

"Where's Gruffydd?" Dafydd asked. The two brothers had moved out of earshot and each understood there was unpleasant news to share.

"I've had no reports," Gwriad said. It was low tide and his eyes were drawn to the partially submerged hulks in the bay and the lone galley on the beach. "I was hoping to get messengers from you or from the King?"

Dafydd shrugged his shoulders. "After the attack on his Palace and the defeat of his forces, Gruffydd insisted on leaving here the next day. He was intending to cut through the mountains to intercept you. That was two days ago."

Gwriad nodded and rubbed the back of his neck. "Teifryn was worried about you. She also asked after Alys."

"She's here." Dafydd raised his thick eyebrows. "However, the Queen insisted on leaving for Bangor, with her children. I understand she has a Northern Lord who will protect her until she knows what has happened to Gruffydd."

"Ah," Gwriad muttered, knowingly. "You must tell me all that has happened." He cleared his throat. "But first, I need a good drink."

· · ·

THE NEXT DAY, THE TERRIBLE news arrived: Cynan ap Iago was claiming to have killed King Gruffydd in the Llanberis Pass and had declared himself King of Gwyneth.

"What will you do?" Dafydd murmured. He was so overwhelmed with emotion he could hardly speak.

"I'm a General, I have to make decisions," Gwriad said. "I will not lead my army into Cynan's mountains to be ambushed. Anyway, I'm against Welshmen killing each other." He embraced his tall brother. "My soldiers don't belong here anymore. I'm taking them back to Deheubarth, where they can return to their farms while we wait to see what the Saxons will do once the good weather returns."

"It's all lost, isn't it?" Dafydd was unable to prevent the tears running down his large nose. "Everything we built up over the last seven years is gone."

"Not everything." Gwriad moved away, and stood looking at the wrecks in the bay. "We have my army, and the Morannwg army's still intact. We'll go back home and lick our wounds."

"But the dream of a united Wales is over!" Dafydd wailed.

"Before long, all the Welsh Princes will be fighting each other, as they always did."

"Yes, some will," Gwriad agreed. "Until another man like Gruffydd ap Llywelyn becomes, once again, King of All Wales. That is our hope."

He walked over to his officers to arrange their withdrawal.

THE END

APPENDIX

NAMES OF CHARACTERS
AS THEY APPEAR IN THE STORY

Lord Gomer ap Griffith: who claimed the Kingdom of Deheubarth. Elder brother to the famous General Cydweli ap Griffith, and uncle to Gwriad and Dafydd

Evan: slave to Gomer

Brother Williams: Priest at Llanduduch

General Cydweli ap Griffith: famous younger brother of Lord Gomer and father of Gwriad and Dafydd. Died 1039 at battle of Rhyd-y-Groes, fighting against the Saxons

King Hywel ap Edwin: Previous ruler of Deheubarth until 1039

Prince Gruffydd ap Rydderch: Self-appointed King of Deheubarth (1047–1055), enemy of Lord Gomer ap Griffith and of King Gruffydd ap Llewelyn. Known locally as Gelen (the leech)

Gwriad ap Griffith: elder son of General Cydweli, becomes General of the Army of the South West and Mid Wales

Dafydd ap Griffith: younger son of General Cydweli, becomes Secretary to King Gruffydd ap Llewelyn

Megan: girl at Llanduduch

Earl Leofric: Saxon Earl and ruler of Mercia,

General Edwin: Saxon, brother of Earl Leofric of Mercia

General Aelfgar: Saxon, son of Earl Leofric, captured at the battle of Rhyd-y-Groes

General Thurkill: Saxon, friend of General Edwin

Rhys: Sergeant-at-Arms to King Gruffydd

Lord Ganny ap Mawr: cavalry officer with Cydweli

Ethelbert: Saxon officer

King Gruffydd ap Llewelyn: King of Gwynedd and Powys, and eventually the King of All Wales, and King of the Britons.

Rhodri ap Tewdwr: officer in King Gruffydd's army, 1039

Emrys ap Mawr: officer in King Gruffydd's army, 1039

Cadell ap Iorwerth: young soldier with Gomer

Elen: wife of Cydweli

Lord Meilyr ap Ithael: cavalry officer with King Gruffydd, 1039

Prince Arthwyr ap Llewelyn: younger brother to King Gruffydd

Lord Cadell ap Bleddyn: King Gruffydd's Seneschal, father of Angharad and Ealdgyth

Angharad: elder daughter of Cadell ap Bleddyn. Future wife of General Gwriad

Ealdgyth: younger daughter of Cadell ap Bleddyn. Future Queen of Wales

Bishop Hywel: the most powerful prelate in Wales and Bishop of St. David's Cathedral

Prince Rhys Fachan of Morgannwg: enemy of King Gruffydd

Prince Anarwd ap Tewdwr of Morgannwg: supporter of King Gruffydd

Prince Rhys ap Mawr of Morgannwg: Second-in-Command to Prince Anarwd

Prince Rhodri ap Williams of Morgannwg: a lesser Prince, later to become Admiral of the Southern Fleet

Catrin: wife of Prince Rhodri ap Williams

Teifryn of Ynys Mon: close friend of Angharad, and future wife of Dafydd

Elen: Angharad's maid

General Owain ap Pasgen: childhood friend of King Gruffydd, General of the Northern Army

Bran: Saxon, intelligence officer to Earl Harold

Earl Harold Godwinson: Saxon Earl of Wessex, defeated King Gruffydd, and future King of England

Earl Tostig: Earl of Northumberland and brother to Earl Harold,

Brandon: servant to Earl Harold

Lord Leofwine: youngest brother to Earl Harold Godwinson

Father Gyrth: Saxon, brother to Earl Harold Godwinson, took Holy Orders, liked by King Edward

Cynan ap Iago: son of the late Iago ap Idwel, rebel tribal chief of Snowdonia

Rhys Gwynedd: new Seneschal, of northern family, lover of Queen Ealdgyth

Elwyn Davies: of northern family, becomes Admiral of Northern Fleet

Lord Wirt: Saxon, one of Earl Harold's officers, friend of Egbert

Lord Alwel: Saxon, friend of Lord Modig, one of Earl Harold's officers, a one-armed warrior

Lord Drefan: Saxon, friend of Lord Wirt, one of Earl Harold's officers

Lord Modig: Saxon, friend of Lord Alwel, one of Earl Harold's officers

Alys: servant to Teifryn

Blodwin: servant to Queen Ealdgyth

Alun ap Iwan: noble, Second-in-Command to General Gwriad

Hwyel ap Morgan: senior officer in General Owain's Northern Army

Dafydd Davies: second officer to Hwyel ap Morgan of the Northern army

Merfyn: a peasant

WELSH PATRONYMIC NAMING

In early times the Welsh family name changed through the male line with each generation. A son was given a first name, and linked to his father. Hence Gruffydd ap Llewelyn was Gruffydd son of Llewelyn, and his son Cydweli became Cydweli ap Gruffydd.

The word *ap* is a contraction of the Welsh word mab, which means *son*. Occasionally, some women were given their full family name: *Angharad* might be known as *Angharad ferch Cadell ap Bleddyn*, or Angharad daughter of Cadell son of Bleddyn.

Over the years, and for reasons including outside pressures, the Welsh took on continuing family names such as Jenkins, Jones etc.

In this novel, the women are known generally by their first name, and sometimes, as with Teifryn of Yns Mon, it is her birthplace that defines her.

I have used the traditional patronymic naming for people of rank, and a first name only for peasants and slaves. In some cases, characters have two names, such as *Rhys Gwynedd*, signifying a lesser status or, as with Prince *Rhys Fachan*, a person of rank who is universally disliked, and held in contempt.

ANCIENT WELSH PLACE NAMES USED IN THIS STORY
WITH MODERN NAMES WHERE APPROPRIATE

Aberteifi: now known as Cardigan

Caerdydd: Cardiff, now the capital of Wales

Caernarfon: port opposite island of Ynys Mon, now known as Caernarvon

Ceredigion: Kingdom in mid-west Wales, including the town of Aberteifi

Cilgerran: ancient village east of Aberteifi near Teifi river

Conwy: port off north-west Wales, now known as Conway

Cornweal: Cornwall

Deheubarth: regional name for south-west Wales

Dinbych: village near border in north Wales, now known as Denbigh

Dyfed: an area within Deheubarth. South-west corner of Wales, including St. David's

Dyserth: village near Rhuddlan in north Wales

Ffestiniog: small village on southern edge of the mountains

Gwent: important Kingdom in south-east Wales, adjoining Morgannwg

Gwynedd: the most important of the Welsh Kingdoms; situated in the north-west, and including modern Snowdonia

Harlech: coastal stronghold in south-west Gwynedd

Llanberis Pass: a famous roadway through the mountains of Snowdonia

Llanduduch: village on the Teifi River known as St. Dogmaels

Llanstephan: village close to Twyi River, south-west of Carmarthen

Llif Pwll: small port, now known as Liverpool

Mold: village near border in north Wales

Morgannwg: Kingdom in south Wales

Offa's Dyke: earth barrier constructed by Offa, Saxon King of Mercia. Stretched from estuary of River Dee in the north to River Wye in the south. Separated Wales from Saxon lands. Thought to be constructed about 770–790.

Powys: a powerful kingdom, second to Gwynedd, mid-eastern Wales

Rhuddlan: village near coast in north Wales, site of King Gruffydd's palace

Rhyd-y-Groes: famous battle near the border with Saxon England

Ruthin: village near the border, south of Rhuddlan

St. David's: Cathedral in south-west Wales, an important religious centre

Vale of Elwy: site of St. Asaph's Monastery in north-east Wales

Ynys Mon: island off the northwest coast of Wales; Druid centre

Ystrad Teifi: an area in south-west Wales adjoining the Teifi River

WELSH VOCABULARY

Arth = Bear
Cariad = Term of endearment
Castell = Castle
Duw = God
Gelen = Leech
Gwirion = Silly or innocent
Gwirionyn = Simpleton
Taid = Grandfather

BIBLIOGRAPHY

I acknowledge the following authors, whose books were of help to me:

Christopher Brooke, **The Saxon and Norman Kings** (Pub. Fontana 1972)

Arthur Bryant, **The Medieval Foundation** (Collins 1966)

John Davies, **A History of Wales** (Penguin 1994)

David C. Douglas, **William the Conqueror** (Univ. of California Press 1992)

Peter Berresford Ellis, **The Druids** (Constable & Co. 1994)

Jasquetta Hawkes, **A Guide to the Prehistoric and Roman Monuments in England and Wales** (Sphere Books 1975)

Richard Kay, **Medieval Anecdotes** (Broadview Press 1988)

William McElwee, **A Short History of England** (Praeger Publishers 1970)

Clayton and David Roberts & Douglas R. Bisson, **A History of England, Vol. I** (Prentice Hall 1980)

G.M. Trevelyan, **History of England** (Longmans,Green & Co 1964)

Dorothy Whitelock, **The Beginnings of English Society** (Penguin Books 1962)

ABOUT THE AUTHOR

Barry Mathias B.Ed., M.A., is a teacher of English and Drama, and author of historical fiction. His *Ancient Bloodlines Trilogy* has sold well throughout Canada, Britain and the USA.

The Trilogy is comprised of: *The Power in the Dark*; *Shadow of the Swords*; and *Keeper of the Grail*. It covers the years 1112 to 1118 and is an exciting exploration of the use of power; in particular it deals with the importance of bloodlines, and the rise of the Knights Templar.

In his latest novel, *Celtic Dreams of Glory*, he focuses on the rise and fall of the charismatic Welsh King Gruffydd ap Llewelyn, who died in 1063 at the hands of Harold Godwinson, the Saxon Earl of Wessex, who later became King Harold of England.

His other publications include *Ebb Tide* (a collection of poetry) and *One For Sorrow, Two For Joy* (a collection of short stories).

Website: **www.barrymathias.net**

CPSIA information can be obtained at www.ICGtesting.com
Printed in the USA
LVOW131735290513

335829LV00002B/6/P